THE RED CANOE

THE RED CANOE

Wayne Johnson

Copyright © 2022 by Wayne Johnson
Cover and jacket design by Mimi Bark

ISBN 978-1-951709-72-3
eISBN: 978-1-951709-92-1

Library of Congress Control Number: available upon request

First Trade Paperback edition March 2022 by Agora Books
An imprint of Polis Books, LLC
44 Brookview Lane
Aberdeen, NJ 07747
www.PolisBooks.com

At that time the great prince, Michael, who stands beside the sons of your people, will appear...
and those who lead the many to righteousness will be like the stars forever and ever.

The Book of Daniel

For those
who have been silenced,
who have not been heard,
who have had no voice.

Fall

1

Buck

The girl came to him on the afternoon of the day he was served for divorce—signed receipt required—and a miracle having just saved his life.

He'd been in his garage shop all morning, the two-car-wide door open, building a facsimile 1880s rowboat for a software designer in Seattle when he heard the shuck of feet on his drive.

"Michael Fineday?" droned a man's voice from behind him, something of the herald in it.

He turned from the boat to face an innocuous middle-aged guy, dressed all in black as if he might be less conspicuous that way, and his dishwater blond, greasy hair in a side-parted comb-over. It took a moment for the name to register—it wasn't his, but when trouble came, and it had over the years, it always came to Michael. To the archangel who, Sister Seraphim at the Catholic off-reservation boarding school had informed him, was his namesake.

All these years later, four decades and counting, Michael still got out in front of him, after which all he could do was follow.

"Sign please?" All-in-Black said. He held out a clipboard and pen, pointed, "Right here at the bottom."

He swept his thermos from his drafting table, poured a cup and took the clipboard.

4

"If you don't mind," he said, and winked, trying to make light of whatever this was now. "I'll take a look-see here. Before I sign away my first born, or—" Center, top was: IN THE THIRD JUDICIAL DISTRICT COURT, and below it: *Naomi Louise Weston, Petitioner.*

Mo, he thought, shit, and an explosion went off in his head. And to get some distance from it, glancing up from the page, he joked,

"Dressed the way you are, how do I know you're not some whiskey priest sent out here to mess with me?"

All-in-Black held up an ID on a yellow lanyard, *Magistrate of the Court.* He was that sort of guy, no affect was good affect.

"If you would, please," he said.

He'd set the clipboard on his hip, like a wing, but nothing was saving the moment, and in him that awful woodenness he'd suffered since having left Naomi's. "I sign this, that's just me agreeing you've gotten it to me, and not anything else, right?"

All-in-Black nodded.

"You know the old saw about the bearer of bad news, right?"

Having heard it before, All-in-Black allowed himself the shadow of a smile, as if warding off a blow.

Behind him were mock tombstones cockeyed on lawns, ghosts in trees, and cardboard witches and vampires on stoops. Halloween was coming up. But standing in the mouth of his shop now, holding the clipboard, *everything* this morning seemed unreal. The odd, too-bruised blue morning light; the too stillness in the air; the too hushed traffic out on the highway. That Naomi had stopped by the house days before "to get a few things," as she'd put it—photos, china, some bric-a-brac he'd mistakenly gotten in his boxes when he'd moved out in June—hadn't alarmed him. After all, it *was* her house in St. Paul and, given she'd told him she "needed some space," he'd gotten his things together and come here, to the house his father had left him.

Counting those earlier "periods of adjustment," as Naomi had once jokingly called them, this was his third.

But now? He glanced down at the clipboard. All that legalese so much mumbo jumbo. *This* was different.

"Just sign, please?" All-in-Black said. "Bottom right."

He did that, with an angry flourish, then handed the works over. All-in-Black grinned, tore the carbon of the petition from underneath and, officiously, nodding slightly, thrust it at him.

"And what am I supposed to do with it?" he said. "Paper the walls, or—I got an idea—it'll come handy in the john."

"Thank you," All-in-Black said, and thrust the petition at him again, "and have a nice day."

"And you do the same," he replied and, with a nod, he took the petition.

He tossed it, so it flapped, all however many pages it was, into a corner of his shop, then dropped to his knee and sighted the length of the rowboat. As true a line as one would ever find.

But the keel was just the slightest bit high in the center, he thought, and took up his plane.

Some time later, he stepped from the boat, sweaty and spent, and it only being late morning. He'd endured all the waiting he could bear, Naomi in every stroke of the plane, every brush of the sanding block, every turn of the steel wool he used to fine-polish the hull. Eyeing it, he bit into the still stickily fresh cinnamon roll he'd bought at the bakery down the block earlier. Even in eating the roll, he was putting off the inevitable. Now just a little bit longer, if he could stand it. The roll was yeasty, rich with veins of butter and cinnamon, and heavily iced. Usually delicious, but now it was just so much nothing in his mouth, tasteless. Even disgusting, but he was eating it anyway. He'd sworn off the rolls when Naomi commented he was "getting a spare" around his middle, but this morning he'd gone to the bakery's back door hours before they opened and gotten two. Carried them hot from the bakery in the bag to the garage, and—sleepless at 4:00 a.m.—had eaten the first, at which time it *had* been delicious, then set the second on his workbench, a reward for the difficult work he was about to set to.

And now, having finished prepping the hull he had gotten to it, the second roll, though, in eating it, he sensed a kind of near giddiness, which he was wise enough to be wary of.

When he'd given in to that feeling in the past, had acted on it, bad things had happened.

"The road to hell is paved with good intentions," Naomi had informed him before she'd asked him to move out the last time.

He swept up his thermos. Put his eye to the dark mouth of it, he had no idea what for. Empty was empty.

In the kitchen, he got the pot going, and while it gurgled he smoked a cigarette at the sink. And so what if the smoke carried through the house now? Who was going to take exception to it? Not Naomi! The phone at his elbow, he thought, No, don't call her, not enough time's gone by. He had some shred of dignity, didn't he?

Calling her now would appear too... *desperate.* Or, was *not* calling her now just being cowardly?

And, with that realization, he dialed. "So," he said, "what's the meaning of the court's little messenger you sent over?"

"Yeah, there *is* that," she replied, "but before we get to it, can I ask one thing of you?"

He would give her what she wanted, he thought. Or try to, and the cycle would start all over again. Just don't beg.

"Like what?" he asked.

In the past, she'd asked him not to bring home any more strays—human or animal—not to take up causes that came back to the house, and over the years there'd been more than a few. So, now, almost with a sense of joy he shifted from foot to foot, waiting to get on with it, what would be more of the same.

"This time: Let. Me. Go," Naomi said, and in her voice a world-weariness that was all too final.

He wrapped the phone cord around his wrist, pulled so hard on it the blood went out of his hand. Shit. This *was* different. When after too long she'd said nothing, he said, "Come on, Naomi, let's just cut this nonsense out, can we?" Begging, when he'd promised himself he wouldn't.

"You just don't *get it*, do you?"

"What?"

"Living with you... is like... like *being a god damned human sacrifice*. I *can't take it anymore*. Not one. More. Thing. I told you I couldn't take any more of your trouble, and then—"

Well, he couldn't deny people came looking for him, and when they did, they were in trouble. As Naomi had been, before this latest mess.

"Look, you tell me someone's stalking you, and you're—what, you're angry I took care of it?"

"You promised no more of that."

"Well, what did you want me to do?"

"*Call the police.* That's what. I mean, Jesus, they brought him in in a C collar and on a backboard."

"Well, if that's all you wanted, why didn't *you* call the police? Why'd you ask me to 'look into' who he was?"

"You promised," she said, "but it means nothing."

"And you're *not* listening to reason, Nina," he told her, using her pet name; it was one of the phrases she'd used on him. Ninamuch— sweetheart—though only at the most intimate of times.

"Shut up, could you? Just *shut up* for once and don't—give me any of your *rationalizing... nonsense.*"

"Hey, that roll of duct tape and other shit in his trunk wasn't for painting houses, Nome, you know that, right? And if—" She sighed, and he cut himself off.

"If you *really* love me, you have to let me go."

"Sure," he said, "but if you stay on the lifetime plan now you'll get a free silver set for six and matching china. And with that—"

"Buck?"

"What, sweetheart?"

"The way you live... terrifies me. I can't take being with you anymore. Not one more minute."

"So?"

"Let. Me. *Go*," Naomi said, and hung up, leaving him holding the phone and a robot voice saying, "*If you'd like to make a call, please hang up and dial again. If you like to make a call, please hang up and—"*

He hit redial, and the phone rang, and rang, and rang, and while he waited he scratched his stomach. The red T-shirt he was wearing had a hole in it, which he explored with his index finger. Tested by pulling at it, and the fabric tearing, all the way around his middle, so the red fabric hung like a sash, like flesh around his middle, and yeah, he had a bit of a happy roll, even though he still ran every other day, three miles up River Road and back.

He set the phone down, threaded the strip of red fabric through his fingers. Shocked.

He reached into the drawer under the phone, lifted up the revolver he kept there, a .38 police special. Six gleaming brass shells, pretty in the gun-blued, milled steel. Humming jauntily to himself, he slipped the revolver into his back pocket and, threading his index finger through his mug of coffee, he scaled the stairs to the attic where he dropped into the chair behind his desk, a window there looking out across his yard. Next door his neighbor, Jerry, had a res mobile up on cinderblocks, was doing a brake job on it.

Jerry's landlord had tried to evict him for running a small business out of his driveway, and Buck had stepped in.

But just now, he was seeing Jerry's place as the landlord did, a veritable junkyard of dead cars, hoods up, and manifolds and engines and tires and wheels and glass everywhere.

Just more of the life in Shakopee, and the reservation and casino miles up the road.

He set the gun on the desk, chuckling to himself. *Yeah, dumbass, you've gone and done it now.* He lifted a quarter from the dish Naomi'd put there for his spare change, fittingly, Naomi in it. A coin toss. Why not? Just for shits and giggles, heads, and he would *not* shoot himself; tails, it'd be lights out. And what harm, since he was only funning?

He balanced the quarter on his thumb and put the gun to his head, flipped the quarter. It arced over the desk, tumbling end over end, then fell to the blotter where it grated in circles, and dropped on its side. He bent to look. Heads. Well, that didn't solve anything. So, two for two?

He set the quarter on his thumb again, flipped the coin, only, this time even before it hit the desktop he was all but pulling the trigger, wincing, when he saw the coin had come up heads again.

He scratched his stomach and, all but chuckling to himself, said, "When the going gets tough, the tough get going...."

Yeah, stick that where the sun doesn't shine, Sister Seraphim. "God has a plan for your life," she'd said to him. Christ. How many times would he have to go through this... fucking "plan"?

The way you live... terrifies me. I can't take being with you anymore. Not one more minute.

And he'd promised himself, long... long ago, he wouldn't rule out an act of God, or The Universe, or Whatever It Was, keeping him around.

If he was needed, which, if what Naomi'd said was true, he wasn't anymore, thank you very much.

With that thought, he flipped the coin again, though this time, exerting that much more pressure on the trigger, cheating, but—the coin rattled to a stop on his green blotter, now for the third time: heads.

He'd gotten a heavy draw so Naomi couldn't accidently shoot herself with the gun, which all too commonly happened. Flipped the quarter a fourth time. Bent to look. Heads. *Really?* Then a fifth, heads. A sixth, heads. And a seventh, all heads, god-damn-it, just get the job done, can you?!

Got the quarter on his thumb yet once more, eight his lucky number, chanted, "Come on, eight!" then flicked the quarter so high it tinkled off the ceiling to drop on his desk where it rattle-rattle-rattled going around and around until, spent, it toppled onto its side and, the pistol pressed to his temple, and squinting against the noise and violence of the coming bullet, he glanced obliquely at it.

Heads.

He kicked back in his chair, thought, Well, he'd never fired the gun. Maybe it didn't work?

He pointed the gun into the brown vinyl recliner in the corner, which he'd always hated, said, chuckling to himself, "Take that, hombre—" and pulled the trigger, blowing a fist-sized hole in the headrest, the stuffing flying everywhere, so it revealed a shaft of sunlight coming through the window.

"Jesus," he said.

His ears ringing, he went to the window to look out, see if his neighbor might have heard the shot.

But—nothing, just Jerry hunched over the car there, and in the yard, the big feral marmalade he'd been feeding stretched in a swath of sunshine.

He slid the gun into the center desk drawer, then locked it with the key on his keychain and, coffee cup in hand, he went down to the shop and stood in the doorway, the late morning light cutting through the leaves in the trees on the boulevard, radiant, as if lit from inside.

Everything, he realized, looked like that just now, a light radiating out of the abyss of his life.

He shuddered. Maybe, later, he'd know what it was all about— his not having died up in his study. But—until then—and when had he ever, really, found out what *anything* was about?—he had a job to finish. The C clamps had to come off the boat, and he could only hope the Tightbond hadn't stained the wood—and that the stem to stern line, exquisite as it was, would eye level, when, earlier this morning, it hadn't.

The keel was a complex curve, a line through three vectors, and given the boat had a champagne-glass stern and the wood was ash, which the software designer had wanted, it was particularly light. But that, exactly, was what made this boat unique. Graceful as swans, Whitehall 14s held a tack beautifully, pivoted easily with a reverse use of the oars, and rode low on the beam and had little drag.

A Whitehall a thing of beauty, as they had been in New York harbors a good century and some earlier, and this one a featherweight.

And thinking that, and almost with a kind of reverence, he got out his tools.

Well into the afternoon he was still working, having removed the clamps and sanded away the Tightbond blemishes, first on the hull and thwarts, and now he finished around the bow plate. Done, he stood in the mouth of the shop, block and sandpaper in hand, as if waiting for an apparition. Or was all of it that now? Was that what this was, one of those moments? The sun butter yellow and filtering down through the trees at the end of his drive, wood smoke in the air, and the birds in his yard darting and calling to each other. Bineshi, pashkandamo, segibanwanish, i okanisse odamaweshi. In their very names the voices of the dead and long lost, and a late afternoon breeze kicking up in the cottonwoods, shaking loose leaves that spiraled down and around like little yellow boats into the street.

Where, just now, a girl in a dirty pink hoodie stepped into them, something injured in the set of her shoulders.

She lifted her face into the falling leaves, and there was something so… melancholy in it, the girl in the falling leaves, hooded as if some acolyte, and he stepped back into the garage to give her the moment. Only, when he did, she noticed. This girl, fourteen or fifteen, who should have been in class—probably over at St. Francis Xavier, the off-reserve school.

"Hello," she called to him. Just that. She was turning to go when she stopped and glanced back.

"What's that behind you?" she called out.

Her directness amused him, she was trying to be tough and reasonable, and he waved her closer. Up the driveway.

"A boat," he said, when she'd made it halfway.

He stood to the side, so as she passed him going into the shop she had a line of escape to the street. She ran her hand over the bow of the boat, gripped a gunnel, pulled a little.

"It smells good in here," she said. This more than surprised him. He was going to comment, when she added, "The gunnels, did you use steam, or soak them?"

"Tank, at another place. Trucked them over. Then bent them

around those forms in back there."

She nodded. "Cool," she said, and he thought that would be it. She'd turn and go.

When she didn't, he lit a cigarette, squinted against the smoke, pinched a bit of tobacco from his teeth.

"Can I smoke?" she asked.

He shrugged. "Bad habit."

"I know. But you do."

"Like I said, bad habit."

"So?"

But he'd noticed the bruises on her forearms now, wasn't about to let her go just like that. He knocked a cigarette from the pack and handed it to her, and she bent into him, an awkward moment, until he realized he was to respond with a lit match. Which he did.

She took a draw on the cigarette, feigning experience, suppressed a cough, turning from him to do it.

"Live here long?" she asked.

There were streaks on her face. She'd been crying. Did her parents know where she was? Or were they the problem? Or was it someone at school?

"You mean the house, or here in Shakopee?" he asked. It was off-reservation, but close to it.

"Both," she said.

"In the house, just since June. But way back, my father was here for work, and I was around."

"Well," the girl said, "you should keep your garage locked. There're a lot of low-lifes around."

"You think?" Was some low-life giving her trouble?

"It's kind of a shithole, if you don't mind my saying." She looked away, her back to him. "I mean, especially just north. Fuckers. They'll take anything that isn't bolted down."

"Uh huh," he said. *They.*

To get her off the subject of her whiteness—she wasn't, which was the sad thing about it; from her eyes, he knew her at a glance for

Native—he motioned toward the shop. Who knew, they could even be related.

Toss a stone any direction near a reservation and you're bound to hit a cousin, uncle, or aunt.

"Get a better look if you'd like," he said, and stepped into the garage and pulled a veneer from the rack.

"Maple," she said.

"Yeah? Why so?"

"It's in the grain. It's fine, see?" She drew the nail of her index finger over the smooth surface. "And it won't dent. Pine's grain is wider. Only, it's not as soft as basswood, or larch, or …. And then you have the super hardwoods, like ironwood, and oak, and…."

She was trying hard, and he felt for her; everything about her was trying so hard to be all right. Was right there in her I'm-Not-Taking-Your-Shit pink hoodie, the tats of barbed wire on the backs of her hands, the ratty holes in the knees of her jeans. Her scuffed black boots.

A girl way too tough for herself, and who knew what manner of difficulty had just befallen her.

Which, when she'd turned, struck him like a blow. She had a bit of a blood stain between her thighs—her little monthly accident? No, since she hadn't tried to clean it up, it was something else.

"So, you know wood?" he asked.

She shrugged again. She was doing that a lot. It had become a kind of reflex, which said bad things, too.

"I'd like to learn how to make boats," she said, though, once said, it embarrassed her, in the still, sad moment his devastation and hers, though neither would speak a word of it.

"Would you?"

"Your work's… *beautiful*. I mean, that boat's really something. Nobody does stuff like that anymore. It's a Whitehall, right?"

This more than surprised him. Who, these days, knew anything about boats, much less the ones he built?

"Smart girl," he said.

14

Of course, at that she shrugged, too, but she was standing more erect now, had lost some of that dejected look. Blushed.

"My dad's kind of nuts about—" she'd been about to say, "shit like that," but caught herself. "*Stuff.* Well, like, you know, engines, and boats and canoes and all that. And guns."

Something had risen to the surface in his mind, but he wasn't sure if he could trust it. She was in trouble, real trouble, but just what kind she couldn't say, which made it the worst kind of all.

And there was the blood there, and—well, he could see she was a late bloomer, so it wasn't that, it was the other, terrible thing.

"I'll teach you if you want," he said, surprised at himself. The tone in his voice, too— What was it, lonely? Or worse, needy? When all he wanted was to be helpful, to give the girl a fighting chance.

"You mean, like—"

"Here. Sure. Why not?"

She considered this. "When?"

Now it was he who shrugged. "Next week?"

She was calculating something. Her eyes darting up and away, and her mind running.

"And only if you'll take orders," he added, and smiled. "I've got tools so sharp you screw up with them they can kill you. So. If you don't pay attention, or show up late—" he didn't want to offend her. "You have to be *alert*, none of this 'I'm half asleep' business. I can't have it."

"For real?" she said. "You're not just saying?"

"Yup. No one's come to apprentice, so I guess you're it. I'll teach you like I was taught."

He put out his hand and the girl took it, pumped it once and dropped it. The handshake a formality that wasn't hers. Or his.

"Okay then," she said, and with a nod, she adjusted her hoodie over her head and marched off down the driveway.

He lit another cigarette, watched as she turned the opposite direction from the reservation. Smart. She was either being safe—which he thought was a good idea—or she didn't want him to know she lived over by the casino, in the run down trailer courts there.

He crushed the cigarette under the toe of his boot. Glanced up into the trees, squinting into the light. He hadn't gotten her name. But what matter? It had all just been talk.

And Naomi? He'd sign the papers. Give her what she'd asked for, because, it occurred to him, that's what he'd been doing in the attic.

Hadn't he?

2

Lucy

He was gone when she came through the door of the doublewide, but in his place was a terrible metallic smell. There was nothing on the stove, so she went to the living room window.

Out on the deck railing was the pan, burned black and the handle set at an angle from her, like a clock. Two, going on three. Only it was nearly four now. She had put out a dish of water for her birds, and sparrows perched on the rim, jockeying for position, some dropping in to bathe, others to drink.

There was a joy in their motions, chests out, and the birds at the feeder darting about, here the one indulgence she allowed herself, feeding the birds, and once she'd begun it, she'd come to know many of them, the chickadee with the bent wing, the dove that strutted, but with a hitch, the albino Jay, the one that always scattered all the smaller birds, the juncos and phoebes and finches and sparrows. And so many, many sparrows. Like herself, nothing to look at, but she adored them anyway. When they all congregated, the birds could empty the feeder in a day, and the money she earned shelving books at school afternoons was just enough to cover the cost.

That was the bright part of returning to the trailer, her birds. And there was the *Essikan*, the raccoon, which lived under the deck—Socks, so named for his black feet. Daily, she saved a piece of hamburger, or a chicken wing, or whatever for him. His ears, frostbitten, were of unequal size, the left only a ridge of tissue on his head. Which, seeing him scoot out from under the trailer now, waiting for her, made her think. Winter was coming, and she'd have to find some way to make a shelter for him—one her father wouldn't object to—or, it occurred to her, she could run some electricity under the deck to a heater of some sort.

A trickle heater, like you'd use for a bird bath, she thought, that would do it, and she slung her backpack off and got out her notebook, wrote in it: *hardware store for extension cord.* The heater, that she could have mailed to the trailer park kiosk, though she had reasons for not wanting to go near it.

The doublewide was quiet, and the heater fan ticked on, whirring, and shortly after came the boom of the gas jets lighting. A kind of roar. She could even feel it in the floor. A contained conflagration. What time was it? 4:15. She'd study for an hour, then get dinner started. Anything not to think about—*it*, what her father's cop friend, Arn, had done.

She pulled her books from her pack. Her green *Introduction to Literature* text; the geometry volume, dog eared; the blue, well worn *Lands and Peoples*, for sociology; her *Our Democracy* civics text.

Turning to the rear of the trailer, she saw her father's blue police officer's uniform hanging from his bedroom door. A signal she needed run a load of wash. She padded up the hallway, snatched the uniform from the door and, the hanger slung over her shoulder, went all the way to the rear of the trailer where she swept up the clothes hamper, then ducked through the door and into the shed, where the washer/dryer sat glowering, lid slung back and waiting. All ritual.

She had to hoist the hamper up to dump the works in and, an almost fearful exhaustion in her, she resisted doing that, attacking the seemingly insurmountable height of the washer.

So, she stood back, gathering herself like some weightlifter—the hamper was half-inch plywood and heavy—a soul deep resistance in herself saying, *This is too, too much.*

But it wasn't. Ever. And she knew that, too. He'd taught her,

"Plan your work, work your plan," always adding, "and even when you're empty, Bebbe Gurl, you can do what?"

Reach down for more.

It was how he'd held his life together, post Army. Had they taught him to do that?

So, order. Ritual. But a kind of blindness in it, so that what didn't fit, he simply ignored or didn't see.

He timed things using his wristwatch, even how long it took to get their food at a restaurant. "Twelve and a half minutes to get eggs and hash browns, from placing our order to the table," he'd say, breezily, to some poor waitress, and Lucy'd feel herself blush right to the roots of her hair.

Fuck! Really?! Which kinda ruined breakfast.

Or she'd take a shower, and when she got out, he'd say, "Lot of hot water, Luce. Remember, we're conserving for the new house, right? You had the water going—" and there he'd tell her how many minutes she'd had the water running, and she'd want to scream—or cry.

She hated it, his over organizing, but loved it, too, because when he wasn't over organizing, he was falling into the bottles he had hidden around the house. Got loose and sloppy and dangerous.

Struggled to get to work, after he woke. Knocked about in the living room in the dark, cursing himself.

"You fucking idiot, what'd you do that for?" he'd say to himself, and her heart would go out to him.

Everything had to be in the right drawer. Just so. Dish towels hung on the front of the stove—just so, seams to the inside, *"a girl should know that like her mother did,"* he said.

Yeah, right.

Don't mix his food. Pair his socks. Pants folded so the crease runs up the front. T-shirts folded in thirds. Uniforms: laundered, on the left of the rod in the closet; coat, shirt, pants, belt.

Fish on Friday. Leftovers in Tupperware to take to work, right side second shelf of the fridge.

Well, it worked. It really did. All but the four drinks he limited himself to, which were never four. And who was she to complain? She loved, but sometimes, like now, resented and even hated him.

Or did she?

And with that thought, she hoisted the hamper up, threw his uniform and clothes into the washer as if into an open mouth, dumped a scoop of detergent in, and set the machine running.

Moments later, she was prone on her bed, the light on, and immersed in her sociology text, far away in Afghanistan. She read with focus, with real engagement, about the war, and the people, because her father had spent time over there, and her father was a terrible mystery. Her father—"The Happy Tank," as she sometimes called him—maybe she might find out something of what had gone wrong with him, here, in her book.

And it was while she was reading about the Kush Mountains and the Pashtuns, her mind struck on something which surprised her.

Maybe the boat guy—it was odd that she hadn't gotten his name, usually she was better with things like that—maybe he could help her?

3

Buck

In the kitchen he turned from the stove, full plate in hand and feeling oddly proud of himself; he wasn't going to be that big-gutted, middle-aged divorced guy eating microwaved meals on plastic trays.

Pork roast, in pomegranate marinade. Squash, with a pad of butter. Broccoli. And a salad. The vinaigrette he'd made himself: two tablespoons olive oil, one of red wine vinegar, a chopped garlic clove, a pinch of thyme and basil. What was difficult about that? But if he was honest with himself, it *was* difficult, just not in the way one might have presumed. Because, what was the point of doing any of it, if it all came to nothing?

Had that coin—just once—come up tails, he wouldn't be here; but *eight* times heads?

And in a state of profound gratitude, he ate. In the kitchen, standing back from the stove, his hip set against the counter.

It was the girl, that's what it was. No, he thought, almost happily, he'd see if he could help her, but he'd have to be careful.

No rushing in, he thought, then laughed at himself. Glanced up at the old clock there: half past six. Waiting drove him crazy.

The pork was tender. But why wouldn't it be? He'd done all the cooking in the last sixteen years, Naomi's duties as a trauma surgeon at Fairview Hospital had taken up all her time.

He lifted his head. Larch cabinets. Green linoleum counters.

The stove there with its lone light on over the burners.

"If you stay here, this time you'll have to remodel," Naomi'd told him when she'd come for her things.

Outside, it had gotten dark, the streetlights haloed in carryover mist from the river. With an easy reach, he got the plastic wrap from the cupboard and threw a sheet over the plate, swung around with it to the refrigerator and popped open the door. Two plates, wrapped in the same way, were stacked on the top shelf, each which he'd promised to eat before making something new.

A line of fear running up his back, he set this night's plate atop them, then retreated to the living room, where he swept up the book he'd been reading, but couldn't seem to concentrate.

He lifted the remote, hit the news channel Naomi had been glued to all those years. Just for noise, to have voices in the house.

Opened the book and read, "The double-minded man stands at a parting of the ways...."

He set the book down, stared off at nothing, the outraged voices on the TV set coming to him as if from another world.

No, the blood on the girl's pants was *not* just an accident. She'd even flinched when she'd inadvertently crossed her legs, had put on an aw-shucks smile to hide her shock at it.

Someone had... *interfered with her*, was how they'd put it back when he'd been at St. Mary's Boarding School, and if there was one thing he'd do now, it would be to find out who.

And the rest would take care of itself, or he would.

4

Lucy

"It's good," her father said, fork held in his fist. "But next time back off on the bread in it. Like your mother used to make. Okay?"

"Sure," she said. "Okay. I'll do that. Would you like more?"

"Just a spoonful." She gave him one, and he nodded. "How was school? Did you ace your geometry test?"

She had, but she knew not to say so, not ever. "I missed a few points." She hadn't. Only one. And she'd gotten the highest score in the class.

He said nothing, only ate with seeming greater focus, as if wanting to sidestep the very issue he'd mistakenly aired now. Her mother. Some private conversation going on in him, so that, while he said nothing, she could see it on his mouth. It was always his mouth she watched, because, when he started arguing with himself, or whoever it was, that's when he hit her.

Had hit her mother, too. So, now she watched for the telltale signs, sitting so she could bolt from the table if need be.

"What about your other subjects," he said, glancing up at her, "are you staying on top of things?"

"Yes, Daddy," she said, and was relieved to have a way to pass the time at the table, so went into it.

And while she rambled on to fill the silence between them, she was careful not to say anything he might take offense at, joked about her sociology teacher, Bill Opitz, who the kids called B.O. Pitts, and her gym teacher, Pocket Pool Lahey, who whistled through the gap in her teeth, and when she imitated her, they both laughed.

And like that they chatted over the stupid little things in their day, and it was all right, since she'd made fun of school.

Her father, Lucy knew, even as sharp as he was, had started working early to help support his family, and he'd signed on with the Army for the technical training, one year into high school, lying about his age, diesel was what he'd been after, or so he said. Which he'd gotten through "with flying colors," as her mother had put it, in peacetime, joining the National Guard shortly after to "stay in touch with his Army buddies" and to pull down the monthly salary. Only, just after he'd gotten his first real job—wrenching for a trucking outfit—the Gulf War started and he'd been recalled to service, into the killing maw of it.

Streets filled with rubble. And the people. Not only soldiers, but just everyday people, too, dead in their homes; dead in their cars; dead in a laundry. She'd seen her father's pictures. And always in them, there stood her father in his sand-tan battle gear, gun angled across his chest, on his dusty face, lines of sweat like war paint and a look of grim determination. Which determination hadn't been there when he'd come through the Lindberg Airport terminal, home again. No, anything but.

Just five, she hadn't recognized him, and she'd screamed when he'd taken her up in his arms.

"Do you remember that, Bebbe Gurl?" he said now.

Rather than asking what he'd been talking about, she said, "Tell me again!" What she'd said when she was little, and things had been all right.

Which he did, kicking back in his chair, and the two of them laughing, so that he was the father she'd loved. Before.

The one who'd been crazy about dogs, and liked to play the guitar and sing sappy country western songs. Who'd hoisted her on his shoulders, saying, "Now you're a princess, Luce! What do you see from up there?!"

"I made some apple crisp," she said. Frowning, he joked, "Why do they call it crisp when it never is?"

It hurt her, and he saw that.

"Hey, Bebbe Gurl, I was just kidding, okay?" he said. "Listen, sweetheart, it's been a long, long day, and I think the game's on."

He went to the front of the trailer, to the couch there, where he plunked down in front of the TV.

"You want to watch the game with me?"

It was odd that he'd ask, since he knew she didn't. She hated football. Or maybe it was just football players, like her father's friend Arn. It still hurt down there. She fingered through her T-shirt the necklace *He*, the one before Arn, the first one, had dropped over her head just weeks ago, after *He* had finally—and on the necklace a crucifix. *Don't take it off*, He'd warned. *And don't show it to anyone, or you know what will happen to your father.*

She got the dishes started, then brought her father the apple crisp, a scoop of ice cream on top.

"Thanks," he said, his eyes on the screen, so she was surprised when he said through the mouthy commentators, "You got your little pal coming over? Help you with your geometry?"

"Jean?"

"Yeah, her," he said. "She's the one with the dyed red hair, right? Too wised-up for herself?"

"Can she?"

"Call her," her father said, and turned back to the TV, and Lucy, happily, did just that.

Jean sprawled across Lucy's bed on her back, an arm flung theatrically over her forehead. "Oh My God," she said, "I mean, did he *really*?" She propped herself on her elbow and eyed Lucy.

"Jean, come on," Lucy pleaded. "I don't want to talk about it."

"So you," she made a pumping motion with her hips, and Lucy blushed, horrified. Yes, that.

She was still bleeding *down there*. After Jean noticed the stain on her pants, she'd had to change, then make something up.

The old guy with the boat, he must have seen it, too, but hadn't said a word, which meant he was kind, and it saddened her to think she was too embarrassed, now, to ever go back.

"You know," Jean said, and slapped her on the shoulder, "you keep this up, you're going to get a reputation for being *that kind of girl*."

"But I'm *not*," Lucy insisted, and she wasn't. She'd just lied about her and weird Ryan to shut Jean up.

"Well," Jean said, and shrugged. "And this was… here, when your dad was on night shift, right? Your dad with the bedroom eyes?"

"Jean," Lucy said, "*please!*" She pointed to her textbook, and they both bent to them, Lucy pretending to read, but her mind was racing. Was Jean really looking at her father that way?

Just now, what with everything, she couldn't have Jean going on about her father. And what if Jean said something to him, even just—being the way she was, kidding around?

God! *Yuck!* It was just too… awful.

Sure, her father was "handsome," and could be, when he wanted to be, disarming—dimples in his cheeks when he grinned. Girls pointed him out; especially when he was in uniform, his policeman's blue black, or his army jacket, a dangerous olive tan, all the deployment patches on it like medals from his time in Afghanistan—the same thing Arn wore, which made her wish her father didn't.

When he came to pick her up at school, the girls waiting with her sometimes asked, "Is he your father? He looks like an actor."

Well, yes, he was an actor, and good one. But she wasn't about to say that, and, anyway, one hard look would tell you her father's happy guy routine was exactly that, an act, a cover for someone barely holding it together. After her mother died four years before, a hit and run at a crosswalk in Shakopee, he hadn't held it together, not at all. Only the promise of a better, more stable home had gotten the SRS to release her into his custody again, and Lucy went back to the trailer.

After which he'd gotten all… fucking Mrs. Doubtfire on her, with the laundry, and his routines.

No, she couldn't have Jean sticking her nose into any of that, complicating things with saying something now.

That her father, terrified of losing her, was working double shifts trying to get them off the reservation, too, didn't help, and those "bedroom eyes" Jean had mentioned were just that. He was sleep deprived, and was irritable, even explosive, prone to rages, and because she hadn't had the… *whatever* she'd needed to… be able to tell him after *He*'d first come to her in the night. And since her father had given Arn his house key to "check in on her," and, god, she'd had no idea it would go on, or that there'd be others, and there being in her this stubborn sense of queasy, sickening… responsibility—she must have done… *something* to bring this on—she still hadn't told him.

Especially not what Arn'd done now, since she was sure her father would go completely, and totally, ape shit—and she'd lose him.

Jean beside her, she was imagining it, what he'd do if she told him, and it made her breath come short.

Jean slapped her on her shoulder, "Jeez, Lucy," she said, "don't be mad," she said, and smiled. "I was just *kidding* about your dad. You don't need to get so… worked up and everything. Gawwwd, Lucy! I was just trying to be… *funny*, okay? I'm your *friend*. I'd do anything for you, you know that, don't you?"

"Uh huh." She glanced over at Jean, propped there on her elbows in her skintight popcorn blouse.

"We have a test on Friday," Lucy said, "so, can we just *really* get something done now?" Anything, to get Jean off the subject of her father; or Ryan.

"You're no fun."

"And you, Jean, you're going to end up in a trailer just like this one if you don't pay attention, and—"

Lucy bent closer, in mock threat, happily her daylight self again, and Jean kissed her. It shocked her. She tasted of grape gum, and it felt… weirdly *good*. Really good. She'd never consciously thought it, but there it was—she was more than a little in love with her friend.

And it hurt, too, knowing it now, because she wasn't going to—*couldn't*—let Jean into her life. When she so desperately wanted to.

Lucy flung her algebra text out on the bedspread between them. "Jean? Right now, and right here."

"Gawd, Lucy," she said.

"Complementary angles in what kind of triangle add up to 180 degrees?"

"*All* of them." Jean grimaced. "You know, Lucy, I may act silly, but I'm not *that* out of it."

There came a knock on the door and Lucy shot away from Jean, set the book there between them. Terrible things would happen if her father so much as suspected what had been going on.

"Yes?" she said.

Smiling awkwardly, he opened the door and peered in around it. The dimples there. The kind father. "Just making sure."

"What?"

"School night, girls," he said, then ducked back into the hall, but left the door open. "I don't have to remind you, right?"

"Noooo," Lucy droned, relieved. Both at his leaving, and at his having interrupted them.

"I should go," Jean said, and she shrugged on her hoodie, then swept her books off the bed.

Lucy went ahead of her up the hallway. As if to confide something in her, Jean darted forward, licked her ear. *Oh, my god!*

"Good night, Mr. Walters!" she called to Lucy's father, who threw a hand over his head.

And like that, Jean went out, leaving Lucy standing behind the door, worried all over again, and struck dumb.

She woke in the dark to the sound of her father weeping out there with the television on— harsh, tearing gasps. Slinging her legs around, she slid off the bed and went to her door and locked it, then stood with her ear to it, listening. She wasn't supposed to lock the door, it was a fire hazard her father'd told her, but the bad things always happened when her father was like this. Back when, her mother would get up and be with him, and her voice was so soothing, and her ability to calm him so complete, Lucy had fallen asleep to it, over and again. Her mother's beautiful, lilting voice, and her sometimes singing in the old language, songs which tripped and ran, tasted like light, and filled her chest with hope.

But then, later, that hadn't worked, and the sound of his gasping became an unending torment, and there had come loud, fleshy slaps. In the mornings, sometimes, she could see under her mother's makeup shadows on her face, and she darted about, the two of them keeping their distance. A once interrogator, her father knew how to hit people and not let it show.

She'd once caught her mother stooping at the kitchen counter, where they kept the gun in the drawer.

Standing in her flannel PJs and wiping the sleep from her eyes, she'd said, "Mom?" and her mother had turned, butting the drawer shut, lifted her coffee cup and asked,

"How's that Mr. Lincoln, Lucy? Are you still crazy about his class? What are you reading now?"

She slid back into her bed, the sheets pilled. She'd get a new set—well, new old—at the Good Will. But her birds, she didn't think she could live without them, so no new sheets.

She lay in the dark, on her back, staring into cavernous ceiling, and her heart beating so she could feel it in her neck. Fearing her father's steps coming back toward her.

He was still out there, sobbing. Making horrible animal noises, ones that both scared and saddened her.

After her mother had been killed, at first she'd cried nights in her bed, silently, while he did.

She breathed deeply, trying to calm herself. So she could sleep, because she was exhausted. And then it was quiet, and in the dark, she felt Jean's mouth on hers. Which was like… light itself. Soft. And tasting of grape. Jean. She'd just been goofing, she told herself, like Jean always did. Jean, a year older, almost sixteen, held back because she'd missed a year of school after she'd nearly died in a fire. Something Jean didn't talk about, or how she'd her lost her parents. Or the scarring on her left side, there by her collarbone, webbed, and pink, which only showed if Jean was wearing something too loose, which she only did when it was hot out, and—

On her back, staring up into the stained ceiling, Lucy longed now to touch Jean in that very place, put her lips on the skin on her shoulder, where Jean always set her hand, to cover the scarring, and, too, because—Lucy could see—it hurt; because of all people now, she loved Jean.

Maybe not in *that* way—or was it just because she knew what people would think? What it would mean? And her father? He was insane about that sort of thing, was that it?

"They should all just shut up about it, those people," he'd said once. "They should just not... talk about it."

Her mother had said, simply enough, "Lee, they're right as rain, and you know it."

"Yeah," he'd drawled. "But do they have to rub it in our faces?"

"They have rights, just like us, Lee. It's the reason you were... over there, isn't that right?"

Ryan was kind of like that, *wrong* too, which was why it was stupid of her to have said what she had to Jean about them... *doing it*, because he just wasn't like that. But then, he wasn't like anyone. Although, whether it was his being Korean—or was it Chinese?—or being so inward as to seem almost Aspergery, but super-smart, she couldn't tell, and Ryan's weird, out-of-nowhere humor something only she seemed to get.

But there was something peevish about him, too, and Ryan always the butt of cruel jokes at school. Milk cartons clunking off his head at lunch—followed by guffaws from the jocks' table.

"Hey, Fucktard!" they shouted, "why'n't you off at the dry cleaners where you belong!" and Ryan ignoring the racial slurs that followed.

Which, even now, in the dark, she wanted to tell Ryan's mother, but knew she wouldn't. Because—there was something truly scary about how she looked at you—like she knew things, terrible things. Or had done terrible things.

She stopped thinking there. Because it always came back to... *that. Her* terrible secret.

She imagined it in a box; one, now, she handed up to God, even though she didn't believe in that.

It was a way to not think about *Him*, or Arn or the two others, and she settled back into the bed, then rolled onto her stomach. Head under her pillow, and in the utter dark, she touched herself, imagining it was Jean touching her, and she was shocked at how quickly it happened, not at all like it did with... *them*, though she refused to think of that now, any of it, so lovely was Jean's touch, she imagined *she* was touching *Jean*, too, and she felt herself as if not her own, and just so, she rose to it, her whole body, her breath catching, and then Jean inside her, in her touch, her gathered fingers, and there was an abandon in it, Jean so inside her, and just there, she got a sensation not unlike tickling, which grew, then got larger yet, caught her up in it, expanded, until, as if she could no long contain it, it exploded outward—Oh, God! Jean!—like a flash-of-light, and she stretched, catching her breath.

After, in that floating... spent state of mind, adrift, she dreamt that her mother came through the door.

Like an angel, one who'd sung so beautifully, and she was crying in her sleep, crying over her.

5

Buck

Up before first light, he carried a bowl of kibble behind the house. To the right of the dryer vent, he set it on the cement walk, though, this time, the slightest bit closer to the back door.

He stretched, hands over his head, dressed but not yet awake, and his mind wandering.

The marmalade feral, her frostbitten ears trained on him, came out of the yews separating his yard from his neighbor's, as she did most days.

If he didn't move, maybe, now—*today*, after all these months—the cat would eat by the house while he was outside. He wouldn't be alone then, with the cat there, which seemed oddly important.

The marmalade stepped closer, moved tentatively over the leaves, and the birds just now starting to wake, too, and he—watching the cat, trying not to so much as breathe too deeply—reached, absentmindedly to scratch his stomach and the cat froze, halfway, and he remembered: His conversation with Naomi, and then *all that up in his study*, and the girl having appeared.

And here he'd been waiting for the cat as if nothing had changed. But it had; *everything* had.

He clucked at the cat, then stooped to make himself shorter, but the cat froze.

Living with you… is like… being a god damned human sacrifice. I can't take it anymore.

The cat, tail up curling sinuously, wasn't going to come any closer. And it *was* hungry. Stubs of ears, its gold eyes on him. What a survivor. On one knee, he reached ever, ever, evvvveerrr so slowly out and—lifted the dish, then slid it across the grass into the yard.

The cat lifted its tail, like a question mark. Eyed him. He held his breath, then stepped back.

The cat came across the distance, wary. Then, set to run, it ate. And Buck smiled.

"Gaagige," he said to her. Life. That was her name. Gyg, for short. And in the cat was the answer to the problem with the girl.

Distance and time. Only he worried there wouldn't be enough, knowing how these things went.

6

Lucy

A hand came over her shoulder and knocked her books out of her arms, so they slapped onto the walk and slid from her. Ryan, beside her, turned to see who it was, but was slow to react.

"You are so gay, Einstein," Booker said, and stomped in Ryan's direction so Ryan stepped back, Booker, in his white and maroon letter jacket, looming over him, skin so black it was nearly purple. Side part razor cut over his handsome face, one broad across the cheekbones.

That Ryan never got it that Booker was just goofing, playing a part, only seemed to further embolden him.

So he overplayed it now, as he had before, here, for the umpteenth nauseating time, Booker just showing up as if by accident, but the three of them not quite falling into it, their little bit of afternoon theater.

"Booker," Lucy said, long suffering.

He'd been there that night when everything changed, but hadn't done anything, and it was exactly that that was eating at him. He'd been about to do something—something that would have been… *catastrophic*—Arn had been in uniform and armed—but she'd stared Booker down, over Arn's fat fucking shoulder, even as Arn *did it*, as it was happening.

No, it was eating away at him, and he wasn't doing well with it, he was even now trying to say something.

"Booker, *please?*" she said, meaning, *don't*. She said it as much for Ryan, because Ryan had been there, too. He and Booker had both gone their separate directions, as they always had, as they would now: Ryan off toward his mother's trailer, and Booker off to... wherever, and Arn thinking she was alone had come out of the dark after, but had seen... *something* in her?

Had it been something she'd been wearing, and had he because of it, instead of... doing what he'd... done before—torn her?

And Booker hearing her shriek turned back, and Ryan, too, saw Arn pinning her up against the kiosk of mailboxes.

Booker had come toward them out of the dark, shouted, "HEY! YEAH, YOU! WHAT DO YOU THINK YOU'RE DOING?!" Over Arn's shoulder, she'd glared, mouthed, "*no,*" and Arn had craned his head around to give Booker one long, hard, angry look.

That Booker had frozen said all sorts of things about both of them that no one had been saying. About people like them. And fat Arn pulling his pants up, so he could stumble off into the dark to his patrol car, which Booker, no doubt about it, had seen coming in.

A cop. Doing what he'd done, and Lucy, all but hysterical at the burning in her, ran to the trailer, and inside.

"Booker?" she said now.

He shrugged. Stooped and swept her books up and handed them to Ryan, who seemed more than a little dumbfounded.

"You carry 'em a bit, okay?" He grinned. Perfect white teeth. "Since you got yours in your backpack and all."

They resumed walking, only Booker at Lucy's side, and Ryan trailing by the moment farther behind.

"Pick it up there, Einstein," Booker said. "S'cold out here. The way you're draggin' ass it'll be dark 'fore we're home, hey?"

Booker shifted from side to side as he walked. "Doin' okay?" he said. Of course, he knew she wasn't. Lucy wished she had her books. Then she could hold them between herself and... things. Her body was changing, she'd be more like Jean now, and it thrilled and embarrassed her.

When Lucy said nothing, Booker turned, glanced back. "What about you, Sir Chow Yun Fat?"

"It's *Chen*, not Chow," Ryan replied, "and I'm good."

Ryan was wearing gumboots and a jacket two sizes too large. Booker reached behind him, caught his arm and swung him up between them. Where Ryan walked now, like Booker, but not meaning to.

"Getting' you a pimp strut there, Einstein."

Ryan mumbled something.

"Can't hear ya."

"Sorry."

"Stop apologizing all the time. What you sorry for?"

Well, Lucy thought, just about everything. Ryan was like that, always apologizing, like he didn't deserve to exist in the world. That he was just about the smartest kid in their class didn't help, either, it just made him all the more a pariah. Ryan always off in is own world, behind his glasses.

"We got us the Three Musketeers here," Booker joked, only, given what was between them now, it fell flat.

They were coming to the cluster of mobiles where Lucy and Ryan lived. Ryan in a single wide. His mother worked over at the Green Giant plant and was never home afternoons. Sometimes, when Lucy's father pulled a split shift, she'd go over and they'd study. Just that. And Ryan's face lighting up—that's what she loved about him, that look on his face he got when he came on something new, so it was new to her, too, and he was excited about it, the world, and his life, even as terrible as it could be, and she needed, over and again, to see it, Ryan's fascination with the "Miracle of the World" as he called it— his fascination with everything. She could go for weeks lifted up by it, just an evening with Ryan. And Booker, he wasn't some dumb jock, though he tried to seem like one.

Since it had happened, he'd appeared afternoons, joking around and picking on them, when all the while he was watching for Arn, sticking with her until she'd gotten to her trailer.

When, after the third afternoon, she'd turned to him in total exasperation, said, "Booker, what is it you think you're doing?" Booker glanced around them, and for the space of a second had become someone else.

"'We know that in everything God works for good with those who love him, who are called according to his purpose,'" he said, a hard something in his face, and then he'd laughed and slapped Ryan on the back.

"Right, Einstein?"

And Ryan, glancing up at Booker in his pathetic green gumboots and his horrible, longed-armed pea-soup-green embarrassment of a jacket, had replied,

"Everybody is a genius. But if you judge a fish by its ability to climb a tree, it will live its whole life believing it is stupid."

She'd never seen it before, in all the years she'd known him, but Booker blushed.

They'd caught each other out, and it changed things.

After a moment, Booker shrugged, then said, "Yeah. You, Einstein, you got you some smarts there, though your sense of style could use some sprucin' up, okay? What's say we work on that, ya think?"

Now they'd come to the mail kiosk, where, after they'd split apart that night it had happened, Arn had come at her out of the dark.

"Ryan," Booker said, and off Ryan went, and Booker walked her to the door of her trailer.

"So, like," Booker said, "this is where you go in 'n' lock the door, right? You all have a nice night, you hear?"

He stomped through the trailers, under the too-blue mercury oxide lights, his shoulders swaying. When he reached busy Highway 13 there, he looked both ways and crossed.

And Lucy, hugging herself, swung inside, pulling the door shut behind her and locking it—for what that was worth—and her breath caught until she got the lights on.

Winter

7

Buck

On the stoop, he lifted the mail from the box and sorted through the junk—direct mailing—what a waste of trees—found a bill from his insurance company, which he tucked under his arm. That and an official looking envelope, one with a logo on it he didn't recognize, printed across the bottom, *Important Billing Information Inside Do Not Discard.* There was something from Naomi, too, which he slipped in with the others, and, grimacing, he turned to the west.

The sun was low, Daylight's Savings Time having ended. In an hour or two it'd be dark, and the trees in the street already skeletal, a hard rain in the last week having taken all the leaves down. Shuddering, as if against the cold, he stepped back into the shop where he set his hands on his hips, thinking to work, but on what he couldn't decide, not with the letter from Naomi—or was it an attorney?—pressed under his arm.

He lay a hand on the boat's transom, the curved shape, oddly, bringing an image to him of Naomi lying on her side, her back to him, mornings, and that oh-so-beautiful curve of shoulder to hip.

Sliding his hand up the gunnel, smooth as skin, he reminded himself he was under a deadline.

This morning he'd gotten the oar locks in, flush with the gunnels, but the thole pins on the oars had been too large, so had been binding, and he'd had to mill them on his lathe. A complex operation, granted getting the pins centered on the lathe took some doing. But now, he saw all that had been a gift. Work. Difficult work that took his mind off things.

He'd been free of having to think about Naomi since shortly after five, when he'd—grudgingly—risen, eaten a handful of leftover Halloween candies, made a pot of coffee, and though it was below freezing out, had gone out to work on the boat. So focused he'd skipped lunch.

Was that why he was so tired? He was going to have to take Naomi off his policy on the truck. And there were the other connections, business and whatnot, that would have to be severed. Phone. Credit cards. Accounts with heat, electricity. All those things that connected them.

And with that thought, he ducked in through the side door and into the house, taking all that with him.

The phone on the counter rang, and he—stupidly—swept it up. As if it might be Naomi.

"This is Holly Jorgenson, and I'm calling for the Policeman's Fund," and on she went. Did he support their "initiatives that would protect the rights of—"

He hung up. Felt guilty, but not. Going all the way back to when he'd first run away from St. Mary's Boarding School, he'd had troubles with the police, and those troubles followed him like a curse into his years playing baseball, but the worst of it coming after.

After the older of his two brothers had been shot and killed, and he'd had to look into it. And, later yet, dealing with his daughter's trouble.

No, the police were no friends of his.

He set the envelopes on the counter, the one on top more fund raising: Lend a Hand. For families in need. Lend a Hand keeps homes warm. Now, he'd give to them. What, twenty, thirty bucks? Even though he was all but broke. Because, god knew, he'd been without heat.

And so as not to forget, he propped that envelope on the counter by the door, where he couldn't miss it.

He sat at the table with a bowl of leftover stew, which he didn't bother to heat. But he had no appetite, anyway. Since yesterday the house had taken on a new and threatening character, in the kitchen now the too-dark seeming cupboards pressing in on him, making him feel suffocated. Should he paint them? White? It would open the kitchen up. And then the thought of all that in the attic, his playing that game with the gun, came to him again, and with it the girl.

Those smudges on her face hadn't been soot. And she'd need to get real with that.

He dipped into his stew, making as if he were enjoying himself, there at the table alone. The cat appeared at the storm door, regarded him with its golden eyes. He reached onto the counter where he kept the box of kibble and, stooping, poured a line of them over the worn linoleum to a dish he'd filled, then swung the door open and sat on the floor, the cold air pouring in, and in it the scent of leaf rot, and wood smoke, and something ashy.

The cat came closer, across the stoop, the furnace roaring on, and his heart thudding. If the cat came in, he'd live, he thought, only that was bullshit, he told himself. Or was it? Because it was no coincidence he'd been thinking of her as Gyg, and for some time. Life. She regarded him, crouched on the rubber weather strip of the threshold, there like a fire, all orange and yellow.

Live or die? The cat almost, but not, coming in. And in one decisive move, it darted to the dish.

Only to dash back outside, in the square of light in the yard crouching, looking back at him.

And it was with a certain ambivalence that he got to his feet and shut the door. Well, he'd see.

8

Lucy

"Morning, Bebbe Gurl," Lucy's father said through the door into her room. "You'll want to get dressed before goin' outside, okay?"

Lucy sat, braced on her elbows. She'd been dreaming. In her dream she was running from someone but could barely move. And at just the moment when—it, or he, or *Him*, she thought—was on her again, she flew up into the trees, and it was that feeling she wanted to hang onto. Of flying. Of being free of it. And then to be awakened to—what did he want, her father?

She went into the bathroom, and in the dark, peed. "No time for a shower now," her father called to her through the door. "And, anyway, you'll want to do that after we're done."

"Can I wash my face?"

"Your eggs are getting cold."

When she came out, she saw that he'd put out a plate for her. Eggs, and two pieces of toast, buttered. She didn't eat bread; and not toast with butter, something she'd told him umpteen times. But when she sat, she ate everything; it wouldn't do to provoke her father, not when he had some agenda.

And he always had some agenda, though he seemed more lit up with it now than usual. Had he been drinking again?

The front door opened behind her. "You just about ready?" he said, poking his head inside.

"Be right with you," she replied, and washed her plate and silverware in the sink and set them in the drain.

She checked the thermometer in the front door window, it was twenty-six degrees, then dressed and stepped out onto the stoop, her father standing in the drive in his tan canvas hunting rig, two knives in hand.

"Arn got lucky in the lottery, so we jumped on it first thing this morning already," he said, "since I used all my sick days...."

And there he turned away, his hands set on his hips and his back to her—yes, *after he'd gone on that bender.*

Her father nodded to his right, and she followed him around the trailer, where a moose hung from its hind legs in a tree. There were sawhorses, too, and a five-by-eight sheet of plywood set on them, covered with the kind of plastic they put over the trailer's windows in January, when it got too cold.

For a second, she felt her breakfast come up. What the hell, she thought, putting on her game face, he'd gone and fucking shot Bambi, joking with herself as she often did around her father.

"Enough meat to get us through most of the winter." He thumped the matted side of the moose. "Chops. Burger. Loins. The whole nine yards. The burger makes great spaghetti and chili. We'll start on that."

She took a deep breath. "Great," she managed. She had to say it. "That's just great, Dad."

"Well, it's time you learned how to render your own game, Luce, since, if we save a little more, we'll be out of here faster," her father said, which set off true warning bells.

Save? And *more*? They were already just scraping by, or were they?

And he had been drinking. She hadn't smelled it, earlier, but did now, that chemical smell on his breath. Vodka. Chased with tomato juice. So, she'd been right to put a happy face on it, his moose.

"Moose hide, if you soften it up enough, you could use it like a quilt, you know, over your bed. Since you said you were cold last winter."

That he was thinking of her kind of touched her; but there was that other thing in it now, too.

"Arn coming over for his portion?" she asked.

"Bagged his own. Why? I thought you and ol' Uncle Arnold were like—" he held up his hand, the index and second finger entwined. "How you two cozied up to each other."

"He's *not* my uncle."

"Sure, but, that's what you used to call him. Don't you remember that? Not any more?"

She felt it on her neck, the flush, but maybe her father had had too much to drink to notice something like that now.

Uncle Arnold. As if! No, Arn had been very careful in how he'd gotten to her, Arn, for all practical purposes the textbook chicken hawk. Arn, after her mother'd been killed, stepping in to help, stopping over day, by week, by month, with a bag of groceries, or cooking when her father'd blacked out again, so by the end of that year he'd become indispensible, and when her father, to pay off debts from the messes he'd made, and to get them off the res, began working the higher paying night shifts, Arn'd offered his ol' Army buddy help then, too, Arn dropping by evenings to "check in" on her, though, sometimes, like when he'd hugged her, leaving, she'd gotten this… creepy, prickly sensation.

And things Ol' Uncle Arnold'd said, casually, had made her uncomfortable, too, because the real question was: Would she, in turn, tell her father these things he was confiding in her?

Like when Arn divulged that Esther Ruhland had shot her husband, Walter, "that wasn't any suicide," but since he'd been beating her, the Shakopee PD had looked the other way.

Even tampered with the crime scene, the one that so disturbed her father, the investigating officer, since it "just didn't look right."

All that, while she and her father were sinking under the leaden weight of her mother's death. And her father drinking when he wasn't working. Lucy herself numb, going through her days, a somnambulant.

And that's when *He* came to her, on a night when her father was working. She'd awakened to find her quilt yanked down.

He'd—at first—just put his fingers in her, and to her shame and disgust, he'd taught her she could respond.

And at the end of the month *He* first startled her, Arn, to her horror, materialized out of the dark.

And the truly sick thing was, she'd gone to her father in the kitchen the following morning.

He'd just come in off night shift—had been on a triple homicide/suicide, wife and two kids, and an estranged father, he told her.

"What is it, Bebbe Gurl?" he said, and on his face a broken look she'd never seen. Not ever.

"I love you, Daddy," she told him, and that had been that.

"Luce?" her father said now. "Bebbe Gurl?"

She waved him off it; reached for one of the knives. She had to do it. Even though she was afraid she'd throw up.

"Show me," she said, and her father stepped with her over to the moose, blade flashing, and his voice directing her when she cut back the hide, to separate the first hind quarter.

In seconds, her hands were greasy with blood and fat, but instead of being sick now, she felt furious. Thinking of Arn, and what he'd done, she slashed into the moose's side, into the meat.

"Hey, Bebbe Gurl," he father said, and caught her hand. "What's gotten into you?"

It was everything she could do not to break into hysterics, as she'd done that night Booker had seen her running, clutching at herself and weeping, stumbling in the dark to get hold of herself.

"Come on now, you know you don't handle a knife like that. What's this all about?"

"Just some… *shit* at school," she lied. She looked away, hidden from him by her hoodie.

"This something I need to look into?" He'd gotten that look on his face that scared her.

"No," she said.

"You sure?"

She, almost petulantly, tore herself from him, before he could turn her as he had in the past to get the truth out of her. "Can we just... *do* this? *Please?*"

"Okay then," he replied, and she nodded and, smiling her best-best fake smile, they stepped back to the moose.

He cut a piece of backstrap. Lifted it to the light. "See how it's marbled? That's the best." He popped the piece in his mouth and chewed. "Moose tartare," he joked. Jabbed Lucy with his elbow. "Try it?"

He cut another piece and handed it to her, and she chewed thoughtfully. She'd seen a movie over at Ryan's, a documentary in which a woman was raising rabbits. The filmmaker stepped in. "Pets or meat?" the woman said, holding up a cuddly bunny. Just like the moose.

"Good?"

"Yup," she said. "Thanks," but in her mind, she was coming up the street toward the garage, the guy there, with the boat.

In the trailer's bathroom, washing up before her father made lunch, Lucy regarded herself in the mirror. There were streaks of blood on her face from where she'd run her knuckled hand over her face—why was it that your face itched exactly when and where you couldn't scratch it? In her eyes was a blank look—so she screwed up her eyes, like in *Carrie*, where, after the shitheads dumped a bucket of pig's blood on the girl at the prom, she got back at them all in a moment of totally satisfying—since the beginning of the film waited for—carnage.

That's what she wanted for ol' Uncle Arn. And even more so... *Him*. That or—and she hated herself for even thinking it—she'd drink a bottle of her father's vodka and put a plastic bag over her head like her classmate had done.

Poor Tony, after the a-hole football guys had relentlessly gone after him for being "queer bait," he'd ended it all—after she'd spoken to him the day before, helped him with his math in homeroom.

Ever since his funeral, she hadn't been able to stop thinking about his having killed himself like that.

"Luce!" her father called.

"Give me five!" she shouted through the door in return, putting a bit of sass in it; if she did it *just a little*, her father backed down.

She shucked off her clothes, then got into the shower, set the water on high, so it was almost scalding. If she could only wash it off, all that with… *Him*, and with Arn, and… but then she thought, You couldn't wash it off, *ever*—that or the laughter. Arn joking about the two others he'd let into the trailer. That was the worst. Or could you, wash it off? If you just had the stones to come back at them? But then, she found herself smiling, really.

The guy with the boat, he was way beyond any of that. You could just feel it. He was the real deal, and nobody was going to be laughing at him.

Monday at school, Jean drew her up the hallway and away from the lunchroom where the kids were chattering like monkeys. Outside, it was bright, and she squinted into the sun. They went down a grassy embankment to huddle in a cluster of older oaks, all still in leaf—they never lost them until spring, why was that? Ryan, he'd know—and they rattled in the breeze.

Jean spiked a joint, and with a lopsided smile held it out to her. Lucy shook her head.

"I shouldn't, either," Jean said, "but I've got B.O. Pitts for social studies coming up, and, hey, I gotta get through that, right?"

That Mr. Pitts taught in a crappy school like theirs seemed a singular act of bravery, given how vicious the kids could be.

"I know, you've got the hots for Bill," Jean teased. "Oh, Bill, give it to me, baby, give me your—"

"*Jean*," Lucy said.

Jean's eyes softened. She swung her head from side to side, pulling a face and being silly in her purple hoodie and knee-high boots.

"Here," she said, and thrust a plastic-wrapped donut into Lucy's hand. "Lifted it from the machine for you."

She spun backwards, imitating kicking the machine. One of Jean's tricks. Lucy took a bite of it. Powdered sugar. Had no idea why she was eating the donut, other than that Jean had given it to her.

A gaggle of boys pushing and poking at each other came down the embankment, and all of them out of sight of the school.

Jean tugged at her. "Come on," she said, "let's go before they see us and come over."

They dodged through bentgrass to a culvert where a creek drained, and sat on a jumble of broken cinderblocks behind it. Here the sun, away from the breeze, warmed them. Jean yawned, and when she did, she threw her arms behind her. Her breasts were a marvel. That she had a boyfriend out of high school was no surprise. All the boys nosed around her.

Lucy's phone buzzed in her pocket, and she lifted it up to see who it was. Her father.

"I gotta get this," she said, and while he told her that he'd be late, and not to hold up dinner, Jean made faces, her mouth a rapturous "*oh*."

"Done!" Lucy said, and slipped the phone back into her hoodie pocket, and Jean put her face in Lucy's.

"What?" she said, and Jean kissed her.

But this time she kept her eyes closed, and there was a tenderness in it. Jean holding her face in her hands, and when she pulled away, they sat, saying nothing, because saying anything would have ruined it.

And in the sun, this warmth in her. Maybe she wouldn't die, maybe she wouldn't come to some terrible end. Maybe—

And there the school bell rang, carrying down to them through the chatter of the lunch crowd.

9

Buck

He was in the shop with the door open, though it was below freezing and his hands were cold.

The Bekins Van that would pick up the boat would be over any time, and it was for that, he'd told himself, he wanted to be ready. So, waiting, he organized. Veneers. Then clamps. Cleaned out the joiner and router and rip saw. Sharpened the blades on his planer, used his emery block, oil, and leather, to get the planer so sharp he could, running the blade along his thumbnail, bring up a band of thumbnail as thin and translucent as onion skin.

He got his bucket and filled it with water—added a soap that smelled of wintergreen—and washed the cement floor. Even in the corners, which required moving things.

Done with that, he got out a folding chair, snapped it open and sat in the cold, jays calling raucously in the pines up the street. Sniffed the air: more leaf rot and dryer vent perfume.

And here, in the cold, was the girl again in the street, in her hoodie. She came up the drive.

"Hungry?" he asked.

She shrugged. Kept her face averted. The girl set to bolt at the slightest provocation.

"One sec," he said, and ducked inside. And it wasn't until he had the sandwich made and on the plate that he realized he was in the house, but the walls weren't seeming to press in on him. That he'd been waiting all this time—for this one thing and this one thing only: the girl.

Outside again, he caught his chair with his foot, slung it around between himself and her.

"Sit," he said, and she did that, and he handed her the plate.

She ate, at first with mincing bites—as if she were eating but trying not to. Was that it? Was she like that? Because Naomi had in her teens almost been killed by it. And there was that in the way she was eating.

The feral came around the side of the house. Sat between them on the asphalt drive. Lifting its head, it tested the air. Looked between them and, with mincing steps, approached the girl.

She pulled a piece of beef from the sandwich, held it palm out, and the cat, brushing her leg, took it. The girl ever so slowly turned, stroked the cat's face, and the cat stretched, purring.

"Yes, aren't you something," the girl said. She looked askance at Buck. "Does she have a name?"

"Gyg?"

"Life." The girl nodded. "That's just right. All orange and yellow like that." The girl took a another bite of her sandwich.

She chewed thoughtfully. She was really eating it now, since she wasn't thinking about eating.

The sun broke through the clouds, bathing the trees around them in light so yellow they seemed to glow. And in it this fated being together, the girl, the cat, and himself.

His phone rang in his pocket—damnit, he thought—and the cat tore around the back of the house.

"Aren't you going to answer it?" she asked.

"No."

"What if it's important?"

"It *is* important."

Six rings now. "So—"

The ringing stopped and he winked at her, something in it she did not like, not one bit.

"The world didn't end, did it?" he joked, hoping, somehow, he could bring her back around. "Sorry, just—trouble. Can't take it too seriously, or it'll kill you. Gotta choose your battles, right?"

The girl had moved down the driveway, the two of them standing the way their people did, obliquely.

She was something—and somebody'd gone after her, this girl, and her face in profile set just so, a duckling, about to become a swan. And her dark hair, in the sun shot iridescent purple.

"I should go," she said.

"Stop by again," he replied, "*if* you feel like it. There's always something to eat if you're hungry."

They were at a comfortable distance now, where you could say something, but not raise your voice.

"Really?" The girl kicked at something in the drive, looked one direction, then the other, then back.

"Anytime," he said.

She nodded, then went off up the street, ducking under the willow by the curb, and was gone, as if she'd never been, and he thought to show her how to make a willow whistle.

To get her started on softwood. Handling a blade which, in the not too distant future, he knew she'd need.

10

Lucy

Booker fell in beside her as she entered the trailer park, but without Ryan along, it felt too close. She wasn't sure what he wanted.

"Booker," she said.

"Mind if I walk alongside?"

"Not at all," she replied, surprised to find herself thinking to sling her arm through his.

She was amused at Booker's formality, enjoyed it. Booker, steering her around the upended Cadillac, and by the reservation boundary sign:

YOU ARE ENTERING
SACRED GROUND
NO ALCOHOL
OR DRUGS ALLOWED

"That damn thing's got more bullet holes in it than a block of Swiss cheese," Booker joked.

Lucy laughed, despite what was between them. Booker was trying. And she was still, against all her misgivings, buoyed up by her time at the boat builder's house. That she couldn't bring herself to so much as ask his name, and that he didn't ask hers, either, spoke of a depth of relation, one unusual, but disturbing. She could be anybody over there. Or, herself, which felt…scary, since she knew where that would go. And, worse, what it would cost.

So, it felt good to have Booker say her name now. She was just

Lucy now, with him.

They threaded through the upended refrigerators, old farm implements, bedframes and junk at the east end of the res. Lucy had gotten ahead of Booker, so as not to have to deal with what he wanted.

And when she thought on what the boat builder had said, when his phone had rung and he hadn't answered it, had said no just then to being interrupted— "The world didn't end, did it?"—she spun around so Booker all but bumped into her, having put him off long enough.

"Booker," she said, "*what* do you want? Really?"

"Looking out for you is all," he shot back, her trailer just up the road and to the left.

"Well," she said, hating herself for it, "I don't need your help," because, the truth of it was, she did.

Coming home, she was terrified that it could happen again. Or worse. Down on the flats, where the river sometimes flooded things, there were scraggly cottonwoods, places where you'd never, never find a body, and there was rumor there were a few out there. All sorts of res girls disappeared, and the parents telling themselves those girls just ran away.

A V of geese flew overhead, high above the crisscrossed gaps of the cottonwood leaves.

"Going where it's warm," Booker said.

"Don't be so nasty to Ryan, okay?" she scolded. "I know you think you're being funny, but...."

"Okay."

"Okay?"

"Yeah," Booker said. "I said okay. So, I apologize. Do you want me to say something to him?"

It so touched her, she wanted to get into the trailer and away from him—to protect him from her, but most of all from her problem—because, someone, or more than someone, was going to die.

"Really, Booker, you don't have to, I'm okay," she said, though, she wasn't okay at all.

"This isn't about Ryan."

"Booker, please. Just leave it alone?"

"That *wasn't* okay."

She felt she might cry. Goddamn it. It had all been sort of all right, until he went and said it. Brought it out in the open between them. It still hurt. Down there, so badly it scared her at times.

"Booker," she said, "you don't know what he's like."

"I *do* know what he's like. I *saw* it."

"And I can't go to the police, and you can see why not, and what's there to do about it now, anyway?"

The way he was looking at her, she was afraid he was going to say something horrible now, something that could ruin both their lives, because she knew how quickly things could go wrong.

"Ryan can't protect you," he said.

She felt her eyes screw up at that. Don't say it, she thought. Don't. But then she was, anyway. "Yeah, like, *really*?" There, she'd done it, even not meaning to; suggested it.

"You need to get out of here, that's what I'm sayin'. That's your only other option here, see?"

"Oh?" She was relieved because she had it in her to say yes to what they'd both been thinking. That Booker might help her.

"Listen," he said now, "I know you lost your moms and all, but she'd be the one you'd go to, who'd get it done or die. Only, she's looong gone, and, hell no, not your pops. And, sure, you *could* go to your school counselor, if you could stomach how horrible that'd be, but that'd all go wrong, too, be all useless and everything, and you know exactly why, and so do I. Which is why you aren't doin' nothing like that. Cause, we both know the best you'd get would be an all but useless restraining order. And most people disbelievin' you 'n' all, callin' you a liar on top of shit's been done already, right?"

She felt her eyes narrow. "Say it, Booker. Why not my dad?"

"Your pop's just a lit match short of an explosion, kind that takes out everything around it, and all his pervo pals being cops, too, well, that's just a total cluster fuck. So, you need help, and from outside."

"You think?"

"Nights your old man's car isn't in the drive, I've passed by your trailer. I seen that fat cop goin' in, but sometimes one or the other of his cop buddies, they be goin' in, too. So, I know it isn't just… him, see? The fat one, who done you like that."

Her face so hot it felt like it was on fire, she spun on her feet and marched from him.

So shamed, she thought again to just kill herself.

"Just tryin' to help!" Booker called from behind her, and she threw her fist up, middle finger extended.

"Don't!" she called back. Even though for a minute there she'd wanted nothing more than to fall into his arms and cry.

In the doublewide having barely shut the door, she got on the phone. Her father had turned down the heat again. *Fuck.* Was it fucking cold in here, or what? she thought, the phone pressed to her ear and looking for the thermostat on the wall. Forty-seven degrees. Here another way her father was saving to get them out this… fucking double wide.

Ryan answered. "Chen residence," he said.

"Can I come over?"

There was a muffled something, Ryan covering the phone with his hand, some garbled conversation.

"You can't stay late," he said, "not like that one time."

She'd been bleeding then, after what Arn had done, and had been terrified it wouldn't stop, so hadn't wanted to be alone. Surreal, that's what it had been. Ryan's mother watching TV, and she and Ryan there at the kitchen table and going over their calculus as if she were fine. And all the while she was wondering if she might die, or—if she was ruined or broken somehow.

"Promise," she said. And then, as if it were nothing, she added, "Can you walk me over?"

Only, she felt awful about it now because, after what Booker had said, she was being selfish.

Prone on the Chen's dirty green carpet, her social studies book open in front of her and the television playing, she could almost think she felt all right. It still hurt, though she'd only been spotting off and on now. But whether it was from... *that,* or from the other thing, she couldn't be sure. And it was as if she were of two minds, the one that was still screaming, I'm *torn!* Something's wrong inside of me! And the girl who lay on the floor, who told herself all over again: *It's your period, finally, Stupid. You're lucky you're not*—which she wasn't, she was pretty sure—*pregnant.*

She bent to the picture in the sociology text. *Margaret Mead with three girls interviewed,* the caption read. Maybe I could be like Margaret Mead, she thought, just pick up and go somewhere, but like... where? The girls in the photo were so beautiful, almond eyed and coffee-skinned. Bare breasted, but the picture cut just below their shoulders.

"...and the nature versus nurture debate, that's going to be on the test, too, " Ryan was saying.

What did she care? What lit her up was the line "unavoidable periods of adjustment."

"Did you hear what I said?" Ryan asked.

"—'discussion of family, adolescence, gender, social norms and attitudes,' that's what Mead brought up."

"It's going to be on the test."

"I know."

She glanced to her right, where Ryan's mother lay sprawled on the couch, Mrs. Chen having drunk too much—her face slack, and the television jabbering away and casting a blue light on her face. Ryan was reading aloud, "Franz Boas," and this and that, and, while he did, what she'd told Jean about her and Ryan came to her, and she rolled onto her back.

What if?

On the ceiling was a brownish-red stain the exact shape of Italy, even with the heel of the boot there, where the ceiling tiles joined.

She took his hand, the one he was turning the pages with, and placed it on her right breast. The furnace ticked on, and a rush of warm air poured out of the floor vent onto them. When Ryan all but froze, she drew his hand down over her ribs, and when he didn't resist, she slid his hand down under her jeans and under the elastic band of her underpants, just there.

"Touch me," she whispered.

There was a distancing, weird embarrassment in the moment, but the other thing was larger.

Ryan went lower, where she'd been bleeding. She needed to know it was okay down there. "No," she said. "Not there."

When he seemed not to know what to do, she set the tips of his fingers just so on it.

"A circle. Make a circle. Not…. on it, around it."

He did that.

"Soft. Not so hard. Lighter."

There was something so strange about it all, it felt like falling through gauzy layers of… just what she didn't know, and, yes, it felt all right now, and the smell of Ryan's mother cigarettes in the room, and the musty carpet, and the television yammering, she caught it, like a wave.

"Don't stop," she said, holding his hand there, pressing down.

She closed her eyes, and daring the moment, *what if*—but she'd entered that other room now, ever-larger and oh-so-hungry, but not with… *them*, it was Ryan who was touching her— and, it was like giving herself over, rising up into it, and she pressed her eyes closed.

Said, her voice husky, "Faster now. Press harder. Right—" she got his fingertips on the side. "There."

And this…wonderful thing rose weightless in her head, sort of right this time, now, here, and through her whole body came an expanding, a rising, and nothing, nothing at all mattered now, and she was clutching his hand, guiding him, pressing, and pressing, and pressing until it exploded in her, and her eyes shot open, her eyes on his, she loved him, just then, she thought, she really did, and when it stopped, she spun around on her rear, and in a second she had him in her hand, Arn had made her fast, and just as Ryan came, his mother, Kitty, stumbled into the hallway, and he shot to his feet. Ryan pulling up his pants and tripping over himself and falling with a heavy thump, going into contortions to stand again, and his mother, drunkenly glancing around her, and then seeing Lucy, said,

"You go now."

Lucy had sat on the floor, her book open to whatever-the-fuck page it was. She had to look down to see.

She put that bland, know-nothing look on her face that she used with her father mornings, after Arn's visits.

Said, over her shoulder, brightly, "We're just wrapping up here, Mrs. Chen. On *Coming of Age in Samoa*. Ryan was really helpful."

It was something Jean would have said, but then she chided herself for it. She wasn't Jean, and she'd never be.

"I-sss almost eleven," Mrs. Chen said, taking pains to enunciate the S, "and tomorrow-sss school day."

She got up from the floor. Her legs shaking. And there was this dreaminess in her.

"Walk me home?" she said to Ryan and, snatching her hoodie from the rack behind the front door, she nodded to Mrs. Chen.

"Thanks for letting me come over to study. It really helped. Ryan's just so—"

Even as bleary-eyed as she was, Mrs. Chen's face went through a transformation: from suspicion and irritation, to a look of fierce love for her son, and, yes, even for her now.

Her son's helper.

"Good night," Lucy said, and Ryan went out with her into the— cutting, cutting cold.

At the trailer, the lights weren't on. Her father was pulling another double shift, wouldn't come in until four. There was an awkward moment at the stoop. Ryan shifting on his feet, stepping closer, then making an overture to kiss her, but so woodenly she darted out and kissed him on the cheek.

He regarded her in that near-reptilian way of his, the look the other kids teased him about.

"Don't ruin it by saying anything, okay?" she said.

Lucy felt herself smile, and just then she felt a thousand years old, and she couldn't help lifting her hand to his cheek.

"Good night, Ryan," she said.

She locked the front door, even put on the chains, all three sets, because she was alone in the dark, and *He* was out there. Went up the hallway. There was the thermostat. Still forty-seven degrees. She'd make her father happy. Climb into bed with her clothes on; and in the morning, she'd take a scalding shower. Dress for school in something warm.

She shut her bedroom door behind her—"Never, never lock your door, Bebbe Gurl," her father had told her. "This tinderbox of a trailer catches fire, and you're asleep, I'm coming for you. Okay?"

But why would he think the trailer would catch fire? She slid under the dirty quilt. And when her ears were cold, she pulled it up over her head, so just her mouth was free, so she could breathe. Cocooned and in the dark, she fell away from the world, as if she were only her mind, and the memory of what she'd done with Ryan there, and falling through that, there was something satisfied, but incomprehensible in it, beautiful, really, but wrong, too, she knew that, and she almost slept.

She'd never let Ryan know she—usually—did better in school than he did; it would ruin things.

She'd try to be more helpful. A better study partner. And Ryan, her most-likely-gay friend, having this… bright, bright future ahead of him, one she was a part of when she was with him.

Which meant the world to her.

11

Buck

He was—again—working in his shop with the door open when the girl appeared at the end of his driveway for the third time.

Wearing a pair of black leather boots that went right up to her knees and a new, even larger hoodie—one that was more flesh pink than the earlier one's dirtied lavender, *Abercrombie* across the chest in black letters, and under that, *Fitch*.

He came out into the driveway, then, recalling what he'd done earlier, held up his index finger. Ducked into the house, then was back with a plate, on it a hot cinnamon bun.

He'd set a pad of butter and a knife alongside it. When she, tentatively, lifted the plate, he told her,

"Do it right. Butter the thing. It's better that way. Otherwise, don't eat it at all. Gifts, you gotta say yes to them, right?"

That she wouldn't look at him after he'd said it, made him—for the space of a second—think he'd done the wrong thing. Kids, especially ones like this girl, were sensitive to being given orders. But having done that, buttered the roll, she bit into it, and her face lit up and there was this—moment—of near rapture, and now an unabashed smile, the girl shifting on her feet, licking the crumbs off her fingers, then shrugging shyly.

She nodded. Swallowing. Then took another bite and, holding her hand over her mouth, she said,

"So," then gave him a mock accusatory look, "I thought we were going to work on that boat."

"It's gone," he said.

She grimaced, stuffed a corner of iced bits in her mouth and, nodding, held up her icing-covered fingers. He'd thought of that, and handed her a napkin, and she dabbed at her mouth.

"Thanks," she said, then nodded. "So? It went where?"

"Seattle."

"Ah," she replied. Truly disappointed, but she was doing her best not to show it. She was good at that. "Who?"

"Software billionaire."

"Bill Gates?"

"I wish."

She shrugged, looked away, her shoulders dropping. "Well, I didn't have time anyway, so—"

"What about a canoe?"

"Like… how?"

"You make one."

"*Me*?"

"Yes. You. I can show you."

The girl smiled, something secret there. Something that made her happy. Something… serendipitous… almost magical in the moment, all of which he palpably sensed.

After all, what was with the new hoodie and the boots? And pants, too, now that he looked.

"So, what's the occasion?" he asked. The girl turned, her back to him. Deciding. "Come on," he cajoled. "Something that good, you should share it."

She half-turned. Closer. But still facing away. She was going to do it; tell him, if he just kept his mouth shut. Today she was a very, very pretty Indian girl, a pretty girl in trouble.

She cocked her head this way and that. If he, too, turned away a bit, faced the street as she did, maybe—which he did.

She shrugged, then glanced decisively over at him. "It's my birthday today, my fifteenth."

"Hey," he said, and threw his arms wide, "Happy birthday—" but he didn't know her name. "Are you Abercrombie or Fitch?" he said, and winking, added, "or are you both or neither?"

"Lucy," she said. She'd been about to put out her hand, but she was holding the plate.

"Buck," he said, and they mock shook in the distance between them, amused. "Should I put a candle in your roll there, make it official? Or we could get started on the canoe?"

Lucy was so surprised she mumbled something through the roll in her mouth; then, embarrassed, said,

"Like, sometime, right?"

"No," he said, "not like *sometime*. How about *now*? It being your birthday and everything."

"Really?"

"Yes, really."

"Can I use your restroom first?"

"Through the back," he said, "first door on the left."

She returned minutes later, followed him into the garage, and he snapped on the lights and pulled out a sheet of wood. Slid it onto the worktable.

"Spruce. Fine grain. No knotholes from branches. But... a little too soft. Especially if you're going to be doing anything other than just floating around in ponds and such."

"It's pretty," she said.

He slid the wood back into the slot. Pulled out another. Laid it, as before, on the table.

"Fir. A bit more durable. Same thickness. No knots to deal with. Stains well."

The girl had come in closer. She was looking at the wood in the light. "It looks the same to me."

"Yup. Same color, but finer grain. By half. See?"

The girl bent to look and nodded. He got out a third sheet. What was wildly colored, cream and a most lovely reddish tan.

"The red portions stain darker," he told her. "Which can look

62

nice, but they usually don't, so you stain the entire hull."

"What is it?" She ran her hand over the wood, palm down, as if caressing something.

"Red cedar. Tough as steel, but flexible."

She stepped over to his workbench, the valentines Naomi had made for him over the years pinned on the wall there, and Lucy following the progression of them, earliest to latest.

"They're really beautiful," she said. She glanced at him over her shoulder, aware he was watching her.

She spun around, then stared down at her feet, and that dejected set to her shoulders again.

"What?"

She frowned. "I should get going."

"Oh," he said, finally getting it. Money. "*That*. Well, see, I can always make it for advertising."

"You can?"

"Sure. You just have to agree to tell people it came out of this shop and it's yours. Can you do that?"

She glanced at her watch—a sort of face-saving, since she didn't know what to make of it all, and since she had reasons, and good ones, for not trusting people. And she was embarrassed.

"Look, I really do have to go." She set the plate on his workbench, then backed down the drive, but facing him. "So. You'll... show me... how to use the tool... *thingies* and all that? *If* I come back?"

"Promise" he said, and the girl spun out onto the street, and heading off and away she threw her hand up.

Yeah, you too, he thought, and went into the too quiet, dust-filled emptiness of the house.

12

Lucy

Right on time, she was thinking to herself as she approached the trailer, and the lights off. Well, he'd forgotten her birthday again, mostly, except for the clothes he'd picked up secondhand for her, and that was better than having to suffer an awkward… weirdness, wasn't it?

She paused outside. Scared half out of her mind to be in the open, but not wanting to go in. Was he drunk in there? Or—

She cocked her head, listening for the usual sounds, the ones she'd hear when her father was home: the TV, and the clattering of the exhaust vent—the one he blew cigarette smoke out of, her father going through a pack now and then.

Heard nothing, didn't smell smoke. And when did he ever turn all the lights out this early?

Something wasn't right, and the hairs on her neck standing up and her breath catching, she got the door unlocked, then swung inside, yanked the door shut behind her and locked it, only to realize, blue orbs swimming in her eyes, and her heart hammering, what she'd been alarmed by outside, was *inside* the trailer: the chemical, astringent scent of Brut, what Arn wore, and even as she was crossing the kitchen to the rack of knives, a scream in her throat, the lights came on, all but blinding her so she threw her forearm over her eyes. A roar of laughter filled the room, and her father, lit up with drink, caught her under her arms and spun her around, and around, and around, and there, in that too small space all her father's cop friends, some even in uniform, and smiles on their faces, and a cake on the counter.

"Hey, Bebbe Gurl! Who loves you!" her father called out, and they all broke into a chorus of "Happy Birthday."

As they were singing, Arn got up from the couch from behind the others, that "Who, *me*?!" look pasted on his face, and he, on the tail end of it, like some… choir director, led them in "For She's A Jolly Good Fellow," something positively bizarre in it, and in Lucy's mind one thought: *I could say it, right now. Say it in front of all these people and—maybe that would be the end of it.*

And just then Ryan and his mother came in. And that's where that died. Saying anything. It would be too humiliating, and Ryan holding a box wrapped in something pink and a blue ribbon around it.

They'd all been drinking, waiting, and the floor of the trailer, with the extra weight on it, bounced like a trampoline. She shared a look with Ryan, for the briefest second, both rolling their eyes. They both hated these sorts of things, and then, everyone was drunk already, she hated being around drunks, worst of all her father, and Jackson, her father's friend, bumped into the lamp on the end table, it was too close in the trailer, and when it fell, it broke. Or, broke the lampshade, so that, when her father set the lamp back up on the end table, it threw shadows, and they danced, her father and his friends, goofing on their shadows, and Ryan's mother cutting the cake, and there was that candle thing, lighting all fifteen, and the pervert, Arn, trying not to look in her direction, bellowing, "Make a Wish, Miss Lucy," which scared the hell out of her because now that they'd all been drinking, it would take nothing to set things off.

"I wish you were dead," she said to herself, "and cut into a fucking hundred little fucking pieces."

"Can't say what your wish is, Bebbe Gurl!" her father shouted, catching Arn in the crook of his arm. "It won't come true if you do."

She bent over the cake. Wished, silently this time, Arn dead again; but even more so the one who'd started it all. *Him.*

She blew out the candles, and they did a circle dance to "Standing Outside the Fire," something she despised. And dragged into it, into the chain by her father, the whole beer smelly, booze smelly, swelling clot of people and hot breath navigating their godawful shitbox of a trailer—her father, even as they went by the counter where the gun was, pulled her close and all but shouted into her ear,

"You'll never guess what I got you for your birthday, Bebbe Gurl, not tonight, but you'll see!"

He spun away from her, grinning, then held his hands up and called out, "Ladies and gentlemen!" and the music stopped, everyone turning to them, and he gestured to Lucy, said, but now with a sincerity that just killed her, "Will you look at my..." and there he got choked up, and everyone laughed, "I was going to say, 'little girl' but look at her, fifteen, and she's a beautiful woman! Isn't she just... beautiful? And—" he teared up, "—and I'm so *proud* of her!"

All of them looking at her, clapping, she just—couldn't— stand— another horrifying second of it, and she bowed, and darted out the door, all of them laughing, leaving poor Ryan in the trailer.

"Motherfucker! Oh, Jesus Christ!" she said on the stoop, wrapping her arms around her shoulders. And, she had to admit it, she *was* choked up.

It was cold out, and there was wood smoke in the air. But at least she knew now that Arn was *in there*—

But *Him?*

And just as she thought it, Booker appeared mysteriously from the maw of trees across the drive.

"Booker," she said, "what are you doing here?" It was something you'd just say, but she meant it.

The moon was out, almost full, and a shelf of clouds bracketing it so that moon beams shot from behind.

"Saw me a werewolf, looked like a man," Booker said. "Went into your trailer there earlier, 'fore your dad and the others showed." She put a hand to her forehead. "Booker."

66

"Happy birthday, 'n' all that."

She sighed. "Really, Booker. *Why* are you here?" She was desperate to say: Go away. You'll only make things worse. But she could see now he wasn't going to do that.

"Why? Why me?"

"You don't ask why something falls into your lap, you know? I'd've come on you 'n' him a minute later, well, I wouldn't've seen it all; or better, earlier, and you wouldn't've been done-to like that. My bad, so—"

She felt herself flush. As earlier, it was one thing to think he knew, and another to have him say it.

"How'd you know it was my birthday?"

"My mom's over at your school, works in the office. Looked into you when I asked her to. Yeah, they seen the bruises, and you got a friend over there, too, watching out for you. Mr. Opitz, your civics teacher."

"Booker," she said, "you don't have to do this, don't you see? And it could all get—and tell me you haven't done anything, please, please, please *don't*, and I really mean it."

"My moms, I had to tell her, that you had trouble, see if she could look into it 'cause—"

She was instantly in tears, fighting off a kind of hysteria. God DAMNIT! She'd been hiding it all so long.

"What'd she say?"

"Well, he's done this before. My moms, she looked into him, and when she gets her teeth on a bone like that—"

There was a thump inside the trailer, then a crash of something, and through the windows, laughter.

"Your Arn showed up at that gas station we pass gettin' home, you know the one, where a—" he shrugged, looking for the right thing to say, "—a girl like you got herself a coke, and disappeared. Happened like... what, four years ago? 'N' pictures of her all over? You member that?"

"Rose L'Rieux," she said, almost angrily, "she went to my school, of course I remember."

She didn't want to believe Arn was any more dangerous than she already thought he was. And, really? She'd never made a connection between Rose disappearing and Arn. And her mother was a friend of Rose's mother, so that, when they'd been little, they'd been cared for by both.

Rose had been years older, so, of course, nothing had come of it but watching TV together.

"She ran away, sent a card from… Chicago or something," she said, hating herself.

"Yeah, well…. *No*. She din't run away, and that card, the one she sent home, they weren't sure it was Rose's handwriting on it. And Arn bein' there, it was on the security video." Booker nodded. "This cop, Lyman Dye, friend of my moms? Native, like you. He caught on to it, seen a pattern, since years back, Arn showin' up and somebody disappearin', but when he pulls Arn over, lookin' into it, he finds Arn's got this… airtight alibi, every time."

"Well, that's it then, isn't it?"

"*No*, Lucy," Booker said, "that's the whole point, *that's* what I come to tell you. His alibi was way, way too tight. So, it isn't just Arn. They're *organized*, Arn and his pals. So, goin' after Arn isn't gonna fix anything. Fact is, it'd make what's going on with you now a whole shitload worse."

She was turning to go into the trailer, the dark swimming around her, when Booker said,

"Hey, I'll walk you home like I've been. And *don't* go out alone, not until we can think of somethin'. Take 'em *all* down, okay?"

She craned her head over her shoulder, said, "Thanks," then swung into the raucous, beery clutch of her father's party.

13

Buck

He woke early, and in the kitchen got his coffee started, then leafed through the mail on the counter. There was a scratching, and when he opened the storm door the cat, as it always did, dashed back into the yard.

When the girl was around now, the cat came into the house after her, and she put out kibble.

He dug to the bottom of the envelopes, the last glaring. *Overdue* stamped in red across it. He slid his thumb under the corner of the flap, tore the envelope open and pulled the bill out. Read the heading and, scanning down the page, got to the gist of it. *Charges refused*. He called the service number and was routed into a labyrinth of useless prompts, any of which, when engaged, rerouted him back to the salutation. *Hello, you've reached—*

He shouted, "Operator!" then got the brief satisfaction of hearing what seemed to be a phone ringing, after which he heard—*Hello, you've reached*—the salutation starting all over again.

The charges were Naomi's, and he slammed the phone down, frustrated, then noticed the light on the answering machine was blinking.

He pressed play, then poured kibble into the cat's bowl, standing behind it to take in the messages. The first was from the software designer. The boat was a work of art, he said, "it rows beautifully." In the middle of the message he pressed the *skip* button. The second message, from Leif, was to let him know his supplies were in. "Don't wait three weeks this time." Again, *skip*. And the last was an inquiry about his cabinetry; it was a large job, and they were taking bids.

The caller ID read: *Unknown Name.*

Could he please call, at his earliest convenience? "I'll be out of the office, but can be reached at"—and there the caller gave a number, which he managed to get down on his notepad.

When the answering machine beeped, having come to the end of the messages, the cat looked up at him, just feet back from the door.

And there it was again—that thought: He'd live if the cat did, if it came into the house.

His eyes on the cat, the phone pressed between his shoulder and ear, he dialed the number, then stepped away from the counter and the cat's dish, and the cat—belly low to the cement stoop, came closer, then closer yet, and the phone ringing, four, then six times—and just when he was about to hang up—his eyes on the cat's eyes, just as it was coming in over the threshold into the house—someone answered.

"Yes?" she said, the voice shockingly familiar.

There was a hum on the other end. Confused, he bent over the phone/answering machine.

"Hello?" Lucy said. "Who is this calling? Hello? Hello, are you there? Is that you? *Buck*?"

Dumbstruck, he held the phone away, as if something evil had reached out and touched him, and when he couldn't think what to say, he banged the phone down into the cradle.

Hit the Caller ID/recall button, found the number this... potential customer had called in on, then lifted the receiver, ringing it.

"Lord Fletcher's on the Lake," a man answered, "would you like to make a reservation?"

"Wrong number," he replied, and hung up, his mind swimming in it, why someone would want him to call Lucy.

Should he call her back? He checked the time; she'd told him her father was there mornings. So, no. He couldn't risk it—he'd have to wait, let her bring it up when she stopped by.

He shrugged on his jacket and went out to the shop, the cat bolting off and into the yard. It was too cold to have the door open, so he worked inside with it closed, now on a dresser.

Assembling it, carefully, painstakingly, he was somewhere in the back of his mind thinking on his call to Lucy.

It could be used as proof of something... truly damning, but he just had no idea what.

Someone had wanted—or was it *needed*?—him to call her; but why?

14

Lucy

Lucy, all morning, felt alternately panicked, and at the same time... oddly cared for, Booker having come by, and she couldn't wait to talk to Jean now, to tell her about what she felt about him, only not... *that*, why he'd come by, and each hour passed as if an eternity, her teachers wah-wah-wah-ing about this and that, and all the while in her head there was a kind of... light-filled deliciousness she was—even in a near swoon—guarding herself from falling into too much.

Booker was watching out for her. And Buck—why did she always have to ask herself what his name was?—he was in his own way, too. He'd called her; but then they'd gotten cut off.

Civics: "Lucy, how many seats are there in The House of Representatives?"

"435, Mr. Opitz," she replied.

In biology, her teacher pointed to a cell on the screen at the front of the room: "Lucy, what is this structure?"

"Mitochondria."

"What does it do?"

She, too, all but droned on now, Wah-wah-wah, "powerhouse of the cell, Adenosine Triphosphate is formed as a result of a transfer of electrons from NADH or FADH2 by a series of electron carriers." Wah-wah-wah. "Oxidative Phosphorylation." Wah-wah-wah.

In geometry: "Lucy, what does the Pythagorean Theorem postulate?"

"The square of the hypotenuse is equal to the squares of the two other sides, Mr. Branson."

The goth girl in the seat behind her poked her with her finger. Right in the shoulder blade, so it hurt. "Shut-*up!*" Lucy found herself staring, wide eyed, at Mr. Branson.

"Lucy, do you have something to add?" he asked.

"No, sir," she replied.

The bell rang, and she swept her books up, slung them in her pack. She all but ran outside, where Jean was blatantly smoking in the parking lot, her back turned to the school.

"Puff?" she said, handing her cigarette to Lucy, who took a deep, deep drag, blew out a plume of smoke, and away they went. Jean locking her arm in Lucy's, and Jean skipping.

"'We're off to see the Lizard,'" she sang, "'the wonderful Lizard of Oz, because because because because because—because of the wonderful things he does!'"

Lucy felt herself caught up in Jean's effervescence. A distance from the parking lot, and in the trees, Jean threw her head back.

"It's ALIVE!" she shouted up into the blue, open sky.

She swung Lucy around to the culvert, and they sat as they had before, perched on the broken concrete.

"Sally Watts is going with Tom Lister," Jean said, her puckish face screwed into a look of horror.

"What?"

"To Tinsel Twirl."

"Oh, that," Lucy said, taking the cigarette again.

"Anybody ask you?"

"No, why would they?" Indian girls, after a time, didn't get asked out. Her mother had warned her it would happen.

"Lucy…."

"I hate those things anyway."

"No, you don't."

Lucy pinched a bit of tobacco from her lip, handed the cigarette back to Jean, who examined it, then looked up.

"Why don't *we* go? Together?" she said. "Shake them up? All those… idiots. Will you? Please?"

Lucy felt herself take a quick, shocked breath. This, now, *was* threatening. She had no doubt what her father would think of it, and he'd find out, somehow—because, well, anything like that in public, it always came out, and she wasn't sure she could stand all that. And, anyway, what was Jean saying? But she couldn't hide it from herself; she was excited.

Jean darted forward and kissed her, and Lucy pulled back. It wasn't a refusal—she wanted to make sense of this… whatever it was.

"Jean, no," she said and, rebuffed, Jean sat back, her hands braced on the cement behind her, then glanced around them.

The place they were in was sheltered, and even warm in the sun. It was one of those days. Jean got this not-at-all funny look on her face, then slid over to Lucy and, cupping her hand behind her head, kissed her, really… and when Lucy, against her own better judgment, opened her mouth, mint toothpaste taste, and Jean's searching tongue was there, she felt it in her, like light, or happiness—and Jean slid her hand down her pants, but not like Ryan. Jean knew exactly what to do, and Lucy thinking *stop, stop, stop, stop!* but the pure pleasure of it, and the weird, wonderful exposure right here in the sun outside, and Jean's fingers doing exactly the right thing, until she was gasping, and Jean's lovely mouth on hers, there was that, like a burst of light.

She opened her eyes, and looked into Jean's. Jean's beautiful eyes on hers, and she slowly drew back.

She didn't know what to say. Her legs were trembling. Jean handed her another cigarette, and they passed it between them, saying nothing.

When the bell rang, they got up.

"So?" Jean said.

She wanted, so badly, to touch Jean now, to give back what she'd just been given, it almost hurt.

When Lucy didn't answer, Jean said, "Well, go with Ryan then. Since you—you know, with Ryan, why not? Hasn't he asked you?"

"Jean, no."

"We can—" she made a sideways motion with her head "—leave him at the punchbowl with my date. I can find somebody, and they'll never know the difference, and we'll be off in the moonlight."

It felt mean to even think it. Ryan was a friend. And she didn't want to use him. But…hey, he'd want to go.

"Okay," Lucy said, and hand in hand, until they breasted the bank to the parking lot and school, they went back.

Her father was at the trailer when she got in, rousting about, tossing his clothes in the wicker hamper, glowering in a fury at the dishes in the sink and the general mess of the trailer, saying it looked like goddamned bomb had gone off .

"Bebbe Gurl," he said, "I thought we talked about this, how, with me away, I need you to take care of things? We need order."

"You're *early*," she spat. She strode to him, took the clothes basket from him. "I was *going to*… but then you—"

"I know, I got off early. And, yeah, it's a lot to ask, and I'm sorry for that, but don't you want out of here, too?"

It shocked her. She wasn't going to get near that conversation. How badly she needed to get away.

"I'll get dinner started," she said. "You just go and do what you need to, all right?" What was going on with him?

"Well, good."

"Is everything okay? Is work okay?"

Her father cocked his head, so she could hear his neck cracking. It was all a bad sign. Her father stared into the countertop, then rapped his fingertips on it, having decided something.

Then he threw her a smile, the one with the dimples. "It's nothing," he said, "I'll take care of it," and nodded in a way that sent her heart pounding.

15

Buck

It was nearly eight and dark and, the truck's left headlight having burned out, it was hard to see the road, just a meandering tunnel through trees. And it was raining. The road was shiny with it and going to ice. And it was only when he felt the truck sliding sideways and a car coming on behind him that he pumped the brakes and steered opposite to correct the skid. The car nearly struck him from behind, then gunned by, the driver hunched low over the wheel, just as the truck's tires caught and the truck jolted to the right. His heart in his throat, the car's taillights dropped out of sight over a rise in the road.

He swung onto the shoulder and sat at the wheel with the wipers cutting the rain on the windshield.

A fox appeared up the road. It looked back at him and, with a shudder to toss the rain from its fur, loped into the trees.

He'd get to Leif's, but not stop for groceries. He didn't want the girl to show up at the shop and not have what they needed to start, and he got the truck moving up the road again.

He was thinking about Lucy, and the bruises on her forearms, and the stain there, on her pants, as he approached a car on the shoulder.

The car that had almost hit him? Or...he bent into the windshield going by. A silver Taurus. He searched his memory.

It *had* been a Ford, for sure, behind him in the dark without its lights on. Someone wanting to know what he was up to?

And was it paranoia, or... did it have something to do with Lucy?

Or was it just that he'd been thinking about her again?

Back at the house, he hit the garage door opener under the visor and the door came up, just as it always did. He stepped from the truck, then slid the first of the sheets of wood out from the camper and, spreading his arms to span its width, he walked the sheet into the garage and set it upright against the wall. Three sheets. And wood for the keel and ribs. Bow and stern plates, thwarts, and end caps. Simple enough. He got it all inside, then stepped back, eyeing the wood with some satisfaction. No knots or runs. Beautiful. Red cedar. And in it the promise of something... he smiled, at the thought of it, working on the canoe. But then recalled the car on the road.

Well, whatever it was, he'd deal with it. And, with a shrug, he hit the button on the wall and ducked out of the garage, and stepped into the house through the side door.

Even in the dark, he knew something wasn't right. There was a residual scent in the kitchen, like cologne, but then some of the flyers that came to the house had cologne samples in them. He told himself, really, he was making something out of nothing, and he hit the attic light going up the stairs.

Mounted the steps and in his study he—for just a second—felt the hairs bristle on his neck. Had someone been at his desk? He usually left his keyboard at an angle so he could log in bills from the three-tiered tray on his left, but now the keyboard was flush to his computer.

Always paperwork—*that* was it, he'd brought his bills up and logged them out at his desk, hadn't he?

He sat—scrabbled through the flurry of paper, all but tossing envelopes here and there—requisitions for supplies, quarterly taxes, receipts. Invoices. Went though it all a second time.

He'd find the offending advertisement with the cologne in it, he promised himself, that odd smell here, too. Or was it the wood? Wood scents were used in cologne. Like Brut—wasn't that sandalwood, which smelled like cedar?

He cocked his head to the side to sniff at the shoulder of his jacket. Or soap? That would do it. He lifted his hand and smelled it. When he'd visited the commode at Leif's, he'd used the bar of soap there. Soap, on a braided lanyard, so you could swing it over your head or whatever in the shower.

Well—he picked up an insurance notice. *Overdue.* Naomi's, and sent to him when Naomi hadn't dealt with it. And why had she refused to pay this one now? He read the fine print. Threats of all sorts, and the bill for all of $69.50. Better to just go ahead and pay it than to have to call her.

He lay his arms on the desk, then set his head on his hands, and in seconds he was asleep.

In the morning he rose early and, stiff from having slept in his desk chair, he all but hobbled down the stairs to the kitchen. He stood at the sink window where he could see the cat in the yard waiting to be fed, then ducked to the faucet, slapped water onto his face and dried off with the towel. Better. And what had been so important last night that he hadn't done? He shrugged, if he could just shake himself awake, he'd look around, find the offending cologne sample. He knew he should take a shower, shave, and brush his teeth, but he did none of it—sliding into what he knew could be a terrible precedent. The weird guy whose wife had left him, falling apart. He ran his hand over his chin. Stubble. No, nothing smelled strange in the kitchen.

Coffee, he needed coffee.

He got it started and put out the bowl for the cat, then stood with his cup at the window, the birds darting to and from his feeder, the cat looking warily around him from her bowl.

He absent-mindedly ate the—he lifted it to his face—cornbread he'd left there the day before. It smelled like sawdust.

There was all that with Naomi's bills he needed to deal with… *That's what it had been last night.* How he'd gotten distracted. He'd been going to look for whatever it was in the house that smelled like Brut, and picked up the bill.

He sniffed at the air, smelled nothing. What the hell, it had to have been the soap at Leif's.

Mystery solved. He felt almost smart having figured it out. And having been nearly run off the road? There was no relation between that and the call from the potential customer.

The call just more... someone messing with him, one of his competitors, or a prank call.

And getting connected to Lucy? She had to have called home from his phone when she'd gone into the house, earlier. So the number had been on his machine. The damn thing auto-dialed, sometimes, which drove him crazy.

Technology, it was magic—until it caused trouble.

Earlier, when he'd first listed in the Yellow Pages alongside The Toy Emporium, he'd gotten prank calls from kids. Ones that played off his ad, and the kids all but peeing themselves with laughter—

"If trees could kill, they wood!" And there followed a hysteria he almost envied, their joy in it.

"What does a stick say when it falls down? 'Wood you help me up?'"

Well, he had a dresser to build for a couple in New Haven, Connecticut. And with that thought he carried his mug out the door.

Some time later, and after having skipped lunch, he told himself he couldn't stand the closeness of the shop with the door down, so worked with it open, wearing gloves with the fingertips cut off so he could feel still, and had put on lined boots, a winter jacket, and a wool hat. Had even got on his heavy sweater that zipped up the neck. It was ugly, but warm. No scarves, ever—they could get caught in the machinery.

And it did feel good to have the door open, but he was waiting. Wasn't most of life waiting?

He slung a plank of oak from the rack, sighted down it. True and straight. Laid it on the milled surface of his ripping saw. He flipped on the switch, and the saw whirred violently. He got—as he often did—a flash of his arm, hand extended, the saw running over his wrist, cutting the hand from it. And why had he thought that? Not wanting his day upset, almost happily anticipating the pleasure of working, he told himself now: I'm not distracted.

Not thinking about having been followed.

Not upset about the girl and her trouble.

Not worried someone might have been in the house.

Only, just then the warning from Newt, his once mentor and friend, came to him.

On his first day in Newt's shop, Newt had taken his hand, pressed it flat on a plank of wood he'd been about to cut, and had run his carpenter's pencil around his fingers.

"What'd you do that for?" he asked.

Newt jabbed his finger into the board there, something like a child's pencil drawing of his hand on it.

"Help you remember your fingers after you've cut them off," Newt replied.

"What?"

"*Never*," Newt said, "feed wood into the saw with your hand in line with the blade like you were just doing, whistling and not paying attention. The wood catches, it'll pull your hand in and take your fingers off, and before you even know it's happened. Got it?"

He had. He'd never forgotten any of it. Don't lean over the wood. If the saw catches something in it, a nail, a knot, whatever, it can kick back, and up, too. Strike you in the face. No radio, not while using the saw. Don't daydream. You're working. Focus. Work from a suitable design. God is in the details, and *always* serve God when you're working. Measure twice, cut once.

And so, once again he emptied his mind of what had been clinging to it, the vague but persistent sense he'd lied to himself, and he gave himself to the work, applied a paper template to a plank and, as if diving into saving waters, he fashioned the top of the dresser, then, from a second plank, cut the legs, into each of which he belt-sanded a concavity, to "mitigate squareness," put together the sides, and set a rising bevel around the periphery of the top on the underside, to be in proportion with the angle of the legs, but not exceeding that, "to make it all look light," as Newt had taught him.

Working with wood was like pitching had been, when he was truly *in it*, and there nothing in the world but motion, and in it grace.

When he could lose himself in it, he loved it more than anything, and was, for a time, free.

But now, having gotten the fluting on the clawed foot just so, and turning to sight down it, there was Lucy.

At the foot of his drive. "Don't stand on ceremony," he called to her, "just come on up."

She did that. Stood in the mouth of the garage in her new pink hoodie, her feet set just so, wide, as if in some possibly difficult confrontation, and this awkwardness in her.

"So," she said, and glanced away. "You can't call me like that again, *ever*. What if it'd been the home phone, and my dad answered? Or... He's... crazy about shit like that. Okay?"

He'd thought he would tell her why he'd called—but—*Damnit*, now the pattern was all too clear.

Somebody *was* messing with him, and for a reason—and they'd been in the house, doing something. But saying it, now, would only sound like nonsense, or, worse, a lie.

So he nodded, just that, and she took it for agreement, and he said, "I got the wood."

Lucy's face brightened. Here was the reason that he'd called, that's what she was thinking, though both of them sensed they were dancing around something odd, or just... not quite right. Even dangerous.

But because there was hope between them, they were trying to find some way around it.

Deciding to let it go, she shrugged and turned to him. It pained him that she was so wary.

"Listen," he said, "you don't know me from Adam, but—"

"What?"

"Well, I can't show you out here, can I? Everything is on the shelves in the back of the shop."

And with that, she followed him into the garage and he slid one of the sheets of cedar from the top shelf, lay it on the drafting table.

"You could play ping pong on this, it's so big," the girl said. She ran her hand over the wood. Smiled. "It's like—" her eyes narrowed "—skin, isn't it? Almost like it's alive."

"Yes." He nodded. "Smell it."

She bent to the sheet, sniffed at it. Her eyes went wide in surprise. "It smells like—like cinnamon, and forests, and—"

He had a book about canoes on his desk in the corner, and he swept it up, opened its glossy pages toward the back.

"How about this one?" he said, and stood alongside her, the book propped in his hand.

She bent to look. Sighed.

"What?"

She shrugged.

"No, really," he insisted.

She kicked at the floor. She was so... like the cat, only, her scars didn't show, no frozen ear or limp, just her always backing away if you got too close, and her shoulders lifted, defensive.

"Listen," he said, "you can always find me here, and if I'm out, leave a note. If you need something."

She visibly stiffened. *Shit.* Now he'd done it. Again. Even suggesting she might come for help had been too much.

She'd turned to the table. "How do you start?" she asked.

They were not going to look at each other. Which was a relief. Strange, the feral had come in from the far side of the garage. Gyg had been grooming, and Lucy, just like that, stooped and swept the cat up.

Pressed it to her, and the cat settling, Lucy ran her hand down it's back and the cat purred.

"Well," he said, "you have to cut the sheets into slats." He nodded. "You want to cut one?"

"How?"

"Ripsaw."

He showed her how to set the feather board and guide, then took her back to the drafting table and, after she'd set the cat on the shelf where he'd made a bed for it, he, so quickly it startled her, lay her hand flat on the drafting table, plucked the carpenters' pencil from behind his ear, and outlined her fingers.

Just as he had decades earlier, she reared back, and he laughed. Newt, long gone, would be proud.

"Help you remember your fingers," he told her, then swung the sheet of cedar over to the saw, "after you've cut them off."

She stood back from it, her hands jammed up into her armpits, just like he'd done.

"You *should* be afraid," he said. "Okay? Keeps you focused. Now, are you going to listen?"

She nodded.

"Okay," he said, and showed her how to butt the wood up against the guide while standing out from the saw, and the two of them ran the sheet, shrieking shrilly up the length, until they had a width of wood too thin to cut yet another strip from, and he pulled a second sheet out, and they cut that, working through the afternoon until they had a stack of slats, a good eighty, and he shut down the saw.

The girl was looking at it, blank-eyed.

"Your ears ringing?"

"No, it's just—"

"Still scary?" She nodded, and he said, "*Never* lose that feeling when you're working a ripsaw. Or about anything dangerous.

"You're making a canoe, and need to cut the wood, and I'm showing you how. One thing at a time."

Of course, it had never been about the canoe, and her eyes, set wide, and now stricken, glassed up, and she turned away. She did that thing with her head. Glanced over her shoulder. "I gotta go," she said. "It's late."

"Then go," he replied.

And away she went, down the drive and into the street where, to his great relief, she threw her hand over her head.

16

Lucy

When she got back to the trailer her father was cleaning his 30.06 on the kitchen table. It was in parts, and he raised the barrel, then ran the brush up it, then sighted the barrel in the overhead light, a hideous—she thought—plastic pineapple of plastic like in a kid's drinking glass.

"What's for dinner, Bebbe Gurl?" he father said, and grinned. "Got something in mind?" When he'd been drinking, he had a way of rounding his mouth when he said *Beb-be Gurl*, and she caught herself at the stove in a near-shudder.

Right. Dinner. "Spaghetti?"

"That'd be just the thing."

She smiled, but it cost her. *Just the thing.* Stared down into the stovetop, the four black burners in the white top like holes into nowhere. How could you be so irritated by someone, and still love them?

She glanced over her shoulder. Policemen liked their guns, and her father was no exception. He'd already cleaned the Glock 9, and his snub-nosed .38—which most days he wore on his ankle—his "backup piece."

"Bebbe Gurl?"

He slid the 30.06 into his multi-pocketed black canvas bag, then hefted it over his shoulder.

"I've got to fill out some forms for my police work, so I'll be in my room," he said. Going by her with the bag, he kissed the back of her head. Dropped the Glock into the drawer under the toaster.

She didn't want to, but she sniffed—no chemical smell of vodka—and how long had it been? A few days.

"You let me know when you have it on the table, okay?"

"Okay," she said.

Spaghetti was her standard, and she put it together like an automaton, a pound of beef in the pot, diced onions—set the right front burner to high… and don't wander off, not until, here it comes, the hamburger sizzles. Back off the heat to four, toss in some thyme and basil. While waiting for the meat to brown, she got out a second, larger pot from under the sink, filled it half full with water from the tap, dropped it on the left rear burner and set it on high.

Shook the salt shaker over it, seven times, any more and it'd be too salty, caught three pieces of white bread from the breadbox on the counter, smeared margarine from the yellow tub in the refrigerator over them, sprinkled on the garlic salt and got the slices on the rack inside the oven. Set it to broil.

"A watched pot never boils," her mother had once joked. "So, don't watch. Do something else."

She checked her wrist. Okay. 5:15. She'd get the bread out by 5:25. Drop the spaghetti in the water.

What to do? There was no mail on the counter, so she dodged outside into the cold to regard the box the mailman refused to deliver to, since he used the kiosk, the box pathetically akimbo on the post, and on the side of it, in reflective letters—*The Walters*. "Jesus," she wanted to say. "Dad, could we get this… *thing* to stand up straight for once? It looks like a bunch of drunks live here."

She peered into the near dark, listening. Just traffic sounds. And no one was moving through or around the trailers.

No Arn there. So, was it safe to check the box? Sometimes, people left notes in it, Ryan, or her father's cop friends, so—

She strode toward the end of the drive now, and her heart in her throat, the snow crunching under her boots, and the sky the most beautiful last-of-the-day rose-blue overhead.

When she got to the box, she threw the mouth of it open. Flyers—*Protect Your Second Amendment Rights*—and something about snowplowing, and keeping the cars off the road. All of which she took out. Crap the US Post didn't deliver, like the thing on top, an add for tree-trimming services.

She glanced at her wrist—all of two minutes had passed—then over at the trailer, ugly box that it was, peeling white paint on the metal skin, and that hideous aquamarine wing over the wheel, as if a piece of shit like their trailer were going to fly somewhere.

There in the cold, and the sky vast and lost over her, something swelled in her chest, Lucy exhausted, and wanting to… just fly, and anywhere, just away, and it burst out of her in a sob, and she was crying.

And just when she worried her father might hear her, there came from the trailer a high pitched, muffled shrieking.

SHIT! She'd forgotten the fucking bread! She jammed the works into the side pocket of her hoodie, and ran inside. Her father charged into the hallway, and they all but stumbled over each other, Lucy dodging to the oven and tossing the door open, from which bellowed a roll of smoke.

"WHAT THE FUCK?!" her father shouted over the alarm. He had that look in his eyes.

In a state, as her mother'd put it, and all but hitting… something, anything, even her. All PTSD crazy and wound up.

"I WAS GETTING THE MAIL!" Lucy shouted, and shoved the junk at him so he—as anyone would—took it. He looked down at the envelopes, as if at something incomprehensible, and there came that shift, he came back to her. Her father blinking, shocked at himself.

"IT'S THE BREAD!" she shouted, then shucked off her hoodie and flapped it over the fire alarm in the ceiling.

The door open, and the frigid air rushing in, the alarm stopped. Leaving a ringing, charged silence.

"What'd I say about paying attention, Bebbe Gurl?! Plan the work, work the plan, right?"

She swept up the burned pieces of bread and held them in his face, and her mouth set just so.

"THEY'RE BURNED. OKAY? I BURNED THEM. THREE PIECES OF SHIT BREAD WORTH... WHAT? TEN CENTS?!"

It was exactly what her mother had said when she'd last burned something. It shocked Lucy to realize it.

"Shut the door, can you?" her father said. "How are we going to get out of this *damn* place if we're heating the whole outdoors?"

"Just," Lucy said, like her mother, again, "go back to what you were doing. I'll let you know when it's done."

Her father frowned, recognizing the weirdness of what was going on between them.

"Go!" she said, shooing him with her hands.

And he did. Go, down the hall and away. It shocked her. And at the same time, she felt herself almost smiling.

She'd just won something. But was there a worse side to it? Because, as much as she felt relieved, she felt... alarmed. All that hadn't worked out so well for her mother, in the end.

Worse yet, she felt as if she'd betrayed her—her memory of her mother, and in a way that darkened it.

So, she'd try. Try not to do again what she'd just done. Even though it seemed the only way to get through to her father.

Putting the dinner together, she stood at the stove, trying to take them beyond what had just happened, to dispel it, saying, "So, should I make a turkey? And everything? I could do that. For Thanksgiving, I mean?" And then, as if a hiccup, she added, to her shock, "Like mom used to make, you know?" *Mom.* Well, now she'd done it, even when she'd promised herself she wouldn't. Invoked her mother again to broach an issue with her father. It had just come out.

"I *mean*, Daddy," she said, setting their plates on the table, "I'll have to plan and everything, and if we're going to have... *people* over, it's different, you know?" She couldn't say his name: Arn.

But he was as much between them now as if he were standing in the room, big as he was. Her father eating and his brows knotted, he said, "Well, come on now, Bebbe Gurl, you know Arn's more than a friend. So, of course I invited him and Caroline and the kids over. He's like… a brother, and—" he pointed his fork, spaghetti on it, at her, "I owe him for saving my life that day everything went sideways, and we lost half our platoon." He glanced up from his plate. "And we owe him for all that help he was after…" he shrugged, "after your mom passed, okay?

"Oh, I know you don't much like him much anymore, he's a bit over the top and—loud and everything, and well, he's *Arn*, you know? I get that. He can be a bit much. But—"

"I *do* like him; it's just…." she shot back, the lie like something caustic in her throat, that she might choke on.

"What?"

"You're… different when you're around him."

"Yeah," her father said, "happier."

Louder. And drunk, she thought. And, she wanted to say, *You might think he's some great friend, but….* They ate in strained silence. That kind where the silverware clattered on the plates, awful.

"So," she said, finally, "*are* Arn and his family coming, or are they *not*?" They'd had Thanksgiving together for years, and this would be telling, whether or not Arn came over.

"No," her father said.

"Well, why not?" She could hear the alarm in her voice, which she'd masked as irritation. There again, her mother. Cutting. She'd have to get control of herself. Kicked herself for it.

"Caroline's sister invited them up to Fridley, and she's not doing too well," her father replied. He looked up from his plate. "That make planning for things a little easier?"

She smiled at him. Well, that sounded like bullshit, didn't it? she thought, and forced herself to eat, her father sullenly forking his spaghetti into his mouth across the table from her.

"Look," he said, "I told Arn I made a bid on a house up in Minneapolis, and he got a stick up. Said, 'What, are you too good for Shakopee?' He—took it all wrong or something."

"When?"

"Arn?"

"No, the house." She'd cocked her head. "Why didn't you tell me?"

"It was a way lowball bid, Bebbe Gurl," he said, "so I didn't get it, and, anyway, it was a fixer-upper. We'd've been here a year or two while I was working on it, and I didn't want you to get your hopes up."

When they were done eating, and she couldn't bear one moment more of it, she stood and swept the plates and glasses from the table.

"I should get you a job," her father said, but a kindness in him now, "one waitressing tables, maybe we'd be out of here… sooner."

"Gotta be sixteen, Daddy," she said.

"Sweetheart, I lied about my age to go to work. Did it at fourteen. And you're far more worldly than I was."

Yeah, and look at what that led to, she thought, and smiled. "I'm going over to Ryan's to study." She dropped everything in the drain. "I'll get to the dishes when I come in," she said and went up the hallway to her room.

"By nine!" her father called out.

Moments later she had her books pressed to her chest, carrying them up the hallway and to the door.

She wanted her breasts not to hurt, but they did. It scared her, and more than a little. She wanted to think it was—"her moon cycle" having started, as her mother warned her it would. And late, like hers had.

"I don't want you spending too much time with Ryan," her father said, as she was going out.

"And why not? He's the—"

"Sure, I know, he's the smartest boy in the class, you said all that before. It's just that, well, they're not going anywhere, Luce."

"Look," she said, shocked at what was in her mouth—DON'T SAY IT!—but then she was, saying it,

"You have Arn, and I have Ryan. All right? And just when are *we* really going *anywhere*?"

Her father's eyes narrowed. She'd got him where it counted, and it showed. "That was under the belt, Bebbe Gurl," he said.

"I'll be back at 9:00," she replied, and pulled the door shut behind her, charging out into the dark, alone.

All through their work on calculus, and then social studies, and even through civics, she wanted to tell Ryan. She'd be getting out of this… hellhole, sometime, her father had really done something, so it wasn't just talk after all, but then she worried Ryan would be hurt, because, she would've been, and, too, she'd been giving him hints about the dance—Tinsel Twirl, it was in a week or so. And, weirdly, she felt compelled to bring it up now, tonight, and, because she dreaded how awkward it would be, she thought of other things to say, to lead into it, so it wasn't so awful.

There was the holiday coming up. Was he doing anything for Thanksgiving? Were they getting a tree for Christmas? Would he bake those weird moon cookies again, like he had last year? Ryan's stepfather had left them the trailer on his allotment, and he sometimes visited, so, would he?

And in all of it was a kind of desperation for connection, for someone—just *anyone*—to listen.

Her father had, really truly, found… *some*place where they could live, and though he hadn't gotten it, he was trying to get them out, away, when… here she'd been too worried sick to even so much as hope, what with what *He*'d done, and Arn after that, and Booker bringing up Rose L'Rieux.

It'd been like she was stuck, and dying, all of it too much, like some suffocating weight she couldn't get out from under.

So she was thrilled now, and sad, and upset. It was a mix of things she was feeling—leaving would solve things, wouldn't it? If they did? Maybe they'd just move away and it would all be over?

Only, when she thought of Jean, she felt sick, and Booker, Beautiful Booker—she loved him, too.

Even weird, impossible Ryan.

An interminable hour passed, all that going around and around

90

in her head and, too, she was wondering whether or not her father, this time, had gotten his shit together enough to really get them out.

He'd been working insane hours, saved enough to try to buy a cheap house in South Minneapolis.

Maybe, once they moved, she'd tell him about Arn and... *Him*? If she told her father now, maybe that'd make moving happen faster? That could bring them together, only, her father'd go ballistic, she knew that, just like Booker'd said, and, maybe, she couldn't ever tell him, because what good could come of it?

No, she could *never* tell anyone, she thought, she wouldn't, because, what would it say about her? That she was weak, because she hadn't, somehow, had the wherewithal to fight them off? Hadn't punched, kicked, and screamed her way out of it? She must have brought it on herself, what had happened. Must have wanted it. *As if.* And all that—Hollywood... *bullshit*, someone always coming to rescue, but before any real harm was done. Well, she'd been alone, they'd gotten to her, and they'd shut her up by telling her they'd kill her father if she "so much as made a peep."

So, this... everyday nightmare, what she'd had to live with? Saying something about it? Well, *really*? She'd seen what happened to women who got "mouthy," and, anyway, if it got out you were forever after *unlucky*.

Stuck with it, with all that ugliness, first of all your own, but worse from everyone else.

And now, when she couldn't stand thinking about any of it even a second longer, the mess in her head, and as Ryan worked a problem set, she asked, "Ryan, would you take me to the dance?"

He blinked, almost reptilian, there with his mechanical pencil, the kind no one else had.

It struck her that he was being... *obtuse* (a word she'd just learned in AP English, from Mr. Brimley, and liked). Or was he just confused?

No. He was going to tell her he didn't want to go to the dance with her, and it made her feelings so plummet she felt as if someone had let the air out of her, as if she were a balloon, and here she was on the living room floor, collapsing into the repulsive, dirty green shag carpet.

She felt, just then, both superior in her experience, and tainted—or, sinking yet further into herself—ruined.

She could always kill herself. With all the guns in the house, it wouldn't take much. Or, she thought, and in that moment of thinking it, her breath catching—she could kill Him, if she only knew who He was, then Arn, and then kill herself. Make a public spectacle of it, like at the police station, get inside, take Arn out there, like some Columbine kind of thing.

It came on her with a shocking rightness. She could take the Glock, which her father had taught her to shoot, and she could—she could shoot him right in public, like an execution, so it was clear what he'd done to her.

She saw herself doing it, "Hey, Arn!" she'd shout, "Yeah, you, you fat fuck!" and people would scramble for their lives when she drew the Glock from her hoodie—"Close in, Bebbe Gurl," her father had told her, "you've got to be near to have accuracy with a hand gun, all right?"—and Arn would look up from his desk, and she'd say, "Hey, Arn, 'you got some slickum on your hangdown?'" what he'd said to her once, and only then would she pull the trigger, pop him five, ten times, just to make clear her doing it was... *motivated*, and not crazy, then put the gun under her chin, and—

"Yes," Ryan said, and with a perplexed look on his face, he added, "of course I'll take you."

"Good," she said, just that. Which ended that fantasy.

Yes, *of course*?! *Of course* said it all. Good god. What had she just done, with Ryan looking at her like that?

He bent over his textbook, put his hand out as if she should take it, and, well, she told herself, he'd figure out things with himself later, and she squeezed his hand, she couldn't think to not do it, and the moment so unbearable after she could only think to pretend to read, too, holding his hand, but the print just seeming to swim on the page, and a terrible heat in her face, her mind wandering.

Yes, of course. Jesus. Was she that ugly, or that awful? Or was Ryan... *other?* She'd make him need her, she thought, the way she'd made Arn need her, had gotten to him, and Ryan's mother passed out on the couch, her sad, moon of a face turned to them, her eyelids bloated.

"Come on," she said, and he got up quietly with her, and in the hallway she got him unzipped, took him in her hand and got it done, in seconds, Ryan almost collapsing, and his mother stirring.

Ryan reached for her, "I want to," he said, even though he didn't really, she knew that.

Ryan's mother rose from the couch. Turning from Ryan, she swung him around toward her and ducked into the bathroom.

She could hear them talking through the door, Ryan saying exactly what, she couldn't be sure, but it was always the same thing. *Mom, I'm taking care of it.* Some version of that.

She got Ryan's... *stuff* off her hands, dried them on the towel there, then made a face in the mirror. Used Ryan's mother's brush to straighten her hair. Well, Jean'd be at the dance, so.

She stepped out of the bathroom, Ryan's mother there, and she quipped, going by her,

"Hello, Mrs. Chen, can I get you something while I'm up?"

"Thank you, and no," she said. "Did you two get done what you needed get done?"

"We're all set for the test," Ryan said, his voice so pitched that he cleared his throat, then added, "it's all good."

"Good," his mother said. "Do you want watch show?"

When neither Ryan nor Lucy replied, Mrs. Chen swept up the remote from the end table and turned on the television. Went through the channels until she, settling back on the couch, nodded.

"Sit," she commanded, and they did.

Her "show" was some inane thing about a too-perky girl, all white teeth and blonde hair and stupidly naïve sayings, ones misspoken, but being oddly wise, "The early worm gets the bird," had been one, and the girl kind of "wormy," so it made a dopey kind of sense, and the whole thing set in a Disneyland version of New York City, yellow cabs and the whole bit, with all the clichéd characters thrown in. The advertising exec boss, horny for the clueless heroine; the genius computer kid next door, autistic, of course, kind of like Ryan, but in a wise way, like one of Shakespeare's fools, like… Falstaff, in her English class, Lucy thought, the kid called over to fix things; the sultry and bosomy secretary friend after the boss, but too hardened, and too wised up, too comically selfish to be attractive, and the ditzy blond heroine, from the moronic mid west, throughout speaking some bullshit right out of *Fargo*, as if—did *she* sound like that? No, she certainly did not.

Oh ya, sure, you betcha, gosh golly, is that really—

None of them did, Ryan, Ryan's mother, her father, Mr. Opitz, Booker, Jean—or Buck. The thought nearly made her laugh. Least of all Buck.

"I've got to go," she said, then stood and went to the door, and Ryan eyeing her from the couch, said,

"Are you all right?"

She clutched her books to her chest—*it doesn't hurt*—but pressed, again, to test whether that was true or not, the way when she'd been a little kid she'd put a tongue into that space where a tooth had been, which brought back a memory of her mother playing tooth fairy, and with it an even older memory, which just now all but caused her to sob, so struck was she by it.

She'd been stung by amoo, a bee, and her mother held in her in her arms, and her mother singing in her ear, a song about waawaabigonooji yag, little mouse, and to not be ningotaaj, afraid, her mother smelling of… lilacs, a perfume she wore…. and just then everything, even though she was in pain, bathed in light.

A thought that made her, again, swallow. I'm *not* all right, she thought, and her breasts were just part of it.

She was not all right *at all*, and this business with her father having told Arn they were getting out?

Like throwing gasoline on a fire.

"Good night, Ryan," she said, "Night, Mrs. Chen." And when she stepped out into the cold, she ran to her trailer.

Slipping, and stumbling, and came through the front door, and it being quiet in the trailer, she went down the hall in the dark, and thumped onto her bed, throwing her books onto the quilt.

She sat in the dark for the longest time, her mind a wide open space of dark nothing, and spots swimming in her eyes.

17

Buck

He stepped from the dresser, a pad of steel wool in hand and the fluorescents buzzing overhead, the salamander still roaring mightily behind him. Checked the thermostat again. Forty-three inside, still not warm enough. Seventeen outside. He glanced through the window in the wall into the backyard, his birds—finches, and sparrows, and cardinals—at the feeder.

The dresser sat on a knee-high stand, and he sighted up it, looking for a shiny spot he might buff with the steel wool. Nothing. Leave well-enough alone, he told himself. Then set a hand on his hip, done.

The shop smelled reassuringly of wood, all those earthy, complicated scents, oak, which was somewhat bitter, but larch now, too (he'd used larch for the box portions of the dresser's drawers), larch having a clean, almost alkaline scent; and here the cedar in the shelves for the girl's canoe, which most would confuse with pine, cedar like an F sharp, to pine's C major, a pure, keening smell, minomagos, something that smelled almost... holy.

You wanted it green enough to be pliable, so it would bend, but not so much that it would reform itself when drying. Thwarts, gunnels, stems, front and rear. Tricky bit, that, curing wood.

The cat was at the side door, scratching, wanting to be let in, she'd done that since the girl had first gotten her to do it, come inside. He let her in, and the cat scooted as far from the salamander as possible. It switched off, and he realized the room had reached the right temperature, but now with cat in, he couldn't spray the finish coat on the dresser, so went out the side door, the cat following him to the house, but not inside, the girl, later, he thought, could get Gyg to come in, and he opened a can of cat food, then spooned the food onto a dish and set it on the stoop, and the cat ate.

And in that moment, he thought he just might live. Again. Because of the cat. But, now, even more so, the girl. Odd, the things you tell yourself. But, really, he hadn't told himself; rather, that sometimes… *voice* had. His otchitchagoma, who was, if he listened, always there. Just as Seraphim, all that time ago at St. Mary's Boarding School, had promised him it would be.

"'Wheels of fire,' Michael, in that voice," she'd said, "and in it you'll find 'cosmic, rich, full-bodied honest victories over desperation.'"

Obviously, she'd been going bug house crazy there—or had she been? Because hadn't she, in the end, saved them all?

Though, not before she'd made him "see." He wasn't now, nor had he ever been, any wabeno, or jessakid, or mide. He was no shaman. It was simply that, through extremis of the kind any sane person would run from, he'd lost his old life, and gained a new one. A hole in him ever after. One connected to something that at first terrified him, and then he'd come to tolerate. Then even seek.

His true, infinitely larger self, his otchit, which was revealed only when his small self was destroyed. Over, and over again.

"Living in the 'Reign of God,' Michael," Seraphim had said, "pain is part of the bargain, don't forget that."

What strange beings we are, he thought, and while the cat was distracted, he went by her, pulling the door closed behind him.

Hours later, in the shop, he gave the dresser one more going over with a finishing cloth in long, rotating strokes. Buff finish. Not gloss. And the wood, having taken the urethane, a deep honey color; buckwheat honey, not clover. Warm hints of purple-red blossoms and sunlight in it. And when he was done, he organized. Sharpened his tools, vacuumed, then, sitting at the drafting table, made sketches of a modified dining set, Swedish Modern, for a venture capitalist in Carmel, and when he'd finished that, he went into the house.

His phone rang, and he lifted it out of his pocket. Late afternoon now, he could see by the time on the face. He didn't recognize the number.

"Buck?" came the voice over the line. Naomi's.

He hadn't been prepared for it, and then, too, he was surprised at the severity of his reaction. Struck dumb. He'd thought he'd been all right. She'd asked him to let her go, and he'd done that. By not calling; not writing. Not anything. But now she'd reached out.

And what about the number? The caller ID? But he wouldn't mention it. That would be small of him, or just not right. Someone who had stayed the night at the house, his phone.

Which was why he'd picked up. Which, of course, she'd known he would. So he said the only thing he could think to say: "Can I help you?"

"I just wanted to let you know my mother died."

"I'm so sorry," he said.

"Well, I'm sorry too," she replied, a whole world of suggestion in it, as if he'd done it; Naomi was like that. Her mother had been suffering from a progressive neurological disorder, one that had all but paralyzed her.

"She left you some things," Naomi said, a diffident note in her voice. "In her will, I mean."

"Oh," he said.

"Yeah, oh. So there's that."

"What about you?" he asked. "Are you all right?" But when had Naomi ever been all right? And working in the trauma OR? All that just seemed to, daily, prove her fears real.

"Buck—"

"If you need to move things from her apartment," he said, interrupting her, which she hated, "you can use my truck. Is that what you want? Is that what you're calling about?"

"God-DAMNIT, you! Could you just *stop it* and…." He could

hear her labored breathing on the other end. "For once, just once, could you... *Not* do what you *think* is right, and do what you *feel*?"

"I *am* doing what I feel. I want to be helpful." Even if it's killing me. Yes. He wanted to be helpful. Even granted he sensed in her now a too ostensible duplicity, Naomi orchestrating something.

"Could you send someone?"

"For what?"

"What Mom had in her storage locker, that... *thing* you had me give to her, you know, back when...." She cursed. "Well, I had to move it *here*. Since— God—damn it. And, why do you have to make everything so...."

"Hard?"

"Like I just said. What did you *think*?"

Well, she'd just told him not to do what he *thought* was right, so how could he answer without causing yet more upset? And what did he *feel*, really? Well, nothing just now. Just that he *felt*—and wasn't that what she'd asked him to do?—like he was falling through space.

After all, what was love, anyway, but putting yourself out? Being there. No matter what?

"What about Leif," she said, "could he come over?"

"What, you need it out of your place right now? Like that?" That she was so set on getting rid of every last bit of him, and now in the form of what he'd once put in her mother's safe keeping, too, hurt him deeply. "Leif is in Seattle."

"Oh. What about Morrie?"

"Ditto."

"Maybe you should move out there?"

"Naomi...."

"How is the feral? Are you feeding her?"

He didn't want to tell her anything about the feral, which was odd. Why? What was it that he was being possessive about there, what was he hiding, even from himself? Well, the girl, she'd befriended it, the cat. When she came over now, the cat all but jumped in her lap. That's what it was. He was hiding the girl from Naomi, because, well, he was doing, all over again, exactly what she'd asked him not to.

"I want this… *thing* out of the house," she said, and her voice all but breaking. "So will you, or will you not, come and get it?"

"I can't right now."

"Well, it's IN *MY HOUSE*, and I want it *OUT*, so…."

And there it was; what she so hadn't-wanted-to bring-up. The house. Would he be fighting her for it, or some part of it, would he drag her into some—interminable legal morass over it?

That's what hung between them, caused the catch in her voice, the house, really, the very stuff of their lives. A once emblem of *us*.

He wanted to tell her, Naomi, just look around you, and right now. It was all right there, what he felt. He'd won her through the house. Hired by her to do the woodwork, he'd poured his very life into it, had turned what had been a hundred-year-old wreck into a beautiful St. Paul Victorian, a Painted Lady on Pillsbury, one that F. Scott Fitzgerald had lived in and that was on the Minnesota Historical Register, so that she got money for repairs.

All of it, a true labor of love. The house was worth a fortune, and only through marriage did he have title to any of it, if at all.

He was tempted to remind her that he'd put on the new roof himself, had removed—with a spud bar—five layers of shingles to get to the decking, which he'd replaced, too. And the double thickness shingles he'd used, each packet weighing a good seventy pounds, he'd carried three stories onto that roof, and in one-hundred-degree heat the summer she'd finished her surgical residency, which she'd celebrated with champagne in the kitchen he'd refinished. And when the guests had gone, when he'd come in off the roof that July evening, dark and as red as he'd ever been, bare-chested against the heat, having gone through the water in his thermos, she'd led him by the hand into her bedroom, and they'd made love there, a breeze blowing in through the curtains so they rolled and furled. And in the morning, she'd asked him to stay, to bring his things over, to be with her, to be her lover, and he confessed, he'd felt this about her from the moment they'd met, but had, out of necessity, kept his distance. Naomi dark, and her Semitic face one he loved, much like his, and so much so, once out with her she was asked if he was her brother, which had amused the two of them, Buck joking he was a descendant of those famous lost tribes, and Naomi laughing.

After he'd finished the house, he'd been up at five every morning to build cabinets in the garage, for Sawhill, until Naomi connected him to her well-heeled surgical peers, and there had started his business.

And in the house, now, new hardwood floors. New sheetrock walls—and he had hated, even back then, more than anything, sheetrock. Working in that abominable and oppressive chalk dust, as a show of his love for her. There was the grand staircase he'd carved, all oak, and to the original pattern, clusters of grapes and grape leaves, and the pattern taken from period photos, from when the house had first been shown to the then-president of General Mills, who'd had the house built.

There were the period chandeliers, all of French manufacture, which he'd found down in Baton Rouge and trucked up on a flatbed trailer, and the pocket doors he'd salvaged and restored, the new plumbing he'd put in, new electrical wiring, new period tile floor in the kitchen.

It had been endless, but in the context of their being together, supremely satisfying. How much do I love you? This much. He could show her, and not have to say a word.

He wanted to say, *Look around you, Naomi, it's in the house, what I feel. Right there, if you'd just look.*

Only now, she'd launched into a diatribe of sorts having to do with her work, which was really an apology, "—and on top of all that, I'm training the new residents, and I'm home even later, which—" She had asked him to let her go, and he was going to do that. He wouldn't interrupt, because he knew she had to say it, her life was so busy she had no place in it for him, and because he loved her, far, far beyond reason, beyond thinking, he let her go on, "Jacobs, you know what a problem he's been, he's after me, I don't know why, and—"

He glanced around his kitchen, the pitch in her voice rising, and her voice speeding up, spilling.

And this house he was in now, dump that it was? He'd hung onto it because his father had willed it to him. He'd set up shop in it, close to family on the reservation, but not on it.

He'd been working out of the house when he'd met Naomi, and had kept his business things here, even after he'd moved in with her.

He ran his hand over the ragged linoleum on the counter, the green fern pattern on it worn through in places.

Earlier, when he and Naomi had been apart, the house had been a space to wait in until she came back to herself and relented, and in that was a kind of penance, because, he had to admit, living with him *had* been dangerous.

And those…. "things" that had happened, that had been *done*, he hadn't back then been able to undo, and couldn't now.

"I don't have the time to find someone to… cart it over to you. So, are you coming for it or—" Naomi said, and then she blurted— "If you *don't come for it—or… have someone come for it—*"

"What? You'll put it out in the street?" It sounded pathetic, and he regretted letting it out.

"Buck," she said now, a tone of exasperation in her voice, "you assume things you shouldn't."

"Like, the sun will rise in the morning? Or that you'll always like your eggs over easy?" He was trying to be funny. In the past that had worked.

"See? We talked about this. How you always deflect if we're talking about something…."

"*Important.* Right," he said, the wrong tone in it.

Well, he'd said it now. But she didn't launch into the usual defensive berating list of his many flaws. Which, admittedly, he had.

"I'll see what I can do," he said, something horribly final in it, since, in saying it he was letting go of the house, but even more so, her. "And, Naomi," he added, "I really, truly, from the bottom of my heart am sorry about your mother. You know how I felt about her." They'd been, oddly enough, the very best of friends. She'd even stored what he'd asked her to in a friend's locker, apparently until just recently. "If you'd let me, I'd like to attend the service."

"No," Naomi said. "I can't have that."

"All right then. God bless."

"You know I don't believe in any of that, so why do you always say it?"

"Can't help it. *I* believe it. No, I *know it*, Nina. Even though it doesn't make one bit of sense."

"If you can't make it this week, send someone else over," she said, a threat in her voice.

"I will," he said and hung up, shocked to find himself in his run down kitchen, granted, during the call, he'd, in his mind, been back in the house in St. Paul. *Their* house. His and Naomi's.

18

Lucy

In the trailer, Lucy was pondering the cryptic note her father had left her on the counter. Typical of him, it read like a command. *Meet me at,* he'd written, then given an address, and directions for using the bus off Highway 13. *Leave a message at the police station that you'll be there.*

She'd come home directly from school, instead of going over to the boat builder's—to *Buck's,* she reminded herself, again—it was hard to think of him that way, because, that wasn't his name, not really— and her good luck she hadn't. Had she not called the police station, her father would have rung the school, only to discover she wasn't working in the library.

She'd have been at Buck's—or Michael's? as he'd been addressed on a bill he'd left in the shop, or whatever.

In the shaded murk of the kitchen, she set the note on the counter, dreading what her father had in store for her. Bus? Into Shakopee? Why? Why didn't he just pick her up from the trailer? It was a good few blocks walk to the stop, alone in the trees, and it was cold out, too.

She checked the thermometer in the window. Eighteen degrees. Dropped into the chair back of the window, then pulled on her boots— army surplus felt and two sizes too large so they made blisters on the back of her feet. "You'll grow into them, Bebbe Gurl," her father had told her. She took the boots off, got on three pairs of socks, two with holes in the heels. Tested the boots.

There, she thought. She shucked on her down vest, bloodstained (the deer she'd shot last autumn), got her hoodie over it, then her anorak, also bloodstained (the damn pheasants, gutted behind a barn).

No doubt, her father had some nasty job he wanted to introduce her to, like the time he'd shown her how to debark fenceposts, and she had to be dressed for it. For rough work. Like the moose, weeks ago. So she got on her old, but warm, leather mittens. And her ugly purple and yellow scarf, on it a pattern of horn-helmeted Vikings (*As if!* Vikings *never* had helmets with horns on them, which, for her, made the scarf something embarrassing), and out the door she went.

Terrified, and the snow squeaking under her boots. Screech, screech, screech, screech, and the path up to the bus stop uneven, so that here and there she threw her arms out for balance. All the kids used the shortcut which wove through trees, and sometimes she'd see one of the mothers from the mobile park returning down it with bags of groceries, and in it shame, since, anyone in the park would know by their walking they'd lost the car or truck for not meeting payments, or there'd been yet another DUI, or—

So, she didn't entirely mind her motley outfit. Who'd recognize her? Probably not even Arn. And especially not *Him*. Who, from the pasty smooth skin of his palms, made him—some… professional, or teacher, or…. Pervert. And her thoughts wandering, she made her way out to Highway 13 and the bus stop and, waiting, the traffic shushing by, she worried.

About…*Him*. He'd… *done it*, put his… *inside her*, as had Arn, and He hadn't surprised her since, let himself into the trailer when her father was away on night shift, which should have been a relief, but which, if she thought about it, now all but paralyzed her with fear.

After He'd—*done it*—he'd put the necklace on her, the necklace and crucifix, and Arn, at the end of that week, attacked her. And out in the open. And—there'd been none of the usual. Her taking Arn in hand, as she'd euphemistically told herself. Her having any control over any of it.

When, all that time before, *He*, and Arn, too, had been so threateningly secretive. So careful. And the two others? Drop ins....

So, maybe, now that they'd... *He* and Arn had *done it*, and she was... different, a woman now, they were finished with her?

And thinking it, she didn't dare sit in the shelter, she wouldn't be caught inside it, not her, not knowing the way they were, and not knowing if they were done with her now, perverts like that, if they didn't want women, they wanted little girls—or boys—and she could bolt if she was outside, if they came after her, because, wouldn't they be worried she might say something now?

Worst of all to her father? They'd have to be thinking it, because *she* was, after all, wasn't she, thinking on it herself?

Wondering why they'd stopped—*coming*, ha ha, perverts, and after the way Arn had hurt her, he had to know, there'd been so much blood she'd barely gotten into the trailer, and—

What if she'd gone to a doctor? But, no. A doctor would have had to have done something already, so... no doctor. But—

Had her father wondered—*did* he wonder?—what was with her having suddenly gone through a few rolls of toilet paper? Her emptying the trash more than once that week?

And what was all this mystery now? Her father dragging her out after school, and to what end?

She paced in front of the shelter, thumped her mitted hands together in an attempt to warm them, the wind blowing right through her, and looked up the road past the traffic. It was rush hour now, a constant line of it, angry drivers, even here in bumble rut Shakopee, and her feet cold, in her "bunny boots," but here came the bus, wallowing into the rutted snow on the shoulder. The door opened with a hiss, and she went up the stairs into the relative warmth.

She plunked down in the seat behind the driver, one of three natives riding, all untouchables on the Green Line, all in ragged, thick coats, and keeping to themselves. When the highway was clear, the driver pulled out, Lucy sitting upright, as if she were going to an execution.

Whatever it was, she was all but sure it wasn't going to be pleasant. Her mother had protected her in the past, from some of it anyway, but she had nothing now between her and her father's cockeyed enthusiasms.

Or, maybe she did? Because, what would Buck think? About any of it?

And maybe she could talk to him, but later?

At the 128th Street shelter she stepped off the bus, surprised to find herself in an area of small businesses and shops. Lit up now, and soon to close. It was well after four, getting dark, and here was her father. Pulling into the lot in his police cruiser, and—of course—in uniform.

"Timed to the second," he called to her, happily, stepping out of the car, and with dread she kicked through the snow over the median to him.

"Hello, Daddy," she said, putting on her face. She wouldn't ask what this was all about. That only made him angry.

"Come on," he said and, throwing his arm around her, he marched her across the lot of the Department of Motor Vehicles. Caught the door and all but slung her inside, warmth again! Thank god, she was thinking they'd get warm, then go off to whatever awful thing he had in mind.

There was a line going all the way to the door and out into the vestibule, but her father took her to the head of it, which was embarrassing.

He nodded to the clerk behind the counter. "Myron," he said, and the clerk nodded, said, "Lee," and pushed a clipboard and booklet and pencil across the Formica to her father, and he handed it to her, then nodded to the desks against the window that fronted Highway 13.

Permit the booklet read, and under it one of those mark sense forms with the little circles you filled in, as she had on achievement tests.

She had, at that moment, an out-of-body sensation. Like when she'd realized—*He* was in the trailer, or Arn, or one of the others, but here the fluorescent lights humming overhead and the other test takers at the thirty or so desks glancing up at her, and her father giving her a push toward them.

"There's an open seat for you, Bebbe Gurl, there to your left," he said, and eased her by her forearm down into it.

Everyone in line seemed to be staring at her, the cop's kid getting some kind of special treatment, and she thought she might die.

Tests terrified her. Each could prove that the last had been a mistake, a fluke, that she wasn't unusual, wasn't special, was too stupid to go to college or even finish high school, that she'd come to nothing. If she was alone, she loved tests and puzzles, loved how her mind worked, could feel it, something almost like gears turning and the answers just occurring to her. Which was why she never made much of her doing well on tests—it was just something that happened.

But she was terrified now. What if it *didn't* come out like it usually did, didn't work for her the way it usually did?

And what did she know about driving? Nothing. She glanced up at her father. Deeply chiseled face, and those dimples, he was looking down at her.

"Come on, Bebbe Gurl, this is your thing, test taking, isn't it? Open your booklet and show them what you can do."

There was an enormously fat man behind her father, and he caught her eye and nodded. She looked down at the booklet on the desk.

She felt as if she might vomit, but she had nothing in her stomach. The pages swam in front of her.

She was in a bright, bright room, lifted high and out of herself, which was terrifying, just like when—Arn… did what he did—or they did—though, this was the worst, as bad as when *He*—with his creepy, too velvety hands, touched her, and she bent to the page, her other self. The one who just got things done. It knew, or seemed to, things she didn't, so—

Signs: Octagonal. Triangular. Round. Rectangular. *Which shape was regulatory?*

She had no idea. But *it* knew, even if she didn't, and filled in the circle with the pencil. Rectangular.

That was the most shocking thing. It did it all. With her there, just some spectator.

After, outside in the bitter cold and the wind blowing, she crossed the lot with her father. He was jabbering on about how well she'd done, "Didn't I tell you, Bebbe Gurl, you got a *ninety-six*—and you didn't even study!"

And all the while she was thinking how, after he drove off for his night shift and she got home, she'd get the Glock from the drawer and kill herself. She couldn't take it anymore. And she couldn't seem to get back inside herself now, either, which was terrifying.

She was numb, deep inside herself, so far back in there, it was as if she were in a cave, and in this world, she could barely feel her hands, her face, her feet, like when she'd taken Jean's PCP once by mistake.

"Okay, Daddy," she said now, "so, can I go home now?"

Her father laughed. "No, Bebbe Gurl!" he said and, again, he slung his arm around her.

She was thinking about the feel of the gun in her mouth. She'd done it before. Put the business end of the Glock in her mouth. Cold, greasy gunmetal, and the piece surprisingly heavy.

He squeezed her, walking her out of the DMV lot and into the blindingly bright car dealership next door, when all she wanted was to get home. Have him leave. And be done with it.

A salesman in the front window stood. Painted on the glass, and partially obscuring him, *Shakopee's Deal Makers, Ron Ready and Dan Done.*

"Daddy," she said, in a voice that seemed to come from that thing that presently wasn't her, "I think they've closed, and they don't want us on the lot." All she wanted now was to get home.

And end it.

"And that, Bebbe-gurl, is where you are wrong!" The salesman waved, and her father waved in return.

"Did you think I'd forgotten, Bebbe Gurl?"

"Forgot what, Daddy?"

But here was the salesman in his tube-top parka, coming out the door, and he had something in his hand.

"My ten-times-smarter-than-me daughter, Lucy," her father said, and she put her hand out to shake the salesman's hand, but he instead handed her keys. "She got a ninety-six on the test, and she didn't even read the booklet! Didn't I tell you you'd better be ready for us to wander over after?"

"Drive safe, she's a good one," the salesman said, and he darted back inside, and to his desk.

She felt herself frowning. She was holding the keys. Her father steered her up a row of cars, at the end of which was a tomato-soup red sedan, one with hubcaps that looked like pie tins.

Her father ran to it and turned to her, threw his arms up. "Happy birthday, Bebbe Gurl! She's all yours. Wheels, sweetheart!"

What was she going to do with a car? And the permit, it was only valid with another license holder over eighteen in the car. So?

"Thank you, Daddy," she said. She had to say it. Or things would go badly wrong. And, what now? Her father would drive the car home? But what about his patrol car in the DMV lot?

But he'd caught on to her confusion, and he ran back to her, like a boy, which was endearing, it really was, she did love him when he was himself like this, like he had been when she was a little girl, and everything had been… different, and her father now all but carrying her to the car.

"I got you a farm exemption, Sweetheart!" he said, setting his hand on the roof over the driver's door, "Says so on the paper permit. You can drive *right now, right here*. All by your lonesome. And you're going to!"

"Now?"

"Yes! Now!" He swung the door open. "Get in," he said, and she slid in behind the wheel. "They even took the sticker price off the windshield, got new oil in her, full tank of gas, and brand new tires."

He'd set his hand on the top of the car, so he could lean in. He showed her where the lights were. The wipers. The heater. Parking brake. It was all—overwhelming—and she was still numb, way inside herself.

Her father held up his forearm. Checked his watch. "I got my shift coming up, so I've gotta—"

He'd missed dinner, to give her the car. She felt her eyes glassing up. He did love her, in his way, and she him, and she jumped from the car and threw herself into his arms, sobbing.

It wasn't the car, it was just that he'd really put himself out. That he cared. If she could only tell him. But not now, not here.

"Thank you, Daddy," she said, in his arms.

He released her and replied, "There isn't anyone one on earth I love more than you, Lucy."

"I don't know how to drive, though."

It wasn't entirely true; Jean had had her get behind the wheel of her aunt's car one night. It had been a stick, and Jean had thought it hilarious, Lucy jerking around, stalling the car time and time again, veering in too-tight circles in the Piggly Wiggly Grocery parking lot.

"Come on, Bebbe Gurl, you get behind that wheel and start her up, you'll know *exactly* what to do. You're that smart, Lucy, you've seen it all before. You're the smartest girl I ever knew, even more than your mom, and, well, she was sharp as a tack and…."

His having invoked her mother struck them both silent, and to fill it, Lucy said, "But that's not like doing it. Seeing, right?"

"You're different, Lucy, even though you try to hide it. And we both know that, so—"

She didn't want to disappoint him, and, too, he'd made it all about proving herself again, even bringing up her mother doing it, so she got in the car. Again, disembodied. Sort of terrified. But if she died, so what?

And she wasn't thinking about going home and shooting herself now. Just the damn… car. She could drive into something—like a bridge abutment, that'd be easier, or there was the train, where it went through town.

She turned the wheel, adjusted the rearview mirror. Looked up at her father and smiled painfully.

"Remember all those things I taught you? How you test the tires on snow or ice, pump the brakes to see if the car'll slide, and how to turn *with* the skid on a front wheel drive like this one?"

She did, and said so.

"Then take her home, Luce—" and he got out his wallet and gave her a twenty "—no, better yet, you drive around a few hours or so, get used to her. Get gas, when you need to, find out how that works. Late curfew tonight, how's that? Come in at midnight if you want, park right alongside the trailer." He nodded. "And no more walking home from school, Bebbe Gurl. No more ramblin' around, okay?"

He slung the door shut, then stood alongside the car until she got it started, and as she was pulling away from him—in a state of near terror, at the car, but at what he'd said, too—he threw her a kiss, then strode toward his patrol car.

It took some getting used to, but the car seemed to go where she pointed it, and stopped, too. And an hour later, she was beginning to lose some of that out-of-body feeling. And her terror—of driving, anyway. As if all that had been some awful, awful nightmare, falling into herself and thinking to kill herself at the house—which was, weirdly, the thinking of someone else now, someone who'd inhabited her, who'd taken the permit test, had been, earlier, driving, and was in her still but was now silent.

Watching, from over her head. As if she'd split, and maybe she'd never get back—entirely—together; like she'd talked to god.

But god was herself, or that vast... *something* in herself she'd fallen into, her otchit, which was everything. Or so her mother had taught her, and she'd believed her, because she'd been like that. Possessed of an unshakeable, inner calm. Why couldn't she be more like that?

Like Buck, who'd joked his nose was French. He was no more French than her mother had been.

Buck would understand, and, focused on driving now, she thought more on her mother, which made her feel lonely, and lost.

So she drove aimlessly, and her mother with her, *Gimikweden ina?* she asked Lucy, while she was getting a feel for the car, how it pulled itself through the snow on the shoulder—*Yes,* she replied, *I do remember, Nima, mother, you come out of a skid by steering into it. Like Daddy said.* And Lucy accelerated briskly onto the dry pavement, turning again sharply, making a U. She took the car into the parking lot of a convenience store that had closed, veered, and circled, and skidded, like she'd seen boys at school do, got the hang of it, how she could slide and go forward at the same time, what distance it took to stop. All good.

And that business about her not walking home from school? Her father didn't know anything, how could he?

At the wheel, she thought: Still, how odd that her father'd given her a way to escape, but in doing it, he had made it impossible to do it—in good conscience—at the same time.

If he'd given the car to her meanly, she'd have had no problem running away. But he hadn't. It was the kindest thing he'd done in years. Such largesse in it. And the—what was it?—joy he'd shown, giving it to her!

"And you thought I'd forgotten your birthday present, Luce!" Well, she had, and entirely.

She knew he didn't have money for a car. So how had he gotten it? His policeman's wages barely floated their life in the trailer, what with him saving for a real house.

She drove all the way north into Edina, a posh suburb of Minneapolis, the houses decorated with red-ribboned wreaths on doors, and Santas and—all *that,* sleighs, and elves, and fairies—on the roofs, the houses aglow in seemingly virginal snow, rich people snow, the purest white, and here children in a yard making an igloo, and she wondered, Could she still have children? Having bled like she had?

And with a shrug she thought, *probably won't be around for that, anyway,* and she turned at the next intersection, Interlachen

Boulevard, and wasn't Interlaken that place in... Switzerland? So, why'd they spell it like that?

She thought to put some gas in the car. Just to see that she could do it, at the pump thinking about her father, that he trusted her, and she felt she couldn't break that trust.

Granted it was a gas station, she looked around her, wary, recalling Rose L'Rieux again.

But, she had to admit it, her father had been right. She *could* drive the car, almost as if she'd been doing it for years.

Which was different, too. Being on his side. But she couldn't go home. That seemed too... dangerous. She didn't trust herself, not yet, and everything had changed with Arn; and the change was... worse than scary.

So, where to?

The bright hum of the city lights seemed too much, and she turned south, drove all the way into ragged Shakopee, then through it into the res, where she, sort of, belonged, only it looked all the worse now.

The snow mounded either side of the highway, there was a solitary figure on the shoulder, his hands thrust forlornly in his pockets and his head down, hatless, and as she went by she saw it was Booker.

She pulled over a distance in front of him, the tires crackling on the frozen slush there; hit her emergency flashers, then reached across the tiny car and threw the door open.

When Booker reached her, he looked into the car from a distance, his eyes narrowing, an incomprehension on his face.

"Get in!" Lucy called to him, and he jumped into the car, then pulled the door shut and nodded.

"Get moving, or you might get hit," he said.

"Okay, Boss," Lucy shot back. She turned the emergency flashers off; glanced over her shoulder and pulled back onto the highway. Booker ran his hand over the dashboard.

"Where'd you get the wheels?"

"Stole 'em," she said. Who was this, saying these things? Jean?

"You did not."

"What were you doing out there?"

"Walking to Mecca."

"Right." She glanced over. "Don't you have a game tonight? I mean, why aren't you playing?"

She only knew because there'd been a pep rally. One she'd skipped. *Go, Gryphons!* Booker was on the rival team, The Spartans.

"Booker?"

He rolled his eyes. "'Cause shit," he said, "that's why."

"'Shit'?"

"I don't want to talk about it." He shrugged, his eyes on the mini mall they were passing. Pizza. Hamburgers. A place with a giant, Pillsbury Doughboy-like character on the roof, had to be ten feet tall. On its head a white poufy hat, like cooks wore in movies she'd seen.

"Fuckin' Happy Chef," Booker said, "whose brilliant idea was that for some burger joint?"

Because she could, she turned into the parking lot, where there were a few cars set parallel in the snow.

"Whoa there, Mario! Gotta double check for pediddles, you cross the highway like that."

"Pediddles?" She killed the engine.

"What we call idiots driving without their lights. Think they save the battery that way. Don't know the alternator's makin' juice whether the lights are on or not. Come at you out of the dark, see?" He smacked his hands together. "Like that."

She threw her door open and stepped out. Glanced back in, holding the door. "You coming or staying?"

Booker got a shocked look on his face. Then frowned. "You think this is wise, Lucy?"

"Yes or no?"

She heard him get out behind her, and when he threw the door shut with a clang she hit the key fob. The car horn beeped. Locked. So, even that worked. It was almost too much.

At a booth inside, she held up a menu.

"Nothing for me," Booker said. "I'm not hungry."

She ordered a full breakfast—*made 24/7* the menu said—hash browns; sausage, not bacon; wheat toast and pancakes. Eggs over easy. Biscuits. Coffee, for two. When the waitress came with the cups and pot, she bent over the table, pouring, set a cup in front of Booker without looking at him; set the other in front of Lucy and, catching her eye, smiled.

"Your order'll be up in a jiff, hon," she said.

Booker watched her go. Grimaced. Moments later, the waitress rushed to the table, a plate balanced on her forearm.

She set it in front of Lucy, and Lucy said, "My friend here, he'd like something for his coffee."

"Excuse me?"

"Booker?"

"Miss, if you could. Cream?"

She turned to him. Smiled. It was, happily enough, a real smile. "I'm sorry. Would you like the flavored? We've got French Vanilla, and—"

"Just the regular, Miss, thanks," Booker said and nodded. The waitress rushed off, and Booker all but glared across the table.

"If you'd given her half a chance, well—you'd see most people are just *afraid*, Booker."

"Of what?"

"*Anything different.* And that's usually me, too. Okay?"

The waitress swung by again, smiled at them both, then set a handful of creamers on the table and rushed off.

"You need anything else, let me know."

Lucy set her fork and knife on her plate just so, then spun it around so it faced Booker, and pushed it across the table.

"'Sup?" Booker said.

"Social lies, Booker. We all tell them. *Eat.* And don't give me any bullshit that you're not hungry."

"You *are* different."

"No. Not really. But I just can't stand the dumbness of it anymore.

And, anyway, it's kind of my birthday. So, eat."

He did, while Lucy nibbled at the toast. Then ate half of a biscuit, slathered in butter. Oh, god, but that tasted good. When they were done—and she was lit up with caffeine—she put what was left of the twenty her father had given her on the table and stood.

In the lot, approaching the car, and it snowing so the mercury oxide lights sparkled like snow globes, she pressed the keys into Booker's hand, and Booker, surprised, turned to her.

"You drive." Again, that look. Incredulity, that was it. "You have a license, don't you?"

"'Course I got a license."

"Hit the locks then. It's on the fob." He did that and Lucy went around to the passenger side and got in.

Booker did too, got in, pulled the door shut and started the car. He turned the heater up to high, rubbed his hands together.

Said, "Where's the light switch?" He was bent over, looking for the switch on the dashboard, and lifted his head. And she was right there. Gently took his face between her hands, and kissed him, and this time it didn't feel like an experiment. Her heart was in it, and it felt good.

Shocked, he reared back, his hands on the wheel at ten and two, as if he were frozen there, unable to move.

She set her hand on his knee, then slid it up to him there, and he caught it, drew it off to the side, and said,

"No, Lucy."

"Are you mad now?" she said, a deep hurt in it. It was what she said when—when they were too rough.

"I'm *not* mad, okay?" Booker said. "Fact is, I'm way, way, way the opposite. Way too much. Honest and truly. But—" He was trying to think how to put it. And then he undid his seat belt and got out of the car. "This can't happen now. And not like this, Lucy."

He ducked in, kissed her cheek. "You know how I feel about you," he said, and ducked back out.

"Booker?" she said, a pleading in her voice.

He turned toward the Happy Chef where a few patrons had blandly lifted their heads from their dinners, watching.

"Seriously," he said, "don't make me say shit neither of us wants to hear, Lucy. Okay? And thanks, and I mean it. So, let's hope—later!"

He marched off into the snow, to the shoulder onto the highway, where he looked both directions, crossed with his hands in his pockets and went up the highway on the opposite side. Head down, as if into a hard wind.

Just the way he'd been doing when she'd first stopped for him an hour ago, before anything had happened.

19

Buck

In the kitchen, talking to a supplier on the phone, he walked his fingers through the bills in the holder on the counter, the supplier, with some irritation, telling him he couldn't pick up his things until he'd paid his last tab. They'd sent the bill out nearly a month ago, hadn't he gotten it?

He had, and he'd put it, of course, right here. Or had he carried it up into his office in the attic?

But what was the point of looking? He'd been telling himself he'd put the bill here when, obviously, he hadn't. Though something now was glaringly not right, but he just could not get what it was.

He stooped. Eye level to the counter. "Sure, yes, my apologies," he said, "I'll stop by the office, square things up, all right? And make that four of the three-eighths, five sheets of half-inch, and—"

The bill wasn't under the toaster, or in the wicker basket which he sometimes stuffed. Which he checked now, too. No. And it wasn't on the windowsill behind the curtains, which he pulled back, and not in the junk drawer, there rubber binders, tape, scissors, glue, twist ties.

"No," he said, "I don't want the larch this time. I want white birch. Right. You don't have half? It's for a dresser."

Back and forth they went, lengths, quantity, no knots. And all the while a sinking feeling growing in him—that someone *had* been in the house: the scent of Brut, not from Leif's.

And that message on the answering machine, connecting him to

Lucy—erased, and not by him.

He was still holding the curtain when he saw it, the tell, and something like a stone dropping in his stomach. Whoever had been in the house had moved the toaster—and with it the toaster's plug—from the AFCI socket, to the ungrounded, standard socket on the right.

The toaster was a fire hazard—and an electrocution hazard, being there beside the dish drain and water—and the AFCI a necessary nuisance, since it tripped easily, and he was often resetting it.

They must have inadvertently gotten the cords crossed when they'd messed with the answering machine.

But here was Lucy at the end of his drive now. A good hour earlier than usual, a tomato soup red Toyota behind her.

Gyg had come out from behind the house, and the girl was petting her; it occurred to him that *here* was something beautiful, even in the midst of awful things, things he'd have to deal with. The girl talking to the cat, and the cat thrusting its head up, enjoying being touched.

"Listen, I've got to go. Can you order twelve planks of the black walnut? And no knots," he said, and got off the phone.

He stood in the window. Felt a moment of… something like… what was it? Fear? For her, Lucy.

And then the phone rang, and he didn't answer it. The machine did, "You've reached"—his voice, and following it, Naomi's—"Buck, you've got to come and get this thing. I want it OUT of the house. It's just like you not to come over for it when you promised, but you have to, come and get it, that is, because I'm not going to… and I'm not driving it over to you, is that clear?

"So. And I won't ship it, because I can't. You don't need to take the truck to get all of it, the other things, too, I mean. You can take—"

But there she recalled she had "his" car. Separation of "community property." And what did he need with a car like that anyway, an old Pontiac sedan, once his brother's?

"If I have to, I'll have an insured mover take it to you. Okay? And that will be expensive. And I know you don't want anyone… looking into—goddamnit!—what's in there, so…."

He watched the girl, resisting Naomi. Pick up the phone? Not pick up it?

"Buck? I know you're there. Pick up." There was a muffled cursing, and she hung up.

Lucy'd brought something; a can of cat food, and she went to the mouth of the garage, where she opened it, spooning some food onto the dish he'd left there, the cat darting to it. It was so lovely, he didn't want to interrupt them, and the angry echo of Naomi's voice too much filling the kitchen.

In the past, before they'd split up, Naomi had gone on all sorts of rants. About how he'd been impossible, how his schedule was unpredictable and work catch-as-catch-can, how it was irresponsible of him, dropping things when someone "needed help," so he couldn't be counted on. She was the one with the real job; real hours and real responsibility. Tragedies on every shift. Well, it was true, her surgery was demanding, and they'd both thought it would become less so, but it hadn't. So he had taken care of everything around the house without mentioning it—just got it all done.

Still, that he'd paid, some months, less of his share of the bills than she had rankled.

"Production and marketing," she'd told him, that last time, "that's how it works in the *real* world."

And he, not realizing the seriousness of the moment, joked, "You forget, I live *in* your world, but I'm not *of* it. Kinda like Sponge Bob Square Pants in a feathered headdress, see?"

"Well, thank you so very, very much, Buck, Jesus Fucking Christ already. *Really*?"

"Hey, it's all just bullshit, isn't it?"

The cat was circling the girl's legs, and it all sat in him like a great weight, his and Naomi's last—and he saw, now, final—bitter conversation.

"That's right," she'd replied, "and you *don't* fit in my world. And you *never* did and *never* will. And *I* never fit in *yours*, either."

The girl had the cat taking food from her hand, and he muttered to himself, "Oh, well," as he had that afternoon, talking to Naomi, then slung his jacket from the rack and went down the three steps to the back door and out.

"Missed you last week," he said. The cat shot away, and a good few yards distant, stopped.

"Kitty-kitty-kitty, come on kitty. Don't run away, he's not so scary, he just looks it, okay?" Lucy said. She stooped, and the cat went to her. "Stay," she said, and the cat, tentatively ate, and the girl, ever so slowly, reached out and stroked its head.

"Can you hear that?" she said.

He could. The cat was purring. Done eating, it darted away again and the girl stood. Brushed off her pants.

"Soooo?" she said, her voice rising.

"The car?"

She nodded. "I can be over here earlier now, see?" she replied, her way of telling him she didn't want to talk about it.

"You have time to work on the canoe? Lunch first?"

"Sure," she said.

In the kitchen, he pulled out a chair at the table, and he sat her there, Lucy quipping, "This is nice, since I'm always the one at the stove." He nodded.

"Pork tenderloin, with pear confit and balsamic vinegar. It's a reduction, and then you—" he stooped to fire a burner "—sear the meat on both sides and—"

"Do we have the time?"

"Takes minutes. Internal temperature just has to get above 170—and it's not tough if you don't overcook it."

Like a three-armed man, he got the pork in the pan, sizzling, ducked into the fridge for the asparagus and potatoes he'd made the night before, heated those in a second pan, while he plated heaps of coleslaw. All of which he did as if in a kind of dance, until he spun the burner knobs off, slipped the pork and confit, asparagus, and potatoes onto their plates, holding Lucy's in one hand, and balancing the other on his forearm. He bowed, at the waist, then swung over to the table, set Lucy's plate in front of her, dropped a fork, left side, knife right, sat, across from her, where he did the same, Lucy watching, amused.

"Is it chef? Or chief?" she said, joking.

"Both," he shot back, then added, "try it," enjoying himself.

She did, then sat back, blinking, "This is really, really good, I'm mean, super good. Where'd you learn to cook?"

"Restaurants—and later, when I guided up north, I cooked. Do it long enough, and pay attention, you learn a few things—don't overcook. Let the meat rest. Don't over-salt. Go for first class ingredients."

She tried the potatoes. "God," she said. "*What* is that? I mean," she glanced up at him, "I know it's cheese, but—"

"It's Gruyère, which is—"

"French, like your nose, right? Look," she bent toward him, in mock irritation, "I'm not dumb, okay?"

He shrugged, then smiled, the two of them eating, and before she'd finished he swung over to the fridge again, pulled out two blue ramekins, dropped them on the table, and sat.

"Low cal dessert."

"You think?"

He laughed.

"What is it?"

"Crème brûlée. Ever had it?"

She rolled her eyes.

"Well, you haven't had mine, all right?"

She pushed her plate away, slid the ramekin over. He handed her a spoon, and she rapped on the glazing.

"Go right on through—you do that glazed sugar on top with a torch." She dipped in, spooned a portion into her mouth, then got that look on her face again. "Like it?"

"Wow," she said, "what is it?"

"Guess."

"I have no idea."

"Lavender and honey," he said.

He kicked his chair back, and in that moment, there in the kitchen, felt at home in a way he hadn't since he'd left Naomi's. And thinking, too, you couldn't live for yourself—it wasn't good.

He watched her, arms crossed, just then happy, and when she got up, he told her he'd send her home with a couple plates, a dinner's worth.

She followed him into the shop through the side door and he got the salamander started. While it heated the shop, she took in the slats of cedar they'd cut earlier against the far wall. And as he'd thought she might, she cocked her head, confused at the hull mold he'd assembled.

She set her hand on the stern section. The mold ran the length of the garage, seventeen feet, to the corner.

"Looks like a... dinosaur skeleton," she said. Each mold partition was wide at the top, narrower at the base.

"Tchiman," he said, testing her. Canoe.

She shook her head, but it didn't mean, "I don't understand." Or did it? Because, she was testing him, too.

She went up the length of the mold, delicately touching each partition, and he found he was holding his breath. And in it a pain so deep, so sharp, he braced himself as if against it.

If she hadn't understood—didn't—a whole world was lost forever. A primordial world of glacial moraines, vast, unbroken stretches of dark forest, and chains of bitter cold, sky blue lakes.

A world in which, legend had it, trees were persons; where stones talked; and the waters of the djigan were populated with spirits.

"Mangonagad tchiman," he said, goading her.

"Enh," she said, finally. "Nin mangon," and he all but caught his breath, so relieved was he.

Some... *one* other person, this girl, Lucy, knew it. And she would, and long after he was gone.

Yes, the canoe wasn't going to be just *any* canoe, it was going to be a broad-bottomed one, and longer, for open, rough water. A Big Lake Canoe.

That kind, and only.

"Here," he said, lifting up a slat, avoiding her eyes, so touched was he, and she helped him clamp the slat to the bottom of the mold, then lay on a thick bead of glue on top of it, and they fit the second slat, all the slats beveled—he'd done that the day after they'd cut them— and they worked, only now and again speaking, but always in the old language. "Nin gwekishin," turn that, "kawin," no, "gwekigina," turn it over, the other side, and she did that, it was the grain, did she see that? It was the pattern, it followed from the last, and, like that, slat after slat, left side, then the right, the canoe came into being, the garage smelling of something like incense—their ministrations having about them something out of an ancient rite—and when they'd assembled the hull in its entirety, there it was.

Done, Lucy stepped back from it, this all but living thing having come into being, as if out of nothing.

"It's—" Lucy said, but caught herself and, so as not to break the spell, said, "—gwanatch." Beautiful.

And it was. The canoe, stretched there across the shop. *A visitation,* Seraphim had said, *you'll know it when the spirit comes, when god is there. And god is* always *there.*

"Well," Buck said.

With his chin, he pointed to his power coping saw, said, "Nin widokododimin?" Why don't we do this together? And Lucy followed him around the canoe to the drafting table.

He handed her a piece of ash, marked in carpenter's pencil, and she held it down on the table as he cut it, one of the seats.

"You know, I can't swim," she said, this coming out of nothing when he'd stepped back.

He made a face, a guffaw in it, and when she shrugged, he laughed. And she laughed with him.

"Bagwanawizi gichi mookomann," she said, and they were all but doubled over in laughter. Like some long knife, a clueless white person come up to the north woods, the kind who threw his weight around.

"Okay," he said, "now hand me that over there," and they worked with the power grinding wheel to dish the seat.

"And, hey," he said, glancing up at her, "they're not *all* clueless. Don't *ever* forget that, right?"

By the time she left, all but skipping down the drive to her car, they'd cut the gunnels, too.

When they got back to it, they'd fit them to the canoe.

She waved to him, long-armed, long-legged: a pretty girl standing at the door of her car. It put him in mind of his daughter. Her mother, holidays, had sent photos, and in them she'd been, like Lucy was now, smiling.

She dropped into the car, then pulled smartly from the curb. Turned the corner and was gone.

And he went inside. Lighter for her having come by. But something in him all the more unsettled.

20

Lucy

Jean was being crazy. Or was it weird? They were outside again on lunch break, had been talking about what they'd do over the weekend, since it was Friday, but now it was cold, truly cold, and while Lucy was shuddering at it, wanting to go back in, Jean was motor-mouthing, her jacket open and her skin chicken-pocked with cold, though she seemed unaware of it.

"You ever think to just... take that little hammer thingy," Jean said, "and smash the fire alarm outside the lunch room, to see what would happen?"

They'd have to go back in, and, anyway, there'd be none of... *that*, she couldn't think what to call it, what they'd been up to before, it was too cold, and Jean jumping up now. Off the cold cement slab.

She climbed the embankment behind them, then rolled sideways down it in the snow, laughing, and her backpack catching.

When she got up, she ran in a dizzied circle around Lucy. Then did it a second time.

"Jean, you're beginning to scare me."

Jean laughed, a high, tittering laugh. "Oh, so you say, Little Miss Stick-in-the-Mud." She lunged at Lucy, kissed her, and her eyes pinpricks.

"Did you take something, Jean?" Lucy said. There was a rumor that some MDMA was going around. That and kitty—ketamine.

"I'm just SOOOOOOOOOOOOOOOO—" Jean shouted, and

threw her hands up over her head, as if ecstatic, "HAPPY!"

Some boys had come to the top of the embankment and were looking down at them.

"Little fuckin' wieners," Jean said. She ran in yet another circle around Lucy. "What I need is REAL DICK!"

Lucy felt something come over her, something dark and complicated, as if the sky had darkened.

"I NEED A REAL LOVE!" Jean shouted, then ran in a zigzag, and, growling, came at Lucy. When Lucy easily sidestepped her, she fell onto her chest and slid on her slick jacket on the snow.

"Jean?!"

"What you need, Lucy, is a nice, hot cock. A big one. That's what he always says, and then he gives it to me!" She laughed, hysterically, and Lucy felt a bolt of terror run up her back.

"Jean, *did* he give you something?"

Jean lifted her right hand, gave the three boys at the top of the embankment the finger. The tallest one, the one on the left, gave it back.

"Yeah, fuck you, too, Rodney!" Jean shouted. She turned to Lucy, "Well, you're not doing anything with those little turds, so don't give me that oh-so-offended face. Not when you've got—" she all but writhed over her feet, making kissy faces and blinking her eyes, "Mr. Black Power."

"His name is Booker," Lucy said, and she wanted to walk from Jean, and as quickly as she could, but she couldn't. No, what she was thinking to do was run inside and get the school nurse.

Because, she felt it rushing at them.

"Once you go Black, you never go back," Jean quipped, then ran full circle around Lucy again.

"Jean?"

"What?"

"Jean, are you all right?"

"I'm—" she flipped the boys off again, then bent over and pulled her pants down, mooning them.

That got their attention. They pointed. Talking between themselves. Poking each other. Laughing, but they were getting it too, now. Because the one on the side opposite the tallest shared a look with Lucy.

They were witness to some kind of meltdown, and Lucy was at the horrified center of it.

"Jean," Lucy said, "what did you take?"

"Not enough is what I took," she shot back. "And I had some for you, too, he's generous, you know, said we should try it together, all excited like, since I told him about us, you know?" She let her head drop back, threw her arms out.

"Crucify me, Lord. I AM YOURS!" she shouted. "That's what he says when he comes! Isn't that funny? Him? Saying that?!"

As if Lucy'd know, but that didn't matter now, it was that there was something horribly, seriously, wrong with Jean.

The boy on the end had come halfway down the embankment, and Lucy ran to him.

"Fuckin' little traitor, Lucy. Where you going?" Jean shouted.

The boy's name was Rolland, Rolland Spencer. And she ran up to meet him halfway.

"Get Mr. Opitz, nobody else," she said. It was a command, and he took it that way; ran.

Lucy went back down to Jean. "Jean?"

"Fuck you, Miss Pretty Pants," Jean said. "Where the fuck is he, when *I* need *him*?"

She looked around, as if someone might be standing there. Which someone was, Lucy.

"Who, Jean?"

Jean burst into tears. "Why did it have to be *you*? Why, when I'm—" she held her hands under her breasts.

"*Me*?!"

"Yes, *you*, Lucy! You made everything wrong." She had no idea what Jean was talking about. "You little Miss No-Tits. You haven't even had your first period yet, have you?"

That the boys had come a ways down the hill, were hearing all of it, made things all the worse. Lucy was terrified now, but she was embarrassed, too—which made her hate herself.

What should she care what anyone else thought? Jean, she was sure, was in trouble.

"Jean, *what* did you take?"

Jean staggered in a circle. "He said to take five, they were so weak, but, hey, I took all ten, and just look at me!"

She lurched, as if some hand had reached up and shaken her, then vomited onto the snow. She held her hand to her mouth and giggled, eyeing it; then turned to Lucy, wide-eyed. Lucy turned to see what she was looking at, there Mr. Opitz at the top of the embankment.

"Lucy," Jean said, then held her hand to her mouth, "I am so, so, so fucked up. I don't know—"

And just then her eyes rolled back into her head, and she fell. Mr. Opitz jogged down, the keys in his pants jangling, and a siren coming on in the distance. He went right down to Jean. Big as a bear. Set his fingers on the side of Jean's neck. Shouted, "GOD DAMNIT!

"Get that pack off of her, and stretch her out," he said to Lucy. "Grab her legs and pull her flat."

She did that, and Mr. Opitz kneeled alongside her. He pressed his hands, folded together, over her chest. Pumped. One two three. Gave her a breath. One two three. Gave her a breath.

The ambulance had pulled up behind the embankment. "YOU," he said to Lucy. "Do it."

She got in where he'd been. Did with her hands what Mr. Opitz had done. Pinched Jean's nose with one hand, breathed into her mouth, so she could see Jean's chest rise. The rescue crew bolted down with Mr. Opitz, one of them with a bag he zipped open.

"Don't stop," he said.

Lucy didn't, not until he took her hand and pulled her back, knelt over Jean and jammed a syringe into her thigh.

Jean's eyes shot open. Fixed on Lucy's. They got her on a backboard, her pack with her, and ran with her up and over the embankment, and in the parking lot slid her into the waiting ambulance. The ambulance shot from the curb, the siren coming on, then growing fainter, until it was gone.

Mr. Opitz stood beside Lucy. He threw his arm over her shoulders and pulled her close.

"You did good," he said, "no matter what happens, you tried," he said, and Lucy burst into tears.

All the kids at lunch had wandered out into the parking lot and were gawking and chattering, and Mr. Opitz directed Lucy around to the front of the school. Just inside the glass doors, a policeman was waiting—tall, and substantial, and intimidating—and they followed him to the principal's office, and her father, like a hurricane, shouting, rushed in seconds after they'd sat.

"Lucy, I got here as quickly as could," he said, then added, "You haven't said anything, have you?" He turned to the other three there: The policeman, Mr. Opitz, and the principal.

Mr. Opitz nodded.

"What is the purpose of this meeting," her father said, "and *why* is my daughter here?"

"We're just… informally, trying to get a little information. That's all we're doing, Officer Walters."

It almost scared her to see her father in his professional capacity, so cold and calculating.

"Lucy," he said, holding up a hand, palm out, "don't say anything you're not sure of. Unless you don't have anything *to* say."

Was he getting between her and the other men in the room to protect her? Or to manipulate the meeting? To prevent something from coming out, something he didn't want coming out?

Whatever it was, he was pushing the meeting, directing it.

"I won't, Daddy," she all but cried, now confused and sickened and, really, more than a little shocked.

He *knew* something, like the time they'd come home to the trailer, and he'd gotten very still, and when she'd reached for the passenger door handle to get out of the car, he caught her arm.

Seconds later, the man burglarizing their trailer dropped out the back, and her father bolted after him.

"So," he said, "Lucy?"

"I *don't... know* what Jean did or what she took. I didn't have *anything* to do with it, other than ... Jean's my friend."

"Officer Walters," the policeman said, and her father, as if having gotten the story he'd wanted, sat back.

A look of concern on his face, but she knew from the way he'd crossed his arms over his chest, more so relieved.

"So, just tell us what happened, so we're all clear on that," the officer said, and when her father nodded, she went into it. What had happened that morning, and only that; which, she knew, was a sin of omission.

But what did it matter? She already knew what she was going to do. And it was going to be bloody.

21

Buck

The day started like any other, and he took comfort in that, though he sensed something coming at him. Made coffee. And while it was brewing he got dressed, so that when he came back downstairs it was ready, and he sat in the relative dark, facing east—it was important to face east, and he prayed. He was no "believer," but he couldn't not believe, either. No, Seraphim had gotten to him. Had forced him to sit, one time for days, and he thinking it was punishment for speaking the old language—which he'd suffered earlier—when she was teaching him first to listen to her, but then to listen to himself. Or, that voice in him. Only, back then he'd had no idea Seraphim was preparing him for something, too, something much larger.

So, most mornings he prayed, beginning with Seraphim, he gave thanks to her, and he prayed for Naomi, that she'd be happy, somehow, and he prayed for the girl, Lucy, and for the day, that he could bring some light into it, be useful, live it with his heart, and as he was praying he went to the back door and let the cat in, and she all but bolted to the dish where Lucy had set it, having gotten the cat to come inside when she'd last been over, and he carefully turned sideways now, as she had done, dropped a big spoonful of food in the dish, and the cat ate. Even let him touch her on her back.

Minutes later, the cat followed him out into the shop, curled in the cubby he had made for it. It occurred to him he'd left his cell in the house, but that was for the best. He had a table and chair set to finish, the Swedish Modern. It would take all his concentration, and he wanted to pre-mill parts for the canoe as well—the seat stays and bow and stern insets.

Still, he worked in a state of anticipation, warding off a distinct unease, until late afternoon when he went inside and the phone rang.

He reached over to it on the counter, lifted it. Who would be calling?

"Hello," he said, thinking it had to be Naomi, since he could hear some kind of hospital PA system on the other end.

"Yes?" he said.

"Buck," a woman's strained, reedy voice replied, one he didn't recognize, but then did. Not Naomi, but Lucy.

There was a muffled something on the other end. He almost said, How did you get my number; but then he remembered, he'd called her, earlier.

"Lucy?"

She sobbed, her breath catching. "There's *nobody*, and—"

"Where are your parents?" She sobbed again, this time only worse. Okay. So that wasn't the thing to ask right now. "*Where* are you?"

She told him, and he said, only, "I'm leaving now," and hung up, not giving her any choice about it.

He looked around the kitchen. What did he need, if anything? He should shave, he thought. But no. There wasn't time for that. He bent to the sink. Brushed his teeth with his index finger. Saw his face in the glass, reflected there. A struck-dumbness in it. Fate, coming at him again. He'd just known it. The cat had, too—or, really, he'd seen it in the cat, first.

This was all going to get complicated. But she'd finally asked, this girl who'd come out of nowhere.

And it was his to deal with now. Right to the end.

If there was one thing he hated it was hospitals, having lost too many people in them. Going by the ambulances in the roundabout, then in the emergency door and through the atrium, rushing by stands of red chrysanthemums, and the white walls pressing in on him, and the floors too shiny, and the antiseptic smells assaulting him, he felt as if he were, once again, crushed.

Naomi was up on the seventh floor on shift, he had to shut his mind to that, and his brother's death here from gunshot, and his father's from a heart attack, and now Naomi's mother's from a stroke; worst of all, Naomi was so close it was all he could do *not* to run up to the seventh floor and say...*what*?

Going to the front desk, he was trying to pull out of it, his feeling of loss, which was useless.

He got directions and, minutes later, stood in the door. Lucy, at bedside, and—her sister? Friend? Whoever it was in the bed, he could see at a glance she wasn't coming back, the girl in the hospital bed was raised as if she were only sitting, in a blue smock, a mask over her lower face, tubes running from it to a machine in the corner, one that hissed, breathing for the girl. An "Indin' girl," and one who'd been way more than pretty, which, ironically, was the very kind who died first.

"Lucy?" he said, and stepped into the room.

"Why don't they shut her eyes?"

He turned to the girl in the bed and, reaching out with his fingertips, he brought her lids down.

"Where's your mother?" he asked, glancing at Lucy, the all-but-dead girl there between them.

When she only looked blankly at him, he said, "Your father?"

"At work."

"Yes, but *where*. He can't come now?"

"He's a policeman. He's got some—there's been some... altercation, and he's on it, and...."

"Does he know you're here?"

"No."

"Why don't you come over to my place. We can..." he lifted his shoulders, "sit in the shop. You can't stay here alone."

"I should go, like this?"

"No."

"What then?"

"Show her, right now, how you feel. Because you're not going to get another chance.

"Do you want me to go out into the hallway?"

She took his hand, her hand trembling something awful, and she bent and kissed the girl on the mouth. When she rose, she stepped tentatively back from the bed and glanced up at him.

"Okay," she said, and he led her out of the room, Lucy looking over her shoulder one last time.

And just then something struck her. And she drew him back to the bed, where she lifted the girl's smock, and the girl's skin, but for where it had been burned, rose petal smooth, and being Indian, the color of caramel.

Lucy, not finding what she'd been looking for, let go a long-held breath, then pressed his hand, and they went out.

In the lobby, it occurred to him where he might find what Lucy'd been looking for, and he asked her to wait, then went up to the room, reached under the bed and got Jean's backpack off the tray.

From Naomi's work, he knew patients' "effects" were kept with them.

In the pack were her clothes, her shoes, a Timex watch, and a piece of cheap jewelry.

He took the elevator down, met Lucy in the lobby and, the pack clutched under his arm, went out with her to her car, where they stood saying nothing.

When, finally, she threw the door open to get in, he caught her by the shoulder, bent to say, "Something you should see."

"Yeah?" She was all but glaring.

He set the pack on the hood, then reached into it, for what he assumed she'd been looking for when she'd ducked back into the room. Lifted up the gimcrack necklace and crucifix, what her friend

136

had been wearing and had been put away for her, and Lucy, out of reflex, covered her mouth.

Stared, while she tried not to let it show.

22

Lucy

He'd gotten out his webbed chairs and they sat in the garage, the salamander roaring behind them. He came into the garage from the house and handed her a mug. A big black one, filled with strong coffee, and she wrapped her hands around it, warming them.

"Her cousins are going over, the Whitehorses." Lucy looked at her watch. "Maybe they're over there now."

He only nodded, then sipped at his mug, a blue one. On the side, in white letters, *Fairview Hospital*. They sat what seemed forever, but when she looked at her watch only minutes had passed.

"Do you have time to sit here?" she asked, feeling like she needed to fill the space.

Sitting, it was sinking in they'd meant to kill her, too. *And I had some for you, he's generous, you know, said we should try it together.* Saw, now, she'd been spared by Jean's having been... impulsive.

Or was it selfish? But that was Jean, and something she'd loved about her. How she'd taken pleasure in things. Only that wasn't Lucy at all, though, maybe that was why they'd been such perfect friends? And why, now, was she recalling that time she'd been ill, when her mother had watched over her? Spooned soup into her? And her father, behind her mother, winking, back when he'd been himself, and Jean, her mouth on hers, tasting of grape gum, and—

The roof beams cracked and popped, the roof settling in the cold. She'd forgotten to take the chicken out of the freezer in the trailer.

So they'd have to have soup. Her father would be angry, or maybe it would be worse than that? He really did seem to believe she knew nothing. Though, from the way he'd pushed the meeting earlier, she'd become aware he was fishing for... something. He was working his own agenda and, somehow, what had happened had not altogether surprised him—just that it had been her friend, Jean.

She felt weirdly numb again, because, well—it shocked *her*, and terribly, to think what all-that-had-just-happened meant.

"Let me get this," Buck said, and he shut the salamander off, "because—well, even though it's still a bit cold, it's too loud."

Which would have been fine, only, now she couldn't hide in the noise, and he reached for a blanket behind them and draped it over her shoulders and head, then tucked it in around her knees so, with her head hooded, she was looking out as if from some tent at her shoes.

Christ, the soles had all but come off of them, and what was she doing wearing tennis shoes in winter?

"I don't know who gave the necklace to me," she said, turning her shoe, Keds, in blood red. Jean's idea.

She'd shown it to him in the parking lot of the hospital, and he'd said nothing, only nodded.

Her elbows set on her knees, head propped in her hands, she kept her eyes on her shoes. She'd always wondered why they put those two metal eyelet things near the arch.

"You got that after... what, some kind of whatever, right?"

Lucy nodded. "Yeah, *whatever*."

"Like a reward."

She let go a deep, exhausted breath. "Yes. Or maybe, something else, because, when," she shrugged, "*that* happened, we got them. I think." There. She'd said it. She'd let it out into the world.

"You, and your friend."

Again, she nodded. And it occurred to her, all over again, but now in a real world sort of way, and not fantasy, that she would track Arn down, and it would have to be someplace public.

"First," he said, as if he'd been listening to her thoughts, "you're going to do absolutely NOTHING."

"And just *what* was I going to do?" She said it with a snide, sarcastic tone in her voice and glared.

"Exactly what I would do."

"They're cops, you know, and I don't know who all else."

"Yeah. I figured as much from the day you showed up here, that you had your reasons."

She felt her face heat. So, yeah, he *had* seen the blood. But then Jean had, too, so….

"Can we not talk about it anymore?" she said, "just now?"

"You don't have to say another thing," he told her, but it came up again all the same, shook her.

Lucy cried soundlessly, like someone drowning.

After, she sat staring and a blank look on her face, spent, as if she'd fallen into herself.

"Can I use your bathroom?" she asked.

Buck, there in his webbed chair, nodded, "Same as before. Straight through the back, up the hallway and first door to the left."

She went out of the garage and to the back, Gyg was there, and she let the cat in, and in that moment, going in, there was that strangeness of being alone in another person's living space, and this one—though it was way better than the trailer—was kind of cluttered, and a little run down, which surprised her since he made such beautiful things.

Like the rowboat, and he'd shown her a dresser and a thing called an armoire, all things she would never have.

The cat at her feet was hungry, and she went to the refrigerator. Canned cat food, a blue plastic lid on it.

There was a spoon, just one, in the sink, and she swept it up, spooned food from the can onto the dish there, and the cat ate, and she dropped to one knee, stroking it, and the cat archied its back, it's once raw, rough coat, now all these months later silky, and just then she felt a great, depthless love for it, the dumb cat.

She knew, if anything in this horrible, broken, twisted, and ugly world, she loved cats, or—just animals.

She went up the hallway, as she had before, but this time, in the bathroom, looked in the medicine cabinet, there aspirin. Toothpaste. Tooth brush. Shaver. Brush. Nothing that said anything about him.

She did her business, feeling oddly exposed, and washed her hands—looked in the mirror.

Threw on a big, hideous smile. Right. Frowned, looking into her eyes. Noticed a baseball card fixed into the mirror. *Cleveland Indians.* A pitcher, in cap and uniform, winding up on a mound.

She plucked it from the mirror, turned it, to take in the stats on the back—her father, old school as he was, loved baseball. But— *wow*—whoever he was, he'd been better than good. And then she realized it was Buck.

Broad shoulders, hatchet blades for cheekbones, and a look in his eyes that was scary.

God, the things you didn't know about people, and he hadn't said a word, but he still looked the part.

The phone rang in the kitchen and she went to it. The phone rang six times, and when a woman's voice started up on the answering machine, for no reason she could think, she picked up the receiver.

"Midwestern Wood, Becky speaking," she said, in a singsong voice. "Our aim is to please. To whom am I speaking?"

There was a long silence, and she was expecting to hear the digital click of a robocaller coming on. When one didn't, and she could hear someone breathing on the other end, she said, "Yes?"

"This is Michael's wife, Naomi," came the reply, a whole world of opprobrium in it. "Could you give him a message?" Hers was a no-nonsense voice, full of barely concealed anger, and under it a tone of all-too-long suffering.

"I could get him," she said.

"Becky," Naomi said. "Now that's a nice, perky name. And you do what for… *Midwestern Wood?*"

I keep the wood waxed and oiled, she thought to say, surprised at herself.

"I do the books. Answer the phone. Get supplies. Put out flyers and things, advertising. Leif isn't delivering anymore, so—I make supply runs, too."

"Well, Becky," this... Naomi said. There was a cutting, sharp intelligence about her. "Maybe you could motivate... *Michael* to come and get—" she sighed, and it was an exasperated sigh "—you'll want to tell him, I *will* set it out on the curb if he doesn't come by for it. I mean it. And this week. Can you tell him that? Can *you* make him listen, for once?"

The cat was turning circles around her leg and she pulled the corded phone to the back door and let it out.

"Yes," she said.

"And Becky. Take it from me, don't let yourself be drawn too deeply into his life."

She didn't know if this was a threat, or—and because Naomi said nothing following it, she replied,

"Where should Buck pick this... *it* up? This would be at your... business? Office? Home?"

"Home."

"And... is there a time in particular, when—"

"I've changed the locks. And I wouldn't want to leave it out on the porch. He knows when I'm here."

"All right, I'll give him the message," she said, as perkily as possible—as much to push back at her, as— "Will he be needing to bring the truck or a trailer?"

Naomi laughed. "He really hasn't told you anything, has he," she said, and it was game over.

There was a dial tone, Naomi having hung up, then a voice saying, "*If you'd like to make a call, please hang up and—*"

She set the receiver in the cradle. Looked out the window over the sink. Buck had opened the garage door, set out two sawhorses, laid a sheet of veneer on them, and was marking it with a pencil.

Granted the rage under the surface of Naomi's call, she knew something had gone wrong there, and badly.

She raced up the stairs and into what was obviously his study, where she tore through his desk. Not even sure what she was looking for, until, in the lower left drawer, she lifted up a stack of bills, rubber bindered together. *Naomi Westin,* was the address on the envelope on top.

Moments later, she stepped outside.

"Sorry for the mess in the house," he said. "Somehow I've never quite moved in."

"Oh, that's all right. It's not *that* messy." It was right there to be said, but she didn't say it: *Naomi called. Wants you to take your... stuff, or thing, or whatever.* Because he wouldn't be doing that.

She told him she had to go, then got in her car and drove around the corner and, barely out of sight, she stopped along the curb. Pulled the bill—scrawled across it, *Paid in full*—from her hoodie. The address: *Naomi Westin, 1785 Pillsbury Avenue, St. Paul, MN 55404.*

She held the steering wheel, and the wheel seeming to want to take her somewhere, and not home, but something compelled her to wait, though she desperately wanted to meet this *Naomi*—it was critical to her survival—but there was dinner to make at the trailer, and now wasn't the time.

23

Buck

The following morning he was up shortly after dawn. It was bright out, almost too bright. He'd overslept, which was unusual and, worse, he had a kind of dread about the day. Already he was fighting some sixth sense that something wasn't right. Something *was* out there, but maybe it was just all that with Lucy's friend, Jean, the bad end she'd come to? And so he fought a kind of resistance in himself. To all the usual things: making coffee, he spilled grounds everywhere; his eggs, he scalded; not burned, but scalded, which he hadn't done in forever. When he got the mess cleaned up, he jammed the frying pan into the lower cupboard, only to have it fall out with the remainder of the pots and pans jammed into the narrow space, so it all clanged hideously, shockingly, onto the floor, and so much so that he fought a momentary impulse to cover his ears.

Everything seemed an irritant. A wake up call. But to what? Which he told himself was, granted his circumstances, an all but unforgiveable sin of ingratitude. What, really, was his problem this morning? Elsewhere in the world, people were—truly—struggling. He glanced out the window over the sink, the hairs on the back of his neck prickling.

Was something—or *someone*—out there, in one of the cars along the curb, frost on their windshields, but for the closest? A Ford Taurus. The right front fender all bent in. And was he being paranoid, thinking it could the same one that had followed him earlier?

It was the same color, but had that one been smashed up? Or was it just that he hadn't given it a good, hard look?

When the cat appeared at the door, he—happily—let it in, the cat all but dancing to the dish. How pathetic was he? He adored the cat. Everything about it: its half missing ear (frostbite); its now sleek fur (Lucy's sardines); its coral pink nose (proof the cat was flesh and blood) and the cat purring so powerfully now that she all but shook with it.

Having eaten, it looked for the girl, and not finding her, wanted to get outside again. Really? It was twenty-one degrees out, and the temperature was dropping. The forecast was for nine degrees by noon, and below zero by the afternoon.

"Gyg," he said to the cat, "I'm *not* going to let you out. Okay? For your own good."

Talking to the cat. He wasn't a cat lady yet, he didn't have five, ten cats, but—what was the difference? Lucy had brought a litterbox into the house and filled it, which was in the corner behind the back door. And what about her? Lucy?

He bent into the sink, looking out the window again, and to his right the cat circling the back door.

The Taurus, along with the other cars, had gone—just off to work, and the owner having been idling in it.

Actually, he thought, he did have reason to be happy. He'd won a bid on a kitchen remodel in Brainerd, one that would cover his expenses for the remainder of the winter. It wasn't even a rush job—which, usually, was exactly when people called him. He'd made the bid in August and had assumed he hadn't won it. But that had just been a delay in the construction schedule. They'd poured the foundation, framed, roofed, sheet-rocked, gotten the bathrooms in, and now they wanted him in the kitchen.

And to get with the project, he needed wood, and a lot of it, which meant a trip out to Leif's.

He dumped another handful of kibble in the cat dish, which made a musical, bell-like ringing. Again, the girl's doing. Now *that* was a lovely sound; a how-many-angels-can-dance-on-the-head-of-a-pin sound.

He reached over the cat and snatched his coat and hat from the rack, then went to the front door.

The cat, for the first time, didn't follow him, and he went out into the cold in his street shoes, not his corks, which he'd foregone because the cat had been at the dish there all but sitting on top of them.

Something he would later think on, that he'd let the cat keep him from getting on his heavy, near knee-high work boots.

Off he went in his truck, and his breath fogging the windshield; it wasn't only cold out, it was damp. He poked at the heater controls. Yet another irritation: the truck was falling apart, the controls all but broken. Why couldn't they just use cables as they had in the past? Like on the old Dodge he'd had? "Smart controls"? When he hit the defroster, it only made things worse, and he rolled down his window to get a cross breeze to blow out his warm, damp breath.

He was thinking about Lucy's friend, Jean, and her having died like that, and what it might mean for Lucy.

Otherwise it was just another day, and because the highway was always a nightmare, bumper to bumper, he took the back road as he always did. The drive to Leif's was a half hour longer this way, but he never got stuck in traffic. And what trouble was driving a few more miles? He bent into the wheel, a pie-plate-sized clearing in the windshield, and in minutes was on the river flats where Lucy lived, all trailers. He went by one steaming slough after another, then north into the estuary, and the ducks wintering over clustered on the open water making hungry, miserable circles, and his heart went out to them—how could anything survive out there, when it got so cold?

He glanced in his rear view mirror. A few blocks back, there was a propane truck.

Gripping the wheel in his left hand, he twisted to scratch at the glass of the rear window, working his broken scraper over it and only seeming to make diagonal slashes in the frost. And turned like that, he cut through it with one good jab and saw there the grill of the truck—impossibly large—looming up at him. He spun around and ducked, thinking: he'll go flying past, crazy son of a bitch—and was struck violently, exactly at the bridge over the narrows, so that in some silent otherworld he fought to keep the truck on the pavement, but hit the guardrail with a colossal BOOM! His face smashing into the windshield, and the truck flipping, as if in slow motion, his body thrown back, glass flying and a broad swatch of river looming up. The cement marker on the embankment a good hundred yards out past the hood *just there*, a bright, white band, from the flood of '66, where the river had capped it—and he hit the water, skipped, once, then came to a stop.

Clinging to the wheel and hanging from his seat belt upside down like a bat, a black—*something*—overtook him.

He came to, the cab all but filled with water. Something was in his eyes and he wiped it away. Blood. And now the truck settling, and the water, he knew, twenty feet deep or so where he'd gone over. The water rising up under him, he saw the shoulder strap hadn't held, but the lap strap had, and that's why he was alive at all. The stick shift jutted down, the knob on the end of it like something he'd never seen before, a ball of black plastic, and the dirty carpet overhead, cigarette butts floating under him like game fish bobbers, the truck shifting side to side, and back to front, like a leaf falling from a tree, going down.

The river was muddy, and he knew he had to get out before he reached the bottom, and he tore at his seat belt. Pressed at the spring loaded release in the center of it. Nothing. *Piece of shit!* It always stuck. But then, it wasn't designed to release under a load, and he was hanging from it. He yanked at it, then got his carpenter's knife from his pocket. Cut through the nylon webbing, took three deep breaths, then ducked down and swam out the window he'd opened earlier. Right there, looking up through what had to be fifteen feet of water, he saw a figure on the bridge, looming there, and he swam as he had as a boy spear fishing, staying down, *reachhhhh*—kick, *reachhhhh*—kick, *reachhhhh*—kick, until he was under the bridge. He rose toward the surface, his lungs all but bursting, though made himself wait, swim to the far embankment where he, desperate for air, came up, mouth open.

Breaking through, he sucked in a silent, burning lungful—in his brain a burst of white like an explosion.

A shadow slid down the embankment—whoever it was who'd been standing on the bridge coming down after him—and he went under again, let the current carry him into the open water on the side opposite into the bulrushes he'd seen the ducks making circles around.

He thought to come up—but whoever it was who'd been driving the truck now stood on the far side where he pointed, into the deepest part of the channel, and a diver in a wet suit got in.

Even from underwater, he could see the truck driver was in a policeman's uniform.

He turned and, with the last of what he had in him, let the current carry him yet farther out into the open, where he surfaced, amid all the ducks, sucked in a ragged, choking breath.

The diver in the channel went by like a shark, kicking his fins and bubbles swelling from his mouthpiece, swam to the right, then left, then back to the bridge where the cop was waiting and got out of the water.

He and the cop argued about something. There was a patrol car, a black and white, parked on the shoulder in front of the propane truck. The cop got into it, then waited until the diver had changed into a maintenance worker's one piece, mounted the propane truck's running board, and swung in behind the wheel.

He pulled in front of the patrol car, the cop nodded, and like that, the two of them drove off.

When they'd been gone some time, the patrol car backed onto the bridge, and the officer got out, big-gutted, and a squarish head; he came down to the water. Looked long and hard.

When the cop had gone, he swam into shore. His feet, numb as they were, post-holed to his chins in the mud. A duck squawked behind him, quack quack-quack-quack, as if scolding him.

He staggered up the embankment. He had his phone on him, but he thought not to use it. Couldn't. Who knew who was following his calls? Since he'd called Lucy that day, he'd lied to himself too much. That had been no accident, him calling her. They'd *expected* him to.

He had to get back to her, because—and he didn't have to guess what they were up to—it had to be stopped.

But what were his chances? He looked down at himself. Already, a transparent sheet of ice had formed over his jacket and pants. He looked around him. The marshland had seemed desolate enough from inside the truck, but now? It seemed altogether and positively lethal. The frozen-over tracks of deer running to the river. Endless ice on shore only broken by bulrushes and cattails, and not so much as a tree to shelter in, to get out of the wind.

He was—desperately—trying to recall if there was any place within walking distance.

At this temperature, he had, at best, a half hour before he'd be insensate with hypothermia. And no one used this road. That's why he'd taken it. No one was coming. Already there was a dense, cottony quality to his senses, as if his ears were stuffed with something—were they? And just there it struck him what to do. He'd done the same a lifetime ago—and a chance passerby had saved his life that night.

It was a desperate measure, but desperate measures were called for. He had to get back to Lucy.

He stumbled down the shoulder toward the frozen bank of the river where the bulrushes grew, shucked off his jacket as he went. Reaching the water, he tore handfuls of the bulrushes free, stuffed them under his shirt and down his back—packing them in as tightly as he could. He got his socks pulled up over his pants, then shoved the bulrushes down his pants too. When he got his all-but-stiff-with-ice jacket back on, he pulled the hood over his head, stuffed rushes in around his insensate ears, working like a madman, stuffing, and stuffing, and stuffing the bulrushes everywhere, until his clothes were all but bursting with them. His feet—he couldn't feel his toes at all—but he wouldn't think about that.

He scaled the embankment and, turning into the wind, lurched up the shoulder. If he died like this, he'd be a sight. And if—somehow—he got out, he'd be a sight then, too. He laughed. And it was a dark, awful kind of laughter, because, even in his diminished state of mind, he knew his being here like this had everything to do with Lucy and her friend, Jean. They were cleaning up, that's what they were doing—the... twisted cops, and who knew all else.

Whoever had hurt Lucy and killed her friend had come after him, assuming she'd told him what was going on.

He looked up the road, which thinned to nothing in the distance, no shelter in sight. The bitter cold wind cutting through him, he started up it.

24

Lucy

At the end of that week her father had a day off—Saturday—and he took it in the trailer, more than for any reason, it seemed, to grill her endlessly on Jean's death. They'd taken Jean off life support, she'd died, and they'd held a funeral for her. Life went on, strangely enough, almost as if none of it had happened. That is, for everyone else but Lucy, who, even now this Saturday morning when she'd intended to go over to Ryan's after breakfast, was sitting at the kitchen table undergoing, all over again, her father's latest interrogation.

He was good at it, too. Sitting across from her at the table, his hands knuckled there over the linoleum. And he did know something—or was up to something—and he all but put her in a cold sweat, digging.

He was a cop, and he tried to trap her, over and again, but she was good, too, he didn't know *how* good, at not sharing things with him, anything really, but the slightest details of her life. And, too, he'd shared his stories of trapping criminals in their stories with her for years and, despite the fact he'd thought at times she wasn't listening, she'd more than listened. She'd taken in every word. Every bit of advice. And the first was: *Never. Never* say anything beyond what was asked for. *Never* give another version of the story. *Never* elaborate. *Never* give in to intimidation. *Never* think a cop is a friend, no matter how friendly he got.

Which made it all too clear now, smiling the way he was, that he was pursuing some agenda of his own.

"Come on, Luce," he said, and gave her his aw-shucks grin, dimples and all, which had once won her over. "Everybody thinks there's got to be more to it on your end, since you were closest to Jean. Where would a kid get drugs like that? Who would have access to pharmaceuticals like they found in her. You must've seen her with… someone, didn't you?"

"*No*," Lucy said.

And that was the truth, too. She could say it with utter and total conviction. That was the trick to acting. You had to believe what you were saying. Play a little game in your head. She *hadn't*. Though, from the necklace Jean'd had on, that she'd taken from Buck, she'd made the connection—between Jean and *Him*, and she was wearing Jean's necklace and crucifix now, both of them, Jean's and hers, as a promise to herself, though just now she couldn't think how she'd get to either *Him* or Arn, and all her options seemed pretty suicidal.

"Look," her father said, "just, since none of this has anything to do with you, what did you see?

"Somebody *had* to have shown up, right?"

Her father smiled, inviting her to open up, to let her guard down. But she was better. She cried a little. That helped. Bringing on the tears, which was easy, since all she had to do was think of her mother, and that "opened up the waterworks," as her father had said in his stories.

Yeah, we played good-cop bad-cop for days, and finally we knew we had him when he opened up the waterworks. Confessed to the whole thing, crying there in the station.

She sobbed, the burned toast there and congealed eggs she hadn't eaten on her plate, lay the back of one hand across her eyes and, blindly, put out the other, which her father took in his. Gripped his hand and he gripped back. Which was weird, because, his loving her in his own awful, and now wrongheaded, way made her all the more determined to take care of this thing herself. Like some Kamikaze if she had to. Because, for what *He'd* done, and Arn, and those, a few times, *others*, she didn't want them just put away. Or, even her father to do something. No, she'd decided she was going to kill them.

It would just take some forethought and planning. And of course, finding out who *He* was—*He* being the first to do what made what Arn did later—and what Booker saw—possible.

She had in her father's guns a 30.06 with a scope, a Glock 9, and a twelve gauge with a two foot barrel. A "shorty." If she couldn't get it done with one of those? Her father let go of her hand and they both sat back, Lucy wiping the tears from her face with her forearm. Real tears, too, for Jean.

The newspaper hit the door with a lumpen clatter, and her father went to get it. Poured two mugs of coffee and, setting them on the table, he dropped down across from her.

He always gave her the front page and headline news, but he took it this time, handing her the Sports section—the… f'ing Vikings, as if she cared—and the *Living* section, which she opened, to find an article on a current fad for collectible furniture, the most sought after 1950s Le Corbusier loungers in boar hide. $20,000 for a couch. Right, that was a world she lived in.

"Hey," her father said, laughing. "You have got to see *this*, Bebbe Gurl. This'll brighten your day. Look at this lunatic!"

He folded the paper back on itself, then turned it to her, there a half page photo of someone who looked like the Abominable Snowman. Someone with—*what was that… stuff coming out of the hood on his head like some crazy fur?—bulrushes*? And his jacket and pants filled to bursting, too, so, whoever it was, he was puffed up like the Michelin Man in the tire ads.

"What," Lucy said, "is it some ice fishing thing?" There was open water behind him, and a patrol car and wrecker.

"Read the caption," her father said, and tapped the page with his finger and missing it, since he was guessing.

She bent forward, and there almost lost her shit, and totally.

Michael Fineday, of Shakopee, the caption read, *Monday survived a crash into the Minnesota River on Route 9, walking twelve miles to*

Denby, where he was rescued by local police.

Think, she commanded herself. Of something else. Anything else. LaLaLaLaLa…. He can't see you know who it is. "The Hallelujah Chorus." That's it. That part at the end. She heard it in her head now. Exultant, *And he shall reign for ever and ever. Hallelujah! Hallelujah!* She focused on it, shocked that *her* waterworks were on the verge of breaking, and all the worse for it. Handel. Damnit, stop it. Stop it! she told herself. And then, as if breaking into some beyond bright light, she was beyond herself furious. It was a blind, wind catching, staring fury. Carrying her to the very center of that soaring chorus.

She'd get *Him,* she'd get Him and Arn and the others. She'd been thinking of it abstractly. As if. Or *if when.* But not now.

"What the hell, Luce," her father said, because she'd forgotten her mouth—she was gritting her teeth.

She reached for her plate. Forked congealed egg off it and into her mouth, then chased it with the coffee, faked choking, then, swallowing the wrong way, she really *was* choking, choking and sobbing, so her father dodged around the table and thumped her on her back, and when that helped not at all, he swung her up by her feet, so she was hanging upside down, and the whole horror in her, she was laughing, hysterically, and choking, and sobbing, and her father hammered her on her back until the egg burst out of her like a cork, and he sat her at the table again, eyeing her. Then sat himself, across from her.

"BEBBE-GURL," he said, putting his face in hers, "You just scared the… living daylights out of me and—

"What the hell was all *that* about, Luce? I mean, sweetheart, you *pay attention* when you eat, okay?"

She nodded.

"I think I wet myself," she said, and she went back to her room and changed—there at her pink vanity—something for a little princess, the one she'd, a lifetime ago, once been.

"You comin' back?" her father called to her.

"In a minute," she shouted.

She sat in front of the three mirrors. Studied herself. Front, right, and left. She put on her blank face. Looked into her eyes. They'd looked kind of dead before, after He'd first—though worse, after Arn hurt her—but now there was a shiny hardness to them, a glitter. That was new. She wasn't scared for herself anymore, that was it. She had a purpose, which she'd never had. She smiled, making her *chit chat face*; worked on her features, her smile, by opening her eyes wider. She'd been wearing things all oversized, like her big, new cotton hoodie, so no one would notice. So she could hide what was going on with her.

And she was all but certain that she wasn't... *that*—in trouble from Arn—but she could see it looked like it.

She'd always been kind of... angular, and even her face now was softer, fuller, and, well, what had taken place much earlier for Jean, was now taking place in her. She had hips and breasts now. Breasts she couldn't hide.

So it looked like that *other thing*—she couldn't lie to herself, and in that was proof—or, Arn, surely was thinking that, and *Him*, and the others, too. Proof they couldn't have getting out.

"Luce?" her father called, "we've got things to do, Bebbe Gurl!"

"Coming!" she shouted.

25

Buck

The cut on his head had been almost surgical, but even then had required twenty stitches. He fingered it now, across the counter, Leif, who, with a laugh, said, "Hey, you're world famous in Minnesota!" It was a stupid joke, and Buck had heard it too often.

"Right," he said.

It was a truly disconcerting thought, his picture in the paper because, now whoever it was who had sent him into the river knew he was alive. Which meant they'd be coming again, only differently.

But here at Leif's he was buying wood, as if nothing had happened. This the very thing Naomi had so hated about him, that he "compartmentalized" his life. In the middle of a shitstorm, he put his head down and worked. And the worse it got, the more he worked and the more he "disappeared," his mind bent on it, and only the husk of him present.

And Naomi? She hadn't been fooled. Not by any of it, him disappearing, after taking on people she'd come to call his "projects," as he had Lucy.

"Hey! Buck!" Leif said. "Wake up, old friend!"

Warehouse. Rafters twenty feet overhead. Wood by the million board feet. Forklifts rumbling here and there, the drivers in safety-yellow hard hats.

He got out his checkbook. Set it flat on the counter, and while filling one out, he thought: He'd have to take Naomi's name off the masthead; since, this time, he wouldn't be getting her back.

"How's beautiful Naomi?" Leif asked. Just to make conversation. He hadn't told anyone they'd separated.

"She's fine."

"Still putting in those long hours at the hospital?"

"Yes," he said, tearing the check out of the book and handing it to Leif, who set it in his cash drawer.

"Doing anything for the holidays?" he asked.

"Flying to Hawaii, going to take ukulele lessons from Don Ho, surf a little, lie in the sun. And you?"

Leif laughed. "Uh-huh. Yeah, me too. I'm off to the Riviera—" he nodded, "when pigs fly. Oh, and someone was in looking for you, a possible client interested cabinets. I gave him your card. He said you'd be hearing from him."

Nice. Someone wanting cabinets, as earlier on the message machine. Was that a coincidence? Or intimidation after he'd gotten away at the river? If so, they were being pretty brazen about it.

"You got a camera on the counter?"

They went into the rear of the office, and Leif ran the video back, until there he was at the counter. In uniform, no less. Big bellied. Tall. But not one of the men who'd run him into the river.

A cop. So, no, not a coincidence, and not a customer.

"You know him?" Leif asked.

"Yeah, after a fashion."

"See you in January?"

"That's the plan," he said, though he wondered if he'd be alive in January, there was no telling.

So, there were, at a minimum, a few of them—though, the kind of men he'd run into so far did the legwork and the brass stayed out of it, so—more. And they knew where he lived now, even his hours.

And with a nod to Leif and a handshake he turned to go out.

He got the wood stacked in his garage, and each time he turned his back to the street he felt exposed. Outside the mouth of the garage he set a hand on his shoulder and stretched. That old injury, from his time pitching, made itself known when he lifted things. Shoulder cuff, it'd need surgery, and soon, Naomi'd told him. That'd be another cold day in hell. Colder than this one.

He went into the yard with a bag of seed, strewed it in far-reaching fans, the birds darting into the trees and waiting.

And where was the cat? Inside, he reminded himself and went in, too. Almost noon, he made lunch, then, absentmindedly eating his sandwich, he checked the phone. Pressed *Play* on the answering machine, and thinking about the kitchen he was remodeling, decided he'd start with the center island.

Amid all the cold calls, and come-ons, "We're willing to offer you a year subscription at a 70% savings…" and "…wounded warriors, we could…" there was something from Naomi.

"Buck? Buck, I know you're there."

He hadn't been, not this time. She hung up. Then came on again. "I saw the picture in the paper. Which made me think…. Listen, I know it's not a good time, but you've *got* to come and get it, really, I don't want it in the house. And I mean it this time. Really."

Nice. No, not nice at all. Did she care that he'd almost just died? He wanted to lie to himself, tell himself her having called proved it. It wasn't about his… "thing" being in the house.

He'd promised Naomi he'd never get her involved in something like that again, and he hadn't, not exactly. Though, standing back of the phone, it occurred to him that Naomi would make a great witness to Lucy's injury. After all, with something like that, there had to be scarring.

And what about Lucy? She hadn't come by in… forever.

26

Lucy

By the end of the following week, and her father gone for days, she'd fallen back into ritual. Up early, make breakfast, then drive to school, endure the weirdness there post-Jean—everyone avoiding her, and the dumb dance coming up, she wouldn't be going to it now, with everyone... talking about her behind her back, and casting weird looks at her, and Ryan acting hurt about it, even though everyone knew Ryan was gay, or was he bi? Or, just, weirdly-Aspergery Ryan? When the day was over, she'd trudge back out to her cold car, drive home, and make dinner. Something carb-heavy that her father could pull out of the fridge in the Tupperware container. He'd promised he'd get a Christmas tree, and he hadn't. Though, sure, she knew they *were* cheaper if you got them the week of Christmas.

Ho, ho, ho! All of it made more awful by the fact she was putting off going over to Buck's.

Dinner done, and it being just after five, she paced in the trailer. Should she go over to Buck's, or not? Her father wouldn't be home until eleven, or even later. She knew she should be studying.

Up the trailer's narrow hallway she went. As if she might find something there. Then back.

The phone in her pocket all but burned, she was so aware of it. DON'T take it out of your pocket, she told herself.

She had her books out on the table. Her highlighters there, and her notebook. But her thoughts slid everywhere, from the picture of

Buck in the paper, to the pain she felt when she thought of Jean, and she imagined the whole kamikaze thing again—the cops at the station knew her and she'd be able to go right in, and when she got to Arn at his desk, she'd pull out the Glock, scream, "THIS IS FOR WHAT YOU DID!"

Put three bullets in his head, then stuff the barrel of the gun in her mouth and be done with it.

Which, now, tonight, started a terror in her. *So, why not, and right now?* something in her said, *aren't you tough enough?* Well, fuck that. Yes, she was.

That she could—not just think about it—but really, really do it, go after Arn herself, came to her as if some revelation. She had the Glock. She had the car. She could drive to the station. Arn would be there, he was on shift. All she had to do was open the drawer now. It was already open a little, so she could see the butt of the Glock there.

So while pacing, up the hallway and back, she swung wide of it. There had to be another way, another—

Booker? Could he help her? Really? He'd *seen* it. But then, what had he seen, exactly? Sure, he *knew*. He'd gotten that. But what, in a… legal sense, had he really seen? *Beyond a reasonable doubt?* Or had it been *just enough to think he knew*—because, she was almost sure it was the latter. It had been dark. And he'd been… what, half a block away? And, the cops would ask, if it had been so terrible, why hadn't she come forward? Right then, right after? Especially with her father being a cop? Really, she hadn't told *anyone*? And could Booker be a believable witness for her against someone like Arn, a cop? And what did she really know about Booker? Was there some reason *he* hadn't gone to the police? Of course there was, and it wasn't good. And what about Arn's—who was *He*, Arn's superior, his boss in all this, the one who'd first come to her in the dark when her father'd been away on night shift, a year or so after her mother had been killed?

She'd been sleeping and had wakened, horrified, to the presence of someone in her room. When He was… *done*, he whispered in her ear: "Don't get up. Don't Look. Ever. One word and your father will die." She'd been tormented, endlessly after, by one question—how had he known to threaten to her kill her *father* only? Her father who, back then, was violent? Who'd been attending meetings, for his out of control drinking and rages and grief?

Did He know them, from St. Peter's, or... maybe through the support group her father had been attending there? Or had it all been through Arn?

Pacing, she'd gotten to the drawer again, the Glock right there, and she paused, standing alongside it. Booker, who had his whole, bright life ahead of him, she couldn't involve him. But what about Buck? She knew, from the way he handled the rip saw, the planer, his carving knives, he was no stranger to deadly things. Buck was the kind of guy who got things done. And had. But all of it was too... horribly awkward, having to explain.

And there something burst into her head. Which, of course, had been lurking in her all along, but she'd been resisting. She hadn't suggested anything, hadn't dared to ask Buck for help because, well, earlier even the thought of it had been too horribly humiliating, and, later, she'd made herself think she might be wrong about him. Maybe, she'd told herself, he just *looked* intimidating? And what better way to make sure about him than through Naomi?

Right—she'd do something useful for Buck, she'd arrange to pick up that... *thing* Naomi had at the house, talk to her.

Lucy all but sighed at her plan; it was good. She'd find out all about Buck, she promised herself, and butted the drawer closed, shocked at herself.

Only, if she were honest, she knew more than anything she wanted to see what kind of woman this... *Naomi* was, too.

The little sedan now seemed to all but steer itself in the dark, and in the sky overhead the clouds lit up by the lights of St. Paul. She put her face into the windshield, watched the sign sweep back over the car, 10th, then turned right, walking her hands over the wheel.

"Never cross one hand over the other," her father had told her, and now she'd done just that. Nervous.

Ten blocks. Through downtown, past the State Theater, then climbing, into an old, old neighborhood. Onto Pillsbury Avenue. Enormous trees, and vast lawns with concrete lions either side of broad cement steps that led to ornamental facades and doorways ten feet tall, bright, but altogether tasteful Christmas decorations over some of them, wreaths and strings of lights.

Could she have the wrong address? Buck, down in Shakopee in that awful little house, had lived *here*?

She swept the bill she'd taken from Buck's study off the passenger seat, but couldn't make out the address in the dark. And she didn't want to turn on the dome light; be seen.

Not yet.

Up a ways, she pulled alongside the curb, which was strangely high. And the street was cobblestone. The house to her right was a Victorian, with ornate gingerbread gables and a wraparound porch. A warm light poured out onto the snow through the curtained windows, all ten or so feet high. Everything about the house was... outsized yet grandly beautiful: the soaring steep roof and tall dormers; the newel posts around the porch, on them complex geometrical patterns; ornate stonework over the double doors and brass sash work. Even in the dark, she could see the paintwork was *just so*—the house periwinkle, and mauve, and purple.

But the front doors, the doors were what convinced her this was—or had been—Buck's place, on either side carved stags, the wood honey blond, and such care taken that that's what you saw first.

The stags—there was something magisterial in them, yet inviting. He was in every bit of them.

She bent down the rear view mirror. Studied her face. She'd gone with the Amy Winehouse look, since everyone said she looked like her anyway, dark, heavy eyeliner swooping up dramatically, because it would make her seem older. And eye shadow, her mother's Passionate Plum. And, under her open, pink hoodie, a black pullover sweater, one with broad, horizontal cream stripes that emphasized her new—

and now not insignificant—breasts.

A look, she'd made sure in the trailer, that all too clearly said…
too-wised-up-for-her-own-good.

She arranged her hoodie now, just so. Torn jeans, and the pair of high-heeled pumps her mother had left behind.

Show time, she told herself, then straightened the rear view mirror. Let's go find out what's what.

And after, we'll get Buck's—whatever.

She got out of the car, a bit tottery. She was unaccustomed to heels, and they played tricks on her ankles. She scaled the steps to those massive doors and knocked, using the brass knocker there, cold in her bare hand. She cocked her head, settling: she knew Naomi was home. She'd called from the crowded vestibule of the casino, from what had to be the last pay phone in existence, one you actually fed coins. Had played Becky, the secretary.

Buck had asked her to pick something up at the house. Would she be in this evening? She'd thought she'd die before Naomi had said she would.

Waiting, she rubbed her foot against her calf, heard someone, or something stirring inside.

There hadn't been a picture of Naomi on the hospital website, and she was prepared to meet someone more than middle aged and, with someone like Buck, blonde. Didn't the native guys, after all, go for the blonde girls? There was some disturbance at the door, the catch of a lock, and the door swung open, there a darkly slender woman in green scrubs, one with enormous, almond-shaped eyes. A gold chain around her neck. Ruby studs in her ears. A full, full mouth.

Lucy kept hers shut, neither of them about to speak—a war of saying everything and nothing at first sight.

"You're a little… *young* to be involved with Buck, aren't you, *Becky*?" Naomi finally said, relenting.

So, she was going to be like that, Lucy thought. Buck's—what was Naomi? They weren't divorced yet, though they were separated, so? When Lucy didn't reply—sure, she was *young*, but she knew how this game was played—knew she'd sunk a hook in Naomi, after all, and if she seemed defensive, it wasn't because she didn't care.

Naomi stepped back, then made a sweeping gesture, her hand trailing suggestively into the house.

"Come in, please."

"Thank you," Lucy replied, and as she stepped over the threshold Naomi swung the door closed behind her. Naomi smelling of roses, a perfume subtle, and complex, and—somehow melancholy.

Inside, the house seemed all the more grand. The ceiling in the entryway all but soaring overhead, it was so high, there fancy, old time glass windows, and brass light fixtures—modernized, now electric—but from the century-before-the-last-century, really, another world.

To her right, and some distance from her, was a beautiful, grand staircase. One that spiraled up to the second floor.

"No doubt this must all be surprising to you, seeing as how Buck lives… in that old house—" Naomi shrugged "is he…?"

"What," Lucy said, "Alone?"

She would let her wonder if she and Buck were… involved. Wouldn't answer her question. And, anyway, she could tell by Naomi's purposeful looks, she was curious, too.

"I put coffee on after you called, so, a cup?" Naomi asked.

"Yes, I'd like that," Lucy replied, and Naomi led her into the dining room where tall windows overlooked the street, and the neighborhood Victorians lit for Christmas, on the roof of the one across the street a Santa in a sleigh, eight reindeer in front of it. She'd seen something like it in an old Coca Cola ad in a *Colliers* magazine in the reservation office.

With a sweep of her hand, Naomi motioned to a chair, one upholstered in blood red leather.

"I'll be right back," she said.

Moments later, Naomi reappeared, carrying two cups on saucers. She handed Lucy one, and sat in the winged chair opposite her, then sipped at her coffee and, with a studied delicacy, set the cup and saucer on the table between them.

"So, he's taken you under his wing now, hasn't he." She said it with a kind of hostility, and disappointment.

"Excuse me?"

"You're in... *trouble*."

Lucy felt her face heat, blushing, shocked at what Naomi'd said, and in it a scalding humiliation.

"Ah, Christ," Naomi said, and all that cutting meanness in her gone. "What are you, all of fifteen? But you're a very *old* fifteen, aren't you?" She sighed. "Does Buck know?"

"I'm *not*, you know," Lucy said, "in *that* kind of... trouble."

Naomi's eyes narrowed, and she frowned. "But you're worried that, whoever it is, thinks you might be. That's the issue."

When Lucy didn't contradict her, Naomi smiled, and it was a sad smile. "You really are in a tough spot, I can see that."

"You know, Becky," she said, "—and, yeah, I know that's not your name—but let's, for now, just ignore that— you're a very, very clever girl. I ring the house, and you pick up the phone, and on the spot you're Buck's secretary, you do his books, you're the gofer, his sidekick.

"You're driving, but... you're barely fifteen. So, you thought to get a farm permit, or whatever....

"Your father... he works nights. And your mother's—" she looked her up and down, "she's gone, isn't she. Those are her shoes."

Lucy's eyes glassed up and her throat positively burned, a pressure in her as if she might burst.

It felt... wonderful to finally *be seen*. But it was awful, too. Did Buck see her like this? Had he? Of course he had, and from that first day she'd come up his driveway bleeding.

"Is your father the problem?" Naomi said. From the too-belligerent stare Lucy gave her, Naomi got it. "Right. No. He isn't, is he. He has no idea what's going on with you."

"We're building a canoe," Lucy said, her embarrassing excuse for being here, at Naomi's.

"You and Buck?"

Lucy nodded, and Naomi laughed, then shook her head and

sighed, and when she glanced back over, she said, "Sure, why not. You can go somewhere in a canoe, right? Paddle around.

"Disappear, up into the Quetico National Forest, maybe? Or go up into Ontario."

"That *wasn't* what I was planning on doing," Lucy said, and all too coldly, surprising even herself.

When Naomi only stared, Lucy got it. Naomi had provoked her into telling her what she had in mind.

"Well," Naomi said, "you've come to my door now and I can't have it, professionally or personally. I won't lie, say you didn't come here, that we didn't have this conversation if, or when, there's reason for someone to ask."

"Why would you, say anything?"

"Because—if it's clear Buck's involved, the police will come to me. After. And since you haven't already gone to the police, since he hasn't, even though that's the *last* thing he'd do, I'd say they were involved."

"No one would believe me," Lucy said, "if I told anyone. How could they when—" she motioned, to her abdomen "—I'm not. And the one who— *found me*, got into the trailer— I have no idea who he is."

"And isn't that the hell of it?" Naomi stood, then bent to sweep up her cup and saucer, motioned for Lucy's. "I'm sending you off— now—under one condition, do you understand me?"

"What?"

"You have to promise me you won't harm yourself, or resort to acting alone. Will you promise?"

"Would you believe me if I did?"

"Yes."

"So, then…yes."

Naomi cocked her head, eyeing her. "You came here wanting to know if he can really help you," she said, "if Buck can. Well, let me tell you, the idea more than scares the hell out of me."

In Naomi's saying it, Lucy felt her spirits lift. Here, Naomi was giving her exactly what she'd come for. "Why?"

"Because Buck is a saint." She frowned, then shaking her head, cut her eyes at Lucy.

There followed a long silence between them.

"And?" Lucy finally said.

"You know what happens with saints, don't you? I mean, saints who won't back down."

"What?"

"Saints who don't back down get martyred, and sometimes, when things go really wrong, those around them do too.

"And *don't* call me. *Don't* contact me after all this is over. *Ever*. I don't want to know. I can't. Do you understand? Because I can't be involved. I've done it before, but I won't do it again—

"Follow me," she said, and Lucy did, through the kitchen, where Naomi set the cups and saucers on the counter, then led Lucy down into the basement, a high and dusty space.

On a shelf against the far wall was a box, footlocker sized. Naomi slid the box off the shelf and Lucy took it in her arms. It was heavy. A good—what?—twenty pounds? Twenty-five?

"What is it?"

Her mouth a sad, flat line, Naomi said, "The very thing that brought you here, what you 'came over here to pick up.'" And then she said something Lucy, later, would recall.

"Tell him I'm sorry," she said, "really. And what's in the box, and my giving it to him just now? He'll understand."

She led Lucy back upstairs and to the tall, double front front doors, and with a grave nod ushered her outside, then stepped back into the house, pulling the door closed behind her.

Out in the street Lucy got the box into the trunk, thumped down behind the wheel, and pulled from the curb.

On the highway, driving south to Shakopee, then into the darkness of the reservation, she didn't know whether to laugh or cry. So she did neither. And at the trailer, she made dinner.

All as if nothing at all had happened.

27

Buck

In his shop, late afternoon and working on a kitchen cabinet—the island he'd finished, now wrapped in foam against the south wall and awaiting pick up—he could not seem to get warm, so stood in the hot blast of the salamander. He looked out the rear window into his yard. He'd been doing that every half hour or so. For the van, he told himself. But it wasn't that. Gyg, the feral, on her hindquarters, watched the birds at his feeder, finches and sparrows.

Who didn't love bineshi? He set his hands at the small of his back. I'm *fine*, he told himself for the umpteenth time, his eyes on the birds.

But he wasn't fine. His back and hip hurt like they hadn't since back when he'd been pitching. And when he bent, so the heat of the salamander was focused on his shoulder, he could feel his collar bone pop out of place again. He'd hoped the swelling would go down, but it hadn't. Being tossed around in the truck had bunged up his shoulder.

Which made trying to finish the cabinet something of a chore, but it wasn't that either.

So it seemed some choreographed miracle when he heard the beep of a car horn, and went to the door.

Not the delivery van, but Lucy. She'd pulled all the way up, which she never did, then went around to the trunk and opened it and, to his shock, lifted out the very thing he'd refused to pick up at the house. A gray-green box, two by two by four. When Lucy, hefting it in her arms, came around to the side, he opened the door for her and she ducked into the shop, went around the canoe to set the box on his drafting table, then stepped back, a look on her face he couldn't in any way read.

But a *there*, in it. That's what she had to say, which, given what was in the box, meant—

"She sent you with this?"

Lucy nodded, standing in front of him, her fingers knotted together, looking.... She was both trying to own up to what she'd done and stricken by his reaction.

She was trying to think of the right thing to say. And then she said it. "I have no excuse for what I've done, and I hope you'll forgive me."

She drew the hoodie down off her head. It was the first time she'd ever done it around him, and he knew the gesture for what it was. She was not a pretty girl, not exactly, more striking and beautiful, but the care in her face, her standing for all practical purposes in front of him exposed like this, and in her hands, held out, was something more than touching, and how could he refuse her—or it?

"I saw what happened, it was in the paper, and I couldn't come over, because.... Well," she closed her eyes, then said, "it has to do with me, and me coming over here. But you know that."

She looked at him, over the table, and over the horrible box, and he felt it settle in him.

"When I went into your house that day?"

He nodded.

"Well, Naomi called and I picked up. And I told her...." She looked up into the garage's rafters. "I lied. I told her I was... your gofer, and helping you around here, like I was your secretary, since I... I see how you don't like to deal with the business end of it, and I thought I could help, with...you know, stuff. So, after I saw what happened to you, I wanted to—and I know this is really, really stupid—I wanted to *do* something for you that you couldn't seem to, somehow." She took a deep breath. She was lying, and she wasn't, too.

Sure, she'd wanted to find out about him, and see what kind of person Naomi was, and the box had been an excuse. He got that.

She braved looking at him, into his eyes, her mouth pursed. "But, now I can see I was... *wrong*, thinking it was all... just about her. Why you weren't going over there to get it, since, well, she said to say that she was sorry." Her brows knotted. "And, anyway, I thought I had to do this one thing for you, to say thanks, because... after what happened to you, I can't come around."

She wasn't going to say why, but it was right there: It was too dangerous for him, and she didn't want that.

"And besides, Naomi, she kinda knew everything, even though she... doesn't, not really. You know?"

"You think that's going to fix things for you, you not coming around?"

"Won't it?"

"You know it won't."

"So?"

Buck slipped behind the table. Stood over her. He set a hand on her shoulder and looked into her eyes.

"I thought I could... help, and—" she was gulping, then hiccupping, and when he stepped back it started all over.

He got her to sit in the arm chair in the corner, where he read blueprints and sketched designs.

"Stay here," he told her, and went into the house, something heavy in his legs—because, he knew *where* this was going now, he just had no idea *how* it would go, or with whom—then stepped back into the shop, handed her a mug and swung a chair up and sat alongside.

"So, how long has this been going on?" When she only stared, blank-eyed, he said, "There are unspeakable things in me, too. Okay?"

"*What?*" She said it in a way that meant, *Not as awful or shameful and self-destroying as what's in me.*

He nodded to the box. "One of mine's right in there."

Lucy laughed. "Yeah, old leaded glass Christmas tree decorations or something, since it's so... heavy. Naomi can't use any of it, because it's all…." She shrugged. "She said you'd understand, what *her* giving it to *me*, to bring to *you*, would mean." She glanced up at him. "See?"

Her nose was dripping, and she drew the sleeve of her hoodie, the forearm, across her face.

"I know," she said, "that sounds awful, like some stupid joke, or whatever… and it isn't funny, but—"

He reached into the cabinet behind them, snatched a tissue from the box there, and offered it to her. She blew her nose, then wadded it into a ball, not sure what to do with it, and Buck, expertly, plucked it from her hand, then lofted it into the wastebasket in the far corner.

"Nice trick, but you can't make a living from it," she said. "Right? Not like you did with baseball, I mean."

It was an attempt at levity, which fell worse than flat, but he loved her for it, for trying, and, in doing it, mentioning the card on the bathroom mirror. He'd thought it had been moved.

"So, don't tell me what happened if you don't want to, but what's in the box?" she asked.

"We're talking about you now, okay?"

Lucy clasped her hands around the mug, turned away from him and her face averted and head down.

"Does anyone else know what's been going on?" he asked.

Glancing up at him, she replied, "Jean did."

"Yeah, I kinda got that," he said. "But I didn't mean her, okay? Like… who are you living with?"

"My father, and…." She took a moment to think about it. "They said they'd kill him if I—" she shrugged "but this, friend, he knows. He saw it. When—it wasn't just… stuff they did—when, one of them… *did it*."

"And this someone is?"

She shrugged.

"But Jean knew, or she was—" he began, and she rolled her eyes, thinking the wrong thing, that he was saying that Jean had been part of her…problem. "Look, I know you loved Jean. It's okay. Really."

Now, for the first time she was resisting, set her hands over her eyes, her head bent.

He told her about the cop showing up at Leif's. "And whoever it was that came to Leif's—he's the one—you know, who's..."

"It *wasn't* him who ran you into the river."

"No?"

"My father works with him, and he was there at the station that day. It was on the roster."

"So, he *is* a cop. And *he's* your trouble?"

She cut her eyes at him. "My father's friend, Arn, he's—*part* of it, only—it's not just him."

"So, before, Arn—did... *that*, they—"

She glared. "They... *did things to me*! Okay?! *Before*. And I pretended I was asleep, at first, anyway, because—" she all but writhed there "—how else could I—and they said they'd kill my dad, and—" She lifted her head, stared off. "But now that I think about it, the one I never saw, who started it all—" She gestured to her neck. She unzipped her hoodie, there, over her T-shirt two necklaces, Jean's, which he'd handed to her in the hospital parking lot, and another, recognizably different.

"After he...." She turned her head away, shrugged. "When *He...* finally *did it*, just before I met you, *He* hung this around my neck."

"Arn?"

"NO!" She lifted the second necklace. "*Him*, the one who started it all—*before* Arn, the first to—"

"To *what*?"

She stared. "TO *PUT IT IN ME*! HE *FUCKED* ME, OKAY?! *HE PUT HIS DICK IN ME*! YOU HAPPY NOW?! And after, He hung... *this* around my neck, which, god, must have meant, since *He* had now, they could *all* fuck me. Do you see?" She'd dropped her head, hugging herself. "But, Arn—he tore me up." She glared at him. "You saw that, I was still bleeding the day I came over."

"Listen to me," Buck said. He got down on his knee, so he could look into her eyes. "First of all, that's *not* what you call what they did. What... *He* did, first, or what Arn did after. Or anyone else.

"It's *rape*, sweetheart. And you're—*just a girl*."

"Arn, a 'pillar of the community' is how they put it, I think," Lucy said, "Arn a real family man."

"So, the first one got into the trailer, when—"

"My dad was on night shift. Arn had a key so he could look in on me, since my mother'd…. She was *gone*, okay?"

"You mean she left, or—"

"About four years ago, that 'hit-and-run'? Remember, the real… messy one?" She grimaced. "'Just another reservation tragedy,' or that's what the… *fucking cops* said."

"I'm sorry," Buck said. "So, Arn let the first one in—or gave him your key?"

"They're like that, all organized, Arn and… his 'friends,'" Lucy said, "and they get their jollies out of it. 'Dropping in.' More exciting for them, since they're all hunters. Survivalists, with weird schedules, which puts them, any day of the week, anywhere and everywhere, see?

"They disappear, show up in our beds. And I think when they're done, they kill people, that's what happens."

"Okay," he replied. "Okay. I get it." But then he said, "No, *not* okay. I have to know. The first one, could you identify him?"

"What, I'm going to ask around a circle of survivalist cops, 'Hey, Arn, Tom, Walt, which of you perverts might know who was in my bed about, like… three years ago, that first time?' Like that? 'And, by the way, who gave me this necklace? So, it'd be okay if all of you—after *Him*—raped me, too?'"

"But, the… necklace, it came from *Him*—you're absolutely sure of it? The first one, who—"

"Started it? *Yes*."

They sat saying nothing, and the shop creaking for the cold outside.

"Can you bring over this… person," he asked, "the one who saw what happened with your dad's cop friend, Arn?"

"Booker?" She stood. "I'll see. And it's getting dark. I've got to get home, act like it's all normal, or my dad'll make a mess of things."

173

He followed her with his eyes across the shop to the door, where she hesitated, "Are you safe?" he asked.

She gave him a look, he was sure, she reserved for the not so perspicacious. No, of course she wasn't.

"Wait," he said, and went to a drawer in his cubby, lifted out what he'd carried earlier, and his father had in the war. Nodded her over.

Lucy crossed the shop to see what he had in his hand. A folding knife, gutta- percha handled. He depressed the button on the side and the blade flicked out. Shiny, and razor-sharp.

"It's double-sided," he said, "and the handle's notched, so you can get a solid grip on it, it can't be knocked away."

He folded the blade back into the handle. "Take it," he said, and she did. "Keep the blade closed, but come at me."

"Now?"

"Yes, now."

Lucy frowned. "Are you serious? And, anyway, what's the use, since, you're like—"

"Three times your size?" He nodded. "Do it. Make like you're going to cut me, and bad."

She lunged at him with the knife and he, all too easily, knocked her hand away. Her head hanging, Lucy looked like she might cry.

"Okay," he said. "Here's the trick, even if someone... *really big* comes at you. Are you listening?" He stood over her, hurt written all over her. "It's simple," he said. "You step *into*... whoever it is. Don't fall back like you did just now. You lead with your left elbow, catch his arms comin' at you, *under*, drive *up* with all you got in your legs, and stab the son of a bitch.

"You don't need much deflection, and you'll get plenty. And—" he pointed to his heart, "here is where you stab, all the way, with your right. Using what's in your legs. Okay?

"So, do it."

"Again?"

"No, not *again*. *Different*," he replied, and when she frowned, he said, "Do it. Take me out."

He dropped back, then came at her and she sprang into him, drove her elbow up, deflecting his arms, tagged his chest with the knife.

"See?" he said. "Your attacker's got his arm's out, there's no way on earth he can fight the leverage."

"Huh," she replied, stunned.

"You keep that," he told her. She got it in her pocket, then pulled her hoodie over her head, this... *something* settled between them. "You'll bring your friend over as soon as you can?"

Lucy nodded. "But you two can't be seen together like, *ever* though, right? If they knew who he was, well—it'd be kind of... bad for everybody. But I'll think of something. I promise."

"Good, I'll wait to hear," Buck said, and with a nod Lucy went out and the cat with her.

28

Lucy

Shortly after one in the morning, she caught Booker bringing two bags of garbage out to the dumpster behind the convenience store where he worked. When she stepped out of the dark, he froze. Van's was the kind of place that was robbed, and it showed on his face.

Had there been a light—which there sure as hell should have been—he'd have been the proverbial deer caught in it.

"Booker," she said. "It's me. Lucy."

He set the bags down. Tilted his head accusingly to the side. But then he sighed. What he didn't say was: Why didn't you just come in the front like a normal person? Because, she thought again, Booker was smart. He knew why. And like her, he tried hard not to show it.

"I've got to get back in there, and in seconds. Okay? They got the cameras going twenty-four-seven. Don't want 'em to think I'm smoking dope on shift or something and can my ass. So, in a word, what is it?"

"You're witness to a rape, Booker," she said, "and I'm witness to a murder now, Jean's. And you saw him—and they know it."

"Fuck, yeah, I kinda figured, and you not going to the cops because they *are* the cops, right?"

"What they don't know is who *you* are, Booker. You're the only reason I'm still alive. That, and—I didn't take that stuff Jean had, which—" she shuddered "—I could have. But they need to get to you first."

"You want me to be a witness in court?" Booker's face hardened—
"Or, better, I'll kill that motherfucker," he said, hurling the bags into
dumpster, "that what you want?"

She took his arm. "No. Because, like you said before, it *isn't just
him*. It's *all* of them."

He glanced at her, frowning. "I'm goin' back in, okay? But I'll
help you. That's a promise. And what about Ryan?"

"What about him?"

"He knows, too, Lucy. He was there the same as I was." Booker
held a hand over his forehead, thinking. "Look, you gotta talk to him,
and then we'll meet somewhere after."

"Why?"

Booker loomed over her, his feet set. "You gotta know Ryan'll
stick all the way with you if it goes truly bad. And your guy, Arn, after
I shouted? He went runnin' right by Ryan. Arn saw 'im there in the
dark as much as he seen me, so, we are *all* in this now, okay?"

He stomped off toward the square of light that was the tiny
fractured window in the back door.

"Booker?" she called to him.

He stopped. "What?"

"Thanks."

With a nod, he went inside. And she was left there by the
dumpster, thinking: Ryan.

She woke early, a little after seven, and her father already up and at the
stove and clattering around. She wandered into the kitchen in her PJs,
rubbing the sleep from her eyes and wondering what all the fuss was.

It was snowing out, big, broad flakes spiraling down, and a cold
creeping through the trailer walls.

"I thought you had the day off today," she said, not meaning to,
but making an accusation in doing it. He'd promised to take her
Christmas shopping, in lieu of trying to find something that was
just right for her, told her, "Bebbe Gurl, now that you're, well…" he'd
ducked his head awkwardly, thinking how to put it, "I shouldn't be

buying clothes for you anymore, okay? And I know that's what you need, so... we'll go over to the shopping center and you pick out your... things, and you want, I'll wrap it up for you, in some nice paper, okay? And if you get *me* something? Just put it in a shoebox or whatever and hand it across the table, tell your dad you love him, and he'll be the happiest man alive. Okay?"

She'd been dreading going out with her father, because she just cringed when he said, as he always did, to a saleswoman, "My beautiful daughter here, she's looking for..." and her father doing that happy guy thing he did, all dimples, asking directions. When, all he had to do was read the directory at the front of the mall, where there was a map.

It was humiliating, even mortifying. So she should have been happy that they wouldn't be going, but she wasn't.

At the stove, he poured the eggs into the pan, the bacon on the back burner just now starting to splutter. Her father, in his quilted vest over a blue plaid shirt, Carhartts, and boots, glanced up at her.

"Can you take a raincheck on our outing, Bebbe Gurl?"

"Sure," she said, "but—"

"We've got the entire week before the holidays. And I'll be on straight shift, have time to finally take care of business around here. We can get that shopping in in the evening."

"So, what now?"

"I'm going hunting with Arn," he said. Stirring the eggs with a wooden spoon, he avoided her eyes.

She got a stab of pain in her heart. Like it had jumped from zero to one hundred in a second.

He glanced up. "It's an end-of-the-year sort of thing. Get a white tail in the freezer before our tags expire." He smiled, an apology in it.

"Where?"

"Where?" He shrugged. "I have no idea. Arn just popped it on me as I was leaving the station. So I didn't get much sleep, but you have to strike while the iron's hot, right?"

"Anyone else going?" She was trying to hide the near panic in her voice. Trying not to be shrill.

"It's just Arn, and a couple others from work, and me." Glancing up from the eggs, he nodded, happy with the thought of it.

Lucy was horrified. If her father went out with Arn, everything she'd hung on to, had suffered to keep him safe, would be lost.

"What?" he said.

Again, she felt she'd failed. A big smile plastered over her horror, she said, "I'm going to get dressed."

"Eggs'll be ready in a minute."

"Be back in a jiffy," she quipped, and went back to her room, where, sitting on the bed her mind spun.

She thought to down all the pills in the medicine cabinet, pretend a suicide attempt. They'd pump out her stomach or whatever, but that would mean a fucking therapist, or her being locked up for observation. A friend of hers had tried killing herself like that the year before, and they'd locked her up and given her zombie drugs. She still wasn't right. Or, she could…set the trailer on fire. But then they'd have nowhere to live. Which defeated everything, too.

Shit. Shit. Shit, she thought. She could burn herself at the stove, but how could she make it look like an accident, when her father was cooking?

And then she struck on the only thing that would work. Really work. And she dressed, quickly. Jeans. Hoodie. Boots. Slipped out of her room, resisting what she was going to do, and taking her seat in the nook. Her father came over to the table, the frying pan held out, and with a bow and a flourish, he slid the eggs onto her plate with the spatula.

"Chef Michelangelo's eggs. And, if you'll indulge me a moment here, I'll get you your bacon, Bebbe Gurl, light of my life."

"I don't eat bacon, Daddy," she said, and as he turned from the table to set the one pan on the stove and sweep up the second, he smiled and said, "C'mon, Bebbe Gurl. Don't tell your old dad you don't like bacon. I know you better than that. It's the holidays, live a little, huh? And, anyway, let your old dad make it up to you just a bit for not following through with the shopping today, all right?"

She did love bacon, but she could bet she'd be vomiting it up for nerves. And just when she was losing it, her father—now all too calmly eating beside her, as she was telling herself she was getting it all wrong, they weren't coming for her father, and, after he was gone, for her, too—he said, "Good?" and she shot back, as if it were all nothing, "Okay. Yes. I *love* bacon."

"Ol' Arn, he's got this new rifle he wants to site in, I suppose that's the real rush. Look, I go now, it'll save me another trip later, see? Kill two birds with one stone. More time for us that way."

She was almost sick right there. Bacon stuck in her throat. She had—abstractly—struck on her plan, but now she'd have to do it.

Even if she was about to shit her pants, and her heart was in her throat, pounding. So she carried on conversation. About those things they were going to do together. Christmas. Groceries. A load of laundry. Uh-huh. Right. Yes.

Arn would pick her father up now in ten or fifteen minutes, her father said, and grinned at her.

She saw herself, as if from a great distance, walk to the sink with their plates. Heard herself talking to her father.

Ha ha. Yes, Daddy, that was a funny one. All the while thinking, *Now, stupid, now and not later, no waiting, no anything, just get that towel on the ring there and get yourself out the door.*

"I'm going to get some firewood, Daddy," she said, and he said just what she knew he would say, "Bebbe Gurl, I'll get to it, I promise. Don't you do it. There's no rush, huh?"

She gushed at his kindness. Pulled on her down vest. Stood in the door. Help me, she thought. God, help me.

"I insist," she said, "since you made breakfast. We'll have a fire later, and it'll be nice, okay?"

He held out his hands, accepting her gift. "But on one condition. You don't use that axe? Right?"

She shot her index finger off her forehead—a kind of goofy salute—Thanks!—and went out the door.

There was an enormous cottonwood stump they used as a chopping block, the axe imbedded in the top of it. And a hatchet. Right. She plucked the axe from the stump and lay it on top of the barbeque, "Never set good steel in snow, Bebbe Gurl," her father had taught her. "Ruins the blade."

She split a few pieces of wood with the hatchet. Just to be safe. To make it look right. Like it wouldn't be intentional. Or was she putting it off? And then Arn, in his rig, turned in from the highway. She set a round of pine on the stump. Held her hand just so, as Buck had when he'd shown her how to use the ripping saw, felt her heart in her throat. Measure twice, cut once.

She brought the hatchet up over her shoulder, then down on her hand, severed the last digit from the little finger. The end of the finger there like some peculiar, flesh colored Vienna Sausage in the snow— hers. Pink-painted-fingernail and all. And blood—it shot right out of her hand.

She screamed, with Arn driving in, screamed right in his face, and her father exploded out of the trailer.

In the ER, she hid the pain killers they gave her under her tongue, Arn having insisted on coming with them. Arn with his big gut and looking all concerned, lurking around, eyeing the nurses, until he was sure it wasn't about—*that*, which it was, of course, but he had to be sure she wouldn't in some anesthetized delirium start ranting, or— and after she'd been sedated, by hypodermic, and she all but melted into the chair they'd sat her in, he excused himself, and went out. Her hand throbbed something awful, but it was her left. She'd thought of that, thanks. And her mind wandering, it occurred to her, so that she nearly cried at it, absurd as it was, she couldn't play a guitar now— and what about that? Not even a little strumming to "Michael Row the Boat," or "Hallelujah," or *whatever*, like her dad had way back when, and there this distance between herself and everything. And the pain, thank God, was something she could hide in, so that she was deep inside herself, her hand throbbing like a damn drum, and her watching herself from a terrifying distance, so far out there this time—what had they given her, what had been in that hypodermic?—she worried she'd never return, sound coming dulled to her, as if she'd lost her hearing, and the bark of the intercom system and the chaos around her muffled, and her father sitting stone-faced beside her, blinking, as if shocked, or—something was going on in him, her father there in his bloodied jacket, holding the end of her finger in a Big Gulp cup filled with ice.

A doctor came in, jabber, jabber, jabbered with her father, who lifted her in his arms, and she clung to him, even as he was trying to set her in the wheelchair the orderlies in green scrubs brought in.

The doctor, some Eastern Indian guy with a kind face, got down on one knee. "How is the pain?"

She shook her head—she didn't want the doctor to get too close to her. His sad face made her want to weep. What if they found out? What it they looked at her—down there?

She couldn't have it, and thinking it, she pressed her knees together.

They'd cauterized the stump of her finger. Burn it to stop the bleeding, or whatever, she couldn't care less now.

They'd put her out, then do it, but the thought of being that vulnerable made her feel even more crazy inside. Still, clutching her left hand over her middle, and sitting in the wheelchair, she thought, with some semblance of clarity, and even a horrible kind of pride,

Well, she'd gotten it done, what she needed to. Proof positive she could do all the other things, too.

29

Buck

"Fixed target," he told himself. And he *was*, sitting in his shop with the cabinets around him wrapped in blue moving blankets ready to go out, waiting for Lucy to call about her friend, the witness. Why hadn't she? Waiting, he'd torn the cuticle of his right middle finger out of nervousness, and it was bleeding, and it would sting and swell and throb. Why had he done it? He'd been telling himself the van would arrive to pick up the cabinets any minute, but it hadn't been any minute, it had been hours—with the box there right in front of him.

If he didn't open it, if he drove to the river (which seemed almost suicidal, given that was exactly where they would come after him) and dumped it, the box would float off somewhere, and he couldn't have that. That would be... irresponsible. And, even then, he'd have to drill a few holes in it, so it would sink. But if he did that, got his hands on it, the box, he'd open it; in fact, now, he was certain he'd open it if he so much as got too close to it. And if he did, well, he knew he'd be— prematurely—tempted to use what was in it. An impulse he couldn't, in any way, give in to.

Which was why he'd kept it at Naomi's mother's place, where he couldn't, on a whim, get to it, but only if he truly had to, if that once-potentially-lethal trouble found him again.

In the fifteen years since, it had been a comfort, and sometimes a torment, knowing it was there.

He jabbed the cigarette he was smoking into the hubcap on his workbench, ten there already, imagined catching Lucy's cop, Arn, out on patrol, and taking him down in his squad car, it being no protection. Until he realized with a start, all over again, he couldn't do that because there were *others*, an organization of them that needed to be flushed out of hiding. And, anyway, that would be the wrong sort of justice. The right direction was exposure, and then, after that—

So, the box—and he was, in an almost dark way, being drawn to it now—and what was in it not the solution. Yet.

He should go into the house and clean, or, better, pay the bills. All those bills in the holder on the counter by the toaster. And that they'd been in the house and so carefully tampered with things? He couldn't see what it would buy them, that, or their having gotten him to call Lucy, unless it had been to establish a connection between them— him and Lucy—but *for* what? Or, was it, *to* what?

Well, he couldn't just sit, not with the box on the table, so tempted was he to open it, and he turned to go into the house—he'd have to ask Lucy where he could find her friend Booker. And just then, there was the clatter of a big diesel pulling up in the street and he went out to it, into the falling snow.

The driver, opposite, dropped down from the cab and came around the front, a clipboard in hand. "Michael Fineday?"

"Yeah," Buck said, wary, but right there, what was in the box and Michael, Seraphim's Michael, came together just the same. "That's me."

30

Lucy

She came to as if out of a warm sea, some dull rhythm in it she couldn't identify, until she became aware it was in her hand, this throbbing, and her arm attached to—she tried to lift herself up. She'd been having a nightmare, one in which she was trying to turn away from—Arn; but it wasn't Arn now, here, was it?—she couldn't get her arm free, something, or someone, was holding it.

"Lucy," came a voice that couldn't be—here, which was—where? She slid up onto her rear. Nauseated. And the light was all wrong, and there was a window where there shouldn't be one, to her left, and the sun, making her squint, cutting between the blinds.

And then it all of it came back to her, Arn driving up to the trailer, and what she'd done.

"The surgeon reattached your finger," Ryan said, in that robotic voice of his, and she turned to him, Ryan in a chair alongside the bed. "Well, the last digit of it, I mean." He shrugged. "You won't have much flexion, but—"

"Thank you so very much for that, Ryan," she said.

"You're altogether welcome," he replied.

Jesus, he just didn't get it. She settled into the pillow behind her, pulled the hospital blanket up around her neck.

"Aren't you going to look?" Ryan asked.

She glanced over—for Ryan, who, she knew all too well, wouldn't stop asking until she did—then really did look. Her arm was fixed to a slat, and her hand wrapped in gauze, a red eye of clotted blood there at the end of her finger. Was she relieved it *was* there, or not? Her right hand was fine, though, trigger finger and all. She flexed her right index finger. All she needed, intact.

She threw her forearm over her eyes. "Ryan, could you?"

"What?"

"The blinds?"

He pulled the blinds shut and the room went dark. She lay back in the bed, as if swimming in it.

"How'd you get here?"

"My mom."

"Yeah, but—"

"I told her if she made me go to school I'd just take buses over here, anyway, so—"

"Nice," Lucy said, in her voice that sarcastic tone she didn't much like. She'd pay for it, somehow, maybe not be allowed to come over to study at their place, and that made her sad.

"Look," Ryan said, and held up a book. "Got you something to read, since, you know…." *Cod: A Biography of the Fish that Changed the World.* Was he being funny? Or? "They said your electrolytes were way off."

"Great."

"That's why you're on the drip. And you were really dehydrated. You need to drink more."

"Wonderful."

"After the first guy left, Arn, right? There was another guy who came by the trailer, like it was some accident. He came over after your dad and you were gone. I got pictures of him."

She turned to him, shocked. "You didn't… talk to him, did you? The guy who came?"

"I did."

She scooted up on her rear, suddenly, fully, altogether awake. She— just— couldn't— breathe, here in this too, too quiet room, and only a curtain between them and whoever was in the bed by the door, which could be anybody.

"Ryan," she said, and motioned him closer.

"Booker came over, too."

"Booker?"

"I called him *after*." Ryan nodded. "He just pretends to be mean. And he likes you."

"Ryan."

"No, he knows about these kinds of things."

"What things?"

"I saw it too that night." Ryan nodded again. "So, I'm in it, just like Booker is. I am."

Holy... FUCK! GOD *DAMNIT*! "Ryan, this—this is *not* something for you. Okay? You stay out of it."

"But I can't."

She was trying to breathe. "Ryan, you don't know what these people are like, not really...."

"They killed my father, for writing things. And they took my mother away. Almost for a year."

Good God. "Ryan, who was it who came?" she asked, and Ryan, with a curt nod, replied, "The 'Re-education Committee.'"

"Where?"

"In China."

It took a moment for what Ryan had said to register. When it did, she laughed. "No, Ryan, I meant at the *trailer*. *Now*."

"The Chief of Police?"

She laughed, again, but it was a high, hysterical laugh. "Yeah, and you'd know, wouldn't you."

He held up his phone. There was a picture of the Chief of the Shakopee Police Department on it.

"I just looked up the Shakopee PD on line." He was going to show her, and she said,

"Can I see that?"

He handed her the phone, and she held it to her face. It was Burgess, all right. That asshole. In the photo, Burgess stood alongside his cruiser, mirrored sunglasses on and a black duffel slung over his shoulder. A meat saw? A plastic hazmat suit? Bleach? Plastic gloves?

"What'd he say?"

"I made him think I was 'retarded,' so he didn't get it."

"Get what?"

"That I was recording him on my cell. I got him to lie, which you can prove if you have to."

She was astounded. "And just… *what* would he have lied about? To you, I mean?"

A nurse ducked into the room, pulled a chart from the rack on the wall, Lucy's, and jotted something on it. She turned to them and smiled, then spun on her white shoes back into the hallway.

"Burgess? *Why* was *he* there?" When Ryan only gave her that blank look, she said, "Jesus Fucking Christ, Ryan."

He took the phone from her, said, "Same reason Arn was. He said he was 'responding to a brawl/family disturbance.' But, see, if he was making it up, there'd be no record of any call out to a 148."

She felt herself frowning, and Ryan nodded, said, "There *wasn't* one. I checked. Okay?" He shrugged. "You could just go to another police department, you know. Or… the newspaper, like the *Tribune*."

"Yeah. Or… hey, why not *Sixty Minutes*?"

"Well?"

"Ryyyy-an. *Jesus*. With *what*? *What* do I have? And, anyway, I don't want to be the poster girl for this, okay? And what proof have I got even with you and Booker? You and Booker saw… *something*. In the dark. And if I—*if this all goes public*, Ryan, they'd try to get to us, before it went… to court or whatever, don't you think?

"I mean, maybe I think they went after my mother because she… *knew something* about Rose L'Rieux."

"Like what?"

She glared. She wouldn't get into it with Ryan. And, again, she had no idea, it was just…. Was she just making it up? But then, she *had* heard her parents arguing about Rose.

There's something not right about that girl, her mother had insisted, *you mark my words, Lee….*

"Can I get a copy of that?" she asked, and Ryan nodded. "You're a lifesaver, Ryan," she said, and he smiled.

There was coughing from behind the curtains surrounding the other bed; the creaking of springs.

When it had been quiet for some time, Ryan said, "I'll read now."

"Sure, lay it on me," Lucy said, "all about how Charlie the Cod saved the world and all that."

"Charlie's a tuna."

"God, Ryan. I was kidding, okay?!"

He lifted a book from the three he'd been holding, *The Secret Garden.* "And I was, too."

She all but stared. She'd known Ryan…how long? Since grade school, or, no—before that. Preschool.

All this time she'd never guessed. He'd been paying attention, quietly, all those years.

31

Buck

Sleepless. So up barely after four and working. The cat in the shop was behaving strangely. Running to the side door, sitting, then dodging to the cubby hole in back where it had been tucked in lately, then out again. He held up the router he'd been using on a sash for a dresser. Whatever it was out there, the cat liked it less than the roar of the router.

Usually, when he was working with the power tools, the cat kept her distance, curled in the far corner. But the canoe was a barrier now, so she curled up closer in the cubby.

He set the router on his drafting table and went to the door. Looked out. Nothing in the yard but birds nattering around the feeder. He'd put a bird bath out, and set a de-icer in it. It made him happy, seeing the ganeshii—chickadees—squat-bodied little birds skittering about, excited to have something to drink, and the birds taking turns bathing, wings fluttering. How did anything, really, anything at all, survive out in that kind of cold?

And then he saw it—a shadow that stretched ominously from the right side of the door. Someone there.

He swept up the .38, feet waist-width apart, prepared to shoot through the door. If he only injured him—his would-be killer—he would run, and he could get to him in the yard.

He ducked down, undid the bolt, then turned the doorknob. Opened the door. Reached over to the table and switched on the router, which danced and roared and rattled.   Perfect cover for— whoever he was; he'd be thinking no one could hear a thing over such a racket.

Light on his feet, he slid inside. Hoodie. Tall. Broad-shouldered. African American.

The man froze there, realizing his mistake. He'd come too far into the room. The router clattered off the table onto the floor. And there he turned. But his head cocked to the side.

He lifted his hands, palms out. Buck kicked the door shut; locked it left handed, the .38 trained on him.

"Move away from the door," Buck shouted over the router.

He did that, but was now closer to the peg board and Buck's carving tools, all of them razor sharp.

Buck dipped down to turn off the router and it was so quiet he could hear himself breathing.

"Sit on the chair," he said and, whoever he was, he dropped onto it, set his hands over his knees.

"I don't have to tell you," Buck said, "if you give me any trouble I'll shoot you right where you sit. Home invasion. No court in the country would convict me. I shoot you, call the cops, and it's all over."

Whoever he was, he was a good-looking kid, powerfully built, but slim—athletic. There was something in his face, though, that didn't fit. A kind of almost disappointed... *forbearance.* That's what it was.

"I'm Lucy's friend, Booker," he said.

"Right."

Buck had fallen for that before, but only once. But then, wasn't that the way it always went? When you stepped into the middle of things assuming they were what they appeared to be?

"They came for Lucy's old man," the kid said now.

"Who?"

"*Them.* And hasn't that been a big part of the problem? That you don't know who they are?"

Still it wasn't enough. Not by half. "Tell me something I don't already know, let's start there."

"They think Lucy's… 'in trouble,' so… that's why they came after you. They needed a father, one they could make go away, and they thought she might've already tol' you what's up, see?"

If it was Lucy's friend, Booker, he had to give the kid credit, he had some balls coming around the house the way he had.

"Look," the kid said, "you don't need to get all Rambo on me now, all right? No need to be waving that… hand cannon in my face." He motioned to the canoe there alongside them, on sawhorses.

"That there," he said, "that's the canoe Lucy said you were makin', one she could go up to the Boundary Waters with it, you tol' her, n' stuff like that. Named your cat there," he pointed to the cat cowering in the wood rack, "Gyg, for life.

"Tell you what," this Booker, or whoever he was, said, "you keep that gun on me, okay, but don't shoot."

"And what?"

"I'll go to the door and call Ryan in. Okay?"

"Ryan?"

"He's another of Lucy's friends, 'n' mine too, and, man, he's gotta be freezin' out there by now. You go back in the corner there with that gun where you can shoot everything all to shit if you need to, okay?

"I'll go to the door, open it, and call him in. So, don't shoot me you don't have to. Fair 'nough?"

The kid—he couldn't be over twenty—turned the bolt, then opened the door and Buck braced himself for it.

And in stepped an Asian teenager. From the way he was broad across the face, eyes, nose, cheekbones, he'd say Chinese-Korean, and, no, Asians did *not* all look alike, any more than Indians did. But the kid was a walking cliché of Asian nerdiness, tape on his black glasses and his hair cut as if someone had set a bowl on his head. Floodwater pants. Jacket that didn't fit.

"You Ryan?" he asked.

"Yes."

"Lucy's friend."

"Yes."

Jesus, was he going to have to deal with somebody who was for all practical purposes Rain Man? But then the kid did look him in the eyes—thank god!—so, just... another poor in-between getting by.

"Shut the door," Buck told him, and the kid was about to do that, when he thought not, and said, "In the house."

Buck made breakfast and they sat at the table in the dark, eating. No one had taught Ryan not to eat with his mouth open, and he did that, smacking and making all kinds of noises that all but drove him crazy.

Booker, now, he was the consummate gentleman. Fork held just so, back straight, no elbows on the table. What was his story?

But Ryan. It was so bad that he had to do something. He set his hand on Ryan's shoulder, said,

"Can I make your life easier?" The kid nodded. "You want to be with a girl someday?"

Ryan lifted his face to Buck's and, with his index finger, he nudged his taped glasses up toward his eyes. The lenses made his eyes enormous. Like fish swimming in a bowl, went the old cliché.

"Chew and swallow with your *mouth closed.*" His brows furrowing, Ryan frowned, hurt. "In Korea, or with your... Korean relations, you do just like them," Buck said, "but here, mouth shut."

Ryan turned to Booker and Booker grinned, happy he hadn't had to say it. The kid had nice teeth.

Ryan suddenly tilted his head to one side, like a bird would. The kid was kind of a flit, but he liked him.

"What?" Buck said.

"Do you have a computer?"

With a laugh, Buck pushed his plate away. Dropped his fork, clanging on the china.

"Lucy said you'd called her," the kid said.

Now he *was* truly confused. What did his having called Lucy have to do with his having or not having a computer?

"I know that you think," Buck said, "I should be wearin' a headdress and buckskins and living in a teepee and everything, but kid, I had computers before you were born."

"No," Booker said, and he turned to Buck, "trust me, he's going somewhere with this." He glanced over at Ryan. "Him calling Lucy, Ryan? What we were talking about, 'fore we come over?"

"How did you know to call her number, when she didn't give it to you?" Ryan asked.

"Someone left a message on my answering machine, about work, and a call back number—"

"—right," Booker said, "and that number was Lucy's." He frowned. "And you didn't think to look into the caller ID?"

"I did. But only after I got Lucy and wondered what was up. He called from a restaurant."

"Nice," Booker said.

"*That's* the issue," Ryan said. "Who called you first."

The three of them sat saying nothing, until Booker comically slapped Ryan on the top of his head.

"Earth to Einstein, Earth to Einstein, come in Einstein. Come on, Ryan," he said, "just…. What's *the issue*?"

"I'm thinking."

"Yeah, we didn't get that," Booker said, and Booker and Buck shared amused looks.

"You called from that message, though," Ryan said, "right?"

"Why wouldn't I? It was a… *job*, it's how I make my living," Buck said. "So I called, and Lucy answered. Which—"

"Made no sense. So, you…used your CID function, called back and got a restaurant, is that what you said?"

"Right."

"So, your computer?"

They all stood, and Buck led them up the stairs to the attic and his little office. At his desk, Ryan thumped down in Buck's chair as if he owned it, picked up the mouse and spun it around and turned on the machine. Buck and Booker stooped behind him, Buck bracing himself there, his hand on the desk.

Ryan bent into the screen, said, "You need a full system update." He looked over his shoulder. "Why do you have such an old machine?"

"What's wrong with it?"

"It's slow," Ryan said, "and it doesn't have enough RAM, and you've got almost no security."

On the screen files flashed and disappeared, shot off in streaking patterns. Ryan pulled a cigarette-pack sized drive from his pocket and connected it to the machine. Sat back while the machine whirred and rattled, then disconnected the drive and bent into the screen again.

"There's a better way to store your business documents," Ryan said. "You want to do it, so, like, only *you* can get to them. Like this... other stuff that's on here now? It's all of it invisible." His head bobbled. "But where you go daily, in your docs, there's nothing."

"Well," Buck replied, "that's a relief. And what's this... 'other stuff'?"

Booker bent in toward the screen. "Just show us, Ryan okay. You don't have to explain."

Ryan rattled something out on the keyboard, then again, then yet again, and a last time, and—

Buck reared back. "WHAT THE—" Children. Men. Skin. All shocking. "Turn— that thing— off!"

Ryan rattled at the keys, and the computer chattered horribly, for what seemed minutes, as if it were eating itself, until a small star appeared in the center of the screen, like a super nova, and it went dark.

"What did you do?" Buck said.

"I killed your computer. Wrote over everything. That's I why said you had to buy a new one, and—"

Buck felt his eyes go wide. "That was my whole *business* in there, kid," he said, "Jesus Fucking—" Leif had told him to back up all that... *shit*, but when had he had time for that? Well, plenty. He'd just had no idea how to do it.

"Kid," he said, in as flat a voice as he could manage, "I hope you have an explanation."

Ryan lifted the drive he'd used earlier from his jacket pocket. "It's all here. I downloaded everything."

"Everything?"

"Everything that was on your computer, and especially—" He grimaced. "You know, what they... put on there. Proof, if you need it later."

"So," Buck said, angry, and sickened that it might attach to him in any way, "it's *gone*. Right?"

Ryan tapped the computer. "*Here* it is."

Booker turned to him. "You use the internet, there's a record of your IP address connecting you to all the sites you—you know—visit 'n' all. You click it, and there's a record."

"They can still come after you," Ryan said, "if the FBI got involved, which they do in cases like this, and if they subpoenaed your provider—what, you're on AOL? That's history, too. Dialup."

Buck felt his face go cold. "So, what was the point of all—"

Booker nodded, "You go there, Einstein, you tell him."

"They wanted a body," Ryan said, "one connected to Lucy. But a body no one could ever get to. The father's, and *no DNA*."

"To blame the baby on," Booker said. "If it came to that."

"How?"

"You called her, right? And—if you... had that sort of thing on your computer and she's been over here. Came in the house all those times. Neighbors had to have seen her goin' in with you."

"But they tried to go after me, in the river where I went in—they sent someone in after."

"But there wasn't gonna *be* any *body*," Booker said, "see? The plan was to call the accident in, say you were... flushed down the river? Since they meant to blame Lucy's 'trouble' on you. Protect Arn that way.

"Gettin' your body was just—well, proof positive they had that wrapped up, rather'n just sort of hopin' the body was gone."

"*My* body."

"Right. They were gonna bury it somewhere, or—put you in a vat of acid or something."

"But if somebody needed to, couldn't they just get DNA from...

196

my shaver, or hairbrush, or—"

"Not if they burned your house down." Booker nodded. "And your truck? Who'd've found it, in the river?

"And later, they'd just happen to stumble on your computer, since you would've stashed it before you ran off. See?"

Buck felt the weight it. They were even more organized than he had feared they were.

More dangerous.

32

Lucy

She was waiting in the hospital reception area, her left hand bandaged like a mummy's and set in her lap. They'd released her, and the neighbor her father called to pick her up was late, the PA system barking announcements, and her thoughts a jumble of desperate plans, which had her arguing in her mind with her father when she couldn't, just couldn't, tell him what was going on, it was too... awful—and how could she get him to go with her, leave everything and run, and to where—if she couldn't so much as tell him *why*?

Her eyes fixed on the traffic in the snow on France Avenue, and rehearsing the things she could never say, she was so distracted she almost missed it, the patrol car pulling into the emergency entrance.

And now she saw it was Arn, enormous, big-gutted Arn in his cop uniform getting out. Unfolding himself, and in him that slow, too-practiced meant-to-intimidate way of his.

Lucy stood, went up the hallway opposite. Forced herself to walk, when she—desperately—wanted to run. She was a minor—she knew that old argument. Arn would have custody, and they could force her to go with him. Worse yet, shoot her up with some... tranquilizer if she really resisted, and— She turned left at a sign—*Oncology*, went through a waiting area with patients in it, one horrifying man with a black cross on his forehead—and a woman without a nose.

Her heart racing something awful, she strode, gathering herself up, to the rear of the hospital and outside, where she stepped into a parking lot, shocked at the cold wind and snow, then bolted around and between the cars there, running, a car horn blaring, and she swerved right, out onto the frontage road, zigzagged through traffic, then shot onto France Avenue, stopped at the intersection, a red light there, ankle deep in snow slop and slippery slush.

Against the light, she bolted across the intersection, too, too visible, and here another patrol car going by, the officer in the windshield catching sight of her, startled, and turning around sharply, lights on, siren on, against traffic, but stuck, and using his bullhorn, "Stop! This is the Police. You are ordered to—"

She tumbled akimbo down an embankment, her splinted hand clutched to her stomach, slid in the snow into the Southdale Shopping Center, she'd been here with her mother, and she got to her feet, went through the west facing doors, women in smart outfits and men in three piece suits having coffees in the food court, all leafy fichus and cacti.

She slipped on the floor and caught herself, and a woman glanced up from her plate, Lucy shaking her head, *No, don't. Don't help.*

She went out the south entrance, running again, to another, yet more upscale shopping area, and she went in the north entrance, looking for something to put on over her pink hoodie.

And there was Arn, up the hallway to her right, Arn and two officers, Arn sending them left and right up intersecting hallways, and Arn coming straight on, only, he hadn't seen her. There was a rack of coats in the way, and when he went into a shop, she lifted a coat from the rack, used the fascia on the window there, the sheet metal, to tear the tracker from the sleeve.

Shrugged it on and pulled the fur-lined tube top over her head, then went up and outside.

Walked, her legs scissoring, willing herself to keep moving.

There was an office complex ahead, but another parking lot in front of it. Another sea of cars.

A bus lumbered north on France, then hissed to a stop, and she sprinted to it, got on and held the two poles there so the coat she'd stolen was facing Arn, who she could see reflected in the window in front of her, Arn sprinting to the bus and slapping the side of it as it pulled away.

Blocks later, she got off. Headed into the housing subdivision there. All fifties split-level. She heard sirens, and she ran into a backyard, a dog barking in the house, lunging at the curtains.

She got out her phone. She had the call in her log. Hit redial.

"Yeah?" Buck said. "Where are you?"

"In Edina. In a backyard."

"They come after you?"

She felt herself sob. She just couldn't help it. And her finger was throbbing something awful.

"Okay. Lucy?"

"What?!"

"Can you listen?"

She couldn't speak. "That's okay," Buck said. "You're in shock, and you're cold."

"What do you know?" she blurted.

And he told her, "I know *plenty*. And don't you dare quit on me, Lucy. Not now. We're not done here. You're not done. Say it, 'I'm not done until it's done.' Can you say it?"

"I'm not done," she said.

"No. Say it, now, *all of it*. And you *mean* it. 'I'm not done until it's done.' Say it."

"'*I'm not done until it's done*,'" she said, and felt something settle in her, and it was in her voice too.

"Good. Okay. Now. You go north. There's a place there called the Convention Grill. You go in, but have the older waitress, hair always in a bun, sit you in a booth at the back."

"What's her name?" she asked.

"Ruth. And how's this all going to go?"

"I'm not done until it's done," Lucy said.

At a table in the rear of the Convention Grill, and the lunch crowd on, she stopped shuddering. Ruth, hearing Buck had sent her, watched over her, set a mug of coffee in front of her, which she warmed her hands on, and the pain in her finger having become something distant, an irritant, an ache. When two officers came through the front door, stomping the snow off their boots, Ruth said, "No, no one like that's come in. I'll clear a table for you in back, if you can just wait a minute," and she cleared Lucy's table, taking her by the arm, as if to show her where the restrooms were, and in that small space swung her into a broom closet, a bucket with a wringer at her feet full of soapy, gray water.

There was a vent into the restaurant, and she could see the cops through it, in the very booth where she'd been sitting, cut off at the head.

Thick fingered hands on white mugs. They argued over some procedure, got something to eat.

"Yeah, Laird, you'd think so, wouldn't you?" the officer with the clunky class ring said.

"Lookit that fuckin' spook, up by the register just come in. He's packin'. See it under his jacket?"

"Dumbass."

"We get lucky he'll rob the place. Gotta be some money in the till this time of day."

"Okay. Here it is. He's talking to the waitress. Whisperin' something." The officer's hand went down to his hip. Unsnapped his holster. He slid his gun out, held it along his thigh.

"Hey, need a refill?" The pot hung suspended over the officers' mugs, Ruth poured.

"Trouble?" the officer with the gun said.

"No. This here's our janitor, comes after breakfast. Between classes up at the university."

There was some grumbling. Seconds later, the door closet swung open. Booker held up his hand, put his raised index finger to his mouth, then took the apron from the hook there, got it on and tied it behind his back. Grimaced, then rolled the bucket out and shut the door.

She heard the clatter of the bucket, saw the mop moving over the floor. The cops stood. She could only see their legs, blue pants over black, thick-soled shoes, scuffed but polished.

"Kid," the one with the gun said. He had it out, alongside his leg. "You got a permit to carry that?"

"'Scuse me, Officer?"

"I said," he said, "'You got a permit?'"

"Got no call to aim that at me," Booker said, his Timberlands pointing now at their thick soled black brogues.

"Just keep your hands up where we can see 'em. No, higher, like I told you to, boy."

"What's this?" the other said.

"A ledger," Booker said.

"This drug money?"

"I deliver pharmaceuticals—that's my book. Those are customers' checks in the back. Never leave it in my car. You don't believe me, you call 'em."

There was some going back and forth, one of the cops stomping off, then returning and throwing a bill on the table.

"They said he works for them."

"Sorry for your trouble," the officer with gun said, though he was anything but sorry.

Minutes later, Booker opened the closet door again.

"We'll go out the back," he said, reaching for her and pulling her out, blinking, into the narrow hallway.

33

Buck

In his shop, Buck stood at his table, the box opened and the lid thrown off to the side, and the machine gun re-assembled. Waiting for his phone to ring, he'd broken the gun down, then meticulously polished and lubricated each part, and the shop now smelled of machine oil—

And still no call.

He shouldered the machine gun, an M249. A Squad Assault Weapon, or SAW. The stock all too familiar. Sighted down the barrel. He had bandoliers of steel-cased bullets, which were illegal. You could shoot through a car, or truck, even inches of armor. As he had when he'd last used it.

The phone rang, and he pulled it from his pocket. Breathed a sigh of relief. Lucy.

"Yeah?"

"I got her," Booker said. When Buck didn't answer, Booker added, "So, what do we do now?"

"Drop her off near the police station and go back to work, since you can't be seen with her." Buck checked his watch. "Her dad'll be off shift in a few, and she can catch a ride home with him." There was something muffled on the line. Voices, muted, then Lucy came on.

"Buck?" she said.

"What?"

"What am I going to tell him?"

"Tell him you don't trust Arn. You can act, right? Tell him you think something's going on with him."

"Yeah," Lucy replied, almost snidely, "good you sent Booker over for me then, isn't it. Now they've seen Booker, thanks."

"They *didn't* see him. Not really. Cops like that? What they saw was a no-count Black kid janitor."

There was a moment of silence again. "Fuck you," Lucy said. "And what would you know?"

"You haven't seen *me* either."

"What?"

"Forget it." He shouldn't've said it. "Listen. Tell your dad when you realized it was Arn coming for you, you took the bus. You do what you always do. Go to school, but with the other kids. Stay in the trailer after."

"Can I drive?"

"Not alone you can't."

"So, then what? My dad'll think it's weird if Ryan and Booker are coming over mornings all of a sudden. "

"Tell him Ryan's dragging you to zero hour Mathletes, or Chess Champs or whatever. Booker, too, see? We'll be in touch," he said, and slipped his phone into his pocket. He lifted the 249 again.

Sighted down the blue-black barrel. It would do. It'd have to.

34

Lucy

They had a sullen, angry ride home from the police station, her father at the wheel fuming, but holding something back, something that had him frowning, then humming, then smiling, then angry again. But in the trailer, making dinner, spaghetti and a salad—a bit awkward one-handed, and the two of them eating, going on about their evening as they always had, and later a football game on the television while Lucy was doing the dishes, and all of it as if some great distance from what had just happened, her having injured herself—her father surprised her.

"All right, so, Bebbe Gurl," he said, glancing up from his recliner. "I know, I told you Maureen was coming for you. Which I shouldn't've done."

Lucy looked over from the sink, her finger, in the splint, throbbing again. This was as much of an apology as she was ever going to get. But there was something studied in it.

"Thank you, Daddy," she said.

He nodded. "But, in the future you don't run off like that for no good reason, all right? You call me, and we'll talk it over. So, I need your word that you won't do anything like that again, because, well—

"When I say, 'Stay put, I'll take care of things,' I want you to follow through on your end. Can you promise?"

She held her throbbing finger to her waist. "Yes, Daddy," she all but droned, "I promise."

"And you being older and all, it wouldn't be right for Arn to ever check in on you now like back... *after*—okay? So you won't be seeing him coming around here unless I'm in. We clear on that, too?"

Blinking at it, and a little shocked, she thought—yes, *after* her mother had been killed.

"Bebbe Gurl?"

"Yes," she replied.

"So, I'm telling you, just so it's no surprise, Arn'll be over soon, since we've got business to take care of. He left me something at work, okay?" He reached into his breast pocket.

Held up a Christmas card, on it a tree.

She stopped scrubbing at the pan she'd made the sauce in, her heart skipping a beat.

"What's it say?" she asked, a strained note in her voice.

Her father shrugged, then winked at her. And she thought, what could that be about?

"It's... something good!"

"Like what?"

There was a truly false note in his voice now; the same false note he used when he lured her out of the trailer to do errands, or get groceries, after which they'd just happen to stop by the dentist's.

Her father stood from the recliner he'd been sitting in, brandishing the envelope like some prize.

"Bebbe Gurl, we're *taking a vacation!*"

"Where?"

"*Where?!*" her father said, his eyes narrowed. "Bebbe Gurl, I thought you'd be over the moon, and—"

"Oh, *Daddy,*" she said, putting on a smile, one that cost her, and terribly. "I *am*! Really!" And she threw herself into his arms, so he couldn't see her face. And if he'd been able, to see?

Happiness. What memory would write it on her face? Instead of alarm. When her mother helped her learn to ride her bike? Wear that. But it almost made her weep, too, because it hurt to remember.

She stepped back from him, smiling, "I thought you said you had to work over break?"

He tossed his hands up. "I went into Chief Burgess's office, and, well, Chief Burgess tells me, 'You been working so many double shifts lately you're due for a vacation.'

"We're going up north like I promised we would, Bebbe Gurl!" He positively beamed at her. She hadn't seen him happy, really happy, in… she couldn't remember how long. Or was it just… wound up?

Still, from the blush in his face, she was sure there was something he wasn't telling her.

"Is there some catch?"

He shrugged. "We *were* going to do our end-of-season review here, but now we'll do it up north." Held up the letter. "It's Pearson's, near Grand Marais. That place I told you about.

"Your mom, she… wanted us to go up?"

It was difficult not to stare. They'd take them out in the woods. Kill them, then bury them. Or—sink them in Lake Superior.

"While we do the review, you can… I don't know, hang out in the cabin, or watch movies or whatever."

She frowned. From the sink. As if she'd just thought of some reason it wouldn't work, disappointed.

Maybe they'd have the whole contingent of… fucking perverts up there? Maybe it was…. What had her teacher, Mr. Brimley, called such a situation? A *fait accompli*, a thing already decided. No. She'd get Ryan to hack into the station schedule for the coming weeks, one not yet posted. That's what she'd do. See who'd be off those days, who would be going up.

She could get to them, and where they'd never see it coming.

"Daddy, you sure I won't be in the way?" she asked. She needed to be certain he'd be taking her.

"If you can put up with me being gone for business a bit, Bebbe Gurl, we're good to go. What do you think?"

He grinned, almost sheepishly, and she made a point of sucking in a deep breath, as if just thrilled.

Good God. Arn, and the others, they really were going to do it.

Or try. They had—and who knew how, exactly—lured her father into it, going up. But it could work for her, too.

Buck, he'd help her. Up there. Exactly where there was no chance of surveillance, no cameras, no witnesses, no nothing.

She smiled as broadly as she could. "Daddy!" she blurted, "that's just *absolutely wonderful*! I'm…."

"What?" her father said.

"I'm just so… *happy*, Daddy," she said. "I'm just so, so happy!" And the truth of it was—she was happy.

Happy to be getting to the inevitable, bloody end.

35

Buck

The call came nine-ish that evening, Lucy at a gas station having run there from Ryan's, breathless, and a panic in her voice, going on about something up north, "They mean to kill us up there," she said, "it's cop business, so my dad's really *got* to go, but they've made it look like it's a vacation, see, paid days and everything, and, I mean, how could he say no?"

His heart went out to her, and though he thought to stop her rambling, because she wasn't making much sense, he listened to the whole stumbling, sometimes choked up mess.

And when she, after minutes, finally stopped talking, exhausted, he said, "I'll come up with you."

"But that's *not* why I'm calling."

"No?"

"No," she said. "I'm calling because they're going to come after you. And I mean—like—*right now*. Because they know we're going, and they'll want to… clean up down here, first."

"You get back over to Ryan's," he said. "And—no more going out in the dark to make calls from—where are you?"

"Jesus! *Really*? Did you hear *any*thing I just told you?"

"Every word," he said, "and, hey, Lucy, thanks."

The following morning he asked a favor of his neighbor, Jerry—the one he'd helped with his landlord—intending to see if the threat

Lucy'd warned him of was real or imagined.

And, too, in it was an opportunity to see who might be involved—in coming after him they'd risk exposure.

"It's just to pick up some wood," he told Jerry at his front door. "The drive shouldn't take you an hour. Leif'll have everything I need ready. Could you? I've got to be here for a delivery."

He nodded, as if recalling something.

"And could I use your car? A minute or two? I need to get groceries—I don't have a damn thing in the house."

Jerry, happy to return a favor, agreed. But before he took the truck, Buck disabled the heater. Nothing to it. He turned a screw and loosened an electrical cable. Jerry'd discover the loose cable for him later, do himself proud. The truck had been in the river, after all, and a few things didn't work right just yet.

And since it was cold, and the heater wasn't working, "not at all," he told Jerry, he'd have to bundle up. Sorels. Tube parka. Mitts.

"Just use mine," Buck said. "Can't beat the best, guaranteed." He had all the gear for sub zero work outside.

Jerry got into Buck's gear, and bundled like that he went out to the truck and drove off. Looking for all purposes exactly like Buck at the wheel, the tube top of the parka over his head.

Sure, Jerry might get his feathers a little ruffled, but if push came to shove, he'd be there to stop anything from happening.

Alongside the house, Buck lit a cigarette, then squinted up into the low sun, a ring around it, colder weather and snow coming.

He'd give Jerry a head start. The route to Leif's was a jog on 13, then straight up 5, and there was no way they'd go after Jerry in traffic, but they'd be out, and, he hoped, he could get a look at them.

He crushed the cigarette under his boot and got into Jerry's car, then went up 13. When he caught sight of his truck, he followed at a distance, the morning rush on.

Jerry got onto Highway 5, and he lost him until Jerry turned off the ramp and he followed, a van on Jerry's bumper. Another tailgater. Or was he just not seeing it? Or them? You could, he knew, tag team, which made a tail all but invisible. And then he saw it, sure enough. A Saturn SUV swung in front of a white Subaru to come up behind his truck.

Only now he was too close, so he turned abruptly right, squaring the west route, all strip malls, and small businesses, to come back onto 5 where Highway 7 intersected with it.

A mile up 5, to the west, the Saturn had been replaced by—an unmarked patrol car.

Clever. Or was it?

He got in the lane farthest over, then shot ahead, and when he passed the unmarked, took in the driver in the rear view. Got a shock. Lucy's father. There at the wheel in mirrored shades.

Lucy'd shown him a photo, in case her father got wise to where she went afternoons and came looking for him.

At an intersection, the Saturn reappeared, got behind his truck, and he pulled in two cars back of them, and Lucy's father, in his cruiser, shot off to the left, back toward Shakopee.

Being a cop, he could run the plates of the cars tailing Jerry, or— was he one of them? Arn, and Burgess, and—

But now—WHAT THE—?!—Jerry was pulling off on a side road, then went a good distance up it toward a liquor store.

As Jerry slowed, to turn into the parking lot, the Saturn jetted forward and smacked into him, sent the truck sliding up the road onto the shoulder, where it lurched to a stop.

"Don't, Jerry, just—*don't* get out, GOD damnit!" he said, then was flying up a side road, paralleling them.

Where the trees ended, he yanked on the parking brake so the car slid a hundred eighty degrees. Jumped from it and unholstered his .38, came across the field, letting off a round, then a second, the side window on the camper shattering, and Jerry hit the gas, pulling away, and the driver of the Saturn firing out his widow.

Jerry raced across a field of dried corn shock, until he reached a connecting road, and was gone.

Buck got back out to 5, too, and minutes later Jerry called him.

"I'm at a gas station."

"Is there a problem?"

"Someone just shot at me!"

"Well, if you were in traffic, someone must have seen it. Road rage, he hit you first?"

There was a pause. "Jesus. I never thought—yes, I slowed... for somebody, and he banged right into me. I was going to stop, but then—Jesus, he shoots out the rear window."

"So, you didn't stop?"

"Are you crazy?"

"You get the plate?"

"DID I GET THE PLATE? NO, I DIDN'T GET THE PLATE. I WAS DRIVING FOR MY LIFE AND—"

"Calm down, Jerry. It's just road rage. Okay? Listen, you're okay, right?" he asked.

"Do you want the wood?"

Now it was his turn to be shocked. "The *wood*?"

"I'm just blocks from your guy's place. Do you want it or not?"

"Of course I want it." He had to think what to say. "Listen, I'm at Kowalski's, how about you stay there at Leif's. Okay? I'll get my groceries and come over and I'll drive the truck home."

"Thanks," Jerry said.

He was in and out of Kowalski's in minutes, bags in hand, and driving toward Leif's. He thought to call Lucy. But what could he tell her? That her father was...up to something?

And, anyway, Booker hadn't got them the burners he'd asked him to, not yet, and he cringed at calling Lucy. Then realized he had to, so did.

"Yeah?" she answered, a wary note in her voice as if she were, already, bracing herself against it.

"It'd be best if you stayed inside for now, since they're not waiting," Buck said. "Just had a little run in with 'em."

"Where?"

He was turning into Leif's lot. On the shop roof was a good foot

212

or more of snow, his truck parked nose in, bullet holes in the gate and the camper windows gone and the bumper all but bent double, having been hit twice, earlier, and now.

"You're armed, right? You've got guns there. Anyone but your old man or Ryan comes to your door, you shoot, understand?"

36

Lucy

In the kitchen nook trying to focus on her biology text, she'd bitten her fingernails down to the quick. Someone knocked at the door, and she trained the Glock on it.

"*None of that dumb, cocking-the-gun Hollywood horseshit, Bebbe Gurl,*" *her father had told her.* "*You get the gun out, you be ready to use it. Shell in the chamber and the safety off.*"

"Who is it?" she called out. She was aiming right where someone's torso would be.

"*Chest's the biggest target. Breathe deep, Bebbe Gurl, squeeze, don't jerk the trigger.*"

If the door moved at all, she'd let loose. That's what she decided. Even the slightest.

"It's cold out here!" Ryan shouted.

Ryan. Christ. She slid around the table, her pants catching on the broken brushed aluminum rim. The whole place was made of Jap cardboard, her father'd said, shit not even fit to burn.

"Get in here," Lucy said and, as Ryan was coming through the door, she caught his jacket and swung him around behind the table. Kicked the door shut and locked it, Ryan staring at the gun, which she set behind the toaster.

She thumped down across from him, and he reached into his pocket and brought out a sheet of paper.

"I got the schedule," he said.

She took it from him, held it under the light. Arn was off over the weekend. But she'd assumed he would be. And Chief Burgess. But Jackson and Tibbets? After all, it *was* a holiday.

"Here," Ryan said, and he spun the pack he'd been carrying onto the table, taking from it a sheaf of papers.

"Emails between Arn and—" He blinked, left eye, then his right, odd fish that he was. "—the other ones."

He was holding onto some… prize or something useful, but she was going to have to see it for herself. Lucy scanned down the first sheet, so many codes and numbers and headings that it was difficult even finding the emails, and when she did, they consisted of cryptic notes:

HTT 4 P Jack, 14Tib, and *Confirm sub, A. A go? Hot 1 for Cheese Burg.*

She rifled through the remainder of the pages. Set them on the table. It was all in this cryptic… almost-code.

A sinking feeling in her stomach, she glanced up at Ryan and said, "Ryan—" but not the remainder—"this is all *useless.*"

Ryan came around the table, stood behind her. "Look," he said, and pointed to a line on the first page. Tapped it with his index finger. "They didn't even use a real code, it's all just *abbreviation.* Jackson, Tibbets, Arn. See?"

"Ryan—if it's *Jack*, for Jackson, *Tibb*, for Tibbits, why a first name for Arn?" She'd set her head in her hands.

"*Arn* isn't his first name. It's *James.* His *last* name's Arnold. He just goes by Arn. And Burg—isn't *Burger*, it's Burgess."

She sat up at that, but then thought—what difference did it make? You couldn't do anything with it. To any of them. And it all came crashing down on her, the futility of her situation, the awfulness of it.

"Ryan," she said, "this all proves nothing. They're careful. What's here, really? And we already—*I* knew—and now *you* know."

"You see the pattern though?"

"Sure, it's all a bunch of cryptic nonsense. You couldn't prove anything with it. It's all just—"

"Gobbledygook?"

Ryan grinned, then squatted and bumped her hip with his, and she shifted over. He swept up the pages. Pointed to, on the first, *NGF ChaP*. She would have shrugged, but she was too disappointed to bother. Second page, another three lines having ChaP in them, and the same on the others.

She felt herself frowning, something coming to her. It came to her as if out of a fog. The pattern.

"They all answer to him. Is that it?" *HIM*. Was it? The one who'd started it all, and she snatched the pages from Ryan.

But just as quickly, she felt sick again. To get so close, but to be so far from it, what she needed.

"God, Ryan," she said, and this time she lay her head on the table. "I don't know *who* that is, or—*where* he is, or anything, and—what's the use? What's the use if we can't find him?"

"Who said?"

"Well, I *know* where… fucking Arn is, but the others? So? How does this help anything?"

"See, they've *all* sent emails *to* ChaP, and I traced his IP address to St. Pete's, one they use for business. But he *never* answers from it, like… all that's just spam, you know?"

"But, if we get *him*, what's he connected to through that, because he's got be going there for a reason, we'll get them *all*."

Lucy lifted her head from the table. She'd gone to St. Pete's. The Indian Catholics living on the res all did. But then she thought, No. Father Burgine hadn't been like that. She'd loved Father Burgine.

Ryan all but set his head on the table, sideways, to look into her eyes. "ChaP. Lucy, he'd never be so stupid as to go on line as himself. So— *who* is he going on line as?"

And she got it. OH MY GOD. What Ryan had brought her. The gift he'd set in her lap.

"Yeah," Ryan said. "He has to *go there*, physically, to get online. To do what he does. Right at St. Pete's. Or, if he's stupid, he works there."

"And," Ryan held up the sheets, "if you look at the time stamps, he usually does it on the first and third Thursday of every month."

Lucy sat up, shook herself. That kamikaze thing ran through her head, bright as day.

She saw herself in the dark, sunbeam lit narthex of St. Pete's, HIM coming through the door, the stained glass rose over his head. She'd say, "Hello, it's Lucy, remember me?"

"You can't," Ryan said, "do what you're thinking."

"Why not?"

"Because. There are others, like Arn, and like you, too. There's a whole lot more," he said, "see?" And he showed her.

She felt herself frown, disgusted. And when she glanced over at Ryan, he didn't look goofy, or funny, at all.

"Like shooting rats in a barrel," she said. "Only, you've got to get them all to crawl into the barrel first, right?"

37

Buck

The cell Booker had brought him was burning a hole in his pocket, over at a ghastly, fluorescent lit warehouse grocery; at a hardware store, in the parking lot and the morning rush on; and at an auto parts, where he got windshield washer fluid, oil, and new bulbs for his left rear blinker and taillight that had been shot out when Jerry'd driven the truck up to Leif's.

He didn't want the cops stopping him for a light violation, not after what Booker had said. They'd stop him for anything and radio it in. Then, when he "resisted," they'd take him out.

"So, what's the deal?" he had asked Booker.

"Deal?" he said. "You carry the burner with you, and when Ryan has done his Boy Genius techie thing, Lucy'll ring you. Let you know who's in it; least, the cops anyway."

She hadn't called, and it worried him. When he pulled into the drive, he parked back of the door and got out, and when he went into his shop, there Lucy was. Sitting at his drafting table.

It was well after 3:00 and he'd forgotten the time. He did that now, and he forgot to eat, too.

He pulled a stool up alongside her. "So," he said, "let's see it, what Ryan came up with."

She pulled from her pocket a sheaf of much rumpled paper, and he took it from her, on it highlighted lines. Communications between Arn and the others—she'd written comments in the margins.

She explained. And even as she did, he saw it all coming together, a plan—this ChaP, if they could get him to come out, it could work.

"In these pages—they're all emailing him, but here, this one time, he sends a group email to Arn, Burgess, Tibbits, and Jackson." She pointed where she'd circled the communication:

SsJLLF?

"This one, the date?" He gave her that look—"this is when…"

"The day before Jean died, and just days before they tried to drown you in the river."

SsJLLF. J—Jean, *L*—Lucy, *LF*—Lucy's Friend? He'd seen this sort of thing before, only back then it had been in a cribbed shorthand, and passed between users on desk calendar pages, and once read, disposed of.

"What else do you have?"

She showed him the duty roster, on it the vacations. She explained it all to him. The resort they were to meet at. Up there. The policemen going up for business, and to, later, "go snowmobiling."

"We still don't know who ChaP is, though he's setting all this up," she said, "and there're more of them than Arn and…."

Buck didn't want to tell her, but he had to. "This is all standard protocol."

"Whose?"

"Career criminals, granted how organized they are."

"So?"

"We get your friend, Ryan, to go deeper into the connections between Arn and Burgess and the others, and this… ChaP'll have to pop up under whatever other name he's using. Because they *are* connected, and going *both* directions. They have to be. It's just… we can't see how. *Yet*. And—we do need to identify them before this goes any further, since they'll be the ones coming at us."

"Us?" she said.

"Right," he said, "and we need to finish the canoe—I mean, *your* canoe, and now."

38

Lucy

"So, Bebbe Gurl, what's for dinner?" her father said, coming through the door, still in his uniform. He pressed her to him, then tossed his hat into the corner behind the table, weirdly jaunty.

"Your day okay? School treating you all right?" He smiled, then gave her a compliment. "Ah, why do I even ask. You're great at all that. You know I'm proud of you, right?"

She frowned at that. It was too much; he was laying it on a little too thick. But why?

"Well, it's Friday, I hope you didn't forget," he said, and turned to go up the hallway.

"I didn't, Daddy," she said. Fridays they didn't eat meat. Real old school Catholic, her father called it. Just something that felt right. But, even more so, it was that order thing of his, and she indulged him in it.

At the stove, she shrugged. The splint on her finger chafed at her hand, and the joint still throbbed.

She bent to the pots and pans. Lifted a lid, right rear: Brussels sprouts with cheese. Left rear: mashed potatoes. And, front right—thanks to her mother, who'd cut out that nonsense with the fish sticks, ugh!—a pound of crab meat swimming in butter, a whole stick of it, thank you, Julia Child!

There was a knock at the door, and her heart fluttered.

"Daddy?"

"Yeah, Bebbe Gurl," he called from the rear of the trailer.

"If I get the door I'll be burning things on the stove, so I need you to get it for me now, okay?"

"Coming!" he called back.

She pulled the drawer to her right open, got the Glock out. Thumbed off the safety. Set it behind the toaster and lay a dish towel over it. Whoever it was knocked again, but this time more insistently, a true thumping.

"Hey, Lee!" Arn shouted, stomping his feet on the stoop, Arn so large the trailer shook. "You there?!"

He was banging on the door a third time when her father, buttoning his shirt, marched up the hallway and swung the door open.

"Get you a beer?" he said, and pulled Arn inside. He swung the fridge door open. Put a beer in his hand. "Got time for dinner?"

"Thanks, but no," Arn said, swaying side to side on his thick legs, and a black bag slung over his shoulder. "Ate already."

Gone to fat, big jowls and marbled, heavy arms, and his legs so fat that when he walked his thighs rubbed together, he looked like a giant, blue frog. That he'd had his fingers stuffed up her, had messed all over her, was right there between them. But worst of all, that final, terrible thing.

Both of them smiled woodenly at each other, the Glock right there behind the toaster.

"So," her father said, but in a way that made the hairs on the back of her neck stand up. "Let's look at those maps."

"Daddy?" Lucy said, her heart in her throat, "this all's going to be ready in no time at all. So, can we? Please?"

"Yeah, Lee," Arn said, "like your sweetie pie there said, do we need to get into all this now?"

"Well, given how we're having our meeting up there, don't you think I'd want to know *where*, exactly, and how much time it's going to take? Because, Arn, Lucy and I have things we want to do, too. I promised her, so, there it is, see?"

Her father smiled, but it was with his—as her mother had called

221

it—SEG. Shit Eating Grin.

There at the stove, she swept up the Glock in the towel, her finger on the trigger, frozen like an idiot behind her father.

"You got the map," her father said. "Let's put it on the table over here and you show me what's what."

Arn, with a nod, got it from his bag, unfolded it, then pressed it flat on the table and her father bent in.

Arn traced a route with a red marker, then stepped back, winking like some game show host.

"Simple as that, by snowmobile, it's forty minutes."

"That's it?"

"It's a straight shot, Lee, you'll be out and back to Lucy—" he actually turned to nod at her "—in no time at all."

"Hey, you'll love it out there," he added, "prettiest country, all in pitch pine and fir. So… we're good, right?"

Arn swung by her to set his beer on the counter, and her father clapped him on the shoulder.

"Oh," Arn said, "check for the deposit?"

Her father wrote out a check and, with a flourish, handed it to Arn, and Arn went out the door, Lucy glaring.

The *fucking nerve*! *Christ*! And Arn thinking he'd just walk away from it all. Well, she'd show him.

"Hey, Luce—" her father looked between her and the door, where Arn had just gone out. "What's up?"

"Nothing," she replied, and she got her face back on, then busied herself with the pots on the stove.

"Well, it sure didn't look like nothing."

With a shrug, she turned to him, waiting there, his hands on his hips, said, "So, can we just… *eat* already?"

She'd gotten the Glock back in the drawer, but she was shaking. She set the plates on the table. Sat across from him.

"Try the crab, Daddy," she said.

He did, his eyes softening. "Well, you're a gen-u-ine cook, you know, and your mother would be proud, too."

"Thanks, Daddy," she said, and forked some potato into her mouth, which sickened her.

After all, it was swimming in butter. Just like this... trip she and her father were taking.

Too, too much butter.

39

Buck

They converged at a roadside restaurant, Buck and Lucy, Booker and Ryan. Lucy doing something on her phone, Ryan too, and only Booker really at the table with him.

Lucy'd called him on the burner Booker'd got her, and she'd been adamant they meet.

"So," Booker said, and poked Lucy with his elbow. "Okay if *I* tell him?"

Lucy nodded, "Okay."

"So, what's so important?" Buck asked, and he jabbed her with his elbow, interrupting her texting.

"I'm missing days at school, I've got to get someone to take notes for me and all that."

"*Really?*"

She looked up. "Well, it would look... *weird*, if I didn't. If I just disappeared, wouldn't it?"

There were two cops in a booth opposite, one with his broad back to them, the other facing away. Buck motioned with his chin.

"No, not him," Lucy said. "And the other one..." It was dark out, and the window fronting the parking lot was a mirror. She shifted from side to side, trying to catch his face there. "I can't see—not with his back turned like that, but, the cops always come here on shift. It's on their route."

"You sure?"

"Sure, I'm sure. I've been here with my dad, that's why I chose it, okay? It's safe. And—it's only the rookies. Never Burgess or the brass."

"This whole thing," Booker said, and turned to Buck, "Lucy going up north with her ol' man and the cops? She had Ryan look into it, found out it was her *pop's* idea to go up there in the first place, turn it into a winter holiday, ho ho ho and all that shit—" he grimaced "—an' get this—he did it *just after* Lucy's friend, Jean, died."

Lucy set her phone on the table, held her eyes on Buck's now. Letting the import of it sink in.

"Ryan?" she said, and Ryan glanced up.

"Lucy's dad," he said, "sent a memo to Chief Burgess the end of that week, and Burges sent a note to Arn—" he glanced up from what he'd been texting, shrugged, then worked his thumbs on his keypad again, nodded, "—and Arn did the footwork, reserved the cabins, and over those days."

Buck slid back in his seat and his thoughts in a jumble. So, Lucy's father *was* on to them.

Their plan, his and Lucy's, would still work, though Lucy's father, he'd have to be taken out of the picture.

Lucy'd have to do it—and she and her father would have to go up, together, so Arn and the others could come after them, later. And, hopefully, this ChaP, who was at the center of it, he'd show, too.

"So," Booker said, and bent over Ryan's shoulder. "What are *you* doin' there, Mr. Thumbunicator?"

His head down, Ryan replied, "Your clichéd trope is not appreciated, Booker. Your namesake wouldn't appreciate it either. It's beneath your dignity."

"Didn't mean to offend," Booker said. "So?"

Ryan smiled, sort of. "Then, no offense taken." His phone beeped, and Booker asked, "What's that?"

"Incoming SMS," he glanced down at his phone, then shrugged, said, "from my mom."

"Yeah, right," Booker replied. "And what's your moms got to say there, Einstein? Got you your milk and cookies waitin' for you you get on home now, and The Enchanted Kingdom on the TV."

Ryan, frowning, looked between them, Buck, Booker, and Lucy. "Booker, you need to go," he said.

"Say what?"

"Out the back. Now."

"Awww. *Really*? Why? Cause of what I said?"

Lucy craned her head around to take in the restaurant. Everyone was behaving reasonably, gossiping over their dinners, a reassuring everydayness in it. But they'd lifted their heads at Booker's raised voice.

Ryan was working his thumbs again. Then nodded. "Go out the back door, and now," he said. "Arn's pulling in. On a 10-14, Citizen Holding Suspect. Came from—" Ryan glanced crossly up. "I put my mom on the PD dispatch site before I left. Well, aren't you glad I did? Has to be one of those two," he nodded to the cops, "who called it in. They get their hands on you, and—"

"Booker?" Buck said. Shielding him, he walked with him to the back door, telling him what to do.

"Yeah, that'll work," Booker said. "But you get the security feed from the office or we're still screwed."

He hadn't thought of it, and he went back inside, the others in the restaurant glancing up from their tables, bored looks on their faces. At the booth, he pulled on his jacket.

"Men's," he said, loudly, "and when you're done there—" Lucy had slid from the booth, but was staring off across the restaurant into the dark windows "—you and Ryan'll take my truck, and I'm off with your friend, okay?" He threw a twenty on the table.

"Right," Lucy said and, catching on to what he was up to, she added, "so you two'll take my car, it's the red Toyota," and they exchanged keys.

In Lucy's little sedan, he pulled the restaurant's camcorder remote-drive from under his jacket and tossed it onto the rear seat. Twenty or so vehicles were in the lot, most of them SUVs and a few older sedans.

Arn came in off 13 and, seeing Lucy's Toyota, he swung around behind an Escalade, a plume of exhaust rising from his tailpipe. Snatched something off his dash—a phone—and waited.

Buck got on the highway, and Arn followed a good half block behind, falling back now and then. A mile or more up the road, Buck turned into the reservation, then shot toward the Mystic Lake Casino, the sprawl of a concert crowd everywhere and cars parked blocks back from the entrance, concertgoers, most of them couples, arm in arm stepping grudgingly through the snow.

Arn got right on his bumper. Hit his lights. Then siren. Yeah, Buck thought, you do that, and pulled to a stop. More than a few of the concertgoers turned to see what was going on.

The casino sign over the little Toyota read, "Barry Manilow, I Sing the Songs." *Christ!* It would be just like him to get shot here, of all places, Barry Manilow grinning down at him.

"Get out of the car with your hands held up over your head," Arn barked over his PA.

Arn stepped from his cruiser and unsnapped the holster on his hip to get his hand on the butt of his pistol.

Buck climbed from Lucy's little car, feeling like some circus clown. With his gun, Arn waved him back, then farther, onto the snow-covered sidewalk where the crowd had shuffled, but was watching. Arn, sidestepping, approached the car. When he got to it, he ducked, then swung the door open, pointed his gun into the rear, looking for Booker, and froze, everything in him registering shock.

Arn poised with his gun, in a two-fisted, all-but-ready-to-fire posture.

When he slouched, a show of resignation on his face, Buck said, "Officer, you looking for something?"

Buck all but grinned—each knew the other; and Arn couldn't shoot him here, not with the concert crowd ringed around him.

"Your taillight's out," Arn snapped. He stepped back from the car, then holstered the gun. "You should get that fixed or you could have trouble. Next time, we'll have to write you a citation. You just get that light fixed," Arn said.

"Gotcha," Buck replied, and Arn, glaring, ducked back into his cruiser, then made an angry U-turn and shot off toward 13.

But Booker, Lucy, and Ryan were, Buck knew, long gone.

40

Lucy

She came by to work on the canoe again, and he showed her how to use the C clamps to fit the gunnels. Sure, he was aware they were being watched, he said.

This, after she told him it had been her father's once Army buddies in the restaurant, both cops in the neighboring suburb, Burnsville. But how could she have known?

Ryan, looking into Lucy's father's unit, had discovered they'd *all* served together. Had shown her a photo.

Lucy's father, Arn, and the two other cops were decorated vets in Afghanistan. Rangers. Though, from the way her father had been standing apart from them, it was clear something had gone wrong.

And thinking on it, the enmity there, they worked, just that, with the clamps, and the glue. Worked for hours, side by side.

She marveled at how he worked with the wood. Driven, and focused, he'd fallen into the old language.

"Gimikwendan ina?" he said now. He pointed with his chin, toward the door, "Miskwaawaak, eh?" Can you get me more of the red cedar out there?

"Daga," she replied. Come on, really? "Aaniin ezhiwebak agwajiing?" What's the temperature?

He bent to the thermometer in the window. "Gisinaa eh noodin!" Cold! He laughed, and reached for a length of spruce, which wasn't there. "Aaniin endaso-diba' iganed?" Spruce too? She went outside, came back in with the wood he wanted, glanced at her watch. "Gichi-gigzheh." Still early.

"Gibichiita?" Take a break?

She held one of the spruce slats she'd brought in flat, and Buck secured it to the canoe with a brass bolt, countersunk it, then capped it so it was all but invisible. In it a final touch.

"Makademashkikiwaaboo?" Coffee?

"Eya," she said, sure, and he went into the house and minutes later returned with two mugs, both steaming.

"Nimbakade?" Hungry?

She shrugged, "Nindanokii," I'm all right, and he nodded, said, "Ondass," come here, and when she stepped closer, he handed her one of the mugs, Buck sharing a joke about a crazy dog, laughing, and there was that give and take, the two of them having people in common, Lucy chiming in about her inzhishenh, her uncle on her mother's side, Zozed, a real trickster, a con artist, but a loveable one. Oh, the wawiyahzh things he did, had Buck heard? How crazy!

And just then came an outpouring of all that she'd stuffed down because her mother had been in it, but not now, not with Buck laughing.

At one point, they were both laughing so hard they were all but crying, and then Buck said they shouldn't be laughing, none of it was funny, at all, and they laughed all the harder. Could barely breathe for laughing.

And then, they both said nothing, and the shop filled with an almost tangible silence.

"I don't even know your name," she said. When he turned away, his mouth set, she said, "Gage' bineh," Everlasting Bird. "Aaniin ezhinikaazoyan?" And what are you called?

"Miskwa' doden," he replied. Red Deer.

"Miigwech," Lucy said, thank you, and he only nodded, and they returned to the canoe.

But there was something different between them now. Larger than either of them, and having a life of its own. They worked side by side, saying everything in saying nothing, letting the size of the threat settle.

Arn, by coming after Booker, had shown them the lengths to which they'd go, how desperate they were.

They fitted the bow and stern plates, then laid heavy beads of tight bond on the veneer, bow and stern, and they were done.

Lucy thought it would "just dry," but he shook his head, got out infrared lamps and fans.

"I need to get home," she told him, even granted how awful things were, joking. It's what she always said.

Her father was on second shift. He'd be back at 11:00, but he'd expect something to eat.

Buck stepped out of the shop. In seconds he came out of the house with foil tins, three of them. Chicken. Rice. Some... green bean thing.

"Take 'em, I made enough to feed an army," he told her, which made no sense at all.

Who was he making all this food for? And then it struck her. Thin as he'd gotten, he'd made it for her.

When, two days later, she returned, he was sewing a patch on a jacket in the kitchen, a needle in his teeth. He nodded her inside, then sat at his table, a pin cushion between his knees, worked the thread through the jacket's Army green fabric, then expertly double-knotted the ends and pulled the jacket right side out, *273* on a cloth badge.

"Your old man's unit," he said. "Pass muster?" he asked, and held it up for inspection. The jacket, but for being larger, was for all practical purposes identical to the one her father wore.

"It'll do," she said.

"Out," he told her, and they went into the shop. With her at the bow, and him taking the stern, they flipped the canoe over so the hull faced up, as it had when they'd constructed it. He handed her an orbital sander.

"Start with the sixty grit."

There were lines in the hull where the glue had squeezed out. He wanted her to take those down first. He needed to finish the jacket and make some calls, he said, and left her there, the sander in hand. She ran it over the tight bond lines in the hull, the sander skittering. It danced all over the place. Slid. Made her hands numb, and if she got the pad too-on-edge, it wandered, made hideous, opaque chevron-like marks on the hull that horrified her. Had they gone right down into the wood? She bent to look. No, thank god.

The wood was so beautiful, she feared messing it up now, and it smelled like... myrrh, at St. Peter's, that's what it was, and a memory of such hope in it, before every all-but-unspeakable-thing since.

The sander held just so, and bracing her feet wide and bearing down with all her weight, she attacked those awful, shocking marks, rhythmically buffing them out, and with them the tight bond lines, and when she'd gotten those removed, as he'd told her to, she switched papers. There was an odd, spring loaded gadget on each end of the sander. She got the one hundred grit in and attacked the hull with that, bow to stern, paying special attention to the places where the slats joined, going back and forth, wrestling with the sander which, with each pass, grew oppressively heavier and harder to manage.

She was all but done and in a hot sweat when he stepped back into shop—her arms heavy and her legs shaking. How did he do it? She'd only been at it an hour and she was exhausted.

"What?" he said, his hands set on his hips, enormous, powerful hands, and his arms ropey with muscle.

"Does it look all right?" she asked.

"Miika'waadendaag," he said, It's lovely, and as he did, he ran his hand over the rounded hull, his fingers splayed, and the wood skin smooth, so that, just then, to her surprise, she felt herself blush.

Because she hadn't, consciously anyway, thought of him like that, he was *way* older —but, there it was.

"Here," he said, and handed her a sandwich off a tray he'd carried into the shop, then picked up his own.

They ate hunched over, the sandwiches wrapped in wads of paper towels, oozing mayonnaise and she felt, oddly, at first that she couldn't eat, it had suddenly become… too close in the shop, and then she was ravenous, ate, and Buck smiled at her, pleased.

"So, you ready for the next bit?"

"Uh huh," she replied, and blushed again. Good God! But, no—he was going to say something.

"We'll fit the ribs. Okay? Put in the seats." It made her feel… still weird, but fine, being so close.

"Ashwii?" he said, ready? and when she replied, "Enh!" yes, without any hesitation, they were in that other place again. Theirs.

When she got home, she looked around, hands on her hips, relieved, sort of—Arn had popped up behind her on the way back in his patrol car, but at the turnoff to the trailer shot away on a side road—to be in the trailer, though she could see things were a total mess, crap everywhere, laundry, dirty dishes in the dish drain, and her father's gun cleaning kit strewn across the kitchen table. And what was he doing cleaning his guns again? She turned the thermostat up: It was only fifty-three inside, and nowhere near comfortable. She could almost see her breath. Her father wanted her to set the temperature when she was home at sixty-three. She set it up to seventy-two, and when the furnace boomed on, with a sense of guilt she ran it back down again. At sixty-three she always had to wear a sweater and the mukluks her mother had gotten for her, and she went into her room for them, shucked them on, then stood in the kitchen.

She glanced over her shoulder at the stove and dish drain. Which to do first, clean? Or get dinner started? She thought of her mother; she'd always been on top of things, but then that hurt too much to think about her.

If she did, like she was doing—it made her feel crazy. Or was it something else now? There was something crawling up and down her spine, a sense that something wasn't right. It made the trailer seem… too quiet.

Something rattled in her backpack. She'd set her phone on vibrate.

Booker? She took the burner from the pack, checked her caller log, and sure enough, Booker. She texted:

You home? She counted five breaths, trying to calm herself, when her phone lit up:

Been trying to get you these last twenty.

Y?

Ryan sent this.

An emoji popped up on her screen, a mustachioed bandito with pistols, and under it, *Sent to Lucy, no rsp.* And Ryan didn't use phone emojis. Or, if he did, they were ones he created. He was very particular about that, to the point of vexation, his and hers. "What good is it, Ryan, if I don't know what it is?" she would ask, and he'd explain, as if she were thick: "It's an Akritirian from the Delta Quadrant," and then would come his exasperated sigh, radiating Ryan's disappointment and loneliness, "From *Star Trek*, Episode—"

But now he'd sent something... goofy, and she had no idea what it meant. It was in her caller log, too, he'd shot it off to her a good thirty minutes ago, when she'd been driving to the trailer. No, the pistols meant something.

Go see what's up over there, Booker texted.

Now?

No, tomorrow.... He attached an emoji, a glaring face. *Take one of your old man's pieces.*

On it, she thumbed back.

She slid the phone into her pocket. Pulled on her jacket and got the Glock out of the drawer. Then recalled what her father had told her: "Handguns in close quarters are all but useless," he'd said. "Your man knocks it away, or gets to it? You're done. Pump shorty. Right here." He'd shown her. "You put it where you can get to it, in a spot like this, so if someone's gotten inside and you're 'playing victim,' backing up?" It was on a bracket behind the fire extinguisher. "Shell's in the chamber. Safety off. You drop down taking it with you, fire from the floor and there isn't a man alive you can't take out, even the Terminator. Trust me. I've done it."

She got the shorty off the bracket. Dropped the Glock in the drawer. Then thought better—hid it behind the breadbox.

Outside, it was bitter cold. And dark. Someone had knocked out the light in the drive. She went up the row of ramshackle trailers. Lights on in them, families watching TV. Everything in the dark looked jagged, and frozen, and threatening. Shitty old river bottom trees, bent all directions, and hammered and bolted and taped together cars at all angles. She came up on Ryan's trailer. Ugly aluminum thing from the fifties with some dopey wings on the side, just like hers, but an off red, like dried blood. The light from the television should have been on, casting a blue light on the curtains in the window to the right of the door. That's how she'd always known Ryan's mother had passed out. The blue television light in the curtains. But there was no light there now, so she circled.

There was a pile of junk at the rear of the trailer. Ryan used it to step down out of his window nights. He didn't have to pass his mother that way, going through the front door. She got up on the slippery, enameled lid of the washer they'd meant to take to the dump. Tried the window. Whoever it was, they hadn't gone in this way. She removed the screen, then climbed over the sill and inside. A whimpering was coming from the front.

She stumbled on Ryan's Star Trek figures, breaking the plastic and arresting her motion.

"You don't do this," Ryan's mother said, and she was whimpering and crying, hysterical.

"Fucking gook," came a second voice, one distinctly southern, "you git this here fucktard of yours to call the others over here, or—"

"But he send, what you want? No one come!"

She got that staring feeling again, her body in the back of Ryan's trailer, where she stood over herself at a great distance, listening. Her heart hammered in her neck. There was a fleshy slap inside. It was them. But not Arn. Or Tibbits or Jackson, this—whoever it was— was from the south. So not Burgess, either. And not—*Him*. She didn't recognize the voice, but he was ranting, and it occurred to her they'd sent over someone from outside, because he seemed to have no idea who Ryan and his mother were or who he was waiting for.

So, what was it? Or, what was it *supposed to be*? A robbery gone bad? And who'd care? Not the police. And thinking it, how expendable they all were, she stepped over the line into something else. Some*one* else. Again.

She, the one who just got things done, had survived what Arn and the others, what *He*, had done to her.

And her otchit there with her now, saying, Don't make a sound. Slow. Gather yourself,

Strike. No hesitation.

She stood at Ryan's bedroom door—swung the shotgun around behind her, slid the safety off with her thumb, then took a deep breath and pulled the door open and stepped into the hallway, a bit sideways. To hide the gun.

Fucking Charles Manson, she thought. In the living room. He was standing over Ryan's mother, her eyes beaten all but shut.

"Bebbe Gurl," came her father's voice in her head, "ALWAYS action beats re-action, so—you hit *first*, and hit *hard*."

But she didn't. She stood there, her heart hammering in her chest. And her father had been right. Everything was wrong now, the whole thing.

"Well, well," Manson said, grinning, like some jack-o'-lantern and, training his automatic on her, he added, "your lil' girl frien' *did* come on over now, din't she!" He wrinkled his nose. "Now you, lil' princess, you go on over to the counter there and you're gonna get on that there phone and bring over your Black boy, hear? And we all are a-gonna have us a party, y'all being so purdy, and your friends here to watch. Cause it's more excitin' that way, you know?"

He waved her toward the phone on the counter, and she moved toward it, shocked and disgusted at herself. If she got to the phone, the island would make getting the shotgun up impossible.

And, much worse, he could drop behind it—crouching the way he was, she didn't have a shot.

"NEVER GO FOR THE HEAD," her father had told her; "it's too small a target, and if you miss, you're dead."

Mrs. Chen on the floor, whimpering, she came on into the kitchen, the gun angled behind her.

"Now, princess, you pick up that old-timey phone like I said, and you call so's I can hear you an all, and you get your Black boy to come on over, else his princess is gonna get it, hear?"

He was losing his patience, if he'd ever had any, his eyes bugging, and the gun in his hand pointing all over.

She picked up the phone with her left hand, and when, with a kind of horror, she realized she couldn't dial with the shorty in her right, she froze. Again.

She shared a look with Ryan's mother, who nodded, then sobbed all the louder. Ryan, pinned beside Manson. And that was bad, too. Even if she could get off a shot, she'd catch Ryan.

"What y'all waitin' on?" Manson said. "If'n y'all don't remember Black boy's number, retard here'll give it you, hey."

And there SHE was, that other girl, the one who did things, and her otchit telling her. Calm. Slowly. You know what to do.

"Ryan," she said, "what's his number?" and even as he was saying it, Ryan bent over his phone so Manson had his eyes on him, and she tossed the shotgun to Ryan's mother, who caught it and snapped it to her shoulder.

"Aw shucks, now why'd you go an' do that, when y'all were behavin' so good?" Manson grinned at Ryan's mother. "And you, ol' fuckface, that's a pump you got there, you gotta rack up a shell," he said, "if'n you're gonna fire that ol' blunderbuss, and I'ma shootcha iffn' you do, okay? Since I got the draw on you here, see?"

Mrs. Chen pulled the trigger, blew him off his feet into the dining table, Ryan struggling under him, eyes wide, and the meth head, gut shot and anything but dead, caught Ryan's head in his elbow, and Ryan's mother sprang from the floor like a jack in the box, racked up another shell, then fired again and blew his brains out, blood spray in a halo on the wall, and Ryan spattered in it.

Into the shocked silence, Ryan's mother said, "Fuckface to you, too," and spat on what was left of him.

She turned to Lucy. Lucy hadn't said to her more than two sentences strung together in all the time they'd, kind of, known each other. Hello and goodbye, and it's getting late, isn't it?

"I keep gun," she said. "I take from you when. You don't shoot. I kill him, all mine responsibility."

Lucy was too stunned to respond. Ryan's mother nodded to Ryan. "Call police. Story is, I shoot. Lucy here to study. Bring shotgun for being in dark coming over. Also true, no? All true."

"Yes," Lucy said. But why—after everything—had she not shot him herself? Coming into the living room?

And, worst of all, her father would want to know how it happened. Exactly. And how she'd let Mrs. Chen, Ryan's mother, get hold of the shorty. He'd be relentless.

"I'm sorry," Lucy said, in it an apology for her having ignored her, which was an embarrassment now.

"For what—you come right time. Save everything."

Ryan got on the phone, and there wasn't in it the least hint of his being some autistic kid; it shocked her. So much of what he'd been doing at school and with her, she realized, had been an act.

"Yes," he said now, and he gave the address, and in a voice she'd never heard, he said, "Yes, officer. I'd like to report a shooting. Yes, officer, we have one dead here, gunshot wound. My mother, Sir. Yes, Sir, that's right."

"I'm sorry," Lucy said, while Ryan was phoning it all in, "but I don't know your name."

"Kitty—" Ryan's mother replied.

A bubble of hyena-like hysterical laughter rose up in her, in the pure, dopey, cockeyed relief of the moment—Kitty, Ryan's mother, had shot and killed the tattooed meth addict.

He was—right there—with half his head blown off, grinning at them from the corner.

"I'm sorry—"

"Again? So sorry for everything. Sure, you laugh. Old lady can shoot, huh? You think that funny?" So, yeah, she'd gotten the gist of it. How weird it all was, after the fact.

"No," Lucy insisted. "But, your *face*." She held her hand up to her own face. "That has to hurt."

"Ha," Kitty said. "You Americans. So safe."

Ryan put the phone down. Looked between them, said something to his mother in—

"Is that Mandarin?"

"Cantonese," Kitty said, wagging her finger. "You never ask Ryan why we come here?"

Again, here, even in the midst of what had happened, was a moment of embarrassment, because she hadn't.

"What if they don't believe it?" Lucy said.

Kitty, her face a mask of pain, looked between them. Ryan said something to her, and she nodded.

"Thank you," she said. "For coming. And now we owe you our life. Now, who took gun?"

"You did," Lucy replied.

Her father came with the other cops, bright bars flashing blue on their patrol car rooftops, and a KSTP news van behind them. It was a shit show, and her father took her under his arm, walked her through it. Lights in her face. Microphone. The asshole reporters turning the whole thing into some cop show melodrama, and her voice that of a zombie, her father having whispered in her ear before it even started, "Only the facts, and when you can, cry."

And while each of them told their story, the one Kitty had put into place, she worried. But about her father, because, while he was genuinely shocked by it all, what had just happened, it was clear, too, he didn't want the police looking into what he'd gotten the detectives calling "just another drug addict robbery gone bad," and her father with his hands on his belt, making it stick.

"So, it was self defense, plain and simple," he told a reporter, which, both she and her father knew, wasn't what had happened at all.

KSTP 9 News came on at 10:00, and Lucy and her father watched it together, Lucy wrapped in a blanket and saying nothing. The cops were still at Ryan's. Yellow crime scene tape and all the rest of it. You could see the lights through the curtains, flashing blue.

Lucy sat in one of the ladder-backed chairs at the kitchen table, staring at the television, and when her father's phone rang, the ring tone a barking dog, her father stepped outside.

Sometime later, he stepped back in, rubbed his hands together against the cold, stood by the heater vent.

"Jesus. Our guy's some peckerwood from down in Louisiana."

"Nice," she said.

"Nice?" Her father paced there. "So, why now?"

She smiled, playing stupid.

"What are you smilin' for? This is serious. We don't know if he's come up here alone or what. And because the cops are calling it a closed case, it's up to me to look into what he was up to, see? So, what did he say that you're not telling me, Bebbe Gurl, to all three of you, huh?" And here came the scary meanness, her nice guy father gone, and this other person there, the one she hated. But she couldn't hate him too much, because, she knew all too well, he had his reasons.

And they had to do with everything, she was sure of it now, going all the way back to… just when she couldn't know.

"Nothing!" she said.

"Yeah, nothing my ass. Was he alone?" He'd come over to the counter, and now he stood over her, threatening.

She wanted to say, He was *going to rape me*, that's what he said, *and of course he wasn't alone. You know that. And I do, too.*

But she had to play her part, didn't she?

"What'd he do?" she asked.

"Sex offender. Went in for five. Got out on good behavior."

Of course. And here she'd hoped he was some… *outsider*, but, no, he was one of them. *Him*, and Arn and the others. It made things worse, that they were down in Louisiana too.

She smiled—well, actually, it didn't. Make things worse. No. It made things very, very simple.

She'd done the right thing, not telling the reporters or police what it was all about. Because with people like that, well, there was only one way to deal with them.

41

Buck

That the whole mess had expanded, gone all the way south now, did not surprise him. At 10:30 that night Lucy'd texted,

Subject up from Louisiana. Sex offender. Out on good behavior.

The news on KSTP 9 he'd taken with a grain of salt—because he recognized a fabrication when he heard one. The police hadn't released information on the assailant, a recidivist from Louisiana, but had flashed a police-blotter head shot. He looked capable, despite all the telltale signs of his addiction: hollow cheeks, the long teeth, and, worst of all, the scabby skin and sunken in eyes. And that Ryan's mother'd shot him came as no surprise, either. Her severe bowl haircut, and eyes that didn't look away. That hundred yard stare you got when you'd seen things.

Using his burner, he texted Lucy: *Stay put. Mouth shut. Stop by when you can.* Switched off the television and carried his phone with him from the living room into the kitchen.

Stared into his eyes in the window over the sink, as if into a mirror. In them an expression all too familiar. His coach, back when he'd been playing ball, had called it *Chief's Killer Look.*

What was it Seraphim had told him? *Life is the destiny you are bound to refuse until you have consented to die.* And that his "life would be hard," and it was a kindness to say so.

"Michael," she'd snap at him, "what are the fruits of the Holy Spirit?" "*Yes, Sister, the fruits of the Holy Spirit are charity, joy, peace, patience, benignity, goodness, long-suffering, mildness, faith, modesty, continency, and chastity."*

"Very good, Michael, and what are the gifts of the Holy Spirit?" *"Yes, Sister. The gifts of the Holy Spirit are wisdom, understanding, counsel, fortitude, knowledge, piety, and fear of the Lord."*

"And Michael, what are the Seven Grandfathers?" "Yes, Sister, *wisdom, honesty, truth, bravery, respect, humility, love."*

He poured himself a glass of water and, studying his face in the window, drank it like a promise. To Lucy. And to Seraphim, his once tormentor and, later, ally and savior at St. Mary's. Seraphim, who by including The Seven Grandfathers in their morning recitation bridged an otherwise unbridgeable gulf.

And in so doing, communicated to him that they were in it together, their difficulty.

He'd get them now, too, and as many as he could.

Then, thinking to fill the cat's water dish, he realized he hadn't seen the cat in days. Maybe it had found another home? But he worried. A Chinook had blown in and it was thirty-five degrees out.

At—he held up his wrist, and the watch there reading: 11:35—and just before Christmas.

Weird. And, all over again, a feeling of fate in the air he stepped out into the yard. It was overcast, and the air felt close with the clouds pressing down. It reminded him of that morning a lifetime ago when his brother'd been shot, something woven into the very air, as if he were swimming in it.

An accident—or so he'd been told, carrying his brother, disfigured and bleeding, to the plane, and the... useless rush, and noise, and effort, until that moment the doctor stepped into the waiting room and it was over, and something died in him, something he couldn't lose.

Jesus. The cat was back. Looking at him in the dark. Poor cat. How had he forgotten her?

Well, she hadn't been around, that's how. How many days? Excuses, he thought. If he'd put out food, well— The cat knew something was going on now, too, though. Animals always knew.

There was something… lurking. In the yard, or nearby. And the cat, at the heart of it, crouched there.

So, since it hadn't come around, someone had been feeding the cat—his neighbor, Jerry? He put his hand out and the cat came over. He scratched its jowls, and the cat turned its head one way, then the other.

He scooped the cat up. Held it against his chest. Something the cat had never tolerated. Not until Lucy. The cat clinging to him, he could feel its ribs under its skin. A swollen something on its haunch.

"Hey, what's this," he said to the cat, and at that moment he felt something cold at the back of his neck.

"Don't move," a voice said.

In the space of a heartbeat, it all came clear to him. One telescoping, shocked second. They'd had the cat, and had starved it so it would run to him and he'd be distracted. It was the cat that changed things. And as he was thinking it, someone stepped from behind the shop. A second man.

"You just stay put there," he said, holding up zip ties and looming closer, "hold tight or—"

Buck hurled the cat at him, the cat, claws out, shrieking. Landing on him, so he knocked it away, as Buck snapped his head back, broke the nose of the man behind him. Spun to catch him by his throat. Crushed his windpipe, lifting him off his feet, then swung him around.

In that confused, shocked second, Buck charged, used the first man's body as a shield. Knocked Zip Ties off his feet and they went down in a jumble. Buck got a knee on his shoulder. Hit him—a hard-knuckled blow across his temple, and his eyes rolled up in his head. The first man, on his stomach, was already out, Buck having so crushed his neck.

He got their hands tied. That they'd had their pockets full of zip ties said terrible things.

A short while later, he stepped back from the two men, who, now, were looking around the shop. The cat, having eaten, had climbed into the shelving where Buck had put her bed. She watched with her golden eyes, wary, but grooming herself. He hadn't bothered with threats. Or questions. Silence was enough and he went about things in the shop. The smaller of the two men, the one who'd come from behind the garage, he'd tied ankles-and-wrists to his drafting table, his tools alongside him; handheld saber saw, the plainer; the joiner.

"We don't show, they'll come looking," he warned.

The big one, jowls, and little red-rimmed pig eyes, he was tied to the chair Lucy always sat in.

"Earl," the smaller said, "tell him what for."

"Shut up," Earl said.

"You don't cut me up, you let us go and—" He stopped himself; glanced over at the bigger man.

"You'll what?" Buck said.

He bent over the smaller man on the table. He smelled of sour sweat. And he'd pissed himself. He was in a mechanic's overalls, green and filthy with grease, *Robert E. Jr.* on the pocket in red stitching.

"You from down south, Bobby?" Buck asked. "You another Louisiana boy, like this one on the news?"

"What's it to you?"

"On the news, the one that beat up the kid and his mother. He your pal? He would be, wouldn't he?"

He glanced over at the bigger man. He was wearing a green Army jacket and twill pants, his boots oiled and well cared for. Earl the manager of whatever dung hole filling station in Louisiana they'd been running.

"You shut your piehole, Bobby," Earl said. "You say one more word and you'll answer to—

"Listen here," he said.

"I'm listening," Buck said, going about his business.

He filled a bucket from the sink at the far wall. Opened the cabinet there and got out buffing cloths. They were a little too tightly woven, but they'd hold water, and that was what he needed. Porous enough, too—that was important.

He dropped the towels into the bucket and carried the bucket over to the table. Set it there.

"No need to go over the particulars," Buck said, "I just want the name of who it was that sent you here."

He stooped, pulled one of the towels from the bucket, water streaming from it, then unceremoniously threw it with a slap over the smaller man's head, cinched it with his fist behind his neck. In seconds Bobby Jr. thrashed on the table. Arched his back, screaming.

When he'd all but stopped thrashing, Buck removed the cloth. Slapped his cheeks.

"Wake up," he said.

"Fuck you," Bobby shot back, and Buck bent to submerge the cloth in the bucket again, lifted it, water spilling from it, over Bobby Jr.'s face.

"No, don't."

Again, when nothing was forthcoming he slapped the cloth over Bobby Jr.'s face and he thrashed there. Gasped when he removed the cloth.

"We're late. So they'll be coming," he threatened.

"No, they won't. No one's coming. Not here. They'll be coming up north, isn't that right?"

He held up his watch. "It's just after 12:00. So, we have plenty of time." He turned to the bigger man.

"What was the plan," Buck said. "Bury me somewhere? After, you know, I got the others to come here?"

He dropped the cloth over Bobby Jr.'s face again, and after he'd all but died of suffocation, he removed it.

"You aren't going to get me on that table," the bigger man said, as if his size was some impediment. "And I got a heart condition."

"What's the plan, Earl? Your name is 'Earl,' right?"

The big man looked around him. Buck went at Bobby Jr. with the towel again. This time it was worse.

"You can cut that out, he don't know nothin," Earl said with disgust, and Buck removed the towel.

"So, who's behind it?"

Earl glared. He was not going to say—for the very reason that he had no idea who was behind it. Of course. Which was all Buck needed to know, because provocation was the thing he was aiming at now.

"So, then—*who* sent you?"

"Can't do that—" he nodded toward Bobby Jr. "—with me sitting up. In this chair."

"Got it. I'll pull your chair down, so you'll be on your back, right? That's what you want me to think? You're down like that, you can kick your feet free of the chair legs, then come at me—what, all two hundred seventy pounds of you, right?"

When Earl's eyes narrowed, he held up the bucket, winked at Earl, then said, "You notice the chair you're in has a metal frame?"

Earl glanced down at it, his brows furrowing, and Buck tossed the water in the bucket on him. Rolled his tig welder from behind the table. Attached one copper headed clamp to the frame of the chair, the other to Earl's now wet jacket.

"Right shoulder," Buck said. "Won't kill you. Unless you really do have a heart condition."

When Earl said nothing, only struggled in the chair, Buck turned to him and winked, "Didn't think so."

Bobby Jr. was silent on the drafting table. He went over to him. "He's alive. Just passed out."

Returned to Earl.

"Who sent you. That's all that I'm asking for, Earl."

"Fuck you."

"That's right. Fuck me." He spun the red box of the tig welder around. Messed with the settings on it.

"You know the difference between voltage and amperage? But of course you do. You run a garage, right? No amperage, and say… 40,000 volts. How about we start there?"

He didn't give him a chance to respond, he just flipped the big toggle switch and Earl let out a scream.

On. Off. On. Off.

"Wax on, wax off," Buck said, and a long way from breaking him. "You see that one?"

When he'd gotten what he wanted, or, as much of it as he was going to get, and both men were limp as rags, he bound their hands and feet in layers of duct tape over the zip ties. Just for show. It would look good in photographs; taped over their mouths, too. Bobby Jr. wasn't hard to get into his truck; the big man, Earl, he had to use a plank to slide him into the back. It was a little after 3:00. Still of the night. He drove into a neighborhood a few blocks from the Shakopee Police Station. Used a slim jim to pop the lock on an older Honda. Well cared for. And an automatic. But new enough to have airbags. That was important, the air bags. Nice, older car. Well cared for. He was sorry for that, but it couldn't be helped.

He got Bobby Jr. and Earl in the back of the Honda, both of whom were making all appearances of having given up, but that was just for show. Of course, they were bent on some last effort.

He was going to drive them somewhere, they thought, and while he was at the wheel, Earl would thrust his arms over the headrest, catch his neck in his bound hands and break it.

"Been there, done that," he said to Earl, and even as they kicked at him, he bound their hands to their feet.

When he was absolutely certain they couldn't lunge at him—the two of them side by side in the rear, straining to lift their heads—they, no doubt, thought he was going to set fire to the car—he swung into the car behind the wheel, and both men sat back, relieved. He hotwired the car, then drove toward the Shakopee PD and parked at the top of the hill there. The police station was at the bottom, where three roads intersected, and behind the station, the river.

He'd had gloves on, so there was no need to wipe the steering wheel. But he did have to fix the wheel in place—he couldn't have the car veering off and them getting out somehow or going into the river and drowning, so, again, he secured things with the tape.

When that was done, he got out. The lights were on in the station and the cops inside just doing their jobs.

He ducked into the car again. "Hang tight," he said, then started the car and wedged the ever-ubiquitous-in-Minnesota long-handled ice scraper between the front seat and the gas pedal, so he got about 2,700 rpm on the tach, then looked each in the eye, Bobby Jr. first, and then Earl.

"Give my regards to the Gipper," he said, then pulled the car into drive and, stepping back, he swung the door closed.

The car dropped down the hill, gathered speed. Down, down, down it went, until it sailed through the intersection, thumped up over the far curb, crossed the PD lawn, shot up the walkway, then slammed, like a hammer, grill first into the police station entryway, glass exploding in all directions, an alarm coming on, shrieking into the quiet night, and the police, like hornets, flying out of the station.

Later, back in the house, he went upstairs and took a shower, and when he got out, he toweled himself off and dressed. Five. It was still early. But possibly not *too* early. He got out his burner and texted Ryan.

Everything you can find on a J.T. Haney. He typed out the phone number Earl had given him.

It was all they had—either J.T. wasn't up on what someone like Ryan could do with a phone number, and they'd get lucky and come up with something, or they'd come up empty handed.

An emoticon appeared on his screen. A smiling green frog, one in a top hat. He replied, *Let Lucy know.*

The cat perched on the arm of his couch, he watched the morning news, there the Honda crashing into the police station entryway on KTSP 9 News. Five times they ran it. The car looming out of the dark and dropping down the hill, then crashing into the entryway, and glass flying. A prank, they were calling it. And not a word about the two men inside the car.

Which said it all: message received.

No doubt he'd set off a shit storm of police looking into what the two men crashing into the building and bound like that meant, since neither Earl nor Bobby Jr. were about to tell them anything.

We're on to you, he'd as much as barked over a PA system, you, ChaP, and your whole rotten contingent. Come and get us.

He switched the television off. Put his boots up on the coffee table, crossed them at the ankles.

He was fast asleep on the couch when the phone buzzed. He looked around him, surprised to find himself in front of the television and a gray, morning light coming through the window to his left. He swept his phone up from the coffee table.

Number registered to J.T. Haney. Deceased.

Typical of Ryan, no salutation, and no mention of how he'd come by what he'd sent, or if there might be more to it. Still—*deceased*. Out of the picture. And not who they were looking for.

So, Earl just flipping him the bird? A made up name? Or—?

Bleary eyed, he set the phone back on the table, then rubbed his face, trying to wake himself. Well, so much for that. From his night, he felt a kind of mild hangover—something like nausea, and in it an almost visceral disgust. And now a deadening anxiety, too. Lucy's father was up to something. And could he, somehow, upset their plan? Ruin things? No, he thought, up north they'd have to get him safely out of it, and he set his feet on the floor.

His elbows on his knees, and his forehead cradled in his palms, he stared down into the table, the phone there.

Something popped up on it, a square with an arrow pointing to the right, what looked like an old floppy disk. He tapped the arrow, and a line of text appeared. Which, even as he bent to take a look at it, was gone. *One of five*, it had read, and a photo appearing now in its place.

Naomi. In her green scrubs. At the house. The photo taken

through the window, which had steamed—the radiator under it vented when there was too much pressure, which—

He tapped the second icon. Another photo. Naomi, in her green scrubs, exiting Fairview Hospital from the rear. Night. Snow. Alone. And here, in a third photo, Naomi at her car, brown paper grocery bags clutched to her chest and struggling to get her key in the car door. Again, night.

He'd told her to never, never do that, be alone in a parking lot in the dark, because, well—they *were* out there, weren't they?

He was, now, afraid to look at the fourth photo. He popped it up, and before he'd even taken it in, said, "Aww—Dammit!"

Booker. And with him Lucy. At her car. Behind a…. He scanned the photo, in neon there: *Van's*. Some kind of… store. Was there a time stamp? Yes. Taken an hour ago.

And the fifth photo? He felt himself wincing as he thumbed the icon and bent over the tiny screen. Ryan. Caught through a part in yellow curtains. Ryan at his kitchen table with his laptop.

He texted: *Ryan. Your mom there?* Seconds later, Ryan replied, *Outside. Getting a photo of our photographer.*

He jumped up from the couch. On his burner, he rang Lucy.

"Yeah?"

"You're being followed," he said. "Someone took a pic of you with Booker." There was a scrubbing sound, Lucy doing something with her phone. "Lucy?"

"Sup?" It was Booker.

"They got a look at you, Booker. A photo. Ryan sent me a photo of you with Lucy, at—"

"Van's. Yeah. But you look, I'm handin' her a bag, like she gettin' something from the pharmacy. S'all it is, see? Sure, they seen me 'n' all that, but it was Lucy they payin' attention to. I got off shift, went into the car wash next door, and she drove through and got me after.

"Been keepin' my head down. Even had a jacket of Ryan's over my head n' all so's they wouldn't see me in Lucy's car and put us together."

"After what happened at the restaurant, I thought we agreed you two should never be seen together? What part of that didn't you understand? And what part of 'stay put' didn't you understand?"

"Yeah, well, Lucy, 'fore things go all to shit up north, wanted to follow a hunch, 'n' I'd say you got your own biz to take care of, too, what with the pics Ryan just sent, so hup to, right?"

"Booker—" he said, about to launch into an angry rant, but even as he was saying it, Booker hung up.

He was at Naomi's house in St. Paul forty minutes later, having driven there in a cold sweat. Went around to the door in back—knocked. Then again, knuckles on wood, banging, really. He heard motion inside, and by the sound of it, both a pattering of feet and a closing of a door upstairs, he knew someone was with her.

Moments later, the curtain pulled to the side. A moon of a face there, a face he loved. Naomi's. She'd crossed her forearms under her breasts, which, granted the sheer material of her nightgown, didn't leave much to the imagination.

When she craned her head up—was she talking to someone on the stairs behind her? or—

"Could you just—*open the door, please?*" he said.

She did that, holding it wide with her slippered foot, in a color she hated, aquamarine.

So, who was it?— He shook himself, damnit, he'd promised himself he'd—not look pathetic.

"What?" she said, but she didn't add, as she had in the past, "and it better be good," because it most certainly wasn't.

"You need to get out of the house," he said.

She stared into the yard, a kind of ultimate frustration in it—she'd *had it*, that look said. All those years ago, when that mess with his daughter had come to them, he'd had to tell her the same. She reached for her cell, which was charging on the counter. Held it out, glaring. On it, a photo of a police cruiser along the curb, an unmarked, and there a face lit by the blue glare of a computer screen.

Arn. In uniform, no less. It struck him as if a quarter'd dropped into a slot machine, and the whole works coming up sevens. That Arn had come to the house spoke volumes.

"Is it *this*? Him? He's the problem?"

"Not exactly."

"So, what *is* it then. *Exactly*?"

"When'd you take that?"

"It's about that girl who came over, your assistant, 'Becky,'" she said. "That's it. Isn't it? She's your new project. And he's—"

"Naomi—" there wasn't going to be any good way to say it "— just get out of the house. And you *can't* call the cops. You can see why not, right? So… get out and stay out."

"Until when?"

"Just after the holidays," he replied, and with a nod, he turned to go, but then stopped.

"I'm sorry," he said. And he meant it. He'd meant it to be about what was happening now, but it covered everything.

42

Lucy

In the car, Lucy had a map over her knees, Booker was driving and Arn was a good three blocks ahead of them in traffic. They'd followed him all the way from the police station to the casino, then into the river flats where he made his rounds—Arn slowing here and there, sometimes even stopping, which made staying out of sight difficult. He pulled in front of the old settlement now, all tarpaper shacks, abandoned cars, and rusty farming implements.

"Go around and park," Lucy said at the Burlington Northern siding, a crumbling, cement silo looming over them.

Booker pulled behind it, tires crunching on broken beer bottles and shards of cement, and Lucy got out. Came around the front, where, with Booker's binocs, she could get a look at Arn.

"Shit," she said.

Arn, in his cruiser, was eating something, then messing around with the dash mounted computer, the windows fogging.

She'd had Ryan send him an email from ChapP, *Need to meet, urgent*, and from how Arn had driven from the Casino where he usually loitered for hours, they'd thought he'd fallen for it.

"Promise, you'll just follow the plan," Buck had said, "can you do that? Stay put and let me take care of things?"

She'd said she could, but hadn't. He rang now. "We've got a problem," he said. She couldn't think what to say, so said nothing.

"Arn was at Naomi's house," he told her.

"She's gone?"

"I told her she had to leave, but she hasn't," he replied. "She's packing and…." She could hear the confusion in his voice. After all, why would she be asking if Naomi had gone? "So—I'll be here until…."

"—it's safe," she said.

"Well, until there's no Arn around, I'm going to—"

"Arn," Lucy replied, "isn't going to be popping up there, you can trust me on that." She cringed, not wanting to say it, but then had to because, how, otherwise, could he know she was right?

"He's right here in front of Booker and me," she said, "at the old Burlington Northern silos on the res."

She was hoping, even as Booker was waving at her to get back into the car, that he'd forgive her, yet again.

"Lucy?! *Don't do anything.*"

"Gotta go. I'll call," she said, cutting him off.

Arn was on the move, and Booker had brought the car around, thrown the door open.

On River Road, they came up behind Arn. "Back off, Booker!" Lucy said, panic in her voice.

Booker shot off to the left to drop back of a bus, the stink of diesel awful. "Okay," he said. "What now?"

They were all but off the reservation, then passed the old sign, YOU ARE LEAVING SACRED GROUND, and crossed into Shakopee, here the streets cobblestone and the tires pattering. Arn pulled into the Sinclair gas station and parked behind the green cement dinosaur there.

"Pull off somewhere, Booker," Lucy said, "somewhere where we can see him, okay?"

He turned at a side street and drove up the hillside there, on it Victorians, Painted Ladies, Shakopee having become a fair weather tourist destination. He parked, the engine running and heater on, the spire of St. Peter's distant—a white finger pointing up over the black,

255

asphalt-shingled roofs surrounding it.

Below them, Lucy could see in the binocs, Arn was busy stuffing his face in his cruiser.

"Yeah, bout as excitin' as watchin' paint dry, isn't that what they say?" Booker said. "Here, lemme see," he said, and she passed him the binocs.

Lucy, her hands pressed between her knees against the cold coming through the door of the car, felt her spirits sink. She'd assumed if Arn got an email from ChaP he'd come running.

It was cold, and dark, and it had snowed again, a blanket of white over everything. St. Peter's was within the Shakopee police department jurisdiction, so, of course Arn would stop by it at some point in his shift. All the cops did. And his fueling up, taking a break nearby now? Nothing.

Her father had complained, and often, that St. Peter's was too far out, too much driving. For a year or so, he'd been at a meeting there a few times a week, when he'd come back "from the 'Stan," as he'd put it, and later, after her mother'd been killed, when he'd truly come apart.

After that, they'd attended services on Sundays, something to say to the Social Services people, that he was trying to put himself back together.

"Can we go?" Lucy said, all but bitterly.

"Not sure we should, Luce. Seems your Arn be purdy nervous."

"Yeah, aren't we all," she replied, dejectedly, and the weight of the whole thing there again.

"No," Booker said, "where I come from, 'Nervous' mean somethin' else altogether."

"Like what?"

"Your man there, he's sittin' on a heap o' coals. He's FOMO, or like my moms says, he be a shaky dog, got him jelly bones. He ain't hungry, he just shovin' that shit in his face." On and on it went. She'd set her chin in her palm, and with the car running it was warm, and she nodded off.

"Yo, Luce! Wake up," Booker said, shaking her by her shoulder.

The car was moving in such a way that, disoriented as she was, it almost made her sick, everything whirling by—trees, streets, and her stomach dropping and the car climbing again. Beneath them, and to their right now, St. Peter's.

Arn, in his cruiser, pulled up in front. He waited a good few minutes, then rushed inside, leaving his cruiser idling.

Booker went up the hill in back, parked in the lot above the church. "Okay," he said, "now that Arn's come here 'n' all, shouldn't we go *down* there and see what he's up to?"

The sun had come out for the first time in nearly two weeks, and the snow made everything brighter. St. Peter's now a beautiful gothic revival church amidst the old black-limbed trees around it, and the river in the distance, a broad swatch of blue gray water.

Booker had the binocs out again.

"What's the sign in front say?" Lucy asked.

"'Take my yoke upon you and learn from me, for—'" Booker said, and Lucy held up her hand.

"'—my yoke is easy and my burden is light.'"

"And there're some services 'n' shit, times 'n' all under it." Booker turned to her. "What?" he said.

"Who's presiding?"

Booker pressed the binocs to his face again. "A... Father Delmonico."

Lucy took her burner from her pocket. Called Ryan's number and held the phone to her ear.

"Ryan?" She told him what she wanted, and he replied, "I'll get it. You got ten, fifteen?"

She hung up, and she and Booker sat in a benumbed silence, St. Peter's below them, a tail of exhaust rising from Arn's cruiser, Booker with his arm's crossed and staring off at nothing.

A black-winged raven with a bone flew over the lot, perched in an elm, trying to eat the marrow.

"Fuck it," Booker said, and, slinging his arm around his middle, he undid his seat belt. "I'm going inside."

"Booker, no," Lucy said, but he'd already sprung out the door. "Booker!" she shouted, then tore out of the car after him. "Don't!"

"You wanna know what he's doin'? I'm findin' out."

"Get. In. The. Car."

"Came all this way, and put up with all this— I'm gonna find out what that cop's doing."

"Booker."

"You stay. I'm goin'."

"How are you going to get in? You'd have to go in the front door. Are you out of your mind?"

"Yeah, with bein' sick of this shit. Creepy a-hole like that, I'm s'posed be afraid of *him*?" Booker bent to her. "Don't gimme none of your backin' off shit n' all cause I have had it. And from the time I seen that cop asshole on you like that, had it up to *here* and then some.

"'Yoke is easy' my ass! Always hated that one. The one I like is: 'If God is for us, who is against us.' And 'Whom he called he justified.' Like that. So, the only question's if we're in the right? We justified?"

Lucy couldn't bring herself to say YES.

"Say it," Booker said.

"Yes."

"All right," Booker said, "then gimme your hoodie. And you give it right now, right here."

"Booker...."

"Goin' in as is, otherwise, no stoppin' me." He held up his phone. "Picture says a thousand words, right? I'm gonna get me some photos of what's going on." He reached out his hand. "Come on. Sling it."

She did that and he put it on, then handed her his jacket.

"That looks like shit," Lucy said. "Like you're some homeless person or something."

With a smile, Booker replied, "That's the whole point."

"Booker—"

"Hey, *some*body gotta cut to the chase here, okay?" He pointed with his head. "Now, you get in the car, and you get ready to get the hell out if we have to. So, keep the car runnin'."

As he was going down the stairs, sliding his hand along the pipe railing, she got in the car and started it.

She cracked her window and cool air spilled in, the sun cutting sharply through the windshield, so she had to squint. A second raven had flown into the trees, and the two now were squawking at each other, fighting over the bone. She scratched at a circle of dried coffee on top of the dashboard. Tore at her fingers, making a hangnail, so put her finger in her mouth—salty, dirty—to bite the cuticle off.

Lifted it to her face. Great. Now it was bleeding, and it stung. She lifted her burner. From Ryan: *Delmonico 0*. Shit.

The ravens suddenly got louder, then flew in a burst of black wings from the trees. Birds didn't just—but here was someone coming out of the trees. Hunched over. He moved toward the entrance of St. Peter's, stocky, thick-chested. Broad-shouldered. In uniform. Arn. He'd come out the back, where you couldn't see from the lot.

She reached for the door handle to get out and warn Booker, but instead popped the glove compartment. Her father's Glock there. Swept it up and racked up a shell, then jumped from the car. This time—she told herself—she *would* shoot, even with Arn being a cop.

Booker came out the arched front doors of St. Peter's. He looked both directions, then headed across the yard and Arn charged from behind.

"Booker!" Lucy shrieked, and Booker looked up, saw her, then glanced behind him and bolted.

It was a good half block to the parking lot, and when Arn, his enormous gut bouncing, saw he wouldn't catch Booker, he slid to a stop and drew on him, and Lucy fired—into the billboard, the glass shattering, anchored herself at the railing just as her father had shown her, took aim again and fired, the bullets sending up puffs of ice off the walkway until she'd run the shots up to Arn, and he leapt off the walkway into the snow, dodging, but still coming on.

Booker made it to the foot of the stairs and glanced back. He'd have to climb the stairs, exposed, to get to the car. Fourteen shells in the Glock. She'd fired—what? Seven, eight times?

Arn looked up at her, deciding whether or not she'd shoot him. Booker, arrested at the foot of the steps, was wondering the same.

Arn charged, and Booker hit the stairs, pulling himself up as much as climbing, the pipe railing singing, and Arn shooting.

Lucy fired in a sweep across Arn's line of motion and Arn zig-zagged, which bought Booker seconds.

In the lot, he slung her into the car. Scrambled over her all elbows and knees and, the tires whirring and whirring on the ice, he fishtailed out onto the street as Arn stumbled into the lot.

Lucy got her phone out—she enlarged Arn's image with her fingers. Hit the shutter icon.

43

Buck

He was in his shop fitting a cleat on the bow plate of the canoe, the cat in the shelving grooming itself, when his phone rang.

"Yeah?"

"Comin' at ya," Booker said.

"I'll be here," Buck replied and slipped the phone in his pocket.

He took one last look at the canoe. It was an arterial red, and long, and low, and lean. Grasping the gunnels, far and near, he flipped it over. Right-side up. The canoe was ready—he and Lucy had sprayed heavy coats of urethane over the hull, and it had dried to a shiny perfection.

Done, all of it. With Lucy's help. And the screws he'd used to fix the ribs to the inside of the hull, to make the canoe all but indestructible, were countersunk, and capped with red cedar.

Even in the poorest light it would be a beacon, visible for miles. A canoe you couldn't miss. Because, later, it would be part of the story.

He ran his hand up the hull. Glossily smooth. Under the fiberglass silk and layers of urethane, the tight grain of the cedar—whorls, and something like a scar, and a pattern like skin.

He stepped over to the Duluth pack he'd put together. Enough explosive in it now to… well, take down a platoon. Because, as Ryan had discovered, that's what they were. Cell service up there was spotty at best, if not nonexistent, so he'd detonate it the old fashioned way.

The trick, the sticking point, would be getting Arn and company to follow him up shore, and to one, finite place.

Something dark slid by his side door window, and he swept up his .38 and stepped around the file cabinet.

There was a knock. "Buck?" It was Lucy, her voice muffled through the door.

"Who's with you?"

"Booker."

He said nothing. Waited.

"Just Booker."

He reached for the doorknob, swung the door open and Lucy ducked into the shop. Wearing a black and silver Raiders jacket three sizes too large—like some gangbanger. Booker trailed in behind her—in a five-sizes-too-small pink hoodie—Lucy's.

"What's with you two swapping costumes?" Buck asked. "Kinda late for Halloween, isn't it?"

"Got this," Booker said, and he thrust out his cell phone, on it a photo. "Take it," he said.

Buck did. A church—alongside—what was it? A river. And the buildings up on the embankment. Old grain silos and brownstone warehouses and cobbled streets. So, St. Peter's.

Lucy had swept the cat into her arms, the cat looking up into her face, entranced. A girl with a cat.

"So, why am I looking at this?"

"Scroll. One at a time," Booker said. "I took some, and Lucy took some, and Ryan put 'em together, figured it out."

"What?"

"Just look at 'em, all right?"

He did that, lifted the phone to his face, three of Arn in a pew, around him stained glass, then Arn going into a stairwell.

"Had to follow Arn down." Booker made a spinning motion with his index finger.

Empty rooms. All too dark to see much. Another corridor. Name plates on doors. And here: A monster of a multi-armed furnace, corrugated hosing, and all that plumbing and gear. Arn, with narrowed eyes, peering over his shoulder, even then turning on his feet.

"What's he doing?"

"Lurin' me in deeper," Booker said, a sneer in his voice, "cause, Arn, he sensed I'd come in behind him."

Lucy, rubbing her nose on the cat's back, looked up between them, hanging on to what it was.

"And—he—"

"Didn't do *nothing*, just turned and come after me, and I barely made it up to Lucy."

"So, what'd you get?"

"Go back there," Booker said, and grinning, he laughed, "yeah, more, all the way to those pics I took in the dark n' shit. Going up that hallway. Can't see barely nothing. Ryan fixed all that."

Buck scrolled back, bent into the screen.

"See the name plates on the doors there, like they got supplies and stuff on 'em, *Linens. Toiletries*. But, yeah, go back one more."

The last was Arn turning toward a door with a plate on it, one that read, *Janitor*. Then going by it.

"Ryan looked into who was in that very room," Booker said.

"Yeah, and I bet it was Arn, like I'm seeing right here, or was it the ghost of Pope John Paul?"

"*J. T. Haney*," Booker said, and with a nod, added, "only, Haney wasn't janitor there six months and died of a heart attack, and the church's all this time kept his phone 'n' computer goin'. And somebody be using ol' J.T.'s log in an' everything, only, Ryan said it was just for what you'd think. Church stuff. That's what it look like, see?"

Good god. Finally. The connection. Even an office. And who was dropping in?

His burner rang, and he answered it, stepping over to the door and looking out into the yard.

"They followed Lucy and Booker over to your place, put up photos," Ryan said, "I'm on Arn's email."

"So?"

263

"You're all proof-positive linked now."

"Who's Arn answering to?"

"No idea. It's masked. But they're looking for Booker. They want him, and it'll only be a matter of time."

"Ryan," he said, "dig deeper on the janitor's computer, okay? Who he writes to, where he goes."

"Already on it," Ryan replied.

He hung up, and the three of them shared looks. Lucy was clutching the cat, and—sensing the awfulness of the moment—the cat wanted to get away. Which it did, climbing down Lucy's pants and its claws making a puckering there.

"You help me out here, Booker?" he asked. "Got one last errand, before we head up north."

They were parked in a shopping area in a car Buck had "borrowed" with the help of a slim jim and a few wires. Buck at the wheel, Lucy alongside him, a light snow was coming down, people dashing from their cars into the shops around them.

He'd dropped Booker at the Radio Shack, and Booker was at the counter trying to scare up what Buck had sent him in for. He needed something that had range, which was the sticking point.

Waiting, Lucy was distractedly playing with the radio. She'd gone off on a tangent.

"But even if Naomi's somewhere else, is she safe?" she asked. "If we're doing all this up north?"

"Naomi?" Buck said. "You have no idea. And, anyway, I already told you, and I'm telling you again, there's not going to be any 'we,' not after you do your bit in the canoe. Got it?"

She was taken aback, stopped messing with the radio to turn and look in his direction.

"And why not?" he said, in response to the question she hadn't asked. "Because you'll be back at the resort.

"You talk to the manager, you spend the night in your cabin. And with an alibi like that, you're good as gold."

"Well, yeah, I know all that, but I wasn't talking about that," she said, "I was talking about *her.*"

He was watching Booker at the checkout counter of the Radio Shack, Lucy trying to be upbeat about how everything between him and Naomi would work out, she just knew it, because Naomi was so angry, and since she was angry, well, she still cared. "Don't you know that?" she said, and in her a kind of naïveté that was endearing, and since he'd so long ago lost it, any kind of innocence, or belief in happy endings, it was heartrending, too.

"Tell me you don't still love her," she said, "and if you'd only *do* something, or *say* something—"

"Uh huh," he said, all the while trying to read in Booker's cocked head if the clerk there was taking exception to what he was asking for. Only, why should he, when Booker had a package of Pampers they'd picked up under one arm, and was shifting wipes and baby clothes in the other?

Why wouldn't a father like Booker want a baby monitor, like anybody else just might?

"Don't you think?" Lucy said.

"What?"

"Naomi'd take you back, if you just—*really* asked her to? Did you do that? *Did* you ask?"

Booker had been out of the car nearly twenty minutes, and Buck was beginning to more than worry. Ryan had shot him a text, just MUST SEE. And he'd sent him Leif's address.

A black unmarked pulled in behind them. Stopped, but his parking lights on. So, still running.

The officer in it was doing something with the screen he had on the dash, his face lit blue.

"You didn't answer," Lucy said.

He glanced over at her. She curled a strand of her hair over her ear. "I'm watching Booker," he said, "and it's—"

"It's *not* going wrong," Lucy said, a note of exasperation in her voice. "See how he's leaned up against the counter, all calm like?" He did. "Has his elbow set there, looking up?" She grinned. "Booker's doing his best Agent J, and who doesn't fall for that, right?"

She cocked her head, and in a voice not her own, she said, "'You know the difference 'tween you 'n' me? *I* make this look good.'"

Cutting his eyes at her, Buck replied, "And just *what* in the world, exactly, has gotten into you?"

"Will Smith," she said, "that's—Jesus, really? Agent J, in *Men in Black*? The movie?" When she saw he still didn't get it, she said, "The clerk... he's like... he's all hunched over, too, like Booker. See?"

He craned his head back, to see what the cop behind them was doing—the cop had a clipboard out, was bent over it, writing something—then spun around again, taking in Booker, and trying not to show his irritation.

"So?"

"It's *mirroring*," Lucy said. "The *clerk*, if it were going bad, he'd be standing upright. Away. But, just like Booker, he's got his elbow down there, going over the directions."

She'd folded her legs under her, the way girls did. It was too close in the car, and it made him uncomfortable.

"Naomi told me you have some 'savior complex,' said I should think about what happened to people like that. She said you were a saint, and I should think about what that meant for me."

Jesus, he wanted out of the lot, out of the car, back to his house and away from all this.

"Lucy," he replied. "Look, I know you're trying to help, but don't, okay?" He had, after all, come into Naomi's life that way, too.

As Seraphim had said, *There is no love which does not become help.* And here Lucy was doing her best.

"She implied you had some great putrid festering *Halloween 5* of a secret that was making you both sick."

"Oh, just one?" he corrected her. "Naomi say that? Or are you just making all this shit up?"

"Well, not *exactly*."

"Terrific," Buck said.

"She said she 'wouldn't do it again.' What did she mean? *What* wouldn't she do again?"

He wasn't about to lie to her, tell her all that had been nothing.

"So…." She'd turned to him, "you never told her, right? *Why* you did what you did, right?"

"Lucy," he replied, "we're not having that conversation."

As if. Hadn't—and wouldn't, not with *anyone*. Three can keep a secret, if two are dead, he thought. And they were.

Lucy turned from him, a pout on her face. "You're *fucking impossible*, just like Naomi said."

Buck shrugged. "'Fucking'?"

"Well, she didn't say *that*, but—" Lucy waved her hand over her head "—she said you scared the hell out of her."

Buck didn't respond. He was counting the seconds until Booker made it back out to the car, the officer who'd been behind them now backing up and going around them, nodding.

"Before—you know," Lucy said, and nodded, "*everything* happened—with *Him* and Arn, and—I went to meetings with my dad. AA and anger management, and I learned some things."

"What, you're a psychiatrist now?"

"No," she said.

Booker and the clerk had gone to the rear, to a display case, and the cop pulling up front. And, now, someone had wandered in—a big, hulking guy in an Army-green-ish jacket. He had a phone out, as if he were taking a call, but was turning toward Booker to get a shot of him, real up close and personal.

Buck got the car in gear, an alarm in him flooding him with a raw, propulsive energy.

"You're only sick as your secrets, that's what they say," Lucy quipped, "you ever hear that one?"

She'd turned to him, her arms crossed over her chest, an indignant, miffed look on her face.

Booker, the Pampers and wipes under his arms, and a bag swinging from his right hand, shot from the Radio Shack, then, sprinting, leapt over a parked car, charging away from them as if he were carrying a ball.

"Lucy," he said, "get in the back."

She did that, then slung her arms over the seat, said, "Jeez, what's the big rush all of a—" But she saw it now, too, the cop in his cruiser, after Booker.

"*Shit!*" Buck said, and he backed up, then spun around the row of cars in front of them.

He slid to a stop, then turned up the parallel access, glad he'd thought to boost a fast car, hit the gas and took them, all but flying, around the rear of the mall, and Booker sprinting for his life, blue gumballs and sirens coming on.

No. He wouldn't have it, the cops bringing things to an end here, in a mall parking lot.

At the corner gas station, where they'd agreed to meet if it went bad, he slid to a stop. Booker jumped in alongside him.

"YO!" Booker said. "FUCKING *HIT IT, BOSS!*" He craned his head around to look behind them.

Buck turned onto the frontage road, raced alongside a bus on the far side, paralleling it. Took the entrance onto the highway, and got in front of an eighteen wheeler.

They were waiting for the sound of a siren, or to see blue gumballs flashing, pulling alongside.

When minutes had passed, and neither Lucy or Buck said anything, Booker laughed.

"Well, thanks so much, Booker!" he said, "And, speaking of, somebody shit the bed, or are you two just buttin' your heads over who gets the Happy Sauce for their fries?"

"Thanks, Booker," Buck and Lucy said, virtually in unison.

"Yeah, 'thanks,' that's more like it." Booker did that boxing thing he did with his head. "And, yes, they *were* inside. Only had to get Rambo here his *Deluxe DB Audio Baby Monitor, Two Way Talk Back* 'n' shit, like Ryan said, and had to go over all the X5-QJ-MPBs."

Lucy frowned. "What's that?"

"Stats, n' shit," Booker said. "Ryan gimme a list of... *whatever* to make sure it had enough firepower.

"2.4 Giga Hertz, range of 300 meters, how's that, Boss? Good enough for callin' to your babies?"

"It'll do," Buck said, and he turned onto Highway 5, headed west, then glanced to his right.

Nodded to Booker, who, looking away, nodded in return.

Sometime later, Lucy thrust herself forward, again setting her arms between the headrests. "Where we going?"

The traffic thinned, and Buck drove with his palm slung over the wheel, Booker shotgun, and Lucy having put something on the radio. Outside, the plows mounded snow along the highway.

"Leif's," Buck said.

"What's there?"

"It's not what, but who." He adjusted the heater; always, with boosted cars, the controls were at first mystifying. "Lucy?"

"What?"

"You're going to be okay on the water, right?" There was an awkward silence in the car.

"Lucy," Buck said. "What did I just say?"

"Well, with life preservers and everything... sure."

He craned his head to the side, his brows furrowed, confused, and she sat back in the rear of the car.

"I told you," she said, "when we were working on the canoe that afternoon, remember?"

"What?"

"I can't swim."

Buck laughed, and when she didn't laugh with him, not this time, he caught her eye in the mirror.

"You're kidding, right?"

She glared back at him. Looked out the side window, then cocked her head and shrugged.

"Well, it was... *funny*, you know, since... everything, but, yeah, um, NO, I wasn't kidding. And—" She frowned. "And what does that have to do with anything now anyway? You don't have to swim to be in a fucking canoe, do you? I can hold a paddle."

He turned left, headed up a county road. Split-levels and ranches surrounded by cottonwoods and here and there small lakes, kids skating on rinks shoveled in the snow.

"You ever *been* in a canoe?" he asked.

"No."

"Not even with your mom?"

"God, no," Lucy said. "Are you kidding? She ran from all that stuff as far and fast as she could. She was a city Indin', through and through. Our ending up back on the res was due to my dad—well, being a mess.

"The… you know, language, I got that from my mother, sure, but even more from my—my nimishomis. Enh?!"

"Hey," Booker said. He reached back and affectionately shook Lucy by her shoulder. "I haven't been in a canoe neither. So, fistbump me!"

They did.

"But you think you could paddle, right?" Buck said and, again, he glanced into the rear view.

"Would I have a life preserver?" Booker asked.

Buck all but laughed, it was just too awful. "I wasn't talking to you, Booker. Sorry, can't have you in the canoe, okay? You're the wrong color." Good god. They were just kids. And even having Lucy go out with him those minutes on Lake Superior was asking too much. "We capsize and go into the lake, we'll be dead in twenty minutes if we don't make it to shore."

"So," Booker said, "if seein' me's a problem, I'll just get more covered up 'n' all, and—"

"Work give you time away for the holiday?" Buck asked, determined to keep him in the cities. Safe.

"You meanin'—" he said, a defensive, and hurt, edge in his voice, "*what*, exactly?"

"Your *moms*, she'll cut you loose to be away? Doesn't she have holiday plans for you two?"

Buck cut his eyes at him, which was both a warning and a threat, and Booker's mouth puckered. Yeah, he'd got him, and good. This time, he'd thought to look into his trouble's—*Lucy's*—friends. And even more so, family.

Something Leif had done for him. Booker being a "repeat truant," he'd discovered, his mother invoking the court's help to keep him away from his father and at home.

It'd gotten ugly, Leif'd told him, but the kid, when he wasn't skipping school, was a model student.

"So," Booker said, "since we're gettin' all... nasty and logistical 'n' all, how bout I keep an eye on Ryan and his moms then?" He grinned, having sunk an arrow into a target.

"Didn't think of *them*, did ya?" he said.

He glanced over at Booker, then at Lucy, then at the road again. Traffic. Thought, shit, he'd been so focused on what he needed to do up north, it hadn't so much as occurred to him.

"You, Booker, and Ryan and his mother, aren't going anywhere but where you're supposed to be, which is *staying out of it.*"

"So," Booker said, "knowin' it ain't safe at home, what say, we go up, too, only you drop us off at a Howard Johnson's? Get us some water wings like little kids have, since no one here but you is some... *fuckin' dolphin*, and me and Ryan and his moms'll be bobbin in the pool singin' 'Michael Row The Boat' n shit while you 'n' Lucy get your Rambo on.

"Sound like a five star general plan?"

"Booker?" Buck said.

"Yeah?"

"Shut it,' all right?" He gave Booker a hard, sidelong look, and the car filled with a sullen quiet.

44

Lucy

At Leif's, a clerk directed them to the back office where Ryan had sequestered himself at a computer, Leif hovering over him, his arms crossed over his chest as if against a coming blow, and Lucy ruffling Ryan's hair.

"So, it's you," she said.

"I took the bus over, like Buck told me I should," Ryan said, smiling for her. "No use calling about what I found, since… you're the one who has to see it for it to make any sense."

"Yeah, like, 'hello to you,' too," Booker said. "And see *what*?"

Leif and Buck shared a look, and Lucy and Booker bent closer to what Ryan had brought up. What appeared to be a screen of impenetrable, glowing green code on a black background.

Ryan had set his face inches from the screen, was writing on a pad, there what seemed more code.

"Just make sure," Leif said, "he doesn't get me connected to things I don't want to be connected to, all right?"

He rushed from the office, and Lucy bent closer yet, and Ryan, with the touch of a button, brought up another screen.

"So, Einstein, where'd that other gobbledygook go?" Booker said. "What was all that sayin'?"

Craning his head around, Ryan looked behind them. For Leif. Nodded at Lucy and settled in the chair again.

"Now that he's gone," he said, "give me a second."

He worked the keyboard, and Booker said, "Yeah, you go there, Einstein. What's takin' so long?"

"It's masked. It's got a military grade encryption code."

"You sure this won't come back on Leif?" Buck asked, and Ryan said, glancing at Buck over his shoulder, "Only if he has people in the NSA or the CIA looking into him. Does he?"

Ryan's fingers were dancing over the keyboard, screen after screen of incomprehensible whatevers flashing by.

"This machine is old," Ryan said, that disapproving tone in his voice, scolding. "And slow. And there's *tons* of spyware on it." He rattled something off, then bent into the screen.

"Okay, killed it," he said.

Seconds later, the creature from *Alien*, glossy black head, silver teeth, and slime filled the screen, a red circle with a bar through it flashing over the image. A horn, like that in a submarine sounded. Then something akin to a screeching home burglar alarm, which set their teeth on edge, piercing.

"Shut it off, Ryan!" Lucy said over it.

Ryan bent into the screen, his fingers hammering at the keyboard and the alarm stopped.

"Timed encryption," he said. "Beat it by—" He bent into the screen. "Three seconds."

"What if you hadn't?" Booker asked.

"Goes nuclear," Ryan said, matter-of-factly.

"On the machine there?"

"Yup." Ryan nodded. "Wipes everything."

"Yeah," Booker said, "like, remind me never to let you near my stuff, 'n' if I do, I'll be on your ass so you don't—"

"Ryan?" Lucy said. "What is this?"

She'd bent in closer, trying to make out what was on the screen. Again, a jumble of headings and cryptic messages.

"Our janitor's computer," Ryan said, "they leave it on, so I remote accessed it and took a look. And... presto!"

He brought up an old confirmation photo, in it Lucy's father, and Arn, and—she recognized the twenty some kids there, all in white robes, boys and girls, most of whom she hadn't seen in years.

"St. Peter's," Ryan said, "your confirmation class. The janitor's got a whole lot like this, but—"

Lucy peered at it. "Why would the janitor have—"

"You recognize anyone other than your dad and Arn, Lucy?" Buck asked. "Like, the priest in back there?"

"No," Lucy said.

Ryan hit some keys, and a series of lines popped up, all tethered to boxes with faces in them. "Facial recognition. I used some NSA software I got off the darkweb." He tapped the screen with his finger. "The only other place these faces came together was in another photo." He rattled the keys. "*Here.*"

It was a photo from Lucy's father's Army unit. Her father, Arn, and a third man, behind them, grinning.

"Who is he?" Buck asked.

"A chaplain."

It was as if some mis-fire had taken place. A bomb detonated with a *ffffuuut* only. They were waiting for the explosion. It was right there in the room, but they weren't getting it.

"So there's a chaplain," Buck said, "when isn't there one? They rotate, so he'd show up all over. And Arn and Lucy's dad served together and, after, went to the same church.

"And this chaplain's in Lucy's confirmation class photo. They're all Catholic, right? So, it's just… coincidence."

"Nooo," Ryan replied, in his tone of voice long suffering.

He booted up a memo, one which detailed how a priest who'd proved resistant to church sanctions had been moved, for oversight, first from the archdiocese in Philadelphia, then to Washington, D.C., and finally to Shakopee, in Minnesota, to a reservation post.

"Chaplain Prendergast," Ryan said, and held his hand out, as if he were introducing him. "*Our ChaP.* Who's been on our janitor's computer at St. Pete's. *J.T. Haney's. Deceased.* But not, by any stretch of the imagination, *dead.* He's been working off that computer, but masked about ten thousand times in subroutines."

"God *almighty*," Buck said, here was what had been lurking out of sight for—who knew how long.

Lucy lifted the crucifixes on their necklaces from under her hoodie. Pointed with her index finger to the screen, in the room only the whir of the computer's fan audible.

Buck was the one who said it, though. "*This*… Prendergast's being at St. Peter's gets us nowhere, though, since he can't be linked to—anything… can he?"

"Other than to Haney's computer?" Ryan said. "Haney, who never so much as looked at a dirty picture? And Prendergast didn't either, he just did church business, as himself. All clean."

"Jesus, Ryan," Lucy said.

"But," Ryan said, and he worked the keyboard, strings of phosphorescent green code filling the otherwise black screen top to bottom. "I followed Prendergast's subroutine links—

"—right to," he said, and with a flourish, his index finger raised triumphantly, he pressed the enter key. "—here."

Here was the explosion: photographs of girls' faces—boys' too. Taken at a distance. In a parking lot. Or through shades. Some being violated. At either or both ends. *Here*, too, communications, between the users of the site. Identifying children. Where they could be found.

"Ryan?" Buck said.

"It's a 'message board.' And, yeah, this is *strictly* dark web. You can post, or you can browse, share information or… find resources…. Like, you should see the boards for Nazi stuff."

One man, bearded, highlighted, was in tens of photos, though his face was always turned away.

"Who posts all this?"

"Anybody," Ryan said, "inside the circle." He tapped his index finger on a photo of the bearded man in the lower right hand corner.

"Can't see his face," Booker said. "Not in any those f'in' photos. That's all you got?"

"Yeah," Ryan said, "that's what *he* thinks. And even when I followed

Prendergast's threads—I couldn't prove he'd posted on the board, because, well, on it he posted as J.T. Haney."

"Could be anybody," Buck said. "That's what he'd be whining."

"He always posted from St. Peter's?" Booker asked.

"Yup," Ryan replied. "There are no threads, not one, linking ChaP to anything on that computer. And who'd ever look for dark web stuff coming from St. Peter's anyway, and from a dead guy, right?"

Ryan went through the jumble of bodies, until he got to a photo taken in a hotel. Sallow yellow curtains in the windows, through which, Buck assumed, a parking lot light shone.

Same bearded man. As always, he was facing away from the camera. Silhouetted on those grimy, yellow curtains A girl under him, young, only—she had breasts, which, Ryan pointed out.

"Ryan," Lucy said. "*Please.*"

"No, " he said. "It's important. Watch."

He enlarged the photo, and in such a way the bearded man and the girl were no longer on the screen. Nothing to see, really. An enormous desk and chair up against a far wall. A cheap light fixture on it. To the right of the desk a closet door, and on it a full length mirror. What looked like a moon, to Lucy, in the upper corner.

"See, he got cocky," Ryan said, not realizing what he'd said, and pointed at the screen yet again. "See that?" he said.

They did, Buck, Lucy, and Booker leaning in.

"No idea," Buck said. "What are we supposed to be looking at? What is it? It looks like—"

"A blur? Yeah. At the top of the closet door mirror there, right? See, what Prendergast didn't realize was, *the closet door's come away from the hinge on the top, so it isn't square with the frame.* See, the gap?"

"Yeah, we all get that Sherlock," Booker said, "so, we're lookin at a dirty sock in a closet door mirror?"

"That means the whole *door* is angled down, maybe… ten, fifteen degrees. So it catches the dresser mirror, see? Which, has in it—" Ryan boxed the blur, there an infinite succession of blurs, telescoping into infinity. The first, of which he boxed, then enhanced, then enlarged, so it filled the screen, a face there, head on.

"—a reverse view—one hundred eighty degrees opposite the one in the closet door mirror." They were all agape at it.

"Jesus Christ," Booker said.

"No," Ryan said, "*that's ChaP*—Chaplain Prendergast. ID positive, and no doubt about it. And he's—you know, *with* the girl."

Ryan brought up the photo from the church's relocation letter. Set it alongside Prendergast's from the message board. Kicked back in the chair he was sitting in, so they could really see, then said, nodding to the screen,

"Bragging rights. Couldn't help himself posting photos. It's kind of a vanity. And it's... *risky*. So, to them... *exciting. Look what I've done.* I mean—" he hit a key, "Prendy visited the site... 147 times over six years. Probably had another computer before this one. And—" he hit another key, looked up again, "he added this photo just weeks ago." He glanced over at Lucy. "I'm sorry," he told her. "Really, I am."

Lucy, her heart in her throat, and something going weak in her legs, said, "You're sorry? Why?"

Ryan cursored down, enlarged the girl's face so it all but filled the screen, and Lucy felt her breath catch.

It was Jean.

45

Buck

In the shop, he assembled his things on his table under the fluorescent lights with a sense of purpose, in the scent of machine oil and canvas, Gyg behind him purring off and on, so that he turned to pet her in the cubby hole—which he'd lined with an old sweater and the cat's legs having disappeared under her, as if she were floating.

"What do you say, Old Mouser?"

The cat deepened its purring. It was more a percolation now, and he thought how he'd miss her—which, of course, was stupid. After this weekend, he was all but certain he wouldn't be missing much of anything. He'd gotten his neighbor, Jerry, to agree to feed the cat over the weekend, had handed him a set of keys.

"What, you're going canoeing *now*?" he'd said. "In this weather?"

Snow was forecast, and following it colder temperatures; really, the usual pattern. Only worse.

He'd told Lucy to stop by on Friday morning, but to call first, only he'd be long gone by then, and he having happily sidestepped the *what ifs*, *what thens*, and well wishing.

And they'd already covered what she needed to do once she got up to Grand Marais and the resort, why go over it again? How, for the plan to work, he'd have to leave shore in the canoe with her visible in the bow in her pink hoodie, and her father by then elsewhere.

And if it all went totally and completely FUBAR, he'd warned her, if the shit truly hit the fan, he'd given her a map. On it a direct route to his cousin's place five miles up shore.

"Just tell him I sent you," he'd said, "no explanation needed, and he'll take you where they can't find you."

His phone rang, the shop phone, not the burner Booker had gotten him, and he answered it.

"Buck?" It was Naomi.

"And to what do I owe this great pleasure?" he replied. It sounded nasty, when he'd only wanted a distancing formality.

"Me, being out of my home, that's what."

"I'm sorry."

"You already said that, is there more?"

"I still love you, you know. More than I can say. Just thought I'd mention it. You know, before... whatever."

Naomi let go a sigh.

"Yeah, I know," he said. "Same old, same old, right? How's it going over there at Fairview?"

"Fine." It was almost the very conversation they'd had over dinner, when it had become clear they couldn't continue.

"Could you ever have just... *pretended*... even a little, that you cared? What *you*, being you, did to *me*?" she asked.

Buck slid the Duluth pack over to him, a bulky, leaden weight, given the explosives in it.

"Buck, you there?"

"Yeah," he said, "I'm here." And in it an exasperation that simply leaked out of him. "Naomi," he said, "it was *never* that. That I didn't care. I never, never stopped caring, and that was the problem, see?"

"You mean, for anyone *but* me," she said, "because, when was I ever first in all this? I was *never* your first, Buck—it was always—one... fucking thing or another. Tell me it wasn't...."

When the silence between them had gone on too long, he said, "Look, I've got to go, or I'll be—"

"Buck, *please*, don't do anything... rash, or...."

There was another strained silence on the phone. Part of him liked that, a part of him he'd never much liked in himself.

"You could go to the authorities, you *have* to. And that girl isn't a stray cat. She's going to need help, and a lot of it. You know that, right? You— going after these people, that's not going to fix that. And she's— She's just a *girl*, Buck. You *can't* involve her."

"I'm not."

"You won't?"

"She'll be miles away."

"But why, just this once, can't you—just really *go to the police*? Because I've got a terrible feeling…."

"They *are* the police, Naomi."

Again, there was that silence. And then Naomi said it, and a cry in her voice, of frustration, but more so pain,

"But why *you*? Why does it *always* have to be you?"

"Because from the second she laid eyes on me she sensed I was the kind of person who'd *do* something."

"It's fate then," Naomi said, "is that what you're saying? That she just happened to show up like that?"

"Fate, character, coincidence. What's the difference? Call it God, if you want, I don't care."

"You *can't* live like this, Buck. No one does. It's all too… there's too much of it."

"Wasn't it you who said, *The only thing necessary for the triumph of evil is for good men to do nothing*?"

She cursed. "Don't— *you*— give me any of your *sanctimonious, moralizing bullshit*."

He'd heard it from her before; back when their lives had been… going somewhere.

"Will you do something for me?" he asked.

"*What*?"

"After—you'll see she gets help?"

"Buck—god damn you."

"Yes, or no?"

"I'm calling the police, Buck."

"Promise me, if there's one thing you will *not* do, it's that. Nome? Tell me you won't." There was only static on the phone, and he added, "And, hey, what do *you* know, anyway, that you could tell them? Or that, even if you tried, you wouldn't be talking to crooked cops?"

When she didn't answer, he said, "I love you, Naomi," and he cut her off, then set the phone, face up, on his drafting table.

Moments later, the phone, set on vibrate, danced and rattled insistently toward the edge the table. He set his mug down alongside the phone to stop it from falling to the floor.

On the table, he had the 249, the .38, and boxes of bullets. It was just a matter of packing now, and sticking to the plan. Lucy would hang tight with her father, go up to the resort. At some point, Arn and the others would follow what would appear to be Lucy and her father up shore.

Only, by the time Arn and company and he came into contact, Lucy would be snug in her cabin, a world away.

Ryan had printed off a map of the resort and surrounding area for him, and in the legend, there'd been a list of trails, on the longest, the satellite cabin, so he could get to it if he had to.

Which he wouldn't think about, what he'd do if Arn and company didn't follow him up shore.

No, he took in everything he'd assembled on the table. Firearms. Neoprene half suits. Outdoor clothing. Sorrels. Mitts. Crampons and rope and his ice axe and ice spikes. And, set on top it all was a palm-sized foil package, on it an Indian chief in a headdress, tobacco.

It was a veritable mound of gear, but exactly what you needed on the north shore of Superior in this kind of weather if you were visiting the ice caves, and it would all fit just so in the canoe.

Which he could make out through the window in the side door of the shop, on the top of Leif's truck.

A red canoe. You couldn't miss it.

46

Lucy

"Bebbe Gurl," her father was saying, digging through the clothes hamper. "We need to get going here, all right?"

He'd come in well after midnight, but even then he'd risen shortly after five, knocking around and waking her, too.

"You know where my parka is?"

In her bed, she was forcing her eyes open, trying to wake herself. "All that's in the back storage bin. I put it there after you didn't go out with Arn. Since you weren't using it."

"Thanks," he said, and there was more thumping about in the trailer, her father talking to himself. Then he was standing over her. "Come on, Lucy, get up," he said, shaking her shoulder affectionately. "I made you some eggs and bacon and even some biscuits."

She rose on her elbow. "Now?" She was afraid she might have to run to the bathroom for nerves. If she did—well, there it was, and she was out of the bed and brushing by him, "Gotta pee, Daddy," she said, and ducked into the bathroom and shut the door.

She turned on the shower. Then vomited into the toilet. Got her clothes off and stepped under the hot water, trying to calm herself. The hot water made her finger throb and itch. And the aluminum splint—doctor's orders, it had to stay on another three weeks—burned her bare skin.

It all seemed... so everyday, she couldn't believe Buck was already up there, doing—what was he doing?

He'd only said, "You just stick with the plan, that's all you have to do. And then *stay out of it*. Can you do that?" He'd made her promise, but she'd intended no such thing.

There came a knock at the bathroom door.

"Leave some hot water, Bebbe Gurl."

She shut the tap off, got her sweats on; she could pack, then dress again. She stood in the mirror, her face showing nothing. She had breasts now. Which made her think of Jean.

That did it.

She brushed her teeth. Then slunk out and up the hallway to where her father was sitting at the table. He went to the stove, then brought the skillet over. Shucked the eggs, bacon, and biscuits onto her plate.

"What's all the fuss?" she said.

"We didn't have much of a Christmas, Bebbe Gurl, since I was working, but I'm going to make up for that, all right?" and there he scared her, touched her nose with his index finger, and added, "Up north we'll celebrate! How about that for a present wrapped in a bow?!"

His pupils were just barely there, small as thumbtacks, and she realized he was speeding again. They were both acting now, as if in some horrible show. Proof positive her father was up to something. Really, though, what could he know? Certainly not what she did.

When he ducked into the bathroom, she looked in the drawer under the toaster. The Glock was gone. Of course.

By the time her father returned she was hunched over her plate, shoveling in the eggs.

"Three eggs, Daddy?" she said.

"We've got to be fortified for the day, Luce, it's cold out there." He bent theatrically into the front window. He was, truly, a bad actor. Checked the thermometer. "Seventeen here, it's gotta be near zero up there." He did a little jig, and, really, he *was* a good dancer, could swing like nobody—but this?

"Daddy?"

"The Exploder's all fuelled up." That he was joking made her all the more nervous. That's when he pulled his fast ones on her.

"When?"

"Last night. Thought it'd save us one stop before we go, we could get there earlier—" He lifted his wrist, checked his watch "—and that way we'll have more time to ourselves."

Lucy smiled. It hurt.

"Think you could be ready in twenty?"

She nodded. But in her mind, she asked herself— Maybe what she was going to do to her father when they got up there was... just—all *wrong*? But then she thought of Jean. And at the thought of Jean she hardened. *No.* And, of course, she didn't for a second intend to leave it all up to Buck.

"Yes, Daddy," she said, and truly grinned now. Light as life itself. "I'm all ready."

47

Buck

Out from the shore of Lake Superior, he J-stroked over the crest of a wave, let the trough carry him, as if surfing. Steered with his paddle. Looked left, into shore yet again, there the caves he'd come for in all their otherworldly beauty, some a hundred, a hundred fifty feet high, glacier blue-green and bedecked in curtains of cascading, alabaster ice.

And everywhere stalagmites. And stalactites. Humped and otherworldly ice, mounded all over, and everything bulging here and there with hoar frost and weirdly crystal-furred.

It would be below freezing in the caves, but here on the water it was warmer. He passed an old buoy, a good fifteen feet or so high, a famous summer spot, good off-shore anchorage for the larger sailboats that went farther north. He looked behind him. It was here. Wasn't it? What he and Naomi had stumbled upon all that time ago? Here, too, reaching out into the water from shore, was a skirt of the ice shelf that the snowmobilers used, one dotted at intervals with the charred remains of campfires, deadwood, and half-burned limbs that craggily reached out of the ice. He looked overhead. It was after seven in the morning, barely light out, and a storm coming in, clouds to the northwest.

A wave crashed over the canoe. Backside. Buck was shaken by it, but then, he'd prepared for that, was using a skirt. And the canoe was a dream, tracked true and straight. Still, he couldn't get careless. He checked his watch. He had to find the exact spot, and soon.

The cold wasn't the problem—he had his neoprene half suit on under his gear, but that would all be for naught unless....

He paddled farther north along the shoreline. Just more of the same. Gray rock faces hundreds of feet high, and trees shellacked in ice. Wasted an hour nosing the canoe into shore, time and again hopeful, only to see, yet again, no. And each ice cave different, beautiful, but not what he was looking for.

So for a moment he despaired. Dumb idea, that he'd be able to find it all these years later. The place where he and Naomi had—happily—once had lunch and marveled at the ice.

Back down near the buoy, scanning the shoreline, he thought to resort to his fall back plan, which wasn't good.

Sure, hitting them at the satellite cabin would get the job done—he shoved an energy bar into his mouth, something that was supposed to be chocolate, only it tasted like wax—but not in a way he could survive.

A piece of peanut had stuck in his teeth, and he lifted his head, probing his teeth with his tongue, then tossed the remainder of the bar onto the ice, disgusting thing, where a bird might come for it.

How, really, did they survive in this climate without real shelter? And even as he was thinking it, a jay darted over the canoe, snatched the remainder of the bar up, then flew into the cave just off the bow.

Seconds later, it shot up into a tree on shore, where it made quick work of the bar, never having flown out of the cave.

In the pines there, watching him, and having eaten, the diindiisi was waiting to see if there might be more. Buck's brows knotted, before the thought came to him: *A bird had just saved his life.*

He stood in the mouth of the cave, under a soaring arch of ice and having drawn the canoe up onto the ice shelf behind him, and snowmobile tracks there leading to the south.

Perfect.

Going in, he all but held his breath. The ice under his feet clear as glass, maybe six inches or even less in places, and the void under him seemingly depthless, and here the currents of warmer water making for the thin ice, a kind of natural river, which he followed, then farther in yet, as if he were walking on water. Into a many-arched blue and white concatenation, the ice here glowing in the morning light, the stalactites humped and ridged, as if in some otherworldly cathedral, which had been and no doubt still was what made this cave a destination.

At the back, he stood beneath what he'd been looking for, in him a certain relief, but dread, too.

The blowhole. Where the jay had flown out. He'd remembered it as having a larger diameter. He stood under it, took his ice hammer and a barbed ice spike from his pocket. Either the ice would hold, or it wouldn't.

He hammered the spike in, and the ice held—but only. It fractured when he put his full weight on it.

"Mo," he said, shit.

He tried higher up, as far as he could reach. Better. That spike held. He could, he thought, tell himself it would get better yet higher up—or, it could be yet more porous. Worse. Still, the cave was perfect. The snowmobile route to it. The canoe outside, red and visible as a flare. He'd carry the Duluth pack in, set all that up. Then wait outside for Arn and the others. Duck in when they came around the point on their snow machines, having seen the canoe. And while Arn and the others stumbled about inside in the dark looking for Lucy and her father—they'd need to talk to them—he'd go up and out the blowhole.

Once out, and certain they were all inside, he'd set off the explosive. End it all, take out the ice underfoot, too, so any and everything that had been in the cave would be carried out into Lake Superior, the water off the shelf hundreds of feet deep, and Lake Superior, as it was said, never giving up her dead.

He craned his head back, eyeing the icy hoar in the throat of the blowhole. Maybe, just maybe, he *could* climb out in time. It was only a hundred feet to the top, and the opening there. He held his hand up, shielding his eyes against the circle of blue-white light.

The jay darted back down the hole, its wings clattering airily, then shot out the front. He stood, his face lifted and eyes closed, so that the light cast a violet glow through his eyelids, and thought—

If only he could fly.

48

Lucy

They stopped in Hinkley on the way up, "just to stretch their legs" as her father put it, but her father taking his time, insisting she read the display on the Great Hinkley Fire in the rest stop, there a tableau of the disaster, pictures and the whole bit, men with shovels burying the 418 "victims of the fire" in long, trench-like graves, while around them charcoal black, limbless trees smoldered, and her father, legs crossed, foot bobbing, drinking a coffee and in a near implosive state of agitation, as if swallowing something he truly did not like, checking his watch, time and again, until he finally marched outside to make a call.

When he finally ducked back inside, Lucy asked, "Who were you talking to out there?"

"Burgess," he said, and grimaced. "Just had to make sure that we had our plans in order."

Lucy shrugged, tried not to appear too interested, when she was sick with the possibility of things going wrong.

"Let's go, Daddy," she said, "we want to get there before they do, don't we? Otherwise, Chief Burgess could ask you to do something. And, I think I'm going to have to lie down—" she stretched, yawning "—before we go out."

He checked his watch again. Rapped his knuckles on the table, then turned to her and grinned.

"Anything for you, Bebbe Gurl," he said, somehow pleased at what she'd said, and they got on the highway.

Later, at a service area near Duluth, her father was paying for the gas inside when a black Lincoln pulled in behind a tanker, over it an enormous sign on stilts that read: *Welcome to Sky Harbor Airport and Seaplane Base, Duluth,* and under that, *Gateway to the North Woods.* Planes with floats and wheels were angled from the tanker where they'd been fuelled. A plane bumped down the runway behind the station and rose into the air, then banked to the south toward the Twin Cities.

The driver of the Lincoln slowly turned his head in Lucy's direction, and their eyes met. Booker. He had to have been following them the entire way up, and had to pop up just now.

And then she felt something softening in her, touched that Booker'd done it. He'd promised he'd be with her, and here he was. *Not now*, she silently mouthed, and her father setting his hand on her shoulder.

"Hey, Bebbe Gurl," he said, "somebody look at you sideways? You see somebody you know?"

"Just some a-hole," she said. "You know, giving me that 'Aren't you Indians supposed to be dead?' look."

"I got you the bag of chips you asked for," he said.

"Thanks, Daddy," she replied.

They got in the Explorer and, when her father turned to check the highway for traffic before he pulled out, Lucy glanced to her right. If he caught sight of Booker in the Lincoln following—

But he wasn't there, just a dented minivan and a overweight guy pumping gas into it.

Her father turned onto the highway, nudged her with his shoulder.

"Why so serious?"

She had to think of some way to get her father to stop, so she could call Booker on her burner. Tell him to go back.

Earlier, when he'd asked, "Who you talking to?" she'd replied, "Nobody," all snarky, and he'd snatched her phone from her. She couldn't risk him doing that again.

They traveled in silence for some time. "You going to eat those chips or just sit with them on your lap, kiddo?"

She hadn't even realized she was all but crushing the bag. She glanced down at it. Vinegar and Salt. Tore the bag open. *Ugh!* She hated vinegar, but they were super salty, which was the point.

"Mind if I—?" her father said.

"Sorry, Daddy," she said, handing the bag to him, "I was, you know, just thinking about how nice it was to be doing something together." It was a horrible lie; but it was half true.

The two of them passed the bag back and forth, and at one point her father jokingly said,

"Penny for?"

"I'm thirsty, that's what I'm thinking," she said and smiled, and they both laughed.

She'd been thinking about how, after she got done what Buck had asked her to do, she was going to find Arn and put a bullet in his head. And Prendergast, first, if she could get to him.

She fingered the necklaces under her shirt. Jean's and hers. Laid her hand over her pocket to be sure she had Buck's knife.

"It's good we're coming up, Bebbe Gurl," her father said. "It's about time we did something fun, right?"

"That's for sure," she said, staring up the road.

49

Buck

On a bluff behind the resort, one that guarded it from the prevailing north west wind, he waited, binoculars pressed to his eyes. Watched the highway for Lucy's father's blue Explorer.

But nothing, just snow driven by the wind, endlessly snaking across the asphalt there.

As in all real-world confrontations, time had to be managed. And, equally, the appearance of things, most of which would not be what they seemed. The canoe he'd stashed behind a cabin. And who would think anything of it? What was more common than a canoe in Northern Minnesota?

When Lucy and her father came in, they'd unpack, but not go out, since they'd be waiting for Arn and the others.

When Lucy had gotten it done, she'd move the Explorer around to the side of the cabin, and then, and only then, would he come down. Change clothes, get the canoe on top, bright as could be.

He'd drive it down to the dock, get it on the water, then stow the Duluth pack between the seats. Arn couldn't miss it. Arn, who was watching even now. Arrogant prick that he was, he'd parked on a moraine, out in the open. In his yellow, hooded anorak, he was glassing the resort, smoking, the lenses of his binoculars facing the sun and catching the light.

No doubt, over in the Middle East he'd been a liability. The others had carried more than a good deal of his weight. Arn, a weak link. Too full of himself, especially now, to think *he* was being hunted.

Buck laid his hand on the .38 there alongside him. If it hadn't been for his needing to get to all of them through Arn, he'd have tracked him down and gotten to him already.

The plan Lucy'd heard, through her father, was for the group to arrive by noon and settle into the cabins.

Arn had shown up hours earlier. He'd circled the resort to be sure Lucy and her father hadn't already gotten in—they hadn't—and had driven to the overlook, where he'd parked and got out, binocs in hand. And there he was now, still. And what was he seeing?

Buck turned sharply to his right, to take in the resort. Leif's pickup in the trees, what would be, in Arn's thinking, just another deer hunter having left his rig there. And Arn and the others would want guests around, or a hunter like this, who could corroborate their story, place them in their cabins when they'd been... elsewhere, doing what they had been doing for... who knew how long.

Well, now it only remained for Lucy and her father to come in, and they'd get to it.

And here in the moment a calm before everything was in motion. Before Arn came down, and the others arrived. For their happy little snowmobiling once-Army-buddies-now-policemen get-together. And, hopefully, ChaP—Chaplain Prendergast, the one who'd found the vulnerable children in his parish and had first groomed them for the others—would be with them.

There'd been a storm advisory warning people to stay in. Plummeting temperatures, three feet of snow, high winds forecast. Perfect, Buck thought. He had exactly the window he needed.

A deer came down to the salt lick the owner of the resort had set up in a stand of pines. Lifted its head.

Was someone other than Arn out there? He swung the binocs in a circle, searching the trees around the resort. An office and six cabins. All in a semicircle that opened onto the lake.

The cops had the cabins on one side of the office, Lucy's father's the furthermost opposite, the Honeymoon Cabin.

And there it was, all but invisible in a dense stand of pines, off a spur

Wayne Johnson

of the main road in: A black Lincoln. He'd all but missed it. And, damnit, now he saw the others, too. Three cars, and even at a distance he could make out the drivers, and not one of them familiar.

Buck dropped the binocs, so they hung from his neck, lifted his wrist to check his watch.

In minutes Lucy'd get to it. He took the package of tobacco from his pocket, poured a portion from it into his palm. Made a circle of tobacco at his feet, dotted it at the top, bottom, right side, left side.

North, South, East, West. There, it was done. He was ready. And... whatever, or... *something*, help him.

293

50

Lucy

At the resort office they checked in, got word on the coming weather. "If you're goin' somewhere, best to do it in the next few hours or so," the manager, a balding, middle-aged guy in a green sweater said, and handed her father the key. They went to cabin six, where there was a pine bough on the stoop.

Her father kicked it out of the way, just as Buck had said he would. Buck's *I'm here*. Didn't think twice. Inside, it was cold. Typical cabin. Blond pine paneling. Two beds. There was a phone in the room on the desk, and Lucy picked it up, as if just inadvertently, got a dial tone. Took note of the number there under the keypad as her father locked the door behind them and got the space heater going. She ducked into the bathroom. Cell service, no bars.

On a piece of paper, she scribbled down the cabin's phone number and slipped it into her pocket. Flushed the commode, just to make it all seem ordinary, then bent into the mirror over the sink.

There were two glasses on the shelf there, wrapped in plastic, and she carried them out. "Look, Daddy," she said. "For your protection. Isn't that nice?" She removed the plastic. "After those chips, I am *so* thirsty!" She checked the refrigerator in the corner. There were complementary sodas in it. Coke, and Dr. Pepper, and 7 Up, also as Buck had said there would be.

Her father was at the window fronting the courtyard. He pulled the curtain back, but kept his head behind the wall. Yeah, he was up to something, that was for sure, but she'd fix that.

"I'm gonna have one of these sodas, Daddy," Lucy said, "got pretty dry eating all those salty chips."

"You want some?" She held up one of the cups. Pasted a Betty Crocker smile on her face.

"What's there?" he asked.

"I'll take the Dr. Pepper," she replied, and nodded, "since I know you don't like it. So, you want the Coke?"

She had the capsule right in her jacket pocket. Her father'd been a Coke drinker forever.

"No beer?"

"No, Daddy. No beer. I'm sorry."

From the window, he looked over his shoulder. "Pour me a glass of whatever, Luce."

Her back to him, she got the cans out. Popped the tops. Emptied the capsule into her father's cup, then filled it with soda.

"Here you go," she said, turning to face him.

He lifted it from her outstretched hand, took a tentative sip from the rim. Winced. But she was cautiously pleased. He was going to drink it, after all.

"Wow. That is *sweet*, but I *am* thirsty."

"Well, we've got sandwiches to go with it, if you reach into the bag there, Daddy. I made 'em with the leftover meatloaf." That would do it, for sure, since her father always drank something when he ate.

And, she'd made the meatloaf extra salty, too.

"Aww, Bebbe Gurl," he said, "you just think of everything, and I do appreciate that."

She jumped up onto the bed opposite, sat back against the headboard and plumped the pillows, faked a yawn.

"You mind if I stretch out here, Daddy, and I'll get up in a bit and we can do whatever, okay?"

He set his cup on the television. Scrabbled in the bag and brought up the sandwiches. Scooted around the bed to hand one to her, then, stepping back to the television, bit into his.

"Mmm. That is just right. Thanks, Bebbe Gurl."

"Thank you, Daddy," she said. "And what's the rush? Why don't you take your soda and sit? These beds are *real* comfy."

The damn soda. Was he going to—accidentally?—knock it off the television, pacing like he was?

The room had come to be filled with a strange tension—her father doing that PTSD thing he did with his head. Craning it one direction, then the other. Which had her heart racing.

Her father smiled, picked up the soda—and she thought, relieved, *drink it, now!*—but he set it on the dresser and turned to her.

He checked his watch and glanced up. "You know I love you, Bebbe Gurl," he said.

"Well, I love you too, Daddy."

Standing in front of the dresser, he was thinking how to put it, what he had to say.

"So, Bebbe Gurl, I'm sorry," he said, "this big ol' blizzard coming in means I've got to meet with the boys now, today, since getting to that satellite cabin will be all but impossible tomorrow. I didn't have it in me to tell you there in Hinkley that our doing anything this afternoon is off."

She felt herself split, just then; as if the very air had been kicked out of her, and her eyes swimming in her head. And her otchit, her infinitely larger self, there again, in her shock. *Wait*, it said.

Something would come to her. It had to.

"But," he took a sip of the soda, winced, then set it back on the dresser, "oof, god, but that's sweet. Anyway, this is better. We'll have the whole day tomorrow. Okay? We can..." he shrugged "see how it goes, all right?"

"But you *promised*," Lucy said. "And—" she'd pitched her voice so she sounded hurt, but was trying, desperately to think of something, anything at all, that could keep him in the cabin.

"What, Bebbe Gurl? Does it really make a difference? Whether it's today or tomorrow?"

There was something all but hysterical in her, wanting to come out, but even now she couldn't say it.

Any of it. Because she could see he was "in a state," as her mother had called it so long ago, was dangerous.

"You good here?" he asked.

"Why, shouldn't I be?"

They held each other's eyes, the heater fan rattling in the silence, each willing the other to say something.

It was right there, dying in her. *Daddy, they—*

And he was thinking this was just about Jean, and maybe—maybe he'd found out something about Rose, and here was her chance to tell him what she'd been holding back all this time.

They... hurt me, Daddy, she wanted to say, it was right there, stuck in her throat, but she couldn't.

And when it couldn't go on any longer, her father nodded, then said, "All right then."

And it was with his soldier's *Plan the Work, Work the Plan* efficiency that he threw his gear together. Jacket, hat, mittens, all rustlings and snappings. Picked up his black tote, in it—she knew, because she'd looked—his rifle and the Glock. Slung it from his shoulder by the webbed strap, his face all angles, and a hardness in him that said *don't get in my way.*

"So, Luce?" he said.

"What?" On the bed she'd drawn her knees up, was hugging them, her mind a hot, stupefied blank.

"Like I told you I would, I'm going to take care of things now, okay? Once I'm out, you lock the door with the bolt and safety chain. And like you promised, you stay put. We clear on that?"

When she didn't answer, only looked away, her father stepped over to the bed and kissed her cheek.

"Sorry," he told her, "really," and, backing out of the unit, he nodded, said, "Bye, Bebbe Gurl," then pulled the door closed.

She waited what seemed an eternity—though by her watch it was only minutes—and went to the door and locked it. Got the cup of drugged soda off the dresser and flushed it down the toilet.

He'd taken his shaving kit out, had opened it, as if he'd meant to shave, there the gutta-percha handle of the .38. His back-up piece.

She took in a sharp breath. She couldn't think—but the gun in the kit said everything.

Her face in the mirror stared back at her; blinking.

There was a knock at the front door, and she turned from the mirror. Got the .38 out of the kit.

It was too early. Or had Buck seen her father going out and come down to see what had happened? She stepped to the right of the door by the window, parted the curtain the slightest.

Good god. It was Booker. And Ryan and his mother?!

She laid the .38 on the dresser, turned the deadbolt, undid the safety chain, then threw the door open and, catching Booker by his jacket, she yanked him toward her, so he as much fell as was pulled into the room.

"Don't stand there, Ryan," she barked at him. "Get in here. And you too, Kitty, now."

Ryan and his mother stepped inside.

"Hey," Booker said, "you gotta fuckin' lotta nerve!" He'd come around behind her.

"Booker—" She had her face in his. "*What* were you *thinking*, bringing them—" she raised her hands, clenching at the air. "Close the fucking door," she said, and Ryan's mother shut it.

"Are you… OUT OF YOUR *FUCKING MIND*?!" she said.

"Hey," Booker said, "who's nuts here? I *tole* you one of ChaP's guys would come back to the trailers, to Ryan's and—" Booker pointed his finger in Lucy's face. "And they *did*, too. Only, Ryan called, and I came and got 'em fore they got shot 'n' all, so there wasn't nothin' for it but to bring 'em. What was I 'sposed to do? And, hey, Kitty insisted, she's got a bone to pick with these a-holes."

Ryan's mother, with her pudding bowl haircut, said, "We help now, good timing."

Lucy checked her watch. *What* was Ryan's mother talking about? She had to move her father's truck, and in minutes. Buck would be coming down to put the canoe on it.

She'd threaded her fingers through her hair, was clasping her skull, staring, mumbling, "No, no, no, no…!"

"Just *tell me*, Luce," Booker said, and she did, and her other self, the one her otchit talked to, stepped right up into her.

It was terrifying, having it come out, and right into daylight.

"Look," Booker said, when she'd finally stopped ranting, "that your old man marched off into the woods by his lonesome makes it all right. What you got going can still work."

"How?" she said.

"Let Ryan's *mom* go out with Buck in the canoe 'stead of you. That solves everything, don't it?"

Her mind a hot, tangled knot of impossible solutions, Lucy said, "Come on, Booker, really? *Kitty* in the canoe?"

"'And why not? 'Cause, that *was* the plan, right? You and Buck head out, and as soon's Arn and the others followed, Buck drops you on shore. You come back here and wait it out, and your old man knocked out cold. Only difference is, your ol' man's out there and gonna make a mess, and he's gotta be stopped."

"Booker," Lucy warned.

"No," Booker said, "it's as simple as this: Somebody's got to go after your pops, and it can *only be you*. Come on. You give Ms. Chen here your gear, your hoody 'n' all, and to anybody, they'll think you're the one in the front of the canoe. Just like it was s'posed to be, and it all still works.

"And, seriously," Booker added, "the only person your old man's *not* gonna gun down out there now is *you*, Lucy. 'Cause, he don't know Buck from a hole in the fuckin' wall, see?

"You're the only one can make some sense to your pops, and there's no getting' around it."

Lucy turned to Ryan's mother. "Can you paddle?"

She gave Lucy a belligerent look. Her face was still bruised from that night weeks earlier.

"She doesn't have to know how to paddle," Ryan said, "sternsman does all the steering, or, that is, he *can*."

"Yeah," Lucy said. "Thank you, Daniel Boone."

"No," Ryan said. "I looked it up on line. And—"

"Enough," Lucy said, and checked her watch again. A good fifteen minutes had gone by.

She'd have to move the truck, and now, to bring Buck down. She swung her father's suitcase from behind the bed. Threw out the things of his she'd brought, a green, rubberized canvas rain suit. Boots. Mittens. A sweater and down vest. At the dock, Buck would wear the army jacket he'd sewn the patches on—and Arn, seeing him there, would mistake him for her father.

That would be the sticking point. Would Arn, seeing Buck there like that, and Kitty in her pink hoodie, preparing to launch the canoe, think it was her and her father? Would it work?

"What about you, Ryan?" Lucy asked. "What're you going to be doing while your mother's out there with Buck?"

"I'll come with you."

Christ. He would think that. "Ryan, no," she said.

She ducked out, moved the Explorer around to the side, and came back in, the three of them, Booker, and Ryan, and Ryan's mother, studying her. "I can find him, your dad," Ryan said.

"Ryan," Lucy shot back, all but rolling her eyes, "this *isn't* the time," and right there she and Booker glanced at each other.

There was a knock at the door and Lucy opened the door a crack, the safety chain still attached.

"They're coming. Arn, and Burgess and the others." Buck bent closer, put his face in the opening. "Hey, what's with the door, Lucy. Open it, will you?" he said. "Your old man is out, right?"

"Yeah, he's out," Lucy said, and when Buck's eyes narrowed, she removed the safety chain and nodded him inside.

51

Buck

To anyone approaching the resort, it would have seemed idyllic. More than picturesque. The log cabin office in tall pitch pine twinkling with colored Christmas lights and the curtained windows warmly aglow. The six cabins set in a semi circle around it all facing the shoreline, beyond which stretched Lake Superior, an ocean of blue-gray water. A pre-storm dark had descended, a stillness in it so the smoke from the office chimney spun lazily and lifted into the trees.

And into it came Arn, first, in his rig, and the others behind in sedans, Arn and Burgess hauling trailers with snow cats on them, and last, in his black Cadillac, was Prendergast.

Arn went into the office to get the paperwork done, and a good fifteen minutes later he stepped back out. Let the screen door slap closed behind him, then took in the lake from the stoop. Buck, at the dock pretending to be busy with the canoe, lifted his hand and waved. Ryan's mother in the front, Lucy's dirty pink hoodie pulled over her jacket, waved too.

And even as Arn was jogging down the shoreline to them, Buck pushed off. "Pull, Kitty," he said, and she did.

She hadn't said anything since she'd dressed in the bathroom of the cabin and they'd gone out.

It was crazy, what Lucy's father had done, and the mess he was making of things, but—everything was always six ways sideways when the shit hit the fan and the only thing to do was to roll with it, use it, the mess, and Lucy having gone out with Ryan to find her father now.

But not before she'd made sure the manager was aware she and her father would be canoeing.

"Just up to the ice caves and back," she'd told him in the office and motioned to Buck at the dock.

Arn called out to him now, "*Hey, Lee! Wait up!* Where you goin'?! We're havin' our meetin'!"

Buck held up his hand. A kind of question mark, then made an arrow with his arm. Up the lake.

Here was the moment of truth. Either Arn would recognize Lee's going up to the caves with Lucy for the opportunity it was, a chance to make them go away for good, or he wouldn't. Even in good weather people went missing on Lake Superior, it happened all the time. Never to be seen again, and never so much as a body. Buck glanced back over his shoulder.

Arn was running from shore to the others in that flatfooted way of his. Arn, he could see in the set of his shoulders, bent on something, and Burgess stepping from his car, and—who was it with him?

Two men, neither of whom had been in the photos Ryan pulled up off the internet. But even at a glance, Buck recognized them, all the same. Squared shoulders, pants "bloused" in their boots.

Ex-military. And meaning business. And Prendergast. Out of his Cadillac now and calling to Arn. Prendergast in black, and the white of his collar at his throat, his cleric's suit on, for show.

Nearly a head taller than the others, he threw his arms up, taking exception to something.

And then, the canoe slid around the shoreline, and Buck was going to say, "Dig, and pull," to Kitty, but she was doing that already.

It was a good forty minutes to the buoy, and the wind was beginning to blow hard and he bent into it.

52

Lucy

Her father was all but impossible to follow, even in the new snow. And the pines here were dense, so they left dry, bare aprons under them, which her father was moving between, going where, she had no idea. He was using every trick he'd taught her to avoid being tracked.

Find hard surfaces. Use a pine bough, or whatever was on hand, to erase tracks. Cross irregular terrain features.

They'd followed him up a dry streambed, one with ankle-punishing stones in it, for a good mile. Ryan had fallen behind, but she'd known he would. Still, it made things harder, and in the worst of it, she truly slowed, so he wouldn't get a sprain, which anyone could.

Behind her Ryan called out, "Stop!"

She'd lost her father's tracks so far back she was all but in a state of despair looking for signs and not seeing so much as one. *Just one. Please.* She was bartering in her mind. *Just one.* But the rocks here didn't show tracks, and the good half mile up she *could* see, they wouldn't.

She glanced behind her and her heart fell. Ryan had wandered off while she hadn't been paying attention. Just the steeply pitched streambed there, and no Ryan. She'd have to go back. She turned, following the streambed, dreading what she might find.

A good block down, there was Ryan sitting on a rock slab,

backpack out and his laptop on his thighs and his phone in hand.

"What do you think you're doing?" she called out. Approaching him, it was all she could do not to weep, and she stumbled, caught herself, but barely.

"Jesus, Ryan!" she said.

Buck would die if she couldn't find her father, and here was Ryan at his... Asperger-y worst.

He was holding his phone to his face, then stretching it arm's length, as if taking a photo of himself, which, just now—

"RYAN?!"

He glanced up at her, blinking. Nodded to himself, then held the phone out. "Here."

"Are you *out of your fucking mind*?" she said. But when it became clear he wasn't going to be budged, she climbed down to him.

"Just look," he replied, and since there was no way around it, she did. Look. From a distance. On the screen the streambed and so many symbols and things over it she could hardly make out any of it.

"*What* am I supposed to be looking at, Ryan?" she said, in her voice something that scared her—true, and total, despair.

"Print signature. In the streambed. He turned off... right up there." Ryan pointed. "Near ninety degrees."

The only thing she could think to say was, "Print signature?"

She was, really, coming to the end of it. She didn't have time for Ryan's weirdness now. Anything but. He lifted the phone closer. On the screen was a glowing red circle, one circumscribing a picture of Ryan's boot sole—he'd taken a picture of his *boot sole*?

"Oh—my—God, Ryan."

"No, see?" he said, and brought up another picture, one of the streambed, and leading up it were progressively smaller orange circles, ones that turned, at one point, off the streambed and over the embankment to their right.

"This way," Ryan said, and he slapped his laptop closed, which, she could see now, he'd wired to his phone.

He slid the computer into his backpack, the one he'd taken to school every goddamned day, and sprung to the right and marched off the streambed, across a space of snow and leaves.

She lunged, from behind him, caught his jacket as if catching a sail, one filled with air.

"Ryan. *No,*" she said. It was like talking to a dog.

"Yes," he said.

He held his phone up again, swept it left to right, so the phone camera took in the ground in front of them. Four or five red circles on the phone camera now, and each spaced a pace apart.

Ryan used his finger to draw a glowing, neon green line through the circles. Up and through the trees to their right.

"It's a pattern. It's there, we just couldn't see it, your father's boot prints. Because of all of the rocks and everything." He was going to hold the phone out again, and she waved him off. "It's a program the NSA came up with for tracking people where there isn't much ground cover," he said.

"How far?" she demanded.

He pointed to a rock outcropping, a fall of scree below it. "We can shoot from, like there, where we'll lose his tracks again. I'll catch the pattern again and we can follow it."

She set her knuckled fist on her forehead. She'd been wrong about him. All over again.

"You go first," she said, and swung him in front of her, Ryan stumbling along with the phone held out.

"And Ryan?"

"What?"

"You did good," she said, and suddenly he wasn't stumbling much, if at all.

53

Buck

Out on Lake Superior the headwind had gotten nearly impossible, and in it the waves were punishing, a stinging pellet snow raking down out of the clouds bunched darkly overhead. He pulled, now, one overly long stroke on his right, which brought the canoe around to face the dark immensity of Lake Superior—the bow had to cut the incoming waves or they'd capsize. Craning his head back, he scanned the shoreline, desperate to see the buoy, and the buoy nowhere in sight.

Kitty—he was thinking of her that way now—turned the canoe to the right with a draw when it began to drift left.

Could they have passed the buoy? But he was sure the shoreline he was seeing here was south of it.

They'd fallen behind, making poor time—which was alarming, since they couldn't have Arn, and Burgess, and Prendergast and the others on their snow machines catching up to them—and the buoy not yet in sight.

Truth was, he couldn't have kept going without Ryan's mother in the bow, anyway. She was bent nearly double. Worked like a machine. Had more than won his respect. He had synchronized his strokes to hers, to keep the canoe on point, but she'd caught on, and almost immediately. Still, the waves were every minute growing larger, cresting now nearly head high. And because they were both in the canoe, he couldn't use the skirt, and they were crusted in ice, and the temperature had fallen precipitously. He'd heard what he'd thought was the buzz of a snowmobile, but the sound carried down from the north. He'd given Kitty his neoprene suit, assuming she'd need it more than he would. Lucy's father's rain gear had helped, but it didn't breathe, and he was all but sweat-drenched in it, and he was freezing now. But what matter. He'd get Kitty on shore, if only that, get done in the cave what he had to, and he swung the canoe around, and Kitty dug in, and they, pulling for all they were worth, cleared a nag head just north, coming into the full brunt of the wind, Kitty not backing off for a second, and his arms burning.

But here was the point and the buoy, and he called out to Kitty, "Right side, hard strokes!"

In they went, until they slid off the water onto the ice shelf. Kitty, getting out of the canoe, slipped and all but fell, and he caught her under her arm, lifted her to her feet and thrust her in front of him. Dragged the canoe up behind them and reached into it for the pack and set it on the snow. Got the machine gun out. Assembled it, then slung it on its bandolier across his chest.

He stooped, facing Kitty, thrust his arms through the pack straps and lifted it, the whole, crushing mass over his shoulders.

"We go now?" Kitty said.

"You," he said, and pointed up shore, "go *that way*. Just follow the shoreline south to the resort."

She put on a face of—what was it, fear? Or he read it that way. Was she too afraid to go back to the resort through the woods? When she'd been... fearless out on the water?

He stood over her, all but numb, and his mind not working well. That was the cold.

"Look... Kitty," he said, "there's nothing in those woods that can hurt you, okay? That's all a load of nonsense and—"

"No," she said.

He wanted to laugh. What, did she really think she could get lost? Or, whatever it was?

He had to get inside the cave and set the pack up. And what

would she do? He'd have to convince her to return to the cabin, though having her walk point into the cave now was a good idea.

He nodded, and Kitty, who seemed to understand, got out in front.

She moved into the maw of the cave, stepping carefully under the arched ice rimming the mouth of it and into the blue light of the antechamber, nothing there, then Kitty a good twenty five to thirty feet in, ahead of him, and it being much darker, she had her hands out, watchful, and not a sound, not a whisper, not the slightest suggestion of motion, and at his first step into the cave, he felt himself knocked off his feet into a great, dark nothingness.

54

Lucy

They had reached a solid set of tracks, ones that led into a dense stand of pines up to a ridge, where her father had gone, no doubt. They'd have to go up and above it, come in from behind, but climbing was difficult, the trail steep and slippery, switch backed, and where the stone was exposed it was icy.

Here and there, the pine boughs were so substantial and over-hanging the path was almost dry, but there the rust-colored pine needles under foot skittered on the ice. Ryan was behind her, stumbling, so she time and time again had to stop for him, as she did again now.

He clomped up behind her, breathing deeply, and his feet splayed, all the worse for the climb.

"Ryan?"

"We've come up six hundred feet vertical," he replied, head bent to his phone yet again.

"If we don't even have cell service, how does... any of that, what you're doing, work?"

"Oh," he said, thinking how to put it. Frowning, framed between two snow laden pine boughs; it would have been a nice picture if not for what they were doing. Getting to her father.

"Satellites," Ryan said, as if that explained it.

"*Satellites?*"

"It's stuff I took off the dark web, military stuff. Only, sometimes you get gaps, because—" She hadn't even known there was such a thing. "Yeah, well, they orbit over, and you have to wait for—"

"Ryan," she said, and getting it for once, he nodded.

"Down on shore, below us. There's a—it's called a 'bald,' and it overlooks the shore, just about—" he glanced at his phone "—well, it's over the... ice cave, where—" He shrugged. "It was all on the resort site. You know, 'stuff you have to see,' when I looked into it, and—

"Here it is."

He held the phone out, there a tiny luminescent green square, as if she could read it from a distance.

"You can call out?"

"Well, sure, to anyone who's connected to a—" he lifted his hands, made finger quotes, "coverage area. Like, 'Can you hear me?' Otherwise, no. Or, if they're hardwired. I can reach any of that."

"Call Booker," Lucy said, and when Ryan frowned, she gave him the number she'd taken off the phone in the cabin, and, as if it were nothing, Ryan got him. He handed Lucy the phone.

"What's he doing?" She meant Prendergast.

"You mean *they*. You got eight men who've come in, counting that asshole Arn. And Prendy, that old fuck, he had everyone doing some Chinese fire drill to move 'em out soon as Buck and Kitty left.

"Lucy," Booker said. "You gotta stay out of their way, because they really mean business. They got rifles with scopes and AKs 'n' shit and lit out of here like commandos. Deer hunting, my ass. And Prendergast was heardin' 'em around like some... fuckin' Patton or something."

"They check out our cabin?"

"I went out as they were comin' in, then scooted back in soon's they went out again."

"You gotta get out of there, Booker. Just... take the car you came up in and go."

"How you callin' me, anyway?" Booker said. "Since we got no cell reception and—"

She heard something below them. A rattle of scree. "Gotta go," she said, hit *End Call*, and handed the phone to Ryan.

To their left, there were pines—and she drew Ryan off her father's tracks and deep into them.

Moments later, Prendergast, light on his feet, came up the trail. He was in an enormous black puffer coat, breathing heavily. He went by so quietly, so expertly, so light on his feet that she marveled she had heard him below them at all, shocked at what could have happened if she hadn't.

If he hadn't slipped on the scree, if she'd been paying more attention to Booker, to the phone.

55

Buck

He came to, his back set against a wall of ice where the snow had blown in and mounded, and his hands fastened behind him. Chilled and a sharp throb in his head. They were deep in the cave, the ice soaring above them, and the blowhole—he could tell from the bitter cold air rushing over him—behind them, and one of the men kicking Kitty, balled up on the ice back of a gas lantern.

"Fucking chink, should've stayed where you came from," the one kicking her said.

He was big-gutted, and it showed, even through the snowmobile suit. Buck recognized him now as Burgess, Chief of Police. He was armed, too, had a hand cannon, some Desert Eagle or— Seven inch barrel, which could be a problem for someone who didn't much use it.

Kitty, on her side, looked across the distance at Buck, her blank, staring eyes defiant, but reproachful.

Here, the ice was especially thin. Clear as glass. A fish swam lazily by under them. Arm length, and powerful. Metallic green. Mouth the diameter of a coffee can, a northern pike. It nosed at the booted feet of the three men, then glided off into the dark water.

A school of perch rose up chasing minnows, which spun in a swath of silver, and the pike shot into them, and, with a muscular flick of its tail, it disappeared into the darkness again.

"Hey, Burgess," one of the men, stocky and broad shouldered, said, "you kill her 'fore we get what we need ain't gonna be no more jailbait for you."

"What difference does it make?" He looked at his watch. "They'll be dead when were done, anyway."

"I don't think you're gettin' through to her," the man behind Burgess, the tallest, said. "Or maybe she only speaks chink?"

The stocky, slope-shouldered one came around Burgess, got down on one knee and put his face in Kitty's. "Gocka gooka chookie?" he said. He stood and kicked her in the stomach so she grunted, then set his hands on his hips.

"It's her son, Jackson, the hacker who's been into our things," he said, "so who needs the old chink?"

"*We* need her, Tibbits, that's who," Jackson replied. "And, anyway, Prendergast will want her. So, ease up there. Unless." He'd been watching from a distance, but now he sauntered over.

And where was Arn?

"What, you think *you* can make her talk?" Tibbits said. "I say we dump them in the lake—save us a world of trouble."

"All we have to do is bring the retard chink in," Jackson shot back, "and *he'll* show us everything. Make it easy. Take out that nigger boy, too. Hidin' in the cabin, fuckin' dumb ass spook."

Jackson got down on one knee, put his face in Kitty's. "Where's your sweet lil' boy, pumpkin?"

Kitty shook her head and Jackson grimaced, then, as if being kind, he patted her shoulder.

"Well, let's say we cut off one of her fingers," Jackson said, and nodded toward Burgess. "We'll show it to the retard, then tell him we've got her. And, you know, he tells us what he knows, to get her free, and—" He patted Kitty's shoulder again, "no chance of things goin' amiss, right, sweetheart?"

They argued the merits of the plan. Cut off her finger? Well, why not her nose, wouldn't that scare the retard better?

Their voices were swallowed up in the cave, and they decided on pressing Kitty for what she knew first.

It had gotten so cold, snow was crystallizing out of the damp air and coming down like a fine ash. Kitty was covered in it, and when Burgess kicked her in the stomach again, it spun around her, sparkling.

"Tickle your fancy?" he said, in a sing song voice. "Like ol' Tibbits said, 'Goochie cha-chi'?" They all laughed.

"Stead of takin' her nose, whyn't we cut off part of her tit, like a nipple, wrap it up like some Chicken McNugget," Tibbits said, "see what the kid says, how about that? That'd get 'im goin.'"

Burgess and Tibbits bent over Kitty, chuckling. Yukking it up. Saying what to her Buck couldn't hear.

Jackson, a distance to their left, lit a cigarette, all but rolling his eyes and shaking his head. They'd gone through the pack, found the explosive in it, and swung it around just off Kitty's feet, the machine gun, the M249, set on top.

Jackson crushed out his cigarette, turned to Burgess and Tibbits, then dropped again to one knee alongside Kitty.

He was no joke. Angular face. Hard eyes.

"Aww, so unnecessary, yes?" he said, "isn't it?" He took a red kerchief from his pocket. Blew his nose into it, wiping it on either side, then smiled into Kitty's face. She was whimpering.

"Sounds like a goddamn pathetic dog is what," said Tibbits, "only I wouldn't trade this old Chink for a one-legged Chihuahua."

Jackson jammed the kerchief into Kitty's mouth and her eyes went wide. She arched her back, huffing, trying to breathe through her nose, and when she'd almost caught her breath, Jackson pinched her nostrils shut and she kicked, hysterically, spinning on the ice so that Jackson pinned her with his knee.

When he let go of her nose, she shrieked through the handkerchief, a whole string of nonsense.

Jackson plucked the handkerchief out of her mouth, and she said, "I talk, okay? Okay I talk now? *Please* I talk?"

Buck watched, at first disgusted, thinking how pathetic it all was. Embarrassing, really. He wasn't about to give them the pleasure. Kitty was whimpering and crying, and, even worse, begging now.

"Please. Please, no more. I tell *everything*," she said. "Where find things. All things. Go where from you find and they be there. Yes?"

They all stooped over her, trying to make sense of it, her going on, the three of them confounded.

"Goddamn chink. Jackson, Tibbits, you get *any* of that?" Burgess said, standing. "What the fuck's she saying?"

Jackson, still on his knee, glanced up. "Could you just *shut the fuck up*, Burgess? So *I* can hear at least?"

"Yeah, you," Tibbits said, "you're the real language expert, you and your Farsi so you could—"

Jackson glared, then got down on both knees, bent yet closer, his ear to Kitty's mouth.

"What was that?" he said.

While they were all bent over her, and she was jabbering, Buck twisted nearly double, got his knife out of his pants pocket, wedged it at the small of his back and, with a sharp upward motion, cut the zip tie, and his hands, even though he could barely feel them, were free.

The machine gun lay on the Duluth pack, fifteen feet or so across the ice, but when he bent to spring at it, Jackson glanced over and he slumped, his hands held behind him.

The men huddled around Kitty, who was weeping hysterically, and what she was blathering all but incomprehensible, Kitty only making sense for seconds, and then not, Kitty speaking—Chinese, or—what was it? And now Kitty, in a near hysterical seeming whisper, spewing some techno babble.

"In trailer, go where I tell, you get code he know all codes CJMQ 85 pass code and get in and *he want send*! I tell him no, no don't do, but he—he do what he want, I say no, he can't be send to newspaper they come for us. So, not send. You can erase all, yes? All he prepared to send out, to newspaper reporter, all link to server, and it won't go out, if—"

She was blubbering, but now even more quietly, and begging and then—exactly when they were all right on top of her—

Jackson choked her again with his handkerchief, and when she could breathe again, she let go a sob,

"Oh, You HURT ME! Oh, you hurt me so much," she cried, and she kicked, as if convulsively, the pack with the machine gun on it, and it spun in a slow, gliding circle across the ice.

She caught Buck's eye. Not a tear there. A glaring, cold eye. And then, just like that, she nodded.

Rose up, laughing, a hideous, weird laughter, a box cutter in hand. She slashed Jackson across his face and he stumbled back, blinded, stabbed Tibbits in the stomach, drew the blade up sharply, gutting him, then turned to Burgess, who, on his rear, was kicking away from her across the ice, clawing at his Desert Eagle, the too-long barrel stuck in the holster.

He slid behind a wall of stalagmites, they all did, crawling and rolling and scrabbling.

Buck brought the 249 to his shoulder. Blew right through the ice. Cut Burgess in half, then hit Jackson, Jackson dancing on his feet. Stitched a line of bullets across Tibbit's chest and Tibbits went down.

A stalactite wobbled overhead, then fell, crashed at Tibbits feet and the ice shattering, and skittering in all directions.

And then it was silent but for the hiss of the gas lantern, and he and Kitty glanced at each other. Either it would happen now, or it wouldn't, the others he'd seen parked earlier in the trees rushing in.

And there it was, off in the distance, the whine of a snow machine. They'd heard the shots. And then two, and then a third.

Buck got his climbing gear out of the pack. Rope. Crampons. Spikes. Carabineers. He camouflaged the pack in the mounded snow where they'd had him sitting earlier, then ran back to Kitty. Caught her under her arm and all but carried her off her feet to the rear of the cave under the blowhole. Ducked to fix the crampons on his boots.

In minutes, they'd be inside. They had to be up and out, or there'd be no escaping them.

Kitty looked up the blow hole, her mouth a hard, lost line. Here, he'd leave her, she was thinking, even as he hammered in a spike, then clipped onto it, feeding the rope out behind him.

"Get on," he said. She did that, and he looped a section of the rope around her waist and cinched it.

"Hang on tighter," he said and started up, using his ice axe, taking long, biting pulls up the blowhole, and the ice barely holding.

Approaching a convexity, he hammered a spike in overhead, tied into it, his safety, then thought, what was the use? He let the safety rope drop and climbed, Kitty on his back, up past and over the bulge, barely getting over it when the men beneath began firing shots, and the men, in a rattle of gear, coming up after them, and Buck a good distance up now.

At an ice shelf, he said, "Here!" caught Kitty under her arms, then thrust her over his shoulders onto it, and above them the glazed ring of the exit so close you could almost, reaching up, touch it.

So close, but it may as well have been a mile.

Buck climbed onto the ice shelf now, too, and when more shots came from below, he turned to Kitty.

"Climb onto my shoulders, and you go on out," he told her, and he reached for her, and she stepped back.

He looked up, the sky in the opening a kind of heaven. He'd get Kitty out, and here the last thing, really, he was going to see, snowflakes big as quarters tumbling down cold onto his face.

A figure bent over the blowhole, dropped a length of rope, then croaked out, "Take it."

Lucy's father. She'd gotten to him, after all.

Kitty snatched up the rope, knotted it around her waist, then gave a tug on it, and as she shot up and away from Buck, she caught the hood of his jacket, two handed, and he was pulled with her out the blowhole, up and into the open, onto the rough, snow-covered bald, where they came to a stop.

Prendergast there with a gun, a rope snaking to his side and a Jumar at his feet. What he'd used to pull them up.

He could swing the 249 around, but Prendergast addressed that possibility in a word.

"Don't."

The end of a collapsible climbing ladder rose, wavering, out of the blowhole, then clanked to the side of it. The rails shuddered, then shuddered again, someone ascending the ladder.

"Get it off your chest," Prendergast said, meaning the machine gun, and he looped the bandolier over his head, then dropped the 249 on the snow. "Push it," Prendergast said, "push it to me," and he did that.

As Prendergast was swinging the 249 around, a head popped out of the blowhole and Buck held up the baby talkie. Prendergast's eyes went wide, and Buck pushed the send button.

There was a ground shuddering KABOOM and a flame shot from the blowhole. The force of the explosion knocked them back, pelted them with shattered ice as if by bullets. In the stunned silence that followed, a shock wave, like thunder, rippled up the shoreline, echoing.

Prendergast, on all fours, shook himself, Buck across from him, the 249 between them. Prendergast scrabbled to it, then swept it up, blinking, screwing his face up, determined to regain his advantage.

A cascading rumble came up the blowhole. A grinding, shifting, falling away of ice and stone, and the three of them braced themselves, uncertain if the ice would shear from the bald—slide with them on it down into what remained of the cave, or over the cliff face yards distant.

When all that had stopped, and there was just the wind, and the falling, ashy snow, Prendergast said, "You," a barely controlled rage in his voice, "are going to make things right.

"Move away," Prendergast said, "up, to the right. And do not stand. If you do, I'll—"

Buck was going to refuse, when Kitty gave him the strangest look—*just do it*—and he got his hands under him. Shuffled to his right.

"More!" Prendergast barked, and he scooted farther over, and Prendergast shook his head, glared, "No, more. More yet, *all* the way," and he slid yet farther away, now beyond any distance he could safely bridge.

Prendergast strode to Kitty and stood over her, and, for a moment, Buck feared a loss of control. It would be suicide to go at him, but he'd get there.

"Now," Prendergast said to him, in a rage, "we're going to wait for your... *little friends*. And when they come, you're going to help me clean up this mess you've created. Understand?!"

When he said nothing, Prendergast said, "I said, *timber nigger*— when they come down, you're going to—"

"I hear you," Buck said, cutting him off, "I hear you just fine."

56

Lucy

They came upon her father over the ridge, spread-eagled behind his 30.06, an eye pressed to the scope.

There'd been a ground-shuddering explosion so violent it had shaken snow from the pines around them. Below her father, Buck and Kitty sat yards apart on the bald, which dropped off abruptly to the lake, Prendergast, in his black puffy on one knee behind Kitty.

Prendergast glanced up shore toward the resort, then the opposite direction, saying something, and Lucy fought an impulse to go down to her father, or to call out to him—because, he'd drawn the stock of the rifle to his shoulder, had his finger on the trigger.

That he hadn't shot Prendergast already made it clear he didn't know what to make of Buck. But he did know Kitty, so he was watching and trying to make sense of it, the three of them there. Lucy had taken white tailed deer down from greater distances herself.

When she couldn't bear it any longer, she said to Booker, who'd run up the shoreline, and Ryan behind her, "*Stay*," and stepped down, and Booker caught her jacket and she shook him off, skidding on her heels and almost falling, got low over her feet, the ground icy, and there no certain footing, no path.

She slid and skidded down to her father, until she was all but on top of him, and she said, "Daddy, *don't*."

He froze. And Ryan, who'd come down, too, said, in a hush, "It's just us, Mr. Walters."

He craned his head around, having gotten the Glock out of his jacket and under him.

Lucy dropped on her knee beside him, whispered, "Daddy, it's not what you think down there."

57

Buck

Gun in hand, Prendergast wrenched Kitty's arm around and up, threatening to break it, and Kitty grunted at the pain. Buck slid toward them, and Prendergast, glancing up, said,

"I'll shoot you," and nodded, "since I don't need you, so, I wouldn't." He put his face alongside Kitty's.

"Your... *boy*, he's going to tell me how he got to that site, what gave me away, and he's going to fix that. 'We see you.' You think that was clever? Having him write that?" He pulled up sharply on her arm, all but dislocating her shoulder—it was a practiced move, and it did what it was supposed to do—it hurt Kitty, who gritted her teeth against it.

Buck was thinking in a way he knew was dangerous. Had already stepped over the line, where nothing mattered but getting to Prendergast.

Kitty would be safe, because—there was only one way to defend yourself against a frontal attack.

If he came at Prendergast, he could get there even shot once or twice, and just as he was settling into it, this now expanding moment-out-of-time, he heard behind him a crush of snow.

Three boot steps, and a voice, one almost lethally jolly, said, "You let go of her there, Padre, and *set that gun down*, and, I'm warning you, don't even *think* to do something, because, part of me would like nothing better than to put your head on a stick, just so for once you could see your sick self, you understand?"

Prendergast turned, and there they were, Lucy's father, and now Lucy and Booker and Ryan. He set the gun down.

The look on Lucy's father's face said it all, he'd told them to stay back, and they hadn't.

Prendergast let go of Kitty's arm, and she crawled painfully in the snow away from him, then stumbled to her feet and swung in a wide arc around and behind Lucy's father, who said to Buck, "I've got you to thank for my little girl's being alive, so—it's a pleasure making your acquaintance."

The two of them eyed Prendergast, on his face a supercilious look, a world of contempt there.

"You can't kill me," he said, that controlling, sanctimonious thing in him yet, "not with them here; it wouldn't be right. And what about the others who are involved? You *need me* to find them, so, you *listen*, and listen good—"

"Now, Padre," Lee said, and he laughed, "that is really something, you telling *me* I should listen to *you*." He glanced over at Buck. "Doesn't that just beat all? Him saying that just now?"

"Let me talk to him," Buck said, "before anything happens—" which was a lie, but what of it?

When no one moved, he said to Lucy, "Give me those necklaces, the ones around your neck."

Lee nodded. "Bebbe Gurl, do what he says."

She reached under her jacket, then had the necklaces out, crucifixes dangling from them—Jean's and hers.

Set them in Buck's outstretched hand, and he went down, Lee flanking him. When he all but got on top of Prendergast, Lee was there alongside him. And he held out the necklaces.

"Now, tell me, why did you give these to the girls?"

Prendergast glared. "What girls?"

"Jean—" he held the necklaces in Prendergast's face "and Lucy— and who else, and you'll live."

Prendergast snorted, of course he wasn't going to say anything, would admit nothing, he'd get through this, again, barter his way out of it, he'd done it before, and seeing how it was going to go, Buck caught Prendergast just in front of his ears and, squeezing, he forced Prendergast's mouth open and jammed the necklaces down his throat. Prendergast, shocked at the violence of it, gagged, and Buck lifted him off his feet and walked him to the edge of the bald. If near suffocating hadn't terrified him, the thought of being hurled off the bald did, and here he truly struggled, kicking and jabbing at Buck, and something let loose in him, as if he'd been punched, a burning in his back. He heard the report, the echo, and was struck again, and yet again, Arn, who'd shot him, rising from the path to his right.

Lee, a gun in hand, came across the bald at Arn, whose eyes were on Buck, said, "Hey there, Arn, good buddy!" and shot him in his chest, three shots in one, pop-pop-pop!

Buck, clutching Prendergast, stumbled off the bald, and just for that moment, weightless, he felt himself soaring.

58

Lucy

In the silence and impossibility of what had just happened, a phoebe was nattering to the others in the trees around it.

Ryan, Kitty, and Booker turned to Lucy. Then to her father, who shucked his gun into the holster on his belt.

"Bebbe Gurl," her father warned.

"I'm going down," Lucy said and, even when her father tried to cut her off, she got by him.

Skidded down the path Arn had come up, her feet shooting out from under her, and a sob in her throat. *No, no, no, no, no,* and only the sumac cane there to keep her from falling.

On shore, she ran one direction, then the other. Out on the lake, Buck's head was set on Prendergast's body, Prendergast's black puffy holding air, rising and falling with the incoming waves.

It was only a matter of time before they'd go under. The explosion had calved the entire ice shelf, which floated, a white island offshore, where there had been a skirt of ice before.

They were behind her now, her father and the others. Up Buck went, then down again. She turned left, nothing but more open water and shoreline.

Turned to her right, and there was the red canoe. Caught in a cleft in the rock face, having floated there. And even as her father was shouting, "Don't, Lucy!" she dove in. Slapped through the water to the canoe and pulled herself into it. Swept up the paddle in the stern and swung the canoe around.

Paddled, desperately, out to Buck, and when she got to him, she pinned his head over the gunnel with her leg. Prendergast's eye's shot open and he lunged up out of the water, caught the canoe at his waist and Lucy, with the paddle, hit him. Prendergast glared, his mouth stuffed with the necklaces, huffing, and Lucy hit him again. He tried to climb onto her, rocking the canoe, once, and again, and when he'd done it a third time, reared up, she reached into her pocket, had the knife out, hit the button, and the blade flashed free.

Prendergast all but clawing himself on top of her, she knocked his arm up—drove the knife into his heart.

Prendergast fell back, and she caught him by his arm, pulled him alongside the canoe, stabbed him in his chest again, to let the air out of his puffy, and then, in a rage, she truly hit him.

Over and over again, until her hand was covered in warm, stinking blood, and Prendergast's puffy so torn it was in tatters.

She thrust him away from the canoe—on his back, eyes blank. And, trailing lines of plumed blood, he sank into the dark.

Buck pinned under her leg, she paddled, dug in on her right with all that was in her.

Then she was on shore, and over the side she went. Into thigh deep water. Dragged Buck in by the hood of his jacket.

In the cabin, she got on Ryan's phone, and she was so out of herself, so—finished, only one thing mattered.

"Naomi," she said, "it's *Becky*. Yeah. That's right. Or whatever the fuck my name is. Buck's 'assistant.' He's shot and shot bad and we can't take him to a hospital up here; he can't be connected."

There was an at-first why-are-you-calling-me silence on Noami's end, "You mean," Naomi said, "*you* can't. *Be connected.*"

She wanted to say, fuck you, but didn't. She said, "We're going to have him there in an hour. At your back door. You figure it out, or don't." She was going to hang up, but she'd gotten to the absolute end. "No, you take care of it," she threatened, "or so help me god, I can't tell you what I'll do."

59

Buck

He came to, where? He'd been flying, or— There'd been an airplane, or had he imagined that? Something was—he was *with* someone. And a heat in his chest like a fire. Or was it his back? He could barely breathe, it burned so badly. And he was tired. Falling into a nothingness, giving himself over to it, when he was bodily lifted onto something flat, and as he was rolled somewhere, sounds came to him, someone shouting, "GSW COMING IN!" "GET A CATH STARTED," and he felt a sting on his arm, "OR 6, CODE RED, ROLL HIM, NOW!" and a woman was moving with him, she smelled of roses, like life itself, and she put her hand in his, squeezed, and so hard it kept him from going back under.

When, just for a second, he lifted his head and tried to look around him, Naomi bent into him.

"You bastard!" she whispered, and in her voice a sob. "Don't you *dare* die on me, or I'll kill you myself."

And Buck, happy to let go, dropped back on the gurney, and a darkness closed over him.

60

Lucy

In the cabin, Lucy and her father rose late the following morning. He made coffee, and they both had a cup, then made a point of stomping through the drifted snow to the office and lodge where they ordered breakfast, overlooking the snowy sweep of the shoreline through the picture window.

The manager in his blue sweater and twill pants lurked at their booth, hungry for conversation.

Two sets of incoming tracks were visible from cabin #6 to the lodge, and the manager, as Lucy's father had intended, took note of them, as anyone would. Even now, pouring coffee.

"From your tracks," he said, "I'd guess, overnight we got… what? Two, three feet or more?"

"That at least," Lucy's father replied. He smiled up at the manager, then over at Lucy.

"What do you say, Bebbe Gurl, was your Old Dad right, or what? Would've been truly awful if we hadn't come right back in, got stuck overnight in it like those others. How cold is it?"

The manager bent into the window, a thermometer there. "Fifteen below," he replied, "and who knows what with the wind chill. Blowin' like that. Gotta wonder how that church group's doing. Though, with all the gear they had on their snowmachines I think they're fine."

"Snow's a great insulator, if you know how to use it," Lucy's father said, making conversation. "Still, it's whole lot warmer here."

A bell rang—ding!—and the manager spun away, then returned with their plates. On them the works. Lucy dug in. Bacon. Eggs. Steak. Ate like a trooper. It was what she was supposed to do—easier for her to keep her mouth shut that way.

While she ate, the manager stood at the end of their table looking out the window into the now oh-so-dramatic storm, and her father said, jauntily pointing his fork at her, "Take another look outside there, Bebbe Gurl." He forked a piece of steak into his mouth, then leaned toward her, "Aren't you glad now we stayed in after all? You just take a look."

His eyes on the storm outside, the manager nodded to himself. "I heard somebody flew outta here last night after the storm hit, though it's probably just a rumor, what with our bush pilots talking trash."

"You'd have to have brass ones to do something as stupid as that," her father replied. "Don't you think, Bebbe Gurl?"

She was looking outside now, too. It was beautiful, in a terrible sort of way. The drifting snow and wind.

"Yes, Daddy," she said, as if they'd spent all of last evening arguing over it, the storm, not racing Buck down to the airport, and getting back so they could stomp around outside the cabin, in a blizzard no less.

Her father and the manager discussed hunting white tail. The manager was a bow hunter. "More power to you," Lucy's father said, laughing, then winked at Lucy across the table.

"What do think, Bebbe Gurl, like to give that a try?"

She shrugged. It was not her conversation. Not her place to fix in the manager's mind the timeline of things. And, because the manager would be asked later, her father pointed to the clock on the wall there.

"Slept so hard, I was all out," her father said, "and believe-you-me, there was no getting *her* up at rosy fingered dawn."

It was well after nine. Her father had liberally doused his Army jacket with whiskey, so he smelled.

She shared a look with the manager. Who, getting it, grinned, then said, "Hey, and thank you for your service."

Lucy's father nodded, just that.

"Well, you all enjoy your breakfast," the manager quipped, backing away and busying himself, staying out of it.

Until as an afterthought he added, "That fellow came around with the red canoe, you run into him by any chance?"

"No."

"Well, weather like this, no one wants to be on the water. Don't think he even got out. You know if he did?"

Lucy's father shrugged. "Lucy?"

"Beats me, Daddy," she said. "But I saw that red canoe there all day yesterday, and even later in the evening, mistook it for ours, until I saw it was one of those plastic ones."

"Kevlar," the manager said, "'spose he got wise and headed home before the storm hit."

Lucy smiled. "How long is it supposed to snow?"

"Three days," the manager said, "all the way into Monday, though, no doubt we'll see the minister and the rest of 'em Sunday night."

"Three days." Lucy nodded. "Should be something when it all clears off and the sun comes out."

Spring

61

Buck

The bullets had broken a rib and punctured his right lung, and that he hadn't bled to death getting down to the Twin Cities, Naomi told him later, had been nothing short of a miracle.

And at that word, *miracle*, he'd thought of Seraphim, once again, though Naomi hadn't meant much by it.

She'd made his being shot look like some gang-related mess, and no questions asked. John Doe. The morning after Buck ducked out the back, on foot and in hospital PJs.

"Gonna call you 'The Phantom' from now on," Booker joked when he'd come by the house to look in on him.

The disappearance of Prendergast and his Devotional Group made the news shortly after, and for weeks search parties were sent out, but the weather was all but impossible. In February, there was an almost unheard of thaw, and the lake opened up early, as it hadn't in a years, carrying off the ice skirt, and the police found nothing—nothing but the remains of an ice cave, a tourist spot, which was thought to have collapsed when a propane tank exploded, which made sense.

The men having taken shelter in it, and the explosion caused by some malfunction of a propane heater killing them.

There were drives for the families of the policemen. Heroes, all of them, decorated veterans and hard-working police officers. An obit for Prendergast, one making him out to be some kind of angel.

Then, in May, Ryan shot links to Chaplain Prendergast's trophy site to six news sources.

And, as Booker put it, "Truth spoke to power, and the boys in blue got their due, and The Church along with 'em."

After which, the Man with the Red Canoe became the big mystery, or "One BM," as Ryan put it. Had he had something to do with the disappearance of Father Prendergast, who the Church should have dealt with, but hadn't? A canoe. It would have been the only way someone could have gotten to the ice cave if not by snowmobile, to Prendergast and his now, perversely, "Devotional Group" inside it.

So, had the Man with the Red Canoe been a father of one of the molested children?

Or had his being at the resort simply been a coincidence, one having no connection to any of what happened? It was the kind of mystery the public loved, and the news cycle mined it for all it was worth, which meant Buck had to keep his head down, granted the FBI's probe into the "movements" of the men in Prendergast's group prior to their having, it was supposed now, been murdered, and even a once famous singer/songwriter brought into it, bearded and gaunt, appearing on television to sing a hoary old tune that had been popular thirty years earlier, "The Wreck of the Edmund Fitzgerald," a dirge that stuck in your head all too much.

All the better then, Buck noted, calling Lucy one warm, May day, that she have the canoe.

It was hers, after all. Why didn't she come and get it?

She appeared in his driveway Friday of that week, shortly after noon. He'd made sandwiches and, with the door of his shop up, and a new kitchen under construction, he sat on a sawhorse in the sun.

"Hey, Lucy," he called to her, but she answered, now, to ninamuch, what he'd said to her on the phone. Darling.

She came up the drive, no longer in her dirty pink hoodie, but in a long-sleeved T, and womanly.

"You going to show me how to use this thing," she said, "like, before I drive off with it?"

"Just as I promised. We could take it through the lakes in town.

Or, whatever. It's your pick," he said, then added, "and you're taking swimming lessons when it warms up."

She shrugged. "Mind if Booker comes?"

"Course not. Or, maybe you should just go out with him? You want, take the truck, I've got work to do here."

She cut her eyes at him.

"Right," he said. "It can wait."

She smiled, and it was a beautiful smile. Her hair was glossy and blue black, and her skin had cleared up. Her face had gone through a transformation, too. Lucy more than something of a swan.

He slid off the sawhorse, threw his arms wide, and she walked into him, set her chin on his shoulder.

"Miigwech," he said, thanks.

"Enh," she replied, for what? Then, pulling away, she looked off shyly. "Naomi's got me going to meetings."

"Saved my life. Is it working for you?"

She shrugged. "Sorta."

"Sandwich?"

She took it from him, and, nodding, she sat on a sawhorse, her face lifted into the sun, it almost being summer, and warm, and he pulled the other sawhorse up alongside her and the two of them ate, the red canoe there on the truck in the street, and the cat came from behind the house, sat at Lucy's feet, its head lifted, and Lucy tossed a piece of meat from her sandwich to it, the cat eating noisily, and the cat glancing up between them, and the sun cutting down through the leaves in the trees.

The End

Wayne Johnson

Acknowledgments

The author wishes to acknowledge the invaluable support, inspiration, and encouragement of:

Editor Chantelle Aimée Osman; Agent (and editor) Madison Smartt Bell; Heather Levy; Makwa (Bear), John Buck, Patrick DesJarlait, Nodin, Odinigun, Delbert; my Opichi—you know who you are; Kimberley Kaufman, Nathalie L. Johnson, and most particularly Heather Row; Jane, Jim, Frank, Sonny, Julian; Jerry, Benn, Gail, Kevin; Dr. Wayne D. and Nathalie L. Johnson, Sr. And to those I have not mentioned: You have not been forgotten. The list is endless....

Miigwech.

Thanks!

335

About the Author

Wayne Johnson is the multiple Pulitzer Prize-nominated author of the acclaimed Paul Two Persons Mysteries *Don't Think Twice* and *Six Crooked Highways*, a thriller, *The Devil You Know*, and many other works of fiction and nonfiction. Of mixed Native and European descent, he grew up in southern Minneapolis, and in the north lakes region of Minnesota on the White Earth and Red Lake Reservations. He currently resides in Salt Lake City.

Find him online at waynejohnsonauthor.com

CPSIA information can be obtained
at www.ICGtesting.com
Printed in the USA
JSHW021732240222
23150JS00001B/1